The Lies Among Us

OTHER TITLES BY SARAH BETH DURST

Books for Kids

The Shelterlings

Even and Odd

Catalyst

Spark

The Stone Girl's Story

Journey Across the Hidden Islands

The Girl Who Could Not Dream

Out of the Wild

Into the Wild

The Lies Among Us

A Novel

Sarah Beth Durst

LAKE UNION
PUBLISHING

Published by Lake Union Publishing, Seattle

www.apub.com

Amazon, the Amazon logo, and Lake Union Publishing are trademarks of Amazon.com, Inc., or its affiliates.

ISBN-13: 9781662514722 (paperback)
ISBN-13: 9781662514715 (digital)

Cover design by Faceout Studio, Tim Green
Cover images: © Rubberball/Mike Kemp / Getty; © suteishi / Getty; © Trinette Reed / Stocksy United

Printed in the United States of America

For Amy Johnson

CHAPTER ONE

It's quiet inside my mother's casket. Also, dark. And it smells of wood and the thick, cloying gardenia perfume she always used to like. I think they doused her body in it to disguise the odor of the chemicals they used to embalm her. Or maybe they knew she would have liked to wear her favorite scent, even now.

It's not wide enough for me to lie fully beside Mother, but I am doing the best I can, pressed against the crepe-covered wall of the casket. Her right arm is beneath me, and it almost feels as if she has her arm around me. Almost, but not quite. There's no warmth from her body. Or softness. She feels no different from the fabric or the wood that surrounds me. As close as I am to her, I have never felt farther away.

"You weren't supposed to leave me," I tell her. "I never left you."

Even when Dad left us, even when Leah went off to college, I didn't leave Mother's side, and now that she's dead . . . I don't know how to be anywhere else.

I don't *want* to be anywhere else. Even though I know she isn't truly beside me, that her body is just a body without *her* to fill it with breath and life, and even though I know I won't hear her voice again, reverberating through the house as she sings off key to the radio, that I won't see her eyes crinkle in the corners as she squints to read, that I won't hear her footfalls, her coughs, her sighs—the thousand little signs that say she's near and alive and with me—I don't want to leave her side.

That's why I climbed into her casket after the funeral home employees completed their work with the formaldehyde, the wax, and the cosmetics. And that's why I stayed through the service, through the ride in the hearse, through the unloading and the positioning of the casket on the winch at her grave site.

I don't know what else to do.

Except to stay.

It occurs to me that I don't have to leave Mother if I don't want to. It's the kind of thought that's backed by so much truth that it shoots through me like a jolt of electricity. It's not as if there's anyone who will try to stop me. All I need to do is remain here when they lower the casket into the ground, and eventually . . . this will all be over.

It will be soon, I think. My sister and her boyfriend, as well as all our mother's friends and acquaintances, will wend their way from the funeral home to the graveside service any minute now. I listen for the rumble of a car—and there it is, followed by a door slam, then a beep, which repeats as others arrive. Somber and muffled voices approach the grave.

"I'm so sorry for your loss." A woman. I don't recognize her voice.

"Thank you." I *do* recognize hers. My sister, Leah.

She's loud, which means she must be close to the casket. I hear her greet the mourners and, in a stilted tone that barely sounds like her, thank them for coming.

I recognize her boyfriend's voice too. Jamie. He's quieter. "Are you okay?"

She met him in a coffee shop a year ago, she told Mother, and they just clicked. Actual story: she met him in a bar, slept with him, intending a one-night stand, and he stuck around. Mother thinks—*thought,* I correct myself—he has too many piercings but nice manners. I have no opinion of him whatsoever.

"If one more person says that Mom was a wonderful woman, I will shiv them." Leah's voice is low, but I hear it. She raises it to say, "Thank you so much for coming."

"Your mother . . . was complicated," Jamie says.

"She wasn't complicated; she was a liar."

I suck in air so hard it sounds like a hiss. Touching Mother's hand, I am grateful that at least she can't hear Leah. Mother's hand feels like it's made of pliant plastic, but my fingers leave no dent.

"What I meant," Jamie says, "is that it's okay if you have complicated feelings today."

"There's nothing complex about my feelings," Leah says. "I'm relieved, I'm angry, and I'm tired. I just want this over and done with." Louder: "Mrs. Harrington, very kind of you to come."

"Oh, my dear, I'm so sorry for your loss."

There's the sound of shuffling feet, and Leah's muffled reply.

"I was hoping to meet your sister, Hannah, today," Mrs. Harrington says. "Your mother always spoke so fondly of both her daughters. She was so proud of you girls. Please share my condolences with her."

It's an unexpected touch of kindness, especially since I never particularly liked her. One of our newer neighbors, she often received Mother's mail, due to a similarity in house numbers, and would bring it over, always opened—by mistake, she'd say—then she'd comment on the size of the credit card bill, with copious amounts of unwanted advice. But now I warm toward her, and for an instant, the pain that I've been feeling since Mother died recedes like a wave pulling back from the shore.

"I don't have a sister, but thank you," Leah says.

And the grief floods back. I know she feels that way, but it still hurts to hear.

"Oh! Yes, of course. Your mother said you and your sister were estranged, but I thought at least today of all days, she'd be here. You need family around you in times of grief and sorrow. My apologies."

"That's not . . . You know what? Never mind."

"Your mother was a wonderful woman. She will be sorely missed."

There's a pause, and I wish the lid were open so I could see Leah's expression. I don't *think* she'd attack Mrs. Harrington, but with Leah, one never knows. "She certainly made an impression on everyone she knew," Leah says. "She won't be forgotten."

For Leah, that's diplomatic.

Leah has always been difficult—Mother's word. As a toddler, her favorite phrase was *I do myself!* Later, as a teenager, she used to slam her bedroom door when she didn't get her way. One morning while Leah was at school, Mother unscrewed the hinges and removed it. She installed a shower curtain instead. Leah moved out for two weeks after that, living with her friends' families. She even tried to reach out to Dad and only moved back in when that failed. As soon as it was time for college, she was gone. Now, nine years later, she only visits for the obligatory holidays, and she always comes with complaints.

The more she pulled away, the more I wanted to stay.

I only half listen as whoever Leah hired to lead the service mumbles through platitudes and reads passages that have nothing to do with who Mother was or what she would have wanted. Mother would have preferred that everyone meet at an ice cream store, order half-gallon tubs of every flavor, and share them while swapping increasingly outrageous stories about her life.

Like the time she backpacked through Europe on her own.

Or the time she drank the US Olympic swim team under the table.

Or the time she climbed halfway up the fake Eiffel Tower in Las Vegas before security chased her off.

Or the time she hiked with friends into the Grand Canyon, got separated, and was lost for three days but survived because she was carrying all the trail mix. She never ate trail mix again.

All her best adventures were from before Leah and I were born. She gave up her "wild ways" for us, she said, and had no regrets. "You never want to live with regrets," she liked to say, but still, she talked about those days often. Only Leah complained about the inconsistencies in her stories. And Dad, of course. But I loved all her tall tales without reservation. I wish I could hear them one more time.

"You were eleven years old, and you missed the bus," I tell her body. "So you 'borrowed' your neighbor's motorbike. You knew how to ride a bike, and you'd watched your father ride the lawn mower, so you thought, How difficult could it be?" She rode it right past the school and didn't stop until it was out of gas.

Outside, the service is concluding, and the casket jerks like an elevator descending. I hear the purr of a motor as Mother's casket is lowered into the grave. Above, I hear the stream of condolences beginning again. So sorry. Much sympathy. Condolences. And the worst: "She's gone to a better place."

This is not that "better place."

I don't know if a better place exists, but I know she's not here, in this box with its fake-silk fabric and mahogany walls. I can't follow where she has gone.

Above me, I hear the plunk of dirt on wood. Someone has thrown the first shovelful of soil on the casket. Another plunk, then another. I think of Leah and wonder whether hers was the first or whether hers will be the last.

One last splatter of dirt, then voices, then silence. The service is over, and the cemetery workers will wait until all the mourners have left before they use the backhoe to fill in the rest of her grave. And I can't help but feel like this is futile, being here where Mother isn't. She won't know if I stay until I fade into nothingness; she's already gone.

Everyone else has said goodbye, and that means it's my turn.

"I would have stayed by your side for always," I say to Mother.

She does not—cannot—answer.

Carefully but deliberately, I push myself up through the lid of the casket, melting through the wood as if it weren't there. It feels less substantial than mist on my skin. Listening to the cars drive off through the cemetery, I climb out of my mother's grave and beach myself on the trimmed grass beside her family's gravestone.

I expect to be alone, but when I sit up, I see that Leah and Jamie remain. Their backs are to the open grave, and Jamie has his arm around my sister's shoulders. He's speaking softly, murmuring in her ear, and I wish that someone would reassure me or at least tell me what to do now, where to go, who to be.

Crossing behind them, I hear Leah say, "Worst part: She can't ever change now. Can't get better. Be better. I'm not mourning her, you know? I am mourning the mother I didn't have, the one she should have been and now can't ever be."

"Makes perfect sense." He kisses her head through her hair. "Go easy on yourself. It'll be rough for a while, and that's okay. That's how it works."

"Strange to think I'm alone now," Leah says. "I don't even have one crappy, slightly problematic uncle or an annoying cousin with lousy hygiene. I've got no one."

He wraps his arms fully around her. "Hey, don't talk like that. You're *not* alone."

Behind her, I say, "You have me."

A thought, or perhaps a hope, whispers through me: maybe this is it, the answer to where I go and what I do and how I keep from dwindling away. Mother may be gone, but Leah isn't. I have family, and so does she.

"Leah, you have me," I repeat.

Coming closer, I try to squeeze her arm, as if I could force her to look at me and hear what I'm saying to her. As always, my fingers do not dent her skin, no matter how hard I try to hold on. As always, she does not feel me or see me or hear me.

As always, to her—to everyone—I do not exist.

CHAPTER TWO

The blue sky feels as if it mocks me. I want a drizzle as gray as I feel, or a thunderstorm, hard and fast, that obscures everything in buckets of rain. But instead, abundant sunshine.

"It's peaceful here," Jamie says.

Leah snorts. "Sure. All the assholes are dead."

Looking out across the cemetery, I see a haze that circles some of the newer stones. It was shed by mourners when they departed. It circles Mother's as well, in wisps untouched by any wind. It's the same cloud-like haze that encircles Leah like a shroud. I return to Mother's grave and kneel beside her family stone. Her name has already been added, to the left of her parents' names, beneath a carved rose:

ELEANOR RIGGS ALLEN

BELOVED MOTHER

Leah wasted no time arranging for the engraving. My finger hovers over each letter, tracing them in the air, and I wonder if she picked the word "beloved" or if she selected it from a menu of platitudes, much like she chose Mother's Day cards: the blandest and easiest option available. Regardless of the card, Mother would always proudly display it on the mantel. After a few weeks, it went into a shoebox of similar cards inside the closet. I wonder if Leah knew she saved every single one. Probably not.

I deliberately do not look at the nearby stone that bears my name. It's not my grave. It's the grave of someone who could have become me if she'd lived, but didn't.

Kindly, Jamie says, "We can stay as long as you need."

"I need to have left twenty minutes ago." Leah begins to walk toward the one remaining car, parked beneath a maple tree. It has duct tape around the side mirror, and rust has eaten half the back fender. I don't think it's her car. So far as I know, she doesn't have one.

"Are you sure?" Jamie asks. "You haven't . . ."

Leah halts. "Haven't what?"

He shrugs, and it's obvious that he's wishing he hadn't started that sentence. There's an edge to her voice that cuts, and I shiver. Used to be, that kind of tone would signal the start of a screaming match between Leah and Mother. "We can leave," Jamie says, trying to recover. "Wherever you want to go. I'll drive."

"No." Leah bites off the word. "What were you going to say?"

I finish the sentence for him: "You haven't cried." Not the way I have, so hard that it feels like I'm crying blood and bile with the salt water. So hard it hurts instead of relieves.

He holds up his hands as if in surrender, and I can't blame him. She looks as if any second she'll spew shrapnel at anyone close enough. "Never mind," he says. "I just . . . I'm here for you, whatever you need."

She stalks toward him. "You were going to say I haven't cried, as if it's required. Stay strong through the service, and then weep on your boyfriend's shoulder, and everything will be okay, because that's how it's all supposed to work?"

"It might help," I say.

Jamie sighs. "I have no idea what you want me to say here."

"I want you to not expect me to cry over the mother who made me cry every week of my childhood, who embarrassed me, *humiliated* me, with her stories and her lies and her constant—" She flaps her arms in the air as if words have failed her the way she thinks Mother failed her. "Whatever grief I'm supposed to feel, I don't. I feel nothing for her. Get that? *Nothing.* If that makes me a monster in your eyes—"

He stops her, his hands on her shoulders. She tenses. Gently, he says, "Absolutely did not say you were a monster."

His voice is calmer than mine would have been, and I wonder if he's seen her this way before or if it's only today that's special. I haven't seen this side of her since she was a teenager under Mother's roof. Granted, these days, she only visits rarely and briefly, so there hasn't been much opportunity to see if she's changed; I haven't truly known her in years. "I'll say it," I say. "You're supposed to cry at your mother's funeral. Or at least care that it's been months since you visited."

Leah deflates, dropping her shoulders as if she's about to fold in on herself. She's shed a lot of the haze, I notice, except the tattered bits that always cling to her. I can see her face more clearly, and the resemblance to Mother, especially around her eyes, hurts. I have the same eyes, except hers sport deep circles under them, caked with makeup to hide her sleeplessness. Mom liked to say both her daughters were younger, better versions of her—Leah chopped her hair pixie short the first time Mom said that—but I match Mom in photos of her in her twenties, especially around the eyes. "Sorry. I'm sorry," Leah says. "You didn't do anything wrong. It's me. It's just . . . I don't want to have to think about her anymore. I want a bottle of wine and a tub of ice cream and to not . . . think."

She definitely didn't choose the word "beloved."

I wish they, whoever carved the stone, could have asked me. I'd have had a hundred words to give them and still not finished describing Mother. She wasn't simple or easy, but she was mine. And now . . .

I have Leah.

Only Leah.

At least I'm not alone. She may have pulled away—and pushed away—but that doesn't make her any less family.

Following them, I slide through the door into the back seat of Jamie's car. It's an easy maneuver that I've done a hundred times with Mother's car. Most doors and walls (and caskets) can't stop me. Leah, in the front passenger seat, rolls down the window and cranks up the radio; then she peels off her shoes and props her bare feet in the open window. She doesn't look back at the grave as Jamie drives away, through the internal roads of Pinelawn Cemetery, but I do. I look for as long as I can, until Mother's grave is blocked by the field of other stones, and all I can see is the maple tree, solitary, with wispy haze drifting around it.

Only when Jamie pulls onto the street do I face forward—and wish I hadn't.

As we barrel down the street, wind rushing in and music thumping so loudly that it overrides my heartbeat, a motorcycle pulls up beside us. Its driver is helmeted and leather clad, as black and faceless as a shadow. He doesn't glance at us before he veers in front of Jamie's car. My heart leaps into my throat. "No!" I shout, knowing they can't hear me, knowing it's too late—

Jamie drives through him like he's made of mist.

A second later, the motorcycle is back, its driver again a shadow.

As my galloping heart calms down, I glare at the motorcycle driver, but the shadow doesn't acknowledge me. Now that I can see its face—or lack thereof—I doubt that it can. I've seen plenty like him, and none have been substantial enough to be aware of me.

One of the flaws of not existing is that I see other things that also don't exist. Like the fog that drifted around the graves and that often imbued Mother's house. Like the motorcycle. Like the wolves made of shadows that once hunted me.

As Jamie merges onto 495, the lanes fill with other shadows of nonexistent vehicles: convertibles and SUVs and pickup trucks and

18-wheelers that appear only in the corner of my eye. They flash in and out of my vision. Some appear solid, but others look like dizzying blurs of blue, silver, black that streak past until my head pounds and my stomach flip-flops like a beached fish.

I close my eyes and try to lose myself in the steady thump, thump, thump of the bass line. The mash of lyrics is indistinct enough that I can pretend they're just syllables washing over me. I don't even realize that Leah is talking again until midsentence.

"Every single school party, every potluck, every welcome-the-neighbors or thank-you, she'd take off the plastic, throw away the box, and then—oh, here's the best part—she'd add her own imperfections. Like stick her thumb in a brownie. Or she'd warp a cookie. You know, just twist them until they were irregular, more like homemade."

Jamie chuckles.

I smile.

Keeping my eyes closed, I listen, hoping for more anecdotes. *This is exactly what I need right now.* To submerge myself in memories and not think about the present or the future. To not think about the fact that I'm away from the safety of home. To not fear the shadows. "Go on," I encourage her.

"I could have brought napkins or cups or forks," Leah says. "There are plenty of options for kids whose parents don't bake. Not to mention, there's zero shame in showing up with a nice box from a bakery. Or how about donut holes from the grocery store? Everyone loves donut holes. But no, she'd insist they were homemade and even rattle off a recipe if asked."

"At least she sent you in with something," Jamie says.

"Do not try to put a positive spin on this." The edge is back in her voice, though not as sharp. There's a tinge of tiredness. "There was nothing cute or quirky about it."

I say, "She was showing you she cared."

Jamie doesn't seem to hear the edge, or maybe he chooses to ignore it. "My dad . . . First time I brought home one of those teacher letters with a school supply list—my dad called the school and screamed at them that he pays taxes and that this is extortion, and if the teacher can't find a way to educate his kid without extra highlighters, then she deserves to lose her job. She was the nicest teacher I ever had too. She used to give me a granola bar every day out of her lunch after that. I guess she figured if my dad wasn't sending in crayons and highlighters, he probably wasn't feeding me enough either. Mrs. O'Connell. Yeah, that was her name. I wonder if she's still teaching."

Leah is quiet for a minute, and I risk opening my eyes long enough to see her expression. Her lips are pressed together, exactly like Mother used to do, though I doubt Leah would acknowledge the similarity. I wonder if my expression is the same as hers. I touch my face, the contours of my cheekbones, the curve of my chin, so similar to hers yet also my own. Younger by a few years. Softer. At last, she says, "I can't tell if you're trying to empathize or distract me."

"Both? Look, I'm really out of my depth here."

"The point is there wasn't anything too small or inconsequential for her to lie about. Did you know that until this week I didn't even know how old she is?" She corrects herself: "Was."

I don't understand why she sounds so upset. Lying about her age . . . that was a harmless lie that hurt no one. Like lying about one's weight. If it made Mother more comfortable, then why should Leah care? Besides, shouldn't funerals be about forgiveness? Or at least closure?

"She had to have her birth date on her driver's license," Jamie says. "Or on her taxes."

"Yeah, and that's where I found out that my mother was six years older than she always claimed. You know how many birthdays we celebrated—" She cuts herself off. "The lawyer called me this morning. Her lawyer. She put 'Hannah' in her will."

Me.

She did?

Jamie is frowning. I can see his expression in the rearview mirror. I ignore the chaotic swirl of vehicles, real and unreal, and focus only on what he and my sister are saying.

"But I thought she—"

"Yeah."

"What is that—How is it even possible?"

"Guess Mom's lawyer never actually checked. It's going to be hell to untangle."

Jamie shakes his head. "You'd think the fact that—"

"That's what I've been trying to tell you," Leah says. "My mother and facts had an adversarial relationship. The worst part is I'm pretty sure she always liked Hannah better." She lets out a laugh that is nearly a cry and then chokes it back.

I let her words wash over me, though I hear the bitterness in my sister's voice, as sharp as the taste of lemon. Mother loved me. Even Leah could see that truth.

"What are you—" he begins.

"I don't want to talk about it. Change the subject. Please. Anything else."

"Okay."

There's silence from the front seat.

Then Jamie says, "I heard it was supposed to rain today."

"Really? All the topics in the world, and you pick the weather?"

I stop listening.

I'm not sure what Jamie sees in my sister—as far as I can tell, he seems like a nice guy who deserves better than her snark and temper— but maybe today is an exception, not the rule. She could be entirely different on a day that isn't the day of our mother's funeral.

I have to give her a chance, I think. After all, I have nowhere else to go.

And she knows that Mother loved me.

That's not nothing. In fact, that's everything.

◆　◆　◆

I've never been to Leah's apartment in Queens before. Mother wasn't invited, and I never thought to come without her. Frankly, it never occurred to me that I could. Climbing up to the third floor of her apartment building, I try not to feel as if there's less oxygen than there should be. The stairwell is absurdly narrow, with chipped paint on the walls and black streaks on the steps, and it smells sour and sharp, like an onion when liquid begins to pool beneath it. I watch the shadows and try to keep my heart from racing faster. I hear Leah unlock her door—two locks, dead bolt and knob, and she pops it open with her hip.

Jamie asks, "You want me to order anything? Chinese? Thai?"

"Can't eat," Leah says.

"Not even ice cream? You mentioned ice cream and wine."

I follow them inside, expecting to breathe a full breath of relief, but it's just as claustrophobic in her apartment as the hallway. Worse, the graveyard fog is here, too, circling my ankles, and the fear rises instead of fades. *Go home*, a voice in me whispers. *You're not safe here.* I aim for the window and lift my face to feel the kiss of the late-afternoon sun. After a moment of warmth, I am able to exhale.

"Metaphorical ice cream," Leah says. "But literal wine." She crosses to her kitchen, which is only three steps from the front door. Everything in her apartment is three steps from everything else: the kitchen is squeezed into one corner—a refrigerator, a stove, and a sink with a minuscule counter that's dwarfed by her microwave and coffee maker. A table that doubles as a desk is jammed in beside the counter. It's half piled with books and papers and bills and half covered in dishes from her breakfast (and possibly yesterday's lunch and dinner). A couch is wedged in next to it and buried under multicolored pillows. Tapestries, decorated with tiny beads and even tinier mirrors, smother the walls. A folding divider blocks off her bed from the rest of the apartment, but from this angle, I can see that it's drowning in pillows and laundry. She has plants everywhere, vines dangling from pots on shelves, and I can't help but feel as though they're stealing air instead of producing it. *I can't live here. I don't fit.* The fact that I take up no actual space is irrelevant.

She pulls two glasses out of a cabinet and squints at them. One has burgundy wine stains, and the other has a chip in the base. Jamie maneuvers around her and retrieves a half-finished bottle of red wine. He pours for both of them. "You want to toast?" he asks.

"Yes," I say.

"Nope." She tips the glass back and chugs it, then holds it out for more.

"You sure?"

"Just pour."

But he hesitates. "Have you eaten anything today?"

"What are you? My mother?" She lets out a bitter bark of a laugh and flops onto the couch. Several pillows spill onto the floor at my feet, but she doesn't bother to pick them up. The empty wineglass dangles from her fingers. Jamie steps over the pillows, puts the wine bottle and their two glasses on the table, and sits next to her. She doesn't look at him as she speaks. "What am I supposed to do now? Before . . . after the hospital called, there were all these logistics, you know? Decisions to be made. Obituary to write. Funeral home arrangements. Minutiae with the hospital . . . Guess there will be more minutiae. Bills. Banks. I'll need to deal with her house." Slumping into the cushions, she thumps her head against the back of the couch. "Ugh, the house."

"Don't worry about that right now," Jamie says. "It'll wait until you're ready."

"I hate that house," Leah says.

"*Our* house," I correct, though she hasn't lived there since before college. She still has a room in it, filled with the dusty debris of high school. Her desk still has sharpened pencils. Her bed still overflows with stuffies.

"You don't have to do it alone. You're not alone." He wraps his arm around her, and she sags against him, curling her legs up beside her. *He's kind. And patient.* I can see why he lasted beyond a one-night stand. I wonder if Mother ever looked beyond his piercings and tattoos to see his kindness toward Leah. I think she would have liked him.

I wish I had that.

I lift my eyes to the wall above Leah's and Jamie's heads, and instead of the mosaic tapestries, I see canvases, unframed, of varying sizes. A second later, the wall shivers and the canvases fade, and all I can see are the tapestries again. I blink, then focus on the kitchen, deliberately letting my eyes relax, and the canvases flicker back into view, but they're still too indistinct for me to see what's painted on them.

Fabulous. It's even more crowded than I thought.

I know Leah majored in art in college. And then art history. And then psychology? Mother told a neighbor she was prelaw, but I see no evidence of law books. There's a book on the history of film, an Indian cookbook, and a few historical novels. Various papers are strewn beside them: bills, a supermarket list, a phone number scrawled beside a date and time. My fingers slide over the papers without stirring them—except for one that flutters.

This one I'm able to pick up. I lift the piece of paper carefully and note that I can see my fingers through it. It's not nearly as solid as the items I can manipulate in Mother's house. Holding it up to the light, I see it has a pencil sketch on it, half of a woman's face, but then the image and the paper it's on vanish like the canvases on the wall. If I wait, maybe it will reappear. Sometimes things do, and sometimes they don't, no matter how hard I focus or don't focus on them. I don't know why. There's a lot I don't know.

Like why I am the way I am.

Like what the haze is that often clings to places and people. Like why I can see, even touch, things that no one else can, yet cannot affect so much of the world around me. Why could I touch my mother's arm, feel her skin, yet my fingers leave no trace? Why could I lift that piece of paper, even crumple it if I wished, yet not so much as shift the others? I can sit on a chair *or* walk through it, whichever I choose, but it doesn't bow beneath me, and I can't shift it, even an inch. Unless I can. Some days, I manage not to let the horrific absurdity of it all gnaw at me. Those are good days, when I can tell myself, *It is what it is.* Other days, though, I drown in my theories and plausible but unprovable explanations—*Am I a ghost?* I can't be; I grow and age and breathe and bleed. *Am I a dream?* I could be, but how and why? *Am I a wish? Am I a curse?*—and the contradictions inherent in my daily existence choke me. Those days, I'm consumed by the fear that I too will dissipate like the haze or vanish like a barely seen work of art. Always, I wish there were someone I could ask the very simple question:

Why?

There's no one to answer that. Just like there's no one to answer why Mother had to die. It was a brain aneurysm, the doctors said, unlikely that anyone could have predicted it, and unlikely that anyone could have prevented it. It was one of those things that sometimes happens. It's no one's fault.

I found her. The TV was on, blaring because she liked it to wash out every other sound, but it was tuned to the news, specifically a show with political talking heads, arguing back and forth about fact-checking some speech. She hated watching the news, especially the pundits and spin doctors. It made her shout at the TV and stomp through the house. I hated it too. There's an ugliness to it that often seeps out of the television like sludge. Thick as tar, it pools on the carpet and oozes across the room. Once, I stepped in it, and it burned the sole of my shoe away like acid. Flayed my foot so badly that I ached for weeks. So I knew to be careful when I came downstairs to see why she hadn't changed the channel.

It was another day before Sonya found her, a friend who stopped by to pick her up for their weekly book club meeting where they discussed books they hadn't read and sipped wine they pretended to like. She'd seen Mother through the window and called 911, twenty-six hours too late.

I had, at least, made sure Mother wasn't alone. In the beginning, I'd yelled at her to wake up, knowing she'd never heard me before and wouldn't hear me now. I'd tried to shake her, even though I knew I couldn't. I'd cried and raged. And in the end, I simply sat beside her until the ambulance came.

They had to break open the door, but there was no rush once the paramedics were inside. It was clear she was already gone. I watched as her body was taken away, wrapped in black plastic. The paramedics stomped through the toxic muck from the television, ankle deep by then, but it did not touch them.

Leah was called to identify the body. She didn't cry then.

She isn't crying now.

She has another glass of wine. I didn't notice when she poured it. She's swirling it absently, not drinking it, as if she only wanted it to occupy her hands. *Just because she hasn't cried doesn't mean she's not in pain.* She's my sister, and she's hurting as much as I am. If only we could reach each other. I, at least, have an advantage, in that I know she's here. She believes herself alone in the world.

"You're not," I tell her. "I'm here. We'll find a way through this."

If I can find a place in Leah's life, then perhaps I can weather this.

When the paper with the sketched portrait reappears, I study it again. I think that it could be Mother—the curve of her cheek, the shape of her eyes . . . but it doesn't have her mouth, her smile. It's Leah's smile, bleak and mocking and empty, like the one she wore whenever she came home. A self-portrait? It fades in and out, and the sketch lines shift. Now I see a stranger's eyes.

There are other papers on the desk, more than I remember seeing before. Some I can't shift, but others . . . I examine them one by one as if searching for clues—clues to understand Leah. More sketches: a cat on a fire escape, the outline of a city skyline, a leafless tree, a bird. Some fade as I study them, and some stay, though there seems to be no rhyme or reason as to which are impermanent.

Now I begin to see the sketches everywhere in the apartment: loose papers on the kitchen counter, piled on her dresser, strewn on the floor. I am ankle deep in drawings that don't exist, and I begin to feel a panicky tightness in my throat. Closing my eyes, I breathe steadily in and out. When I open them again, I am looking at Leah, only Leah, not at the detritus of her dreams or the wolves of my nightmares.

"You wanted to be an artist," I say.

She loved art class when she was in high school. Used to fill up notebooks with her sketches. I remember being jealous that she could create something that had permanence. She tried pottery once—on the mantel, Mother had a lopsided vase Leah had made—but it was mostly drawing and painting. Looking again at the wall, I'm certain these canvases are hers—or would have been if she'd kept creating. *She wanted to.* All these sketches . . . they're the art she never created but wanted to.

"What happened?" I ask. "Why did you stop?" She's able to make art, to create something that others can see and respond to. Why would anyone give something like that up?

What happened to her?

It bothers me that I don't know. She's my sister, so why does she feel like a stranger?

"You know the worst part?" Leah says.

I answer, "That I barely know you anymore, or that you don't know me at all?" Both painful in their own way.

Jamie says, "What's the worst part?"

"None of the people that came today knew her as she was," she says. "They all knew their own version of her. One of them told me how much they admired her, how brave she was for hiking through South America on her own. She never set foot anywhere south of Florida. Another man—okay, this was the worst—he talked about her volunteer work at a soup kitchen. Every time he saw her, that's where she'd say she was going. She never set foot in a soup kitchen in her life."

"She always meant to," I say. "Just like you always meant to paint all of these." Mother liked to imagine herself as the person she wanted to be. Was that so terrible?

"All of them saw this great woman, this great mom. It would have been enough if one person had told me they knew she was a fraud. Then the day would've been bearable."

"It's kind of more traditional to say nice things to the family at a funeral," Jamie says mildly.

Leah snorts.

"Seriously, what kind of person would go up to the daughter of the person who died and list out her flaws?" He fakes an accent. "Excuse me, miss, but your mother used to floss in public."

She almost laughs. "That's the worst you can think of? Not, you know, emotionally abusive. Manipulative. Narcissistic." Each accusation feels like a punch, though they're aimed at Mother, not at me.

He tries another accent—Australian this time. "Excuse me, miss, but your mother used the company microwave to heat up fish."

She joins in. "Excuse me, miss, but your mother took off her socks on the subway."

"Excuse me, miss, your mother chewed with her mouth open."

"Excuse me, miss, your mother ate the last cookie."

Jamie pauses. "What's wrong with eating the last cookie?"

Leah rolls her eyes as if the answer is obvious. "You're supposed to leave it so that the person who wants it the most can have it."

"But what if I want it the most?"

"Then you can have it," Leah says.

Jamie clasps his hands to his heart in mock horror. "But then *I'm* the person who ate the last cookie! All this time, I have been the lowest of the low. How can you even look at me, knowing I'm the kind of guy who would eat the last treat?"

Leah laughs at last, and it reminds me of a bubble bursting, the way it always sounds surprised it could pop. "Guess our relationship is doomed."

"That's a shame," he says, smiling at her.

"Indeed. Especially since you're such an excellent kisser."

And I feel as if a knife has been slid into my side while I wasn't paying attention. I was thinking it was just Leah and me now. But it's not. She has this—him, Jamie, someone who can make her laugh, even on the direst of days, *especially* on the direst of days.

It's not Leah and me, now that Mother is gone. It's Leah and her life, all squeezed into this apartment, with no room for me. She may know of me, but she's never made space for me in her world. Why should she start now? She doesn't know how badly I need her.

She slides on top of him, straddling him.

"Oh," I say. "Yikes, no. Could you not? Not right now?"

"Make me forget," Leah orders him. "I want to forget today."

Reaching behind her, she unzips the dress she wore to our mother's funeral and pulls it over her head. It catches on strands of her hair, and she yanks them out. The dress drops onto the floor, a puddle of fabric.

He takes the wineglass out of her hand and lays it on the edge of the table, near the books and the unwashed dishes, and then he's kissing her. His hands slide up her back and fiddle with the hook of her bra, and I look away.

I laugh, brittle. "And here I thought today could not get any worse." I think about leaving, about going home, but I don't know which way home is. I know how dangerous it is out there for someone like me.

They stumble, hands all over each other, to the bed behind the divider. *This was a mistake. I shouldn't have come here.* This isn't my home. It's no safe haven. Wishing I could disappear, I fix my eyes on the wall with the canvases that fade before I can see more than a flash of a shape or a color. The sketches that don't exist are ankle deep around me.

I thought the problem was that I don't know Leah well enough, but that's not it. Between Leah and her boyfriend and her plants and her dreams and her regrets and her desires, there's no room for me. Given how she feels about me, I doubt she'd make room if she could. I should have realized that before following her home. She's always resented me—or at least resented the space I occupied in Mother's heart.

I don't belong here. Without Mother, I don't belong anywhere.

How foolish to think I did.

CHAPTER THREE

Leah rode in the back of an Uber to her mother's house in Garden City and wished she could tell the driver to keep driving past it. Just keep going as far east as he could go until they reached the ocean. Or better yet, turn around and go home.

Come on, Leah, you can do this. Suck it up.

"It's the beige house, third on the left," Leah said. "You can pull into the driveway."

He parked.

She stared at the house.

"Shit," she murmured.

She did *not* want to do this. As much as she told herself that this—Mom's house, which squatted like a neglected animal on a tiny parcel of unkempt lawn—was just another task that she had to deal with, like the lawyer and the funeral home and the obituary and the insincere sympathy cards from people she'd never heard of who, thanks to Mom, seemed to all have her address . . . this was *not* just another task. From age six until the first day of college, this house had been her home. She'd spent countless hours flopped on her bed, headphones on her ears and a pencil in her hand; countless nights tiptoeing into the kitchen to scrounge for food because Mom and Dad had argued through dinnertime again; countless mornings in the bathroom, staring in the mirror as if that would transform her into someone old enough to leave.

Thanking the driver, Leah forced herself to get out of the car. Behind her, he drove away as she fumbled for her copy of Mom's key and tried not to feel the weight of a thousand memories settling on top of her. The last time she'd been here, for an obligatory Thanksgiving dinner, she'd offered to help clean up the yard—get rid of the crap on the porch, eliminate the weeds that threatened to choke the azalea shrubs, and clean the windows—but Mom had waved her offer away, saying she had plans to fix it all herself. Mom always had grand plans. Never saw them through. And now . . . *It's a wreck.*

She was dreading what she'd find inside.

"You can do this," Leah said out loud. "It's only a house. An empty house. Can't hurt you. Can't do anything to you."

She wished she hadn't come alone. Jamie had said he could take the day off if she wanted, but no, she'd told him she could handle it. Not a big deal. Just a house. She hadn't lived here in years, so why would this bother her? It wouldn't.

Staring at the front porch, Leah wondered what it would have felt like if she'd had a sister to do this with her. What would this day have felt like if Hannah had lived? If Leah had gotten to share this house and all its memories with her own sister?

A lot would have been different.

She squashed thoughts of Hannah down, the way she always did. There was no point in dwelling on a past that never was. She was here to facilitate moving on, not dwell on what-ifs.

Behind her, Leah heard a car pull into the driveway. *See, you don't have to walk inside alone after all.* She'd dithered long enough that the real estate agent had arrived. Procrastination for the win! She plastered a smile on her face, hoping she looked as if she were intentionally delaying out of politeness instead of dread.

A middle-aged woman in an ivory suit stepped out of the car with a friendly wave and flashed an extra-wide smile at Leah. Her lipstick shade, Leah noticed, matched her purse precisely. Leah wished she'd made an effort to be more presentable. Her jeans were clean but hardly the same level of dress as a pencil skirt, and her ChapStick was colorless.

The woman's heels clicked as she minced down the walk, avoiding the loose bricks that Mom had always claimed she'd fix but, of course, hadn't. "Margaret Addleman from Premiere Homes," she introduced herself. "You must be Leah Allen. I am so sorry for your loss."

"Thanks for coming to meet me." Leah sidestepped thanking her for the obviously perfunctory condolences. The last thing she wanted to do was discuss her mother's death with a stranger; it would be better if they focused on the task at hand. She had the sense that Margaret Addleman would agree. She didn't look like a woman who did emotions. "So, this is the house. What do you think?"

Leah knew what she must be thinking: It was a mess, a disaster, a shithole. It reeked of all the unhappiness built up over so long and manifested that in peeling paint, a stack of molded phone books on the porch, and a welcome mat with half the letters rubbed away.

The real estate agent studied the property with pursed lips. "Curb appeal is hugely important in raising the value of a house. Some up-front investment—fresh coat of paint, a little landscaping." She pointed to the azaleas. "Tear out that snarl of bushes—"

"Not those," Leah snapped.

Wincing, she took a deep breath. She hadn't meant to react so strongly. Certainly hadn't expected to. But those azaleas—they'd been here since she, Mom, and Dad had moved to Garden City, after Hannah . . . They were the one beautiful thing about the house, blossoming a vibrant pink that brightened the home every spring no matter what was happening within.

"A trim, then," Margaret Addleman said. "To make the yard appear more manicured."

Leah agreed to a trim. And fresh paint. She also promised to clear the junk off the porch. She then led the real estate agent inside, trying to ignore the way her heart was beating against her rib cage as she stepped across the threshold.

The air inside the house was tinged with sourness beneath the pervasive odor of Mom's perfume that clung to every surface. Leah instantly wanted to flee. It was too much. It would choke her. Telling herself firmly to quit being melodramatic, she forced herself to walk farther in.

She halted just inside the living room, beside the old upright piano that Mom had gotten cheap at a yard sale. While the real estate agent poked around, Leah trilled a few notes. She stopped when they echoed discordantly. Had the piano ever been tuned? She doubted it. She wiped the dust from her fingertips on her shirt. "She never played. She always said she did—could've been a concert pianist, she said—but I never heard her plunk out anything more complex than do re mi . . ." She trailed off. Maybe it wasn't a good look to be sharing that kind of detail with someone who'd never met Mom. "At least, I don't remember her playing. She had me take lessons."

"Mmm," the real estate agent replied politely. She poked her nose around the corner and said louder, "Hmm."

Leah followed her into the kitchen, and the smell smacked her as she walked through the doorway—the pungent stench of rotting fruit and sour milk. She swallowed hard. It had never smelled this bad. But then, the house had never been abandoned. She felt her cheeks heating up in a blush, as if any of this was her fault. *It's not my home. None of this is my fault.*

"It could use updating," Margaret said delicately.

Leah dumped a blackened banana into a trash can. A few flies swirled up when she opened its lid. "I'll clean it up," she promised.

"That would be a first step," the real estate agent agreed. "You could hire a professional cleaning service. I have folks I can recommend."

"That's okay. I'd rather . . ." She'd rather dump the entire house and all its rot into a dumpster, but she knew she couldn't. She had to deal with it. The fact was that Leah couldn't afford to hire a cleaning service, not on top of all the other expenses that had come with her mother's death. Yet another fun treat, courtesy of her mother. "I'll take care of it."

She wished she'd dealt with the mess *before* Margaret Addleman from Premiere Homes with her pink lips and pink purse could judge this place. This felt a bit like lying on a doctor's exam table and realizing your underwear had holes in it.

Cleaning had never been Mom's strong suit, to put it mildly. For as long as Leah could remember, Mom had been bored by the very thought of housework. She'd always had bigger, better, brighter things to do, which was fine, but it would have been nice if she'd cared that a very young Leah was pouring cereal into stray cups because there were no clean bowls, or at least cared enough to teach her daughter how to clean dishes. Instead, Leah had had to teach herself—which, again, was fine. There were far worse hardships, and dishwashing wasn't difficult to figure out. It was just that . . .

Forget it. It's the past.

Like Mom was now the past.

She can't disappoint me anymore.

"I'll empty the house before we go on the market," Leah promised.

"Not empty," Margaret said, sweeping through the house. "The idea is to stage it so that prospective buyers can imagine themselves living here. You want to display only the bland pieces, framed by as much open space as possible. Keep the couch. Get rid of the love seat. Piano can stay, but only one end table. Remove all the knickknacks, books, decorative pieces, personal items, photos. All of it. You want it to look clean." She lifted the edge of the rug. "I recommend a new rug, or if that's not in the budget, you could have it professionally steamed. Fresh paint on the walls, of course. Neutral colors only. Nice, clean white preferred." She continued through the rooms, pointing out what could stay and what had to go.

Reaching Mom's bedroom, Margaret waved her manicured fingernails at a canvas on the wall. "Amateur artwork has to go. You want inoffensive, tasteful pieces. Each room should resemble a page in a home-decorating magazine. Think aspirational! You want this to look like someone's dream home!"

She swept on, but Leah lingered. She remembered this painting: a bridge over a lake. She'd painted it when she was thirteen for an art class in school. The perspective wasn't quite right, and it looked as if the bridge was twisted as it straddled the water. She remembered she'd been so proud of it, at least until Mom had pointed out its flaws, under the guise of helping her artistic development.

"I didn't know you kept this," Leah murmured. "You hated my art." She lifted it off the wall.

The wallpaper was brighter beneath it, and the contrast left a crisp outline of the canvas. She stared at the pink roses on the wall. Mom and Dad had put up this wallpaper together after reading a DIY home-repair guide. Mom used to tell anyone who asked that this was what killed their marriage.

Leah thought of Jamie at the cemetery, saying her mother was complicated. It felt too much like an excuse. Or like forgiveness.

She was a liar. About everything.

The sooner the house was stripped of her lies, the better.

Bright and early the next morning, Leah hauled cleaning supplies and garbage bags back to her childhood home. She'd tied her hair into a ponytail and wore an old, stained T-shirt and her least favorite, baggy jeans. *Today is for getting things done.* No matter how hard it was. She just had to get through it.

And she wasn't going to do it alone. Her best friend, Jersey, had offered to help. They'd been friends since they were eight, and Jersey knew about Mom, Dad, Hannah, and all the messy ugliness. At least with Jersey, Leah wouldn't have to explain or defend or counter whatever they found.

"Thanks for coming," Leah said, blinking at her. Leah had dressed for dust, dirt, mold, mildew, and whatever else they found; Jersey, on the other hand, looked prepared for an afternoon in a coffee shop. "Um, are you sure you're ready for this? It's going to be messy."

Jersey was wearing paint-spattered jean shorts that were more a fashion statement than work clothes. Leah doubted that the paint originated with Jersey—she'd most likely purchased the shorts that way. She'd paired them with a white shirt, cut to show off the cherry blossom tattoo on her clavicle. The pink petals matched her pink hair. "You don't think this looks cute?"

"I'm sure the mice and cockroaches will be really impressed."

Jersey laughed.

Together, Leah and Jersey unloaded the supplies from the trunk of Jamie's car. *Should I have prepped Jersey better for what we'd find inside?* She just hadn't wanted to talk about it—any of it. The lawyer had called again . . . More money, more time, more mess. It was hard not to be furious at Mom, even knowing that was a pointless way to feel. She'd spent too much of her life furious at her mother with zero effect; it certainly wasn't going to accomplish anything now.

"Well, it's . . ." Jersey paused, searching for a compliment that wouldn't be a lie. ". . . a house. Definitely a house. Door, windows, roof." One of the things Leah loved best about Jersey was how sunny she always was, but this was stretching even her abilities.

"It lacks curb appeal," Leah said dryly.

"I'm sure it's better on the inside."

Leah snorted. "Want to bet on that?"

It was strange to look at the house and know it wasn't Mom's anymore. *It's mine.* Sort of. Once the lawyer finished untangling the absurd mess that was Mom's will. She remembered coming home from the school bus and running up the porch steps. The front door always creaked, so she could never enter without Mom noticing. Mom would swoop in, demand to know how Leah's day was, and then not listen to the answer. Just launch into a tale of whatever she did—or more accurately, didn't—do while Leah was at school.

She instinctively tensed as she unlocked the front door and pushed it open, but no one rushed forward to steamroll her with implausible anecdotes. Going inside was easier this second time around. *It'll be even easier once this place is clean.* Then she'd feel better. Then she'd be able to move on and forget about all of it—every disappointment, every bad memory. After today, she'd be like Mom: beyond caring.

"Wow . . . it, uh . . . What's that smell?" Jersey asked, poking her head around Leah.

Setting the box with Lysol, sponges, and gloves just inside the door, Leah reminded her, "You volunteered."

"Yes! Absolutely! I'm here for you! But . . ."

"It smells like home," Leah said.

"Oh! Sorry! I mean, I didn't . . ."

Jersey dithered until Leah held up her hand. "Jersey, stop. I'm kidding. I know it smells worse than a garbage day in August."

"Sorry," Jersey repeated, then added, "I know this is hard for you. I'm here to help however you need. Just tell me what you need."

Leah sighed. What she didn't need was to shoulder Jersey's issues on top of her own. "All I need is help with the mess. I didn't ask Jamie because I didn't want him emoting all over me. And, well, he wouldn't understand. I just want to get this place cleaned up and sold." She didn't want to wallow in thoughts of what was and what should have been. And she didn't want to explain the gory details to someone who didn't know firsthand how bad it had gotten. "Can we not talk about how hard it is or isn't for me?"

"Got it. Yes, of course. We won't talk about anything you don't want to talk about." Then, "Is everything okay with you and Jamie?"

"Yeah, everything's fine." She'd spent the last few nights with Jamie being oh, so solicitous, the perfect boyfriend really. He'd plied her with food. Even cooked dinner for her last night, with wine. And washed the dishes. Yet he kept encouraging her to talk about her mother and her feelings. He couldn't seem to accept that, when it came to her mother, she didn't have any more feelings. She'd used them all up in the years before her death, and now . . .

Now she just wanted this over and done.

"Maybe let's not talk about him either?" Leah asked.

Jersey nodded. "Got it."

Leah felt a knot in her neck muscles loosen. *See, she understands.* Jersey always wanted to make things easier not harder, even if she didn't know how—yet another reason why Leah loved her.

Leah trooped through the living room and halted in the doorway to the kitchen. She wrinkled her nose as she surveyed it. It wasn't worse than yesterday; it just wasn't better. She thought she'd be inured since she knew what to expect, but it still stank. "Start in the kitchen?"

"Sounds good," Jersey agreed.

It didn't sound good, but it was necessary.

They hauled the trash out of the trash can and carted it outside. Leah propped open the fridge door and began dumping everything into a garbage bag: the take-out containers, the milk, a ketchup bottle, and at least two dozen partially used salad dressings. "Why?" Leah asked, making her voice light, as if this were humorous instead of awful. "Why so many salad dressings? There are five—no, *six* different kinds of Caesar dressing. All open."

Across the room, Jersey was tackling the spice cabinet. She held up an unopened bottle of ground cumin. "Do you want to keep any of these?"

"Toss them all." Leah dumped the salad dressings into the bag. She thought she knew her mother's every flaw, but she had no explanation for this many bottles of salad dressing. *Why, Mom?*

Why did you make the choices you made?

Why did you live the way you lived?

"Spices are expensive," Jersey said. "You'd never have to buy them again."

"I want it all gone." Every single item that her mother had touched and hoarded and valued more than Leah or Dad.

"Can I keep some of them?" Jersey inspected another bottle. "Vanilla. You know how much this stuff costs? It's practically liquid gold."

"Don't bake. Don't care."

Jersey hesitated, holding the vanilla over the trash bag. "Is that a yes or a no? If it's going to upset you at all, I won't keep it."

Leah lifted a bag of half-liquefied lettuce out of the crisper and dropped it into the garbage. "Take whatever you want. Just don't tell me about it. I don't want to know there are pieces of my mom in your apartment. I want to be memory-free."

"Got it," Jersey said. Leah didn't look up to see whether she'd pocketed the vanilla.

She wasn't ever going to get answers, and it didn't matter. All that mattered was emptying out this house. *No. Not emptying it. Making it bland.* She had to strip it of memories and unanswered questions.

Also, salad dressing.

Jersey crawled onto one of the counters and began emptying the highest shelf of a cabinet, the one filled with flour, baking powder, and brown sugar. She worked in silence for a while, then said, "Wow, she really did like to pretend she was a baker."

"She once told the guy at the bagel store that her homemade ones were better." Leah immediately wished she hadn't said that. It brought back a flood of memories and feelings she didn't care to deal with.

Jersey seemed to sense that. "Did I ever tell you about the time I tried to make my own bagels? You know how you're supposed to boil them, right? Well . . ." And then she was off and running with an anecdote about bagels that tasted like soggy cardboard, then another about an attempt at a peanut chicken that had so much peanut butter your tongue stuck to the roof of your mouth.

Leah thought of all her mother's stories, each more implausible than the last.

You can do this. She can't hurt you anymore.

Once they were done and all traces of her mother were eradicated from the house, then she'd feel better. As she cleaned and cleaned, she kept telling herself that she was tossing memories into the garbage bag along with the other trash.

CHAPTER FOUR

Here is what Leah sees when she looks at Mother's house:

A drab one-story beige home with peeling paint, cloudy windows, and a porch cluttered with junk: a bike with a warped front wheel, a stack of empty planters, a pair of boots with cobwebs between them, and a moldy phone book still wrapped in its plastic bag that was once tossed on the driveway.

And here is what I see:

A cheerful two-story yellow house with white shutters and a white porch with a swing. Blazing pink azaleas frame the steps leading to the front door, and the flower beds are a riot of colors, sometimes daffodils, sometimes tulips, sometimes roses. Inconstant flowers, but I've learned to enjoy the array as a whole. It is the house that Mother wished it was: impeccably maintained and perfectly manicured.

For twenty-three years, I've lived within the beauty of Mother's good intentions. I do not know what will happen now that she is gone and the house is, or will be, Leah's.

Worry claws at my throat. Surely, Leah won't—*can't*—erase all that Mother made. This is our family's house. She must feel the same pull to it as I do. Or does she? She must.

But she's inside now, with her friend Jersey, tossing out everything she touches. I heard her tell Jamie at the cemetery and then Jersey in the kitchen that she wants this "over and done"—as if that's possible. You don't get to be over and done with the person who made you who you are, even if you forged yourself in opposition.

As hard as she tried to leave, Leah has found herself back here again. *Better if she'd never left.* Once, I thought I'd leave. It was a few years after Leah left for college, and I decided it was time for me to strike out on my own as well. That's what you're supposed to do, what everyone did. Spread your wings and leave the nest. Back then, I clung to the idea that I could be like everyone else if I tried hard enough to pretend that I was.

I had a plan: follow Leah to college, live on a couch in her dorm room, hang out in the student center, and sit in on any classes that interested me. It wasn't as if anyone would demand tuition or to see an ID. I'd learn about . . . well, I never settled on what. Anything that struck my interest, I suppose. And then I would see the world. I had visions of traveling and seeing the places that Mother used to talk about, like Europe, where she backpacked with friends or on her own, depending on which anecdote she felt like telling. I'd start in London, cross the Channel to France, and then continue on. Maybe take a train to the Alps. Continue south to Italy. I'd have liked to see Egypt too. Not just the Pyramids of Giza but all the way up the Nile. Or I'd head west across the US. See Yellowstone, the Rocky Mountains. Go all the way to the Pacific Northwest where I'd stand in the rain and look out at the ocean. Or I'd travel south, all the way to Peru to see the Andes.

Maybe I could travel now.

But I know I won't.

It was a Saturday when I tried to leave. I remember waiting until Mother woke. As she made her coffee, I said a lengthy goodbye, carefully laid out all the reasons why I'd decided to see the world, and then glided out the door, imagining that she was waving from the window. I didn't look back to see that she wasn't.

The garden was lush, overflowing with roses. Heavily fragrant blooms coated every bush, their flowers so heavy that the stems drooped.

As far as Leah was concerned, Mother had never successfully grown a rose bush before, though she'd tried once or twice, but to my eyes, she was a prizewinning gardener whose green thumb never failed. I made it to the end of the driveway without losing my nerve, checked the traffic, and strode purposefully across the street. I had never walked outside on my own, and I remember how free I felt, as if I could walk anywhere.

But then the shadows began to creep from the houses. So I walked faster. More poured from the nearest church. Even more from the elementary school. With them came the sound of crying, a thin kind of wailing that wasn't from any particular throat.

Glass shattered.

And the shadows took shape, svelte as wolves. Blending into one another, they stalked me silently, their numbers swelling the farther from home I walked. I caught a glimpse of a jaw, then the silhouette of lean legs running by. I could almost convince myself they were my imagination, except that my skin chilled and my breath tightened when they came near.

But I wasn't truly afraid until the road disappeared.

Cars kept driving, but I saw nothing ahead of me. As they reached the edge of the pavement, the cars vanished as if swallowed.

The wolves closed around me.

I told myself, *They aren't real; they can't hurt you; they don't exist.* Until they attacked. When one bit my arm, it felt like shards of glass shoved into my flesh. I remember screaming so loudly that it hurt my throat, my lungs, my skull. People passed by—a woman with a stroller, a jogger with headphones, a delivery woman. No one heard my screams, and that broke me.

I don't remember how I wrenched myself free, but I did. As I ran, they followed, flowing around me like the wind. My arm throbbed with a slicing pain. Until that moment, I hadn't known that anything could hurt me.

Wildly, I threw myself onto Mother's yard. The smell of roses surrounded me, and it seemed as though *that* was what stopped the wolves. Thinking back, I don't know why that would be true, but maybe it was. Regardless, they did not follow me inside. And I did not leave again.

Always, they lurked, waiting for me to stray. I saw them sometimes through the window. For years, they didn't give up their hunt, but so long as I stayed close to Mother and stayed within the confines of her world, they kept their distance from me. If I were to leave . . .

But maybe after all these years, they wouldn't find me. I haven't seen them through the window in a very long time. Maybe enough time has passed that they have forgotten me, and I'd be safe. Or maybe they would finish what they began that day and rip me to pieces while I scream—and no one hears.

The world outside is a strange and scary place. It's nice to dream of traveling through it, but that won't happen, at least not for me. Better to stay here. Or it would be if I could stay.

I imagine what it would be like if I *did* stay:

All Mother's belongings, all her memories, all her stories would be stripped from each and every room the way Leah was doing to the kitchen, and then the house would be sold. Another family would move in, occupy it, fill it with their hopes and dreams and hurts and dramas. At best, I would linger. Like a ghost. Haunting the place.

Unless I fade away before that happens.

I lift my hand and study it in the sunlight. For an instant, I think I can see the azalea bushes *through* my palm. Shuddering, I squeeze my hand into a fist. My fingers feel solid. Real.

What will happen to me after Leah erases everything?

I scoot inside and try to ignore the clattering from the kitchen as Leah and Jersey tear apart my everyday. Surely Leah must have good memories here that she wants to hold on to and not see stripped away by "updating" and "curb appeal." I think of Christmases when Leah would tumble bleary eyed into the living room. Mother always went all out for Christmas, with decorations in every corner of the house. She collected nutcrackers, which she'd display on every surface, and she'd tell stories about how she got each one: a find at an estate sale for an old millionaire, a bargain from a yard sale where they didn't recognize its value, a souvenir from a trip to Germany, a gift from a grateful friend for a favor that changed in every retelling.

Stopping next to the upright piano, I can almost see the picturesque scenes unfolding in front of me. All the wonderful memories packed into this house. Can Leah remember Mother at the piano? She'd glide her fingers over the keys softly, not pressing them, and talk about how she'd nearly been a concert pianist. She had stories of her piano teachers: an elderly woman with thick glasses who couldn't see the sheet music but had perfect pitch, a younger man who liked his students a bit too much, a high school teacher who gave lessons on the side and had always praised her innate talent and told her she should pursue it professionally. But life got in the way, and she never did. Sometimes I could hear strains of music from the piano when no one was there.

If I concentrate, I can hear the faint sounds of Debussy's "Clair de lune." It was Mother's favorite. She'd hum it sometimes. Or play it on the stereo, volume turned all the way up. She always turned the volume all the way up on everything.

I don't let myself look at the couch in front of the TV. I don't check if the pillow is still askew from where she lay. I don't look to see if her slippers lie on the carpet. One of the paramedics must have turned the TV off. It sits quietly now. Even the muck that oozed from the pundits on screen has dispersed. Only tattered bits of it cling to the corners of the room, thickening the shadows.

Truthfully, in that deep place inside with no voice, I never expected to survive Mother's death. Perhaps my dissolution is inevitable.

Mother, why did you have to go?

Sinking onto the floor, I pull my knees to my chest and squeeze my arms around them. *What am I going to do now?*

Nothing. There's nothing I can do.

I'm losing the fight against my fear when the living room plunges into darkness.

◆　◆　◆

A second later, it's light again.

But the light in the living room has shifted, falling at a different angle across the rug, as if it's suddenly hours later. Jumping to my feet, I search for an explanation. I don't think I fainted or fell asleep. Yet hours seem to have passed.

I have lost track of time, or time has lost track of me.

My heart thuds in my throat. What happened?

I rush into the kitchen to see if anything happened to Leah—and I halt just through the doorway. She and Jersey are still in the kitchen, but the kitchen itself . . . All my life, Mother's kitchen has rivaled any magazine spread, with marble countertops, copper pots hanging from the rafters, and skylights overhead flooding the room with light. Every fixture is stainless steel, and she has an extra refrigerator to chill wine. Fresh fruit always adorns the counter in creamy white bowls: white- and yellow-flesh peaches, black-red cherries, and plums with dew on their skin, alongside pyramids of homemade muffins, rolls, and croissants.

But that's not what I see.

Before me, the marble is old, stained Formica. No fruit or muffins. The wall above the stove is speckled with grease, and the linoleum floor has bubbled with water damage. There are no copper pots, and the ceiling presses low, without any skylights.

But then, a moment later, Mother's kitchen reasserts itself. My galloping heart begins to slow, and I feel as though I can breathe again. I pluck a peach and bite into it. The juice dribbles down my chin, and I catch it with my finger.

Everything's still here.

Except it's not. Leah and Jersey have emptied every cabinet and cleared every shelf. Pots and pans are heaped on the floor. There are boxes now, stacked with plates and bowls. Jersey is wrapping glasses in bubble wrap. Perhaps Leah intends to keep them, but then I think, *No.* She must intend to donate or sell it all.

I look at the peach, and it's shriveled with a coat of gray-green mold. Its skin collapses under the pressure of my finger, and I feel the slick wetness of the juice. It chills me to my core, and I can't help but think it's a deliberate warning:

You're next.

Right now, I feel, to myself at least, as solid as ever. But what happened before, in the living room, when I lost hours? Did I imagine that? No. No, I don't think I did.

Maybe this is the way it happens. You're here until you're not.

Mother hadn't expected to die either.

A glass shatters and I jump. For an instant, I'm on the half-vanished street again, and I feel the shadow biting my arm as if it intends to saw through my bone—but it's only Leah. She's dropped a pitcher. She kneels in the glass shards, picking them up.

"Hey, careful there," Jersey says. "You'll cut yourself."

Leah doesn't reply. She just shovels the shards into a trash bag. They clink as they collide within the plastic. I stand rigid, trying to contain the feeling of terror that floods every inch of my body—it feels as though it's coming from everywhere, both my past and my future.

Squatting next to Leah, Jersey catches her wrist. "Stop. Leah?"

Leah lifts her head, and I see her cheeks are streaked with tears. "I can't do this. Just . . . can't do this. Don't want . . ." She sucks in air, unable to finish the sentence.

"It's okay. Just tell me what you need. Do you want to talk? Do you want to hug? Do you want me to distract you with idiotic anecdotes like the legendary tale of what I did when that kid would leave old tuna fish sandwiches in his locker in tenth grade? Whatever you need, whatever you want, I'm here for you. You know that." Jersey is wrapped in gauzy pink that curves around her in the shape of armor. It vanishes when I blink.

"I want you to get me out of here," Leah says.

"You want to get drunk?"

"Exactly that. Yes. I don't want to feel."

Jersey nods. "If that's what you need, then that's exactly what we'll do. We can talk it out, cry it out, whatever, later—when you're ready. Come on. I know just the place to go to forget the world. Music so loud you can't think and drinks so strong they're practically hostile." She helps Leah to her feet, carefully, as if Leah is fractured and will shatter into a dozen pieces if she's not handled gently enough. "First, though, we have to change our clothes."

When they disappear into Mother's bedroom, it's at first a reprieve, but then I look around myself at the kitchen I barely recognize without its lush fruit or copper pots or marble countertops, and I know I can't stay here and just let myself disappear—perhaps permanently the next time.

They emerge, and Jersey guides Leah out of the house, leaving the broken glass and overflowing bags of trash behind them.

Uncertain if it's the right choice or not—uncertain if I have any choice—I go with them.

CHAPTER FIVE

It's not the right choice.

I know it isn't as I follow Leah and Jersey into an Uber, and I'm even more certain as I climb out in front of a bar in Queens that boasts the name SWEET VENOM in faux-blood letters above the door and in neon in the grimy window.

"Definitely a terrible idea," I say.

Lately, it feels as though I'm making one bad choice after another, but maybe it's only that without Mother, there are no good choices anymore. Not for me. "Sweet Venom?"

Leah seems to be having second thoughts as well. "We could go someplace nicer if you want. Up to you," Jersey says.

"It's perfect," Leah says firmly.

"I don't think anyone has ever called Sweet Venom 'perfect,' but I thought . . . You want to pretend you're someone else, you go to one of those bars that charge five dollars per olive. You want to pretend your life doesn't exist, you come to a place like this." She waves her hand at the red neon sign.

"Like I said. Perfect. You know me better than anyone." With a fierce grin close to a grimace, Leah leads Jersey to the door, and they both show their licenses to the bouncer, who only briefly glances at them.

Only two options now: stay outside or follow Leah in. Night has fallen, and streetlamps bathe the sidewalk in a sickly yellow. The same toxic muck that often flowed from Mother's TV oozes through the gutters in thick, sluggish rivers. It collects in pools by the drains. Cars whip past on the street, splashing through puddles of water while leaving the deep morasses of toxic muck untouched. At least I don't see any shadow wolves—only a man on the corner with a cart lit by a string of white lights. He holds out a gyro to a college-age couple. I see it first as a pita piled with meat and lettuce and tomatoes, and then it's a pulsing mass of deep red that drips down his hand, and he is handing them a living heart.

I scoot inside the bar.

Through the murky glass, the street looks as flat as a painting. A smokelike haze, thicker than in the cemetery, fills the already-crowded bar. I wade through the mist, looking for my sister, careful to sidestep the splotches of muck between the tables.

She's at the bar with Jersey, who is tugging on the sleeve of the bartender. He turns around, and I see a flicker of faces overlaid on his: a bearded old man, a young woman with a half-shaved head, a young man with a goatee. Their features shift and blur. Under so many layers, I can't distinguish which is the bartender's true face. Perhaps he, or she or they, never shows it here.

"Two sweet venoms!" Jersey orders.

A woman so thin that she's merely a spine between her breasts and hips exits the bathroom. Another, closer to the bar, is covered in boils the size of my fist. On one stool, there's a man entirely enveloped by a swirl of white mist. Then I blink and see them as they are: ordinary people, laughing and shouting at one another over the swell of the music.

There's not much real here.

Of course, there isn't. It's a bar. Nearly everyone here is pretending to be someone they're not. I take a deep breath and try to focus on the bits that don't shift and blur.

There's the bar itself. It's wood. Solid. Coasters litter its surface, and the varnish is rough with bubbles from drinks that sat on the wood too long. Behind is a wall of liquor. The levels of liquid in the bottles rise and fall when I look at them, like a tide pulled by the moon.

Opposite the bar, benches wrap around the wall. Shadows lurk along the benches, and on the floor, water creeps toward my feet and then recedes. Waves lap against the floor as if the scuffed wood were a sandy shore. Refocusing my eyes, I see that an ocean fills the farthest corner of the bar, receding into a darkness that could extend a few feet or many miles. I look away from its impossible depths, back at my sister.

Leah is holding her glass up and examining it. Red swirls within amber liquid. "What's in it?"

"Exactly the question we don't ask," Jersey says.

They're both shouting because the music is pounding through the bar and through my head. Maybe I can lose myself in the music. This might be exactly what I need, a chance to stop thinking and feeling. I spend too much time thinking.

Crossing to the bar, I begin reaching for drinks. My fingers slide through the first, then the second, the third. I don't stop. Though I don't *need* to eat, I know that I *can* eat the fruit and the cupcakes and the breads in Mother's kitchen. I can often find vegetables, too, since she always swore she was on one diet or another. There will be drinkers here who make similar promises: only one more drink; this is the last one. And there will be those who pour a drink into a drain or a planter and claim they drank it all. Those who say their soda is alcohol and their alcohol is soda. Those who say they aren't here at all—they're home, studying; they're at work; they went to the movies with friends; or they stayed here all night and never left with anyone and won't ever set foot in a bar again.

This place is thick with people's intentions.

My hand closes around a tumbler filled with a dark-amber liquor. I lift it to my lips and drink, and it burns as it trickles down my throat.

"Grenadine?" Leah asks.

"Among other things."

"Is one of those other ingredients pepper spray?"

Jersey plucks the glass out of her hands. "If you don't like it—"

Leah retrieves it and knocks it back, swallowing half in one gulp. "I don't."

"They call it venom for a reason," Jersey says. She swirls on her barstool and leans her back against the edge of the bar. I see stray liquid—beer, liquor, not water—soak into the back of her shirt, but she doesn't seem to notice or care. Her focus is on Leah. "Want to dance?"

"There's no one dancing."

There is. She just can't see them. Shadows are gyrating between the tables. They slide ghostlike through the other customers. They're faceless and often formless, but their silhouettes tangle together as the waves crash around their feet.

Jersey has clearly decided she knows what my sister needs—I notice the pink gauze around her that only I can see has hardened. She pulls Leah toward the center of the bar, where the ocean begins, and they wade into the shallows, though they can't see how it laps around their ankles. One hand in the air, one holding a tumbler full of sweet venom, Jersey swivels her hips. "Don't think. Just dance."

"This is embarrassing," Leah says. "I'm a terrible dancer."

"We're here for unhealthy self-care," Jersey said. "You can't care about what strangers think."

"Of course, I don't care," she lies.

She's always cared. If she didn't, then she wouldn't have been so upset about what Mother claimed about her baked goods. Or her piano playing. Or me.

I put down the glass and don't look to see whether it vanishes. Following Leah and Jersey, I wade into the waves that lap the floor. The pink flows from Jersey and wraps around Leah as they dance together, hips swiveling as the rose-colored ribbon swirls around them.

As the music pulses, I dance with the shadows and flirt with the darkness. The music vibrates through the floor, and I feel the cold of the seawater that no one else can feel seeping into my feet. The lights swirl as I spin, and I don't know if it's because I am spinning or because they are. Or both. But they settle when I eventually stop, breathing heavily, sweating in my armpits, and soaked to my ankles.

I've danced for at least an hour. Maybe more.

Blinking, I look for Leah.

She's in a corner, one of the darker ones where the ocean pools, pressed against a man with thick hands. She's sucking on his lips as if she's trying to swallow him. Jersey is—I don't see her, or her ever-present rose mist. Perhaps she went to the bathroom. Perhaps she left. Perhaps she drowned in the sea.

I cross to Leah. "Hey, what about Jamie?"

She doesn't reply. Her hands are roving the man's chest, and his are squeezing her ass. I try to poke her shoulder. In as loud a voice as I can, I shout, "You're making a mistake. Drink. Dance. But don't do this. You're going to regret it."

She pauses, and I feel a shiver rush through me. The water recedes from around my ankles, and the bar brightens. I am able, for a moment, to see the place without the layer of unreality.

She heard me.

But she didn't. She heard her phone or felt it vibrate. She yanks it out of her back pocket. The man's meaty hands have migrated to her breasts, and she bats them down as she answers the phone, but she doesn't leave his lap. "Jamie!" she says into the phone. I feel as if I summoned him, though I know that's impossible.

Coincidence or fate, I am grateful either way. She has the chance to make the right choice before she does anything unforgivable.

"Jersey took me out," Leah says. "Just couldn't handle being in the house another minute. Yeah. Girls' night out. Me and Jersey." A pause.

"Of course, I'll be careful." Another pause. "You don't need to come." Her voice sharpens. "I just need to forget for a few hours."

Poor Jamie.

Maybe I thought better of Leah, and maybe I shouldn't have. It doesn't take a fortune teller to predict where this is going, and suddenly, I don't want to hear any more. I have no right to judge—I don't know her, not anymore—but I know that I don't like what I see. If she's going to make a mistake that I can't stop, I'd rather not watch.

I return to the bar and begin sliding my hand through glasses again, looking for another that I can drink. My fingers pass through beer after beer until they're stopped by a tumbler.

There's another hand holding the glass.

I stare at it.

It's not a shadow.

My eyes travel from the hand to a wrist, to an arm, to a shoulder, to a face. Strong arms. White T-shirt. Also, white jeans. Black hair. I can't see his eyes—he isn't looking at me. His gaze is fixed on a woman. She's a slim Asian woman with pink eye shadow, and she's fending off the attentions of a much-older white man in a suit. He has the kind of stubble that looks trimmed to resemble a five o'clock shadow, and his teeth are so straight and white that they gleam in the bar lights.

"Let me buy you a drink," the suit man says. He's leaning in so close that it must be impossible for her to breathe anything but his exhalation.

She demurs as she slips off the barstool. "Sorry. I have a boyfriend."

Standing protectively behind her, the man in the white T-shirt and jeans rests his hand on her shoulder. Somehow, he manages to look both comforting and threatening. At this angle, I have a better view of his face: Asian like her, with a square jaw like a classic movie star. It's a wonder that every single eye in the bar isn't on him, he's that good looking. "She has a boyfriend." His voice is smooth and deep and resonates, even though he doesn't raise it.

The suit man holds his hands up in mock surrender. "You came here alone. I assumed . . ."

"He's in the bathroom," the woman says. "He'll be back any minute. You might want to be elsewhere." She strides away from the bar and away from the hand on her shoulder.

Still looming, the man in white glares at the other man, but he's already turned away.

Obviously, the man in white can't be the woman's boyfriend—she said he was in the bathroom. I doubt he is. In fact, I doubt whether she even has a boyfriend. Sipping his beer, the suit man is eyeing the bathroom as if he doubts her as well. I wonder what he'll do when no one emerges. I wonder what the woman's wannabe rescuer will do.

"Don't even think about it," he growls at the suit man.

The suit man ignores him.

"Decent of you to step in," I say to the man in white.

"It doesn't take a genius to tell she's not interested." He's glaring at the suit man, but I pretend he's replying to me. "Only thing subtler would be a neon sign that said, '**GO AWAY.**'"

"Still, not many would have tried to help," I say.

I used to do this with Mother often—slide into her conversations as if she were talking to me. It helped that she talked to herself. And the TV. And her dinner. And the books she didn't read. And the mail she didn't want. And the computer that wouldn't work the way she wanted it to. Sometimes she'd take calls, and while she sat in the kitchen talking, I'd sit on the other side of the wall, holding up my end of the conversation.

"How are the kids?" she'd ask the phone.

"Fine," I'd say. "The baby slept through the night for the first time."

"Don't know where the time goes," she'd say. "I swear, I'm not a day older. Remember the time in junior high we told your parents we were sleeping over at each other's houses—" And she'd be off on a half-remembered anecdote, and I'd listen, pretending she was relaying it to me.

The suit man signals for another beer, and the bartender fills a glass and hands it to him with a warning: "You're going to get another drink in your face if you keep this up."

"Nah, not tonight," he says. "Got a good feeling about this one."

The bartender snorts.

"Wow, he's either dense or delusional," I say.

The man in white gives the bartender an easy grin. "Don't worry. This isn't my first rodeo. I stop by this bar and a few others in the neighborhood almost every night. Over the years, I've seen plenty of guys like this one. The world might change, but these guys don't. They're only interested in easy prey. I'm good at making it difficult."

Instead of responding, the bartender takes an order from a college kid who shouts a request over my guy's shoulder. So I respond instead, "I take it you've been doing this for a while?"

He eyes the suit man. "Someone has to."

I shiver a little. I *know* he's talking to the bartender, but my timing was perfect on that.

The woman has retreated to a corner where she nurses her drink. She's not watching the bathroom door, conspicuous for someone waiting for her date to emerge.

The suit man chugs his new beer and wipes his lips on the back of his hand. He's eyeing the woman, and it looks as if he's decided that now is his moment. He puts his glass down and crosses the bar toward her.

"Uh-oh," I say. "Looks like he didn't believe her."

Glancing at the wannabe hero, I'm certain he won't ignore the suit man's actions. "Happens sometimes," he says. He then hands me his drink. "I didn't drink any, if you want it."

My fingers close automatically around the glass, and then I freeze, staring at him.

It's not possible.

Did he see me? Hear me? No one has been able to before.

He slips between the other customers, and I hurry to follow him. People cross between us. I start to walk around them and then realize I can't see him. *I can't lose him.* Gritting my teeth and squeezing my eyes shut, I slide directly through the people, as if I'm a ghost—or as if they are. On the other side of the crowd, I open my eyes.

I don't see him.

Panic slices through me. I have to find him again. I have to know—

I scan the bar for him. There are more bodies pressed together than before, shouting, talking, laughing, flirting, pretending to be whoever they want. So many bodies that I can't see through them. I rise on my toes, but it doesn't help. In the corner, the man in the suit has slid beside his prey, but she quickly and smoothly extracts herself and plunges in between the dancers, without the help of the man in white.

"Where is he?"

I know he was heading for her, so where—

By the door, I see a flash of white. He's leaving the bar.

Weaving through the bodies, I chase after him and spill onto the sidewalk. He's halfway down the street, walking at a brisk pace. Without any hesitation, I run after him.

CHAPTER SIX

"You're sure you don't want me to come?" Jamie asked, his voice nearly drowned out by the thrum of music and the buzz of conversation in the bar.

Leah tumbled off the lap of the man she'd been kissing. "Really, I'm fine!" She brightened her voice. "All good here. Just having fun with Jersey." Lying to the man who loved her—she felt lower than low.

"Hey." The man had noticed his lap was empty. Bleary eyed, he squinted at her. She hadn't even told him her name or asked his. God, this wasn't like her.

What had she been thinking?

Jamie can't see me like this. Tomorrow, she'd pull herself back together. It was only that she'd worked hard today, and Mom's house was a lot. She wanted to shake it all off and pretend nothing existed beyond this moment—not the house, not the lawyer, not the bills from the funeral home, not the fact that she was supposed to return to work tomorrow. She hadn't wanted to deal with the sympathy of her friends or condolences from her coworkers or with Jamie's puppy dog eyes as he asked how she was for the millionth time.

"You shouldn't be out drinking, not with everything you're going through right now," Jamie said. Her grip on the phone tightened as his worry flooded into her ears, eyes, throat. Even miles away, he could still ram his emotions into her. She felt as if she were back in Mom's kitchen, with the stench of spoiled food choking the air, and she wanted to end this slice of awfulness as quickly as possible.

"Gotta go," she told him. "Jersey needs me."

Where was Jersey?

Why didn't she stop me?

Coming here had been a spectacularly terrible idea. Making out with an extremely inebriated stranger had been an even worse one. She had a boyfriend, the kind who made her dinner and stood by her at her mother's funeral and tossed out words like "our future" and "forever." No matter how unhelpful he was being while trying to be helpful, he didn't deserve this. She was not the type of person who cheated on her boyfriend, the man she was supposed to have a future with. "I'll call you in the morning," Leah promised Jamie as the music wailed louder.

"What?" he said. "Can't hear you!"

"Tomorrow!" she shouted into the phone. "I'll call you!"

He told her he loved her, and she heard herself saying the words back to him, feeling as if she were kicking a puppy; then she shoved the phone back into her pocket. Exhaling, Leah scanned the bar for Jersey—her friend was dancing, hips circling and hands overhead, oblivious to everyone around her.

Leah wanted that: to be lost in the thrum of music, caught in the moment. Briefly, with her hands on a stranger, she'd had that, a kind of oblivion—but then Jamie called, and the past and future came crashing in to shatter the moment. She envied Jersey's ability to willfully tune out the world. Sure, it wasn't always a healthy skill, but as Jersey frequently claimed, it enabled her to be sunny the rest of the time. "Going to get a drink," she told the man she'd been kissing. "You should find someone else. I'm taken."

He caught her wrist as she turned to go. "Sure, but—" He released her and held up his hand. "If you change your mind, I'm here."

She shook her head and felt the floor undulate—the sudden movement made her dizzy. *I drank too much. Or not enough.* One more drink, and then maybe she'd forget about kissing a complete stranger, lying to Jamie, and making an ass of herself.

"Sometimes a person just needs to forget for a few hours," the man said, and she realized he'd been listening to every word she'd said to Jamie. That made her feel worse. "It doesn't have to mean more than that. Your choice."

She stepped back, unsure what to say and wishing she could disappear, and the crowd closed around her. She wormed her way to where she'd seen Jersey undulating to the music. Leah bumped into a woman, mumbled an apology, and tried to steady herself. *Definitely drank too much.* She'd never felt so unsteady.

Her friend caught her hand. "Hey, having fun?" Jersey asked.

"Sure," Leah lied. And then: "Actually no."

"Get another sweet venom," Jersey suggested. "On me."

"Not sure that's the best idea."

Jersey flashed a grin. "All my ideas are the best ideas!" And then she looked at her with that mix of pity, understanding, and frustration that only a best friend could wear. "You're brooding, and it isn't good for you." She gave Leah a little shake, so gentle that it felt like the equivalent of a hug. "Get out of your head."

She wasn't brooding. She was . . . She tried to think of the word but failed. It fluttered, just out of reach. The music was too loud. It echoed against her skull. Maybe Jersey was right. She needed to numb her mind. Didn't she deserve a little peace? Leah made her way to the bar and ordered another sweet venom—still didn't like it, but it tasted flatter than the first. Less sickly sweet.

Okay, maybe Jersey *wasn't* right. But Jamie wasn't either. Leah just needed . . . She didn't know what she needed.

Leaning against the bar, she watched the people dance, flirt, talk, shout, laugh.

She wondered how many of them were lying with their voices and their smiles, acting as if they were having so much fun when all they wanted to do was scream. She downed another third of her drink. Blinked her eyes. She was starting to have that gummy-eyed, clogged-ears feeling and knew she shouldn't have gone for another drink. Obviously. There was a lot she shouldn't have done. Like try to maintain a relationship with her mom.

Fresh air. That's what I need. Clear my head.

She stumbled out onto the sidewalk.

The night air was sharper, edged with the stink of car exhaust and the tang of garbage, but not the stench of sweat and beer. *Better.* She inhaled deeply. Her head swam.

She never should have tried to compete with Hannah's memory. She should have excused herself from her mother's life as soon as she realized she was never going to measure up, not to Mom's image of who her sister could have been: the perfect daughter.

Maybe that's who Hannah would have been if she'd lived, and maybe it wasn't. *I would have been a good sister.* Or maybe she would have fucked that up too. Maybe a living Hannah would have been worse, amplifying every one of Leah's mistakes.

"Stop thinking!" Leah said out loud. She was supposed to be distracting herself. Ugh, how did you shut off a brain?

A voice behind her asked, "You okay?"

She waved at the speaker. "Fine. Just . . . fine."

"Feel sick? You can throw up in the gutter if you want. I doubt anyone will notice." It was a man with a gentle voice. He was looking at her with concern in his eyes. She noted that he was holding a flask. "Or do you want more?" He held it out. "It's whiskey."

She considered it, but all the drinks before hadn't helped so why would more? She felt as if her skull was stuffed with oatmeal. "I think I want food." Her eyes landed on a gyro cart. She weaved toward it, but the sidewalk seemed to be sticking to her feet.

Leah felt a hand on her elbow. "I'll buy us both gyros," the man offered.

She wasn't going to argue, especially since she was fairly certain she'd spent most of her cash on those horrible sweet-venom drinks. "You don't have to."

"Onions or no onions?" he asked.

"No onions. Extra tomatoes."

He ordered for both of them, and they carried them to a curb and sat. She felt better sitting—the world didn't spin quite so much. "Thanks," Leah said. She rolled the aluminum foil to expose the end of the gyro and bit into it. Tzatziki sauce spurted out and spilled on her fingers. He handed her a paper napkin, and she thanked him again.

"If you're trying to pick me up," Leah said, "you should know I have a boyfriend." Wow, this tasted amazing. She wasn't sure she'd ever tasted anything this good. She stuffed another bite in her mouth.

"Not trying anything," the man said. "Just wanted a gyro. And you—well, you remind me of someone. A friend of mine. She—" He cut himself off. "You remind me of her."

Leah didn't really want to know the details, but she asked anyway, "Is she dead?"

He blinked. "How did you know that?"

She thought about how her voice had sounded when she called the funeral home, when she talked to the lawyer, when she called work to say she'd need a day or two off. "The way you said it."

"Oh."

She knew she should follow with all the sympathy and condolences that everyone had been parroting at her, but she couldn't bring herself to do it. None of the platitudes had made her feel one whit better. They just made her feel like biting someone. She noticed a few stray onions had sneaked their way into her pita, and she plucked them out, flicking them into the gutter. "You know, I heard once that if a baby orca dies, its mother will carry the dead infant through the icy waters for days," Leah said.

"Huh. Okay."

"And elephants are supposed to have graveyards. They'll visit the bones of the deceased. I think I'd rather be a goldfish. Three-second memory."

"I've heard that's a myth," he offered. "They can remember things for at least five months."

"Oh? You asked one?"

He grinned. "They're not great conversationalists."

She knew she should ask about his friend, how long ago, what happened, et cetera—that's how a polite conversation would go. She'd then offer up the fact that her mother died recently. He'd say he was sorry, and they'd bond over their losses. But she didn't want to have that conversation.

Still, she regretted mentioning the orca and elephants. That had been a weird thing to say. She took another bite of the gyro, unable to think of anything she *did* want to say. Her thoughts felt sluggish. Maybe all the alcohol was finally doing its job.

"If you did have a three-second memory," he said, "you wouldn't have much personality. Who we are is who we've been. And who we've known."

That got much too close to what she didn't want to think about. She swallowed her bite of gyro; this time it was like a lump of cardboard. "Selective memory then," Leah said.

"I'd agree to that. Erase everything embarrassing and idiotic I've ever said, beginning with the time in college I worked in a sporting store, and someone bought a canoe, and I said, 'Would you like that in a bag?'"

Leah felt herself begin to smile. It felt unfamiliar, as if her cheeks hadn't moved like that in days and days. She wondered when she last laughed. A day ago? A year? She deliberately cut off any memories before they could arise.

"And then I'd move ahead to yesterday, at a coffee shop, where the barista asked if I'd like an extra shot of espresso, and I said, 'No, thanks, I'm not in a hurry.'"

Now she laughed.

He smiled back at her. "I'm Sam."

"Hi, Sam. Can I have a sip of that whiskey?"

He handed her the flask. "You're trying for selective memory?"

Leah took a swig. "I am the goldfish."

CHAPTER SEVEN

Outside, shadows slip across the street, as if frightened by the headlights of the passing cars. Ordinary shadows, for the most part, but here and there, tucked against a building or a doorway, there's a sharpness to the dark. I deliberately avoid those areas and instead scan the sidewalks.

Muck runs through the gutters, thicker here by the bars and restaurants than it ever was near Mother's house. A gaggle of tipsy friends clusters on the opposite sidewalk, and the man in white is beyond them, across the street. Avoiding the stream of toxic ooze, I dart out as the taxis whiz by. I feel the wind of one rush past. *You're being an idiot.* Not all cars will necessarily flow through me. If I'm unlucky enough . . . But my need to catch him, to know if he can see and hear me, overrides all common sense.

He's turned down a side street clogged with faceless pedestrians holding umbrellas. As I follow him, the street becomes overrun with a flood of even more men, women, and children, all with umbrellas held up against a nonexistent rain. A moment later, it's merely umbrellas held by shadows. All the pedestrians have dissolved into smoke. Chasing after him, I push the umbrellas out of my way, my hands slapping the fabric. The shadow bodies evaporate beneath them, but the umbrellas continue their march through the street. I continue shoving them aside, trying to see beyond. I know he's ahead of me—but where? He's gone.

I halt at the street corner. Which way? He can't be far; he's on foot. White shirt and white jeans, he should stand out against the shadows. "Come back!" I yell. "Please! I have to talk to you!"

But no one responds.

People flow up and down the sidewalk beside a steady stream of toxic muck.

And then, ahead of me!

I see the man in white round a corner, lit by a streetlight, and I run. The concrete crumbles into sand that pulls at my feet, slowing me, trying to trip me. It pours into my shoes, so I kick them off. Carrying them, I run faster, watching out for the toxic muck. The beach sidewalk is hot beneath my soles, and I feel the crunch of a crushed shell, the sharp bite of a rock. Ignoring the pain, I run until I am on pavement again, but I don't slow to put my shoes back on. I don't understand how I haven't caught up to him yet.

He can't be ordinary.

He can't be real.

He has to be . . . what? Like me? It feels so impossible that I can hardly form the words in my head. I haven't dared hope for this, not in years. There has never been another like me. All the shadowy people I've seen . . . Every single one has dissolved. None have spoken to me or seen me.

Only the shadow wolves have ever touched me, and that was with the intent to harm.

I used to dream that I'd meet another like me. Used to watch kids wait for the school bus from my bedroom window, watch parents with strollers, joggers, the shadows . . . Every time I saw someone who seemed indistinct, I would race outside—straight through the door or window—and drop down amid the flowers, which shimmered and vanished when I landed, scraping my knees. Once, twisting my ankle.

But it never worked. Like the flowers, they'd fade away. Or they'd be too insubstantial to interact, like the motorcycle driver that Jamie drove through the other day. Shadows of people. I don't know why I think it will be different this time.

He handed me a glass. He spoke to me. That should have been 100 percent impossible by everything I knew and understood. I want to ask him how he did it. I want to ask—

How. Why. If.

If I catch him.

Ahead, I see a train bridge over the street, the Long Island Rail Road. People are hurrying up the steps, and I see my white knight dodging between them, and—wait, where is he? I can't see him, and I am running again. My bare feet pound on the sidewalk. Pain shoots through my leg from the sole of my left foot. Pausing, I yank out a shard of glass, pull on my shoes, and continue running.

Ahead of me, the sidewalk has been consumed by toxic muck. Spilling out of doorways and windows, it's swallowed half the street. No one else can see it; they wade through it as if it doesn't exist. The waves of muck slosh over the pavement. I give it as wide a berth as possible and try not to think about what would happen if it flooded the entire street.

At last, I reach the stairs. He's already at the top, then out of sight. Has he boarded a train? I would have heard one, wouldn't I?

I hear one now, in the distance. Its horn wails like a rush of wind. I pound up the stairs, charging *through* the people. It feels like running through the rain.

I'm panting hard when I reach the platform. It's full of people heading home and people heading out. On one end, there's a man playing an electric keyboard. He's wailing out a song with unidentifiable lyrics. A violin plays, discordant beside him, upheld only by shadows. There are drummers on the opposite platform. A woman's voice wails in an operatic solo. All the music clashes together, and I can't tell what is real and what isn't, except that passengers toss coins in the keyboarder's hat. *Real.* I weave through people. *Real, real, real.*

Where are you?

The train slows as it pulls into the station. I have to find him before he boards, if he hasn't descended again or vanished. He could fade to a smoky shadow like everyone else I've ever tried to talk to. Unless he isn't like the shadows. He said the words "over the years" as if he'd lived a life.

I have to know.

It's a need that pulls me like hunger.

The train squeals as it brakes. It lurches to a stop, and the doors slide open. I'm still weaving through the crowd, careful not to touch any of the passengers, but now there are even more people spilling out. A guy with his bike shoulders past, his arm moving through me, but I feel the metal of the bike—and when I look again, he isn't carrying anything. It distracts me long enough that I almost miss it: my white knight boards the train.

He steps on between two older women in saris. I zigzag between passengers as I run toward his train car doors, and then the doors are closing. They shut before me, and for an instant, I feel like howling. He can't escape me!

I am only dimly aware that this is the sort of moment that can change a life: to stay or to go, to follow or to forget, to choose yes or no. As the train lurches forward, I throw myself at the closed door and slip through as if I'm made of nothing. The train pulls away from the station, and I am carried with it.

◆ ◆ ◆

I jerk to the side as the train chugs forward. Spreading my feet, I try to balance myself. Buildings begin to slide past the grimy windows, and I feel my heart thud harder within my rib cage.

Leah is back there.

I didn't intend to leave her.

For an instant, I think of hurling myself back through to the platform, but then the opportunity is gone: we're picking up speed, and Queens is flickering by faster and faster, the lights from the buildings and cars blurring. I don't know where I'd land, or how broken I'd be if I jumped now.

I've never been on a train. A bus, once. Mother preferred to drive herself. I'd ride with her, eyes closed so I wouldn't see any wolves, or stay behind and wait for her to return. But I try not to let panic swallow me. I have a purpose: find the man in white. Focus on that. Find him. Ask if he can see me and hear me. Ask . . . oh, God, the things I could ask if someone could answer! My hands are shaking so hard that I'm vibrating.

Resolutely, I stride through the crowd, directly through them. I spread my arms wide and walk straight through their bodies—if I encounter the man in white, I'll feel him. And if not . . . no harm to anyone, as far as I know.

I hate the way it feels. No, I hate the way it makes *me* feel, as if I am insubstantial, as if I am irrelevant. I *can* feel them if I concentrate enough, the same way I could touch Mother's arm as she lay beside me and Leah's arm in the cemetery, but this . . . I slide through people as if I or they don't exist. Baseball fans coming home from a Mets game, college students decked out in ripped jeans, tired travelers with suitcases on their way back from wherever—my arms glide through them all. My fingers brush against a purse, and I feel the leather on my fingertips; it's held by an elderly woman, and when I reach out to touch her shoulder, my hand melts through her flesh. She shivers as if an errant breeze has touched her. "Can you feel me?" I ask. "Any of you? Can you hear me?" I shout louder, "Can anyone hear me? Please, I know you're here somewhere!"

I hear the tinny sound of music thrumming from a commuter's headphones, a hush of voices as two college students talk about an exam on Monday, a man loudly answering his cell phone, the Mets fans singing off pitch at high volume. Very soon, I reach the end of the car.

Where is he? I saw him board this train car.

At least I think I did.

Maybe it was the next one?

Gritting my teeth, I push my body through the door. The wind whips like a shrill screech, and the connection between cars squeals. I toss myself through into the next car. And then I keep going, train car after train car, breaking into a run.

The train jerks to the side, and I'm knocked off balance. I crash through a woman with pink hair and fall on my knees. My shoulder jams into the side of a seat—I don't know why I can feel it when I couldn't touch the woman. I don't know why I can't find the man in white. Or why no one can hear me scream, because I am screaming now. I can feel it tearing at my throat and echoing in my ears.

It's easy to scream when no one can hear you. Harder to stop. I think if I just keep screaming louder, pouring every bit of anger, frustration, and helplessness through my throat until I feel it burn, then it will somehow break through. But it doesn't.

Beneath me, the train squeals. I hear the whistle as it pulls into the next station. If I don't find him right now, he could exit the train, and I'd never know where he went.

Resolutely, I charge toward the doors as they open, and spill onto the platform. And I run again—past every train car, my arms wide again, searching for the man in white. I reach the end of the platform as the train doors close and hurl myself back on board. Methodically, I search every car again and frantically check the platform every time the train stops. By the fifth stop, my lungs are heaving and my legs are aching. I still haven't found him.

Once, I catch a glimpse of white, but when the man turns his head, I see it's not him. Somehow my wannabe hero has eluded me. Perhaps he's vanished, like the pedestrians with umbrellas. Except he seemed so solid, so real, so reachable!

Maybe I was foolish to think I could find him. I've been alone my entire life—

Not alone. I always had Mother. She loved me.

But she's gone. And now . . .

And now I'm on a train, and I don't know where I'm going or where I want to be.

There are no screams left inside me. No tears left either. I feel as dry and empty as a husk. I don't watch out the window, but I feel when the train lurches to a stop at each station, just as I hear when the conductor calls, "Babylon, last stop. Babylon. All passengers must disembark."

Numbly, I exit the train and stand on the platform as passengers flow around me. None of them are the man in white, and I think I've made a terrible mistake.

At last, there's only me.

Feeling emptier than I've ever felt, I curl up on a bench in a corner of the platform where the shadows seem softer. Closing my eyes, I wait for either sleep or clarity to claim me.

Sleep comes first.

CHAPTER EIGHT

Hannah died on a Tuesday.

Leah should have known it was coming, but she'd been told over and over that everything would be okay, and she believed that lovely lie with all her heart. She couldn't be blamed for believing what she was told; she was only six on that terrible Tuesday.

Six-year-old Leah knew it was Tuesday because she had her piano lesson with Mrs. Murphy, who had wrinkly knuckles and liked to drink iced tea. Leah was eking out the notes to "Twinkle, Twinkle" when her father arrived early to pick her up. He whispered to Mrs. Murphy, who clucked her tongue and said, "Oh, I am so dreadfully sorry," and gave Leah a sticker, even though she'd missed half the notes. "You poor dear," Mrs. Murphy said to her.

Her father wasn't the one who usually picked her up. That was Mommy. Daddy was supposed to be at work, but Leah didn't ask why he was there or why he was early. His lips were pressed together hard, as if they were all that was keeping a swarm of bees from spilling from his mouth. She stared at his lips and imagined wasps, hornets, and bees.

He still didn't say anything as she buckled herself in the back seat of the car. Instead, he squeezed the steering wheel and watched Leah in the rearview mirror. Fiddling with the strap of her backpack, Leah pretended not to notice his grip on the wheel or the worry in his eyes.

I won't cry. No matter what's wrong. She had already decided at a very young age, without ever really thinking about it, that crying felt too much like letting the world win. She'd rather bite the inside of her cheek until it bled than cry.

He parked in their driveway, and when Leah reached for the door handle, he said, "Hold up a minute, honey." And he released the bees.

Her sister, Hannah, had been very sick. She'd been sick since she was born, in and out of hospitals. Leah knew that. The last time she'd seen her two-year-old sister, Hannah had so many tubes and wires connected to her that Leah didn't want to look, even though she knew it wasn't the kind of sick you could catch, as a doctor had told her. Her sister was sick because something inside her hadn't grown right when she was inside Mommy's tummy. Leah had asked if they could put her back, let her finish growing, and then take her out again when she was better. The doctor had laughed, but it was the kind of laugh that didn't sound as if she'd heard anything funny. Leah hadn't thought it was funny. Weren't doctors supposed to fix you?

"Do you understand?" Daddy asked her. "Hannah died."

He was the only one to say those words.

Later, she heard other words: *She's at rest. She's at peace. She's in a better place. She's beyond pain. She's sleeping.* That last was the worst. For weeks after—and sometimes randomly even years later—Leah would lie awake at night, terrified of closing her eyes, even though she knew it was just a thing people said when they didn't want to say the uglier, truer words.

During the funeral, Leah stared at the polished wood box and wondered how her sister could really be in there. She wondered if she still had all the tubes and wires with her, tucked inside. She pictured her in that pale-blue hospital gown and hoped Hannah was wearing the dinosaur onesie with the ruffle instead. Leah was wearing her itchy black dress and tights that twisted no matter how carefully she tried to pull them up. She didn't want her sister to be uncomfortable inside the box.

"Mommy, what is Hannah wearing?" she asked.

Her mother flinched. "I don't . . ."

"Is she wearing the dinosaur onesie? The one with the ruffle?" Suddenly, that seemed like the most important thing in the world: that Hannah had on her dinosaur onesie instead of the pale-blue gown. If Leah's sister had to be in that box forever, then she should be dressed in her own clothes. "She should be wearing it. She loves it. Is she wearing it?" It had a T. rex stretching its arms out with a cartoon bubble that said, *I love you this much!* The first time Hannah had worn it, Leah poked the picture again and again so that the dinosaur closed its arms, hugging her finger, and Hannah giggled so much that she fell over. Leah clutched her mother's sleeve. "She won't be happy if she's not wearing it. She needs to be wearing it!"

"Yes, yes, sweetie, of course she is. That's her favorite."

And then Leah felt as if she could breathe again.

She let the strangers from Mommy's and Daddy's work hug her and pat her head, even though half of them wore flowery perfume that smelled like a just-washed bathroom. While they talked about the flowers, the weather, the casket, how tall Leah had grown, and how sorry they were, she pictured Hannah giggling at the T. rex with his tiny arms.

It was only weeks later that Leah found the onesie in Hannah's hamper. She didn't say anything about it, but she took it and stuffed it in her drawer instead, beneath her pj's.

◆　◆　◆

The odd thing was how she'd sometimes forget.

She woke one Sunday morning, bounded into the kitchen, and asked when they were going to visit Hannah at the hospital. It had been a while, she said, and Hannah must be lonely.

Her mother was at the sink, with soap up to her elbows, and her father was spreading butter on a piece of toast. He dropped the knife, and it clattered on the counter.

The silence was thick.

And then Leah remembered.

"You understand she's not at the hospital anymore," Daddy said to his toast.

"Yes," Leah whispered. She didn't know how to say she'd forgotten. It was a large, horrible thing to have forgotten, but sometimes it just didn't seem real, and it slipped away like a shadowy dream. She didn't know how to explain that. Every day, she half expected to come home from school to hear Hannah in the living room, playing with blocks. They'd stack them until Leah had to stand on her tippy-toes, and then Hannah would bash them with her head and giggle wildly as they crashed down on the carpet. Looking down at her feet, Leah said, "I'm sorry."

"She's not there, and she's not coming back," Daddy said. His voice sounded as if he'd swallowed sand, and she wished she could slink back into her room and bury herself in blankets.

"Aaron." Mommy's voice was sharp.

"She needs to understand."

Leah felt hot tears fill her eyes. She *did* understand, but some days it felt like something that had happened to some other family. She remembered visiting Hannah in the hospital. It was easy to picture that; it was harder to believe that she wasn't there anymore. Leah bit the inside of her cheek to try to keep her tears from falling.

Mommy knelt in front of her. "You remember that nice man at the funeral talking about Heaven? Do you know what that is, Leah? Some people believe that's where people go after they die. It's always sunny there. Always warm. You're always happy. And you have whatever you want. If you'd like, you can think of Hannah there. Always playing. Never in pain. No wires. No tubes. No yucky hospital food."

"She's in Heaven?" Leah asked. Several people had said that at the funeral, that her sister was with angels, even that she'd become God's newest angel. Leah had thought it was just a fancier way of saying that she was asleep.

If Hannah was there, why hadn't her parents said so?

"Can we visit her?" Leah asked.

"You'll see her there someday," Mommy said.

"Saturday?" Leah asked. That was the next day she didn't have to go to school and her parents didn't have to go to work.

"A long, long time from now."

Daddy slammed his hand down flat on the counter. "Dammit, Eleanor."

"This is exactly why religion exists," Mommy snapped at him. "And it could be true. You don't know. Millions of people believe it's true."

"Millions of people believe in Santa Claus and the Tooth Fairy," Daddy snapped back. He then winced and ran his hand through his hair. "Sorry, princess. How about I take you to the cemetery this weekend? We'll visit Hannah together."

Leah's throat felt clogged. She shook her head vigorously. She wished she hadn't left her bedroom. Or her bed.

"We'll bring flowers," Daddy said.

Hannah didn't care about flowers. She was two. She liked blocks and dinosaurs and bananas, especially when Leah pretended her banana was a phone. She'd act as if she were talking to an apple in the refrigerator, and then she'd hand the banana to Hannah.

"What do you say?" Daddy cajoled. "Come with me?"

Leah opened her mouth. "I forgot to brush my teeth."

She fled the kitchen.

Behind her, she heard Daddy say, "I thought we agreed—"

"*You* decided," Mommy said. "*We* didn't agree to anything. She's *six*. She shouldn't have to go through this. I think we should say whatever will make this easier for her. It's a kindness."

"It's not kindness. We tell her we love her, and we'll get through it together," he said. "We don't fill her head with fairy tales that clearly don't make sense to her. We have to be consistent. We can't suddenly pretend to be religious because it's easier."

"Why can't we?"

Leah shut her bedroom door.

◆ ◆ ◆

Leah always loved when the teacher came into their classroom for art. She loved starting with the snow-white page and then filling every inch with color and shapes, and she loved the smell of the paint and the way she could sweep the brush across the paper.

Usually, their art teacher was Mr. Sullivan, who would launch into endless monologues about the color wheel and perspective while the kids painted whatever they wanted, but this Friday there was a substitute, Ms. Bailey. She had curly hair, a hoop in her nose, and an armful of watercolors. She gave them a new assignment: paint a picture of your family, however you see them. It didn't have to be exactly what they looked like; it just had to be what they *felt* like.

Lots of hands shot into the air: Can I paint my dog? What do you mean "felt like"? Like, are they squishy? My daddy's smushy in the middle. My mommy smells like toast. Can I draw toast? Do *you* have a dog, Ms. Bailey, and what's its name?

Leah just started painting. She chewed on her lower lip as she concentrated on adding as much color as she could: a wash of blue and then three figures at the bottom of the page. She painted Hannah at the top, in Heaven, of course. She thought about adding squirrels behind their house because they were there so much, raiding the bird feeders, that Mommy said they were practically part of the family, but she didn't think Ms. Bailey meant to include jokes. She wanted a real picture of their families.

When Ms. Bailey came around the room to see how everyone was doing, she paused by Leah. "Who are they?" she asked, pointing to the figures on the bottom.

Leah thought it was clear. She'd painted her mother all in purple, because that was her favorite color, and she'd done her father with hair that flopped into his face. The paint bled into where his eyes were, but she hoped that was okay. She'd done herself, too, in between her parents, with their arms overlapping. She wasn't certain she could do hands in watercolor. Hands were hard enough with crayons and pencils. It was okay if their sleeves meshed into each other. "Me, my mommy, my daddy, and—" She pointed to the top of the paper at the baby floating in blue. "—that's Hannah."

"Who's Hannah?"

"My sister," Leah said. "She's in Heaven."

Ms. Bailey looked as if a spider had dropped on her lap. Her eyes widened, and her mouth formed an O. "Oh, sweetie, I'm so sorry." She wrapped Leah in a big hug while everyone else in the class stared and whispered. When she released Leah, Ms. Bailey was crying, fat tears dripping down her cheeks. She sniffled, and Leah didn't have any idea what to do or say.

Mommy was wrong. It wasn't one bit easier than saying her sister was dead. With Ms. Bailey's cheeks all wet, Leah felt as if she was going to cry, and that was the last thing she wanted in the middle of school. School was not for crying. Everyone looked at you funny when you did, and they whispered about you in the cafeteria. She'd had enough whispering after the funeral, when everyone tried to be extra nice by inviting her to sit at their table and then not talking to her because they didn't know what to say.

"Can I keep painting?" Leah asked.

Mommy always liked to say whatever was easiest.

"Oh, of course, I love banana bread."

"You haven't aged a day."

"I was almost a concert pianist, but I had to choose between a career in the arts and raising kids. All the rehearsing. All the travel. I never regretted the choice for an instant."

"I don't mind."

"I was here first."

"You must have lost the reservation. I made one weeks ago."

"I'm sorry, but we can't come to your holiday party. Leah's been throwing up all day, poor dear, and I just don't feel comfortable leaving her with a sitter." With the phone to her ear, she winked at Leah, who was watching TV while shoveling pretzels into her mouth. "Oh, no, Hannah's fit as a fiddle. Stomach of steel, that girl. Yes, please give our regards to Harold and tell him we're sorry we'll miss his bagpipes."

Leah was staring at her when she hung up.

"She didn't know," Mommy explained to Leah. "It would have made the conversation awkward. This was easier."

For who?

◆ ◆ ◆

The next time it happened was at Target, approximately eight months after Hannah died.

Leah was following her mother through the cleaning-supplies aisle and wishing she could have stayed in the toy section when a voice rang out from beyond the sponges. "Eleanor?"

It was a woman with a flower-print skirt and platform shoes.

Louder, she said, "Eleanor Riggs?"

"Eleanor Allen now," Mommy corrected, squinting at the woman. Leah thought she wore a lot of makeup and wondered if her art teacher would ever let them paint their faces. She'd use more blue, she decided. Less pink.

"Sasha," the woman said. "Remember? From Greenville High. Go, Timberwolves!" She struck a cheerleader pose. "You were voted most likely to be in a music video, and I was most likely to marry my high school sweetheart."

"Ah, Sasha!" Mommy beamed at her. "So great to see you! And did you marry . . ."

"Josh, and yes," Sasha said. "Although we took a break for college, but now three kids later, and we're happy as clams!"

Glancing longingly at the toy aisle, Leah wondered how happy clams were.

"And you?" Sasha asked. "Is this gorgeous pumpkin yours?"

I'm not a pumpkin.

Mommy steered Leah in front of her and smiled brightly. "Yes, this is Leah. Leah, this is my old friend, Sasha. We went to school together."

Sasha laughed, close to a bray. She had very yellow hair, Leah thought. Like a crayon. She thought about drawing her. "Oh, don't say old!" Sasha said. Then to Leah: "How old are *you*, sweetheart? Five? Six?"

"Six and three-quarters," Leah said. She'd requested a bike for her birthday, or a skateboard. She didn't know if Daddy would approve of either. Their street had a lot of traffic, he'd said. She'd need to wear a helmet, knee pads, and elbow pads, and she could only ride in the park. With work so busy, he didn't know when he'd have time to teach her.

"So precise!" Sasha clucked. "You have a little mathematician here. My oldest is a whiz at math. He's taken math two grade levels above."

"Leah's teachers say she's advanced for her age," Mommy said. "We're thinking of having her skip a grade, but we're worried that will shorten her childhood. It's so fleeting. You don't want them to grow up too quickly." *Skip a grade?* Leah wondered. She'd never heard her parents mention that. Maybe they'd talked to her teacher and hadn't told her? Or maybe this was just another of Mommy's stories.

"So true," Sasha said with a sigh. "Is she your only?"

"She's not," Mommy said and then stopped.

Leah suddenly felt as if the store were too hot. She thought of the box underground and the dinosaur onesie hidden in her drawer. Somehow, she'd gone almost the whole day without thinking of Hannah. Guiltily, she looked again at the toy aisle and tried to think of what Hannah would have liked. She wondered if the next time she went to the cemetery with Daddy, she could convince him to bring a toy instead of flowers. Hannah would have liked that better.

Sasha glanced around the aisle like she was looking for someone. *She doesn't know.* Leah thought of Ms. Bailey. There was rarely anyone in Leah's life who didn't know—all the teachers, all her friends, all her classmates, even the school bus driver, knew. Leah tensed. She knew the kind of sympathy that was going to come. It would ooze all over them. It made Leah uncomfortable.

But Mommy said, "My youngest is spending the day with her grandmother so that Leah and I can have some quality time together." She placed both hands on Leah's shoulders.

Sasha nodded wisely. "Ah, it's so crucial to remind the oldest that they're still important, especially when the youngest sucks so much attention. I make sure to take each of mine on a special outing each season. Last month, the zoo with my youngest. Next month, a play with my middle—she loves musical theater, so we're treating her to the revival of *Oklahoma!*"

Leah felt her mother's grip on her shoulders tighten. "Hannah loves the theater too," Mommy said. "You should hear her sing. Voice like an angel."

A neighbor had told her Hannah had become an angel. Leah didn't think that was what Mommy meant, though. She wondered what

Hannah's singing would've sounded like. Maybe Mommy was imagining that?

"How wonderful! Does she perform? My middle girl is in the youth choir over at Lady Catherine's. She had a solo last Sunday. Wowed everyone."

"She was once recruited by an agent," Mommy said, "but we elected to wait. It's so important that young kids have a normal childhood, free of feeling like they have to compete."

Leah didn't know what an agent was, but she knew no one had recruited Hannah. Unless it was God recruiting her to be an angel? Maybe Mommy was just trying to explain in a way her friend would understand. Grown-ups did that sometimes.

"It does require a particularly mature child to handle the pressure," Sasha said. "You're wise to protect them as long as possible." She waved at her nearly full cart. "Well, I have to be going. I promised my husband it would be a quick trip to pick up a couple items, and now look at me!" She brayed a laugh again. "So great to see you, Eleanor! We should get together sometime. Coffee or lunch."

"I'd love that."

Sasha waved and pushed her cart out of the aisle. When she'd disappeared from view, Mommy squeezed Leah tight and kissed her on the top of her head. "Let's go home." Abandoning their cart, they left the store.

◆ ◆ ◆

Ten months after Hannah died, Leah was told they were having company for dinner: a new colleague of her father's and his family, which included a seven-year-old girl—wasn't that nice? They could play in Leah's room while Mommy and Daddy prepared dinner.

Emma reminded Leah of a rabbit. She had tiny eyes, a tiny nose, and soft brown hair that looked pettable, though Leah knew it would be weird if she touched it. She darted through Leah's room, examining everything. She picked up and put down all Leah's stuffed animals, peered at the books on Leah's shelf, and fiddled with Leah's hair ties.

"What do you want to play?" Leah asked her.

"House," Emma said. "I'm the mommy, so you have to do what I say."

Daddy had given a speech about how Leah had to be a good host, play whatever Emma wanted her to play, and be a nice, good girl so that his friends would think they were a nice, good family. "Okay."

"We're going to make pancakes," Emma declared. She began bossing Leah around, demanding that she fetch ingredients—a handful of dirt from one of Mommy's potted plants, shampoo from the bathroom, and pencil shavings from inside Leah's pencil sharpener. She mixed them together in Leah's trash can. "We have to be done before the baby wakes up. Babies *love* pancakes."

And then Emma pointed to Hannah's crib.

Daddy had said they needed to give it away, and Mommy had said, "Not yet." She wasn't ready yet. Leah had said she didn't mind. Most days, she barely noticed it, even though it filled a corner of the room. Hannah had been close to outgrowing it. She'd tried once to climb out, before she'd gone to the hospital.

"Where's the real baby?" Emma demanded.

Leah opened her mouth. Gone, she almost said. In Heaven. In the cemetery. Asleep. Instead, she said, "She's at the zoo, with her grandma."

Emma's rabbity face squished up. "At dinnertime?"

"She likes to feed the giraffes," Leah said. "They have long tongues." She'd seen a picture once of a zookeeper feeding a giraffe. Its tongue had wrapped around the woman's hand. "And she likes to watch the monkeys."

Emma nodded as if this made sense.

Leah continued. She wasn't sure why she did, but she couldn't seem to stop talking. "She likes the elephants too. When she's older, she's going to work in a circus and be an animal trainer." It could have been possible. She remembered how much little Hannah had loved her stuffed elephant with the floppy ears.

"Our dog sits when you give him a treat," Emma said.

"She's going to train elephants," Leah said. "That's why she's at the zoo. She's practicing." She didn't think they let you practice training elephants at the zoo, but the words were already out of her mouth, and she had no idea how to reel them back in.

Emma considered this for a moment. "I think you're lying."

She could have said yes, it was just a story she made up, but she didn't. "I'm not lying. Hannah is at the zoo. Ask my mom if you don't believe me."

And then Leah looked up to see her father standing in the doorway. He stared at her, and she stared at him.

By the time she came home from school the next day, the crib was gone.

Within six months, they'd moved to a drab one-story house in Garden City with a porch and no memories of Hannah at all, except what they brought with them.

CHAPTER NINE

I wake to the whistle of a train and the glare of the sun. Sitting up, I run my tongue over my teeth, trying to make them feel less sticky, and rake my fingers through my hair. It's late morning, and I don't know how many train whistles I've slept through.

If it was sleep.

Holding up my hand, I try to determine whether it looks less distinct than it used to. Am I fading? Did I wink in and out of existence while the morning trains blared, losing hours the way I did in Mom's living room? It's possible. In fact, I think it's likely, given that it feels like I slept for only a few minutes but clearly much more time has passed. I shudder and lower my hand.

That's twice now. It's never happened before, not to me.

At least I did wake or come back or . . . whatever. I'm still here. And the shadow wolves haven't appeared. Maybe they won't. Maybe they don't exist anymore. They could have faded with my childhood . . . except that I don't believe that—they lurked outside my window for too many years for that to be true.

They haven't found me yet. That's enough for now.

I have, as I see it, two choices:

Get on a train heading back west, toward my sister and her life. Or board a train in the opposite direction and keep heading east, as far as the train will take me. Right now, both sound as appealing as Mother's casket.

So I let fate decide.

I take the first train that arrives: eastbound, to Montauk.

I don't bother to look for the man in white—it's beyond unlikely I'll find him now. Instead, I let the conductor walk through me as he checks tickets; then I sink onto the floor as the train pulls away from the station. As we chug eastward, I try to think as little as possible.

Two hours later, the train lurches when it reaches the end of the line, the very tip of Long Island before it vanishes into the Atlantic, and I think about staying exactly where I am. Just ride the same train back in the opposite direction, back to Leah . . . but I don't. I can't. There's nothing for me in that direction. There's only forward.

What's out there?

As if I'm a passenger like any other, I disembark, careful not to walk through the family of three ahead of me. The kid is shoving pretzels in her face as she walks. She's gawking at the blue sky, the platform, and her flip-flops as if every sight is new. Her mother is carrying a beach bag. The handle of a plastic shovel pokes out the top.

"Do you like the beach?" I ask the girl.

I pretend she answers.

"Sand does get everywhere, and your parents are right to make you wear sunscreen," I tell her. She doesn't look back as her father pulls her by her free hand along the platform. "You should listen to them. As much as you can. And they should listen to you." He's pulling a suitcase with his other hand, and her mother waves toward a car in the parking lot. I wonder if it is a grandmother, grandfather, sister, friend, uncle, cousin, but I don't wait to see who emerges.

Instead, I take stock of where I am: the Montauk train station. The station itself looks like a house, white with black shutters, and while the usual mist swirls around the train platform, it doesn't extend beyond the station, perhaps because people don't linger there—they board a

79

train, or they drive away. I don't see any shadow wolves, and there's no toxic muck near the station either. It feels a bit like a different world from either Queens or Garden City, but it may only be because there are fewer people this far east, especially right here, right now.

I walk across the parking lot and breathe in the salt-tinged air. It smells like seaweed, and I hear seagulls crying to one another. I breathe in deeply and tell myself there will be another train heading west whenever I want to take one. For now . . . I follow the road leading away from the station.

Soon, I'll see the ocean.

Already, I can taste it, and I can feel it on my skin, the salty droplets in the breeze.

And then before I'm ready, it's there, the Atlantic.

You'd think that, having lived on an island my whole life, I would have seen the ocean before, but Mother wasn't a beach person—she didn't like the sand, the sun, or the salt. She preferred a pool, ideally owned and cleaned by a neighbor, heavy with chlorine. Our house was—is? was? is it our house anymore?—inland, sandwiched between a family of four that constantly bickered and an elderly man who loved to putter in his garden and criticize everyone else's yard. There wasn't much within walking distance, except the elementary school where Leah went. I used to go with Mother and Leah to the school playground on the weekends when my sister was little, and Leah would swing so high that Mother would warn her she'd flip over. The top of the swing set was festooned with sneakers, memorializing the kids who'd sworn they'd swung a full circle around the crossbar—dozens of sneakers that only I could see. Once, I spent an entire afternoon trying to figure out how to knock down a pair that I liked. I ended up prodding one off with a neighbor's unused fishing rod.

Loved those shoes.

The ocean stretches before me in all its varieties of blue. And the sky is as blue as a kindergartener's crayon art. I stop in my tracks, staring at the blue meeting the blue, with a smear of purplish land between—Rhode

Island or Connecticut—far in the distance. I don't know how long I stand there, awed. There isn't a hint of haze on the horizon. I think it's the only view I've ever seen that isn't marred by the unreal.

Veering off the road, I head for the beach. My feet sink into the sand, and its heat penetrates through my shoes. I walk straight toward the water, shuck off my shoes, and wade ankle deep into the edges of the crashing waves. The water is cold enough to bite. I can feel it even though it doesn't curl around my feet the way it would anyone else's. Holding my shoes in one hand, I stroll along the shore, feeling but not disturbing the sand.

They call Montauk "The End," and I wonder if this is where I will end.

It's not so bad.

It's beautiful. Peaceful.

Eventually, I see houses. Mansions. First, a sprawling mansion with an infinity pool, then a New England–style estate with a widow's walk, then a beach cottage. They're wreathed in a sparkling haze, and they shift before my eyes. My stomach plummets, and I feel the peace dissolve. It's here, too, the haze and the shadows.

Of course, it is.

It's everywhere. Or at least it's everywhere I've ever been. Out there in the vast blue, maybe there's a place free of the haze. A place where I wouldn't have to fear the shadow wolves. A place where nothing could hurt me, and I could just . . . be.

And if that place could hold someone else like me, someone who could be like Jamie was to Leah, a person who could hear me, see me, make me laugh, then what would it be like to be in such a place with such a person?

I continue to walk toward the houses, watching them shift. The center one stays relatively the same, I notice: a beach house with wide windows and a deck. I stop and try to separate out what's real and what isn't. It's impossible to tell just by looking at it. It could be like Mother's house, overlaid with dreams and intentions, or it could be fully unreal, an entire mirage, though I've never encountered a place that was entirely illusory before.

I realize I'm walking up to it when I reach a gate in a white picket fence that's drowning in beach roses. I think of Mother's roses, riotous in her front yard. Tentatively, I stretch out a hand, expecting my fingers to slide through, but they're stopped by wood. I close my fingers over the latch. It feels like metal, solid, hot from the sun, and it clinks as I lift. Inside, the yard is perfectly manicured, with a stone walkway of blue slate that leads to the pool and patio. Hydrangeas are in full bloom, big fat bunches of blue blossoms, though I'm certain they're not in season. Like Mother's yard, I don't think that matters here. The grass under my feet bends as I step, and when I glance behind myself, I see I've left footprints.

I've never left a footprint before.

I walk up to the patio. Touch a lounge chair. Run my fingers over a glass patio table. There's a pitcher of lemonade with ice and glasses next to it. Lifting the pitcher, I pour lemonade into a glass. The ice pours with it, splashing as it lands in the lemonade. I raise it to my lips and take a sip. Sharp but sugary.

The pool looks pristine, blue and shimmery and perfect. I'm sweating from my walk, so I strip off my clothes and cross naked to the water. Nakedness isn't an issue when no one can see you.

The water has been warmed by the sun and feels soft on my skin. I walk down the steps until I'm waist deep, then submerge myself. The chlorine stings my eyes, but I keep them open. The blue tiles below me are distorted.

Bursting out of the water, I suck in air and then drop under again. There isn't anything that can hurt me here. I feel utterly safe, as I haven't since my mother's body was carried out of her house. The water cocoons me, and it can't tell whether I'm crying.

On the surface, the sky warps through the water. It's blue everywhere: blue sky, blue tile. A smear of red passes overhead, and I burst to the surface again in time to see a woman saunter inside a set of sliding glass doors. She's carrying a glass of lemonade.

◆ ◆ ◆

Lemonade.

It takes me a second to realize the implications, and then I shoot out of the pool and tug dry clothes over my wet skin. My hair instantly soaks the back of my shirt, and I note that there's a puddle under me on the patio deck. That's new, but I don't linger to admire the spread of water around my feet or study my soggy footprints as I sprint to the sliding glass door.

I halt in front of it and reach to open it rather than walk through it. Like the gate, it feels unwaveringly solid beneath my fingers as I slide it open. Extraordinary. I walk inside to be greeted by a blast of air-conditioning. Prickles immediately rise on my wet skin. Shivering, I call, "Hello?"

I don't expect an answer.

I don't get one.

She couldn't have been holding my glass of lemonade. There had to be real glasses amid the unreal. She must be the owner of this house, spruced up by her imagination, like Mother's house. But after the man in white, I have to be sure. Hope feels like the pool water, stinging my eyes, but I don't want to close them.

The kitchen is bright and cheery, everything white and stainless steel, with sparkling marble counters and a tiled floor. There's a bank of ovens on one wall and two kitchen islands in the center of the room. A breakfast nook by a bay window. There's a pile of books on the table, as well as remnants from a meal. A lone blueberry sits in a glass bowl. I cross to it and hesitate before picking it up.

I hold the berry between my fingers and then pop it in my mouth. Its juice spurts out as I bite down. Is there anything here I can't touch, taste, feel? I cross to the refrigerator and throw it open. It's stuffed full of food: shrimp cocktail, deviled eggs, other appetizers, all sealed in cellophane as if prepared for a party. I touch each one, and they squish beneath my fingertips. I turn to the stove and twist the dial, feeling the burner heat. Next, I test the sink. Everything works for me. There's nothing I cannot touch, lift, twist, slide, break.

What is this place?

Who lives here? *Why, why, why?*

"Hello? Is anyone here?" I hurry through the rooms. A dining room connects to the kitchen. Its walls are painted blue like the sky, and it has views of the Atlantic beyond the table. Through the dining room, there's a living room with a vaulted ceiling. White couches. I walk in and feel the carpet beneath my feet, the fibers between my toes.

This must be someone's dream summer home. There's no other explanation. Someone made it up out of whole cloth, and that's why I can see it and touch it and feel all of it. But what of the woman in red with the lemonade? Is she the dreamer or the dream?

I check every room: the guest bedroom with its yellow comforter and shell-motif furniture, the marbled bathrooms with claw-foot tubs, the main bedroom with the canopied bed and walk-in closet, the game room with a pool table and air hockey, the TV room with a screen to rival a movie theater, and the garage with a classic Corvette with white paint and red leather seats. But the woman, she isn't anywhere inside.

I return to the pool and spot a woman with dark-bronze skin and a red bathing suit doing laps. Her hair is braided tight against her scalp, and she has poppies tattooed in red ink on her arms. I'm afraid to call out, so instead, I watch her, the Atlantic beyond, a white bird skimming the surface of the ocean.

"You know, I never knew what I was missing," I say. "My mother used to talk about all the traffic in the Hamptons—one-lane roads to discourage too many tourists, at least those who can't take their own personal helicopter to their summer home—so I thought it would be crowded all the way east to the tip. But this, here . . . it's so peaceful."

The steady rhythm of her strokes is like music, undercut by the steady sound of waves breaking on the beach. I watch the white foam dissipate on the sand.

"To think I might never have seen the ocean," I say.

I almost missed out on this.

If I'd stayed in the casket. If I hadn't followed the man in white. Maybe I was never meant to find him. Maybe I was meant to find this place and see the ocean. If my clock is ticking before I fade away forever, then I can't waste even a single second. "I used to dream about traveling. Mother would talk about trips she'd taken before Leah was born . . . She had so many stories. I always thought we'd travel together someday. I believed I'd be able to, with her. But she never did. It was never the right time. Or it was too expensive. Or . . . I don't know what kept her there. Maybe she was afraid the reality wouldn't live up to her memories or her dreams. Inertia kept her in place." *Fear keeps me,* I think. From the pool, I hear a splash. Out of the corner of my eye, I see the woman in the red bathing suit climb out of the water. She grabs a towel and squeezes her braids. "I wonder if Mother ever would have left if she hadn't died."

It's not as if I don't know that Mother had her flaws. She'd make these grandiose plans—she'd go to Paris and then rent a car and drive straight until she reached Spain. From there, why not Morocco? It was just across the Strait of Gibraltar. She'd promised Leah a trip to a location of her choice after she graduated from college. In the beginning, they'd talk about the places they could go: See the northern lights in Iceland. Visit New Zealand. Climb Kilimanjaro. Take a helicopter ride over a volcano in Hawaii. See Machu Picchu. Go to Carnival in Rio. All the world was waiting for them—but then there were the arguments. Mother hadn't set aside enough money for college tuition. She wasn't particularly good at saving. Or working. She flitted from job to job. She managed to keep the house, but there were loans for college. Loans that Leah had to repay, never mind that she wanted to make art, not work a desk job. Certainly, now there wasn't time to travel, but someday, Mother would promise, she'd give her the world. "She used to say she'd give us the world. Both her girls."

"Screw the world," the woman says. "I'd rather someone give me the stars."

CHAPTER TEN

Glistening with water, sun, and sunscreen, the woman saunters over to the lemonade and pours herself another glass. She takes a sip, then swirls it so the ice clinks against the sides.

"You . . . Can you hear me?" I ask.

She doesn't answer.

It was an illusion. Like with Mother, when I'd slide into her conversations. I was so familiar with the rhythm of her words that sometimes, for an instant, it felt real. "You can't. It's okay. I'm used to it, or I should be." Hope is such a funny, vicious thing. It sneaked up on me, lemonade in one hand and knife in the other.

"Hard to ignore you," the woman says. "You have a tendency to monologue."

"You *can* hear me," I breathe. "And see me?"

"Saw more of you before." With a wink, she grins at me, then chugs the rest of her lemonade. "Pool is yours if you want it." She sets the glass down, stretches with her hands laced over her head, and then strolls back into the house.

I'm stunned, motionless, for a second; she's so nonchalant. But then I rush after her. I won't let her disappear on me like the man in white. I reach for her arm but stop just shy of touching her. What if my fingers slide through her? "Who are you?"

"Sylvie." She flashes me a brilliant smile and tosses her braids. "You?"

"Hannah. Hannah Allen."

"Ooh, you have a last name. Fancy."

"Can you . . ." I lick my lips. I don't know how to phrase what I want to ask. There are a million questions inside me all clamoring to come out. How can she—How can I—"Are you like me?"

She scans me up and down as if determining my dress size, and her pursed lips remind me, briefly, of the real estate agent, but that's where the resemblance ends. "Unlikely."

"But . . ." I reach for her again and, this time, let my hand close around her forearm. She's slick with pool water. My fingers indent her skin lightly, and my breath hitches in my throat.

Startled, Sylvie pulls back, out of my grip. "Rude." Wrinkling her nose, she wags her finger at me as if I'm a disobedient puppy and trills, "Consent first, please!"

"Sorry. Are you *real*?"

"Oh, sweetie, it's not the right time of day for an existential conversation. It's nearly sunset." She flicks her fingers at me. Droplets of pool water hit my cheek, and I touch them as if they're jewels. "Go on. Shoo. Take your melodrama elsewhere."

Turning her back on me, she flounces toward the bedroom. I trail after her, puppylike, but she doesn't acknowledge me as she beelines for the closet. Flinging open both doors, Sylvie pulls out dress after dress and tosses them over her shoulder onto the bed.

"You *have* to be like me," I say, and I can hear the desperation in my voice. She can see and touch the items in this house, exactly like I can. She can hear me. I can touch her. Feeling flooded with . . . what is this? Hope? I sink down on the bed as my knees wobble.

"Really don't see the resemblance."

"Can other people see you? Can they hear you? Because . . ." I am mangling this. I've never talked like this to anyone before, at least not to someone who can answer. I try to formulate what I want to say. Last thing I want to do is alienate this woman before I have a chance to . . . I don't know what. Ask her everything I've ever wanted to ask anyone? Ask who she is, *why* she is, why I am? Does she know?

She selects a black dress that flows like it's made of shadows. "This will do nicely." She turns back to the closet and pulls out a blue sundress. "And for you. Go on, try it. Might as well, though honestly, anything would be an improvement." She slips it off the hanger and tosses it to me.

The chiffon flutters around me.

"This isn't real," I insist. The dress, the house. It's all proof that she *is* like me. She wouldn't be able to touch any of it if she weren't. "You aren't real." I'm sure of it. Mostly sure.

Sylvie gives a little laugh that sounds as light as wind chimes. "So personal! I'm as real as you are, honey. Just with better fashion sense, though I get that it's not your fault."

I pounce. "So you admit it. You're like me."

Stepping into the bathroom, she sings, "Privacy!"

I stand there, holding the sundress. I might as well wear it. My clothes are soaked through from not drying off after my swim, and here are clothes that I can touch. It feels almost rebellious. I've always just worn whatever was in my bedroom closet—Mother had envisioned me with everything I needed: every shade of jeans, the softest cashmere sweaters, velvet dresses for holidays, shoes of every kind. Once, in the spring of what would have been my senior year in high school, I opened my closet to find a half dozen prom dresses. But I usually wore whatever was the most comfortable. It wasn't as if I had anyone to impress.

Leah would've loved to have the clothes I never wore.

I wonder if she knew all that Mother gave me and couldn't give her. *Yes, she knew.* On some level, in her own way, she must have known. And it must have hurt.

I find dry underwear in one of the many dressers and change into the sundress. It feels light and airy, and I hope it won't vanish. "Are you sure these clothes won't disappear?"

She doesn't respond.

She's vanished. All this was a hallucination, or a momentary blip. It is a phenomenal coincidence that I found first the man in white and then the lemonade woman on the very first time that I ventured out . . . Maybe there are many like me out there, and I assumed there weren't because I never ventured far enough from home. There could be hundreds. Thousands. Millions? Not millions. I still believe I'm rare.

I knock on the bathroom door. "Are you in there?"

No answer again.

I shove my shoulder against the door until it pops open. The marble bathroom is empty and gleaming.

She's not here.

Vanished. Faded. Rotted away.

"Shit," I say.

I'd hoped. Never mind. I'm a fool.

I cross to the mirror and stare at my reflection. It's rare that I have a reflection. The blue sundress makes me look as if I'm a woman on vacation who expects an evening of champagne, instead of one who is lost in every way. My still-wet hair is matted to my cheeks. I push it back behind my ears and think that I look like a variation of Leah.

Leah.

I can't stop thinking about her.

Did she stay in that bar with the stranger, or did she have the sense to go back to Jamie? Did Jersey intervene or cheer her on? Was that what grief looked like on her, a mistake she'd regret?

Who am I to judge? I jumped on a train to chase a man who couldn't be found and rode as far east as I could. My grief isn't any more sensible. And now a new grief is rising within me. At least for a few moments, I felt hope that I found something new, a change to my existence, and now that hope has vanished like the haze.

A gauzy curtain waves in the breeze.

I wonder . . .

I lean out the open window. Sylvie is standing amid the hydrangeas, wearing the shadowy dress. "You're still here!" I smile so hard that my cheeks hurt.

"Of course! I never miss the sunset!"

I look for a ladder or stairs. "How did you get down?"

Sylvie spreads her arms wide and spins, barefoot in the grass. "I'm a mystery!" Her braids whip with her as she turns.

She certainly is. I feel giddy. Almost dizzy. She didn't disappear! She's here, and she can still see me and hear me; she knows I'm here, with her. Granted, she doesn't seem to care.

"Lovely to meet you, darling!" She waves and saunters across the lawn.

"Wait—where are you going?"

"I told you: to watch the death of the day!"

There's a trellis attached to the wall. She must have climbed it, but I don't trust myself not to fall and break my neck. There are no hospitals for the nonexistent. "Wait for me!" I order her.

"Then hurry if you can! I don't miss the sunset for anyone!" She says the last word in singsong as she continues to stroll toward the gate.

I have the sense that if I let her go without me, I wouldn't find her again. Just like the man in white.

I take the stairs two at a time and spill outside. Sylvie is by the gate, as if waiting for me, despite what she said. "You *did* hurry. Huh. And you made it before the sun kisses the waves." She regards me with slightly more interest than before.

She expected me to vanish too. I shiver and, for a minute, fear wars with elation. My throat feels tight. *She knows what's happening to me.*

Sylvie seems to come to some kind of decision because suddenly she grins at me. It feels like sunshine splashed on my face. She has that sort of smile. "Come on, Hannah. Glory awaits!"

Hearing her say my name—it's beautiful, and I realize with a shudder that no one has ever, ever said my name *to* me before. About me, yes. To me . . . never.

Occasionally, Mother would talk to me as if I were in the room, but her eyes would never focus on me. She was seeing another version of Hannah, her daughter as she imagined she would have been. She'd ask for my opinion on what she should wear or what she should eat for dinner, but she never waited for my answer.

If Sylvie keeps saying my name, I will follow her anywhere. As it is, I follow her onto the beach. She's right about the sun: it's beginning to sink toward the horizon. It sprawls as if it's a yellow marshmallow about to burst. It hurts to look at it, so instead, I stare at its reflection on the water. The water cups it in a thousand curves that rise and fall with the swells of the waves.

We cast no shadows on the beach. Here, beyond the house, our feet leave no imprint in the sand. It's the same for both of us. She's the same as me. It's a marvel and a miracle. "I can't believe I found you."

"Belief has nothing to do with it," Sylvie says with a shrug. "Or perhaps it's everything."

What does that mean? Is she just being poetic, or am I supposed to understand what that meant? "Who are you? What are you? What am I? What do you know?"

She laughs again. "You are so intense. Relax! Enjoy the evening! Breathe in the air. Feel the sand between your toes, the breeze on your skin. Isn't it glorious?"

Yes, it's very nice. "But there's so much I want to ask you! Do you live here? Are there others like us?" I want to ask if she's ever lost moments of time, if she ever fears fading away into nothingness, if she's ever seen the shadow wolves. I want to ask how she's survived to see

91

her sunsets, if she has someone like Mother, and if she's lost someone like Mother.

"There's no one like me. I'm unique, by definition." She dashes forward, and the hem of her dress drags in the water, but she doesn't lift it.

That isn't much of an answer. Following her, I stop just beyond where the waves reach. "Have you met others like us?" I press again.

"You say 'like us,' but you barely know me. You don't know what I'm like. I would bet, if I had to guess, that you don't even know what *you're* like."

"But you—"

"Hannah, enough with the questions! Questions won't make you happy. You need to just *be*!" She catches my hand and pulls me.

We run together down the beach, hand in hand.

Out of breath, we reach a curve in the beach, and Sylvie flops down against a dune. "Ahh, perfection!"

She's correct: it is the perfect spot, facing west—the shoreline curves here for a direct view of the sunset. Already, the sun has tinted the sky a rosy orange. A few of the clouds glow a brilliant lemon.

"There are a thousand questions I need to ask," I say.

Sylvie exhales with an exaggerated puff. "Fine. Pick one. But I warn you: all I truly know is how to find the best view of the sunset. It's my secret power. Place me anywhere in the world, and I'll find the best sunset vantage point."

I have one question: "Why?"

"Because you can rely on the sunset. Always happens. Always beautiful."

I shake my head and want to shake her. "Why are we the way we are? Why can no one see us or hear us? Why can't we touch what's real?"

"Who says what's real and what isn't? Maybe *they're* the illusion."

Nice idea, but there's a constancy to the real world that ours lacks. "Things vanish and appear for us. They're solid for them."

She shrugs as if it doesn't matter, or she doesn't care. Or she doesn't know? "Watch. It's about to touch the horizon."

"But—"

"Just watch, Hannah."

My name again.

By Sylvie's side, I watch the sun kiss the land and sea. It looks as if it elongates from the bottom, as if the earth is pulling a drop of sunlight closer to it. An embrace. It hurts my eyes to stare, but I can't stop.

"I think we're dreams," I say. "I think we are the wishes and hopes of people." Like Mother. I have thought this for a long time. It explains me. And our home. And her garden. The fruit in the kitchen. Even explains the art in Leah's apartment. Those were her hopes and dreams.

"How sweet," Sylvie says.

It isn't a perfect theory. It doesn't explain all of it: the shadows or the wolves. "Or we were born of both hopes and fears," I say.

"Mmm, that's beautiful," she says.

I'm not certain if she's talking about the sunset or about what I said.

The sun is melting into the horizon, sinking into a distant strip of land that looks as purple as a bruise. Above, the clouds are a ruddy red and burnt orange, and below, the water glows. The water darkens—the farther from the sun, the blacker the sea. Lying back, I see the first star, so faint that I'm not even sure it's there, against the deepening blue.

"But it's bullshit," Sylvie says.

"Sorry?"

"We aren't hopes and dreams. Or even fears."

The sun sinks lower.

She is silent as we watch it fall to the earth. Soon it shrinks and vanishes.

"Then what are we?" I ask.

Sylvie looks at me and smiles. "We're lies."

CHAPTER ELEVEN

Leah was eleven years old when her father gave the ultimatum.

"Get help, or I leave."

Mother promised she would. And then she promised again. And again.

He left on a Thursday.

Later, Leah would wonder: if her mother had kept that promise, what would have changed? But back then, she only knew that someone—God maybe, if He existed, or her parents—kept making terrible mistakes, and it wasn't her fault.

Covering her ears with headphones, Leah would lie on her stomach and draw in her sketchbook—scenes of places she'd never been and people who weren't here. Her parents' shouts would still seep through the music. She'd crank it up so high that Mom would have to pound on the door at dinnertime.

He lasted one more year before, true to his word, he packed up his clothes, his toothbrush and razor, his favorite mugs and books, until the shelves looked like mouths with missing teeth. He left the furniture, the dishware, the photo albums, and his now-twelve-year-old daughter.

Then that Thursday came. She'd walked home from the bus stop with her backpack and seen his car in the driveway with the trunk open. He was loading boxes. Halting by the mailbox, she watched him.

He didn't see her at first, and she watched in silence as he pushed and shoved the boxes to fit and then stepped back and sighed. His face relaxed and his shoulders sank. He looked like an exhausted man who was finally told he could sleep, but then he spotted her, and his face tensed into a fake smile, his shoulders stiffened again, and his entire body seemed to clench like a fist. Leah felt an ache in the pit of her stomach.

"Today?" Leah asked.

Why didn't he mention it over breakfast? Mom had been in the shower; it had been just Dad and Leah. He'd sat with his coffee while she babysat the toaster until it spat out her Eggo waffle. Plenty of time for him to have said, "*Hey, today's the day I'm moving out and making you a statistic—yet another kid with a broken family.*" But all he'd said was, "Do you have a math quiz?" She did, so they'd spent the rest of breakfast reviewing the Pythagorean theorem. Mom still wasn't out of the shower when Leah snagged a waffle to go and headed out to catch the bus.

"New lease already started," Dad said, motionless by the car trunk. She half expected him to sprint for the driver's seat. "It's for the best."

Is it?

She'd noticed those words didn't always mean what people thought they meant. For one, they were unspecific. Best for who? And how? And when? Permanent? Because temporary sucked. "Can I come stay with you sometimes?"

He looked like a trapped mouse—ready to bolt in all directions simultaneously. "It's a small apartment. Only there temporarily. When I've gotten a house, gotten settled, I'll make sure it has a room for you. Your own room, with your own bed. Then you can come whenever you want and stay however long you want."

"I can sleep on a couch."

"I promised your mother . . ." He ran his fingers through his hair as he trailed off. Over the last couple of years, his hairline had been creeping higher up on his forehead. Sometimes he wore baseball caps.

She wondered if he'd remembered to pack them. "We agreed that we'd make things as normal as possible for you during this transition. As soon as I have a place that's kid friendly . . ."

"I don't bite."

"Sorry?"

"You make me sound like a dog," Leah said. "I don't bite. I'm even housebroken. Why can't I come with you?" What she didn't ask was, *Would you have let Hannah come? Would you be leaving if you still had two daughters?*

He put his hands on her shoulders. "Because this is your home. You'd have to switch schools again, and then switch schools a third time wherever I end up. All your friends are here. Your room. This will be the least amount of upheaval for you after all you've already gone through. Don't worry—I'll still call all the time. You'll be sick of hearing from me, that's how often I'll call. But I just . . . have to get my feet under me first. I need a fresh start. Okay, pumpkin?"

"Not a pumpkin," Leah said. "But okay."

What else was there to say? It was done. He was packed. He had a lease. She wasn't entirely sure what that was, but he had one.

He hugged her, a big bear hug, like he used to when she was little. Back then he'd scoop her up and swing her in a circle so her feet flailed out. He didn't do that this time, but he did squeeze her hard before getting in his car with all his boxes and his suitcase.

She watched as he drove away. Only then did Mom come outside. They stood side by side on the porch. "He'll be back," Mom said. "This is just temporary."

Leah kept watching until Dad's car rounded the corner at the end of the street. He could have just been driving off to the supermarket or back to the office or to the gym. She wondered if any of the neighbors guessed that he wasn't coming back. Like the old man with his dog, across the street. Or Mrs. Harrington, the local busybody, who was weeding her front lawn.

She felt exposed, as if she'd been peeled naked and stood on the porch for everyone to see.

Mom slung her arm around Leah's shoulders. "Did I ever tell you how we met? I was working as a waitress at a diner—saving up money for a trip to South America—when in walked your father. He had a leather jacket on. Let me tell you, your father looked absurd in a leather jacket. Like he'd found it on some biker's motorcycle and just picked it up. But he looked at me and said, 'You. I'm going to marry you.'"

Leaning forward so that Mom's arm slid off her, Leah said, "Dad said you met at a friend's party. You were drunk, and he held your hair while you puked."

Mom gave a tight laugh. "He told you *that*? Definitely not the version we agreed to tell our impressionable tween." She reached out again and tucked Leah's hair behind her ear. "Alcohol is bad for you, and you shouldn't have any until you're at least twenty-one. Twenty-five, to be on the safe side. Come on. I'll make you a snack."

"I can thaw my own Eggo," Leah said.

"He'll be back," Mom said again. "Everything will be fine. You'll see. He won't stay away from his own daughters." She went inside, the screen door swinging shut behind her.

Softly, Leah corrected, "*Daughter.*"

◆ ◆ ◆

A fresh start, he'd said.

Leah hadn't thought it would take until she was fourteen. Worse, his house had no additional bedroom for her. Just an office for his new wife.

But now he wanted her to come, he'd said.

He'd filed for full custody.

She didn't understand why. Why now, after years?

"I'm so sorry he's doing this to you." Mom was getting dressed in a gray tweed skirt and a white blouse to meet her lawyer. She added a necklace with a chunky blue pendant, then removed it. "It's selfish. And cruel."

Leah was sitting on the end of Mom's bed.

"He has no right to turn your life upside down," Mom said. "Zero. And I'll tell that to the lawyer. He hasn't even tried to be a part of your life over the past two years. How often have you seen him? You can count it on one hand. A few holidays. A weekend last summer."

The weekend had been Dad's wedding. Leah had met her new stepmother-to-be on a Friday, and he'd married her on Saturday. On Sunday, they'd left for their honeymoon in the Caribbean after bringing Leah to the Long Island Rail Road and watching to make sure she was safely on the train back to Garden City, where Mom was waiting for her.

The only nice part of it was Katelyn herself. ("You don't need to call me 'Mom,'" she'd told Leah. "I know you have a mother, and I would never try to replace her. I do hope we can be friends.") She apologized upward of six times for the suddenness of it all—not that it was sudden for her and Dad, but it was sudden for Leah. Katelyn had wanted Dad to tell Leah months ago, but Dad had said no. He hadn't wanted any hint of the event to get back to Leah's mother. "She'd have found some way to make you miss it," Dad said to Leah. "Concocted one of her lies—said you had chicken pox or were in the Arctic."

He's probably right. Still . . . "You could have told me."

"It's like a surprise party! Who doesn't love a surprise party?"

Me. I don't love surprise parties.

Katelyn had three bridesmaid dresses waiting for Leah—Dad hadn't known Leah's size—she wanted Leah to be in her bridal party, if Leah was willing. She asked so nicely and so sincerely; how could Leah say no? And she'd bought dresses in three different sizes, just to be safe. So Leah had worn one of them and been a bridesmaid. Smiled in all the pictures. Cried in the bathroom later, acutely aware that if Hannah had lived, Leah wouldn't have had to stand there all alone, dolled up for a wedding that should never have happened. On Sunday night, when Mom asked what she'd done over the weekend, Leah said, "Nothing."

Later, after Dad had posted his photos all over social media, Mom said, "He only wanted you there for the pictures. Because people would have asked where you were. Just wait. He won't invite you over again."

Leah had wanted to defend him, but the words stuck in her throat. And the worst part: Mom was right.

He hadn't.

Every time he called, Leah hinted. Sometimes she outright asked, and he'd always say, "Now is not a good time. Another weekend. You understand, pumpkin?" He was working on the house. Or he had a business trip. Or they had to attend a wedding or a cocktail party or a dinner. Or he had too many chores or errands or extra work. But "soon," he always said.

Every time had felt like a punch to her heart.

Mom selected a plain silver necklace. "You remind him too much of Hannah. That's the truth of it. He can't handle looking at you and remembering what he lost when he walked out that door. It won't be any different if you live there. He won't spend time with you. Hell, he doesn't even know you."

She's right. Had he ever asked her what she thought or felt? Whether she was happy? Whether she missed Hannah too? Instead, it was all, How was school? How were her grades? What did she do last weekend? Any extracurriculars? Had she thought about a sport? Or taking up piano again? He never even asked about her art. He didn't know anything about her, not really. It would be like moving in with a stranger. "Then why does he want me?"

"He doesn't," Mom said. She paused and reached out to lay a hand on Leah's cheek. "I'm so sorry. I know, I shouldn't talk badly about your father, but you need to know. This isn't about you. It's not about him. It's *her*."

Hannah. It's always about Hannah.

"It's all that woman, Katelyn," Mom said. "I didn't want you to hear the news like this, but she's having a baby. Due in six months. She hasn't even started showing yet, but it's certain."

A new baby.

A half sister. Or half brother.

Leah tried to absorb the news. A sibling. She tried to feel excited, but all she could picture was the hospital with all the wires, tubes, and monitors, always beeping and whirring, all that noise, and the cemetery, always much too silent.

"He's replacing Hannah," Mom said, "or trying to. And she clearly needs a babysitter. She plans to return to work after her maternity leave ends, and you are the perfect solution to her childcare needs. You're the right age. And you're free."

Leah felt her stomach sink. It made a horrible kind of sense. Dad never had any use for her before now—she had no place in his life—but now, she served a purpose, as free help. She'd have to switch schools, leave all her friends, and move to where she knew no one to be a live-in nanny to a newborn. "But I don't know anything about babies."

"If he gets full custody, you'll learn," Mom said. "Two parents working full time? And with the number of vacations and business trips and dinners and cocktail parties and the like that they go to . . . you'll learn fast."

She didn't want to learn fast.

She wanted time with her friends. She wanted to stay in her own school. She wanted to be somewhere where she was wanted, not where she was needed. Mom wanted her. Why else would she be trying so hard to keep her?

"But we can fight this, Leah." Mom took Leah's hands in hers and sat down on the bed beside her. "All you have to do is testify in court. Tell the judge you want to stay with me."

Leah nodded. She could do that. If it meant she didn't have to leave everyone and everything she knew and move in with a virtual stranger, to live a life she didn't want. "I want to stay with you."

"If you don't say all the right things . . ." Mom trailed off, shaking her head grimly. "You won't be able to come back here. Your father will make sure that I don't even get visitation rights. You won't be able to see me again."

Could he do that?

"I can't lose you, Leah." Mom had tears in her eyes, stuck on her mascara. "So you have to tell the lawyer and the judge. You have to tell anyone who asks . . ."

"Please tell me what to say," Leah said.

"You just have to tell them that of course I know Hannah isn't here."

CHAPTER TWELVE

We're lies.

I hear the words ricochet inside my head. Loose bullets, tearing through my mind. Can't think. Can't breathe.

We're lies.

Lies.

Lies.

I want to deny it.

We're hopes. We're dreams. We're the bone-deep wishes of people who want us. I think of Mother's roses that she never planted, of the muffins she never baked, of the music she never played. I think of Leah's sketches strewn throughout her apartment.

We are possibilities and promises and unfulfilled potential, the ghosts of what could have been.

We are good intentions.

Or . . . we are lies.

I taste the words, and they taste like salt. Like copper. Like blood. Like truth?

Years ago, after Leah was born, Mother wanted a second child. God, it sounds like a fairy tale. Once upon a time, a woman wanted a child. She was desperate for one, a second daughter to fill a hole in her heart, to save her failing marriage, to make her feel that her life was complete. So, she had one. It was an easy pregnancy. Touch of morning sickness, but she worked right up until her water broke. Or she was on bed rest for a few weeks, but it all worked out fine. No complications. It all happened fast, no alarms that blared or nurses that raced her to the operating room, and suddenly I was there. Or it was complicated, a C-section, then a blood transfusion, but worth it. So very worth it. And after, easy-peasy! Latched with no hesitation, not like her first. Slept through the night after just a few weeks. Oh, her first had been difficult, but this was smooth, smooth, smooth. She knew the instant she laid her eyes on me that I'd be an easy baby.

I was napping whenever anyone wanted to see me. Couldn't be disturbed.

I was with my father. Couldn't be reached.

Or I was in day care. Or with the wonderful nanny she'd found. Tried an au pair, but she didn't work out. Can't pass along the name of the nanny. She's not taking new clients. She's moved back to California to be with her elderly parents. She died.

Certainly, I wasn't in the hospital. Why would you think that?

There was a brief scare early on, when Hannah was two years old, Mom would sometimes admit, but it was easily resolved. Misdiagnosed, in fact, but no, they weren't going to sue. It was enough that they had their precious girl at home, their little miracle.

Hannah's just shy. She's up in her room. Always with a book, that girl. Learned how to read at four years old! Isn't that extraordinary? Gets along so nicely with her sister too. Yes, her sister's a handful.

Mother would sigh here.

But Hannah's an angel. So obedient. My little companion. My miracle. The doctors said she wouldn't survive past two years old, you know. They called it an incurable genetic defect, but ha! Shows what they know.

Mother would talk about me to neighbors, to relatives, even to friends who should have known better than to believe her, and all the while, I would be at her feet, quietly playing with a toy that would morph in my hands from a book to a truck to a doll to crayons. No one ever offered to play with me or talk to me. No one so much as glanced at me, and for years, I hungered for it so badly. They call it skin hunger. Touch starvation. I ached with it.

I remember how I would try to play with my sister, Leah, and how much it would hurt, like a physical hurt as sharp as a stab, when Leah wouldn't answer me even when I shouted so loudly it felt as if my throat were shredded, until I figured out that it wasn't her fault. She didn't believe I was there. But Mother did. Or she wanted to.

Closing my eyes, I try to forget one conversation, before Dad left. It was in the kitchen. A Saturday?

"You were talking about her again," Dad said.

"I wouldn't," Mother said stoutly. She was at the sink, dish soap up to her elbows. He was beside her drying the dishes. Except he didn't do that. The dishes always sat in the sink until morning, and he'd be off at work.

Not at the sink then. At the breakfast table? Dinner. It must have been dinner, except I don't remember Leah being there. She could have been in her room, finishing homework. Yes, it was after dinner. The plates in front of them were stained with clumps of unfinished food. The sauce was congealing in thickening pools.

"Stopped by the post office today," Dad said. "I know you've been talking about her again."

"I haven't," Mother insisted. "You know I promised. They must be remembering from before. Can't exactly go back and tell them—"

"Sure, you could."

She let out a bark of laughter. No mirth in it. "And how awkward would that be?"

"You made the awkwardness."

"Well, I don't know them well enough—"

"You need to say it."

Mother shook her head as if he were being ridiculous. She would have laughed it off again, except he was staring at her so fiercely that she froze like a deer. There would have been silence, except that I filled it. "Mother. Mother, you don't have to. You don't have to say what he wants you to say. You don't have to talk to him at all if he's going to be like this. You can talk to me instead. Tell me about your day. Tell me who you saw. Tell me about the garden you planted. I saw an iris and a daffodil. What else did you plant? Any roses?"

Mother swallowed, her eyes glued to Dad's.

"Say it," he ground out.

"I'm right here, Mother." How I pleaded. Or maybe I didn't. Perhaps I am speaking only in my memory, pleading because I know what comes next.

Her voice heavy, Mother said, "I lied."

"Go on."

"It wasn't planned. I swear it wasn't. It was just . . . easier. They asked about her, and it was easier to follow the flow of conversation. I didn't mean to lie again. I know what I promised, but it was only to smooth over a social situation—I couldn't very well admit right then and there . . ." She followed him to the kitchen. "It was meaningless small talk, the way you say you're fine when someone asks how you are. They didn't want to hear the whole ugly truth. All they wanted was a simple answer, so I gave them one."

And then more.

"I know Hannah isn't real," Mother said. "You know I know that. I wanted to make a casual conversation more pleasant, that's all, and it was simpler to just go with it. Anyone would have done the same."

"I wouldn't," he said. "And I didn't."

"Well then, I can never go to *that* post office again."

"You should have thought of that before."

She knew exactly what I was. There were times when I think she successfully deceived herself, but in her heart, she knew.

I am a lie.

I am Mother's lie, told to whoever would listen. A lie she carried to her grave, literally. I think of what it felt like beside her in the casket, the feel of her plasticky skin, the scent of the chemicals and the wood. I feel as though I am there again, trapped between her flesh and the fabric that lines the walls.

But I can't hear the silence of her grave—beyond my feet, the waves crash rhythmically, as steady and unrelenting as a heartbeat, beating back the memory.

Focusing on the waves, I emerge from the whirlpool of my memories and breathe again. My hands are clenched so hard that, when I pry them open, I see half-moon indents from each of my nails, so deep they're purple.

Sylvie takes one of my hands, splays out my fingers, and runs her palm over mine as if she can smooth away all pain. "You freaked out a little there," she says, calm, almost amused.

"I did," I admit.

"You never knew what you are?" Sylvie asks. "Because—no offense—that seems pretty unobservant of you, unless you're new. Are you new?"

"You could be wrong," I say.

"Sure. Could be. Except I'm not."

"Couldn't we be ghosts?" It was a much nicer, neater explanation.

"Highly unlikely, since I was never alive. Feels like that should be a prerequisite. But you go on and think whatever you'd like." Sylvie releases my hand and lies back in the sand. A few more stars are scattered across the sky. The clouds have turned from wine red to a deep blue-gray.

We are both silent. The waves continue crashing.

"We could be dreams," I venture.

"If we were, there would be a shit-ton more ballerinas and astronauts."

"I'm serious."

"So am I. Ever met a preschooler? If dreams were alive, we'd constantly be chased by deranged clowns. Also, dinosaurs. There would be a lot more dinosaurs."

Propping myself up on an elbow, I stare at her. I don't know her well enough to read whether she's mocking me. "That can't possibly be the extent of your evidence."

"Believe whatever the fuck you want to believe, Hannah Allen with the last name." She flashes me an overly bright smile. "I am what I am, and I know what I am. I really don't care what you think."

I want to insist she tell me every shred of evidence she has for her claim. I want her to argue like an impassioned lawyer. Walk me through her reasoning. Explain how she came to this conclusion—and why it feels so right. But it's not her job to help me through my existential crisis. And if I push, I could drive her away. I have to be patient. Remember patience? It's how I've weathered twenty-three years without getting any answers. "I'm sorry. It's just . . ." I'm about to make an excuse, to explain how I've never met anyone like her. Like me. But I think maybe she doesn't want to hear that either, so instead, I repeat, "I'm sorry."

At least she hasn't left. That has to be a good sign.

I hold still, as if I may scare her off by breathing too loudly, and wonder if this is what social anxiety feels like. It's a fluttery, nauseous feeling. Whatever I am, whatever this means, I know I don't want to be alone right now. It feels imperative that Sylvie doesn't leave me before I know . . .

I don't complete the thought. I don't want to formulate the one question that looms over me, unspoken, now that I know what I am.

"You know what's nice about being a lie?" Sylvie says. She reaches her arms up toward the stars and twists them as if examining her flawless skin. "No mosquitoes."

I let out a bark-like laugh. "What?"

"No one ever lies about mosquitoes. I mean, why would you? You're either bitten up or you're not. Either way, no one ever lies about that." She considers what she said. "I suppose someone might have. People lie about the most surprising things."

"Like gardens," I say.

"Exactly! Why lie about daffodils?"

Because you meant to plant them. Because you didn't want to be nagged about having bought the bulbs but not put them in the ground. Because you wanted your friends to think you were so on top of your life that you'd even enhanced the yard. Because you felt it was something you "should" have done. Because you wanted to participate in a conversation. Because you wanted the cashier/librarian/doctor/neighbor/friend to think better of you. Mother always had a plethora of reasons why she lied. "People do lie about daffodils," I say, heavily.

"Yes, they do. You should see the gardens attached to some of the summer houses—wait." Sylvie bolts upright. Her braids are askew from lying in the sand, but she leaves no imprint behind. "That's it. Tonight's plan. I'm going to show you the best lies, before you go on your merry way."

Go on my merry way? But I just found her! Before I can object, she jumps to her feet, reaches down, grasps my hand, and yanks me up beside her.

She touches me so easily, and it takes everything within me not to cling to her hard, just to see if I leave a mark on her skin. But she's already released me and turned toward the shoreline, studying it as if it had answers.

"Why? I mean, I thought you didn't care whether I believe you or not, so why do you want to show me lies?" I examine my hand, where she touched me. There's no trace, but I felt the pressure of her fingers. Like a burn. I think of the jolt of pain when the shadow wolves bit down on my flesh, the only other time I've been touched.

Sylvie is trotting down the beach. She's at the edge of the water, the waves teasing her toes. She has a butterfly tattoo on her ankle. "Come on! We'll hit Southampton and Bridgehampton. You ever steal a car?"

"What? No! Why?" And more importantly: "How?"

But she just laughs and runs along the shore. I follow her as the waves nip at our feet and the stars scatter across the sky.

◆ ◆ ◆

You can't steal a car if you can't press down on the gas pedal or turn the steering wheel, so that renders a fleet of vehicles in the parking lot of the Sunset Beach Motel unstealable. Sylvie strides past Subarus and BMWs and Audis, even a Bentley, only stopping in front of a gleaming white Corvette. Convertible, top down. Cherry red inside. Classic.

"Yeah, this is the one," Sylvie says.

"What do you mean?" I ask.

"It's a 1953 Corvette." She caresses its hood, her hand gliding over the curves until she reaches the windshield. "Only three hundred were made. Estimated two hundred twenty-five still exist. All of them with a Polo White exterior, red interior, and a black soft-top. And this, this is *not* one of them." Opening the driver's side door, she slides inside. "Oh, yes."

Gingerly, I lay my hand on the car door and am both surprised and unsurprised that it's solid beneath my fingertips. *It's not real.* An entire car that doesn't exist, except to us and whoever dreamed it up. *Or lied it into existence.*

She pats above the sun visor, then checks the glove compartment. "Easiest is if they leave the keys in the car. You would not believe how often that happens. You never see it with actual cars—seriously, that's what pockets and purses are for—but *lie* cars . . . I think it's because three-quarters of the time their liars are picturing cars they've seen in movies, and people in movies are constantly finding keys left inside cars, probably because it's easier than stopping the action to hot-wire a car. So always check for keys first, before you go for the wires." As she talks, she pulls her skirt up to reveal a strap around her thigh with a variety of tools. She selects a screwdriver and a wire cutter. "Helps to be prepared."

Squirming lower in the seat, Sylvie unscrews the casing around the steering column. She removes it and lays it on the passenger seat, then feels around for the wires.

"You have tools you can use?"

"Super easy to get high-quality tools, if you bother to look," Sylvie says. "Just find yourself a guy—I know, sexist of me, but it's nearly always a guy—who claims to be handier than he is. These gorgeously useful babies, they're from a man who was constantly telling his in-laws that he fixed everything himself. Remodeled the kitchen himself. Reinstalled the bathroom toilet himself. Rewired the lights in the dining room. Truth was, he'd hired a contractor to take care of all of it. He didn't own a single screwdriver, much less a wire cutter, but he had an entire nonexistent workbench full of high-end, brand-name, nonexistent tools."

Huh.

I never thought of scavenging for items like that.

She shifts to give me a better view. "Okay, what you're looking for are the brown wires. These red ones here—that's for power, but brown connects the starter. Sometimes there's just one brown wire, and then you have to cut and strip the reds and touch the brown wire to them, but if there are two brown . . ." As she talks, she cuts and strips them with the ease of someone who's done this a hundred times. "You expose the bare wires and then—" She taps the exposed wires together, and the engine rumbles to life. "Voilà!" She tucks the wires back beneath the steering column. "Ideally, you'd wrap those in electrical tape. Nasty shock if you touch them, so please don't electrocute yourself. Not sure what that would do to you, but probably wouldn't be pretty." She replaces the casing with a few twists of her screwdriver. "All set. Hop in!"

She made it look so easy. Scurrying to the other side, I pull open the door, drop into the seat, and marvel. Usually, I just melt through. I hadn't realized how hard you have to tug to make a door close, or how satisfying it would feel when it shut.

"Seat belt," Sylvie says.

I pull the belt across my lap and buckle in. Like a real person. Caressing the seat belt, I admire how it curves over my body, firm against me. Everything about this is new, and I hadn't realized how much I craved new. "Wondrous."

"You're easily impressed," Sylvie notes. "This is going to be fun."

She throws the car into reverse and peels backward out of the parking spot. As she squeals the brakes and then turns, I'm knocked into the side. Laughing, she hits the gas.

"Who taught you how to drive?" I shout as the wind slams into me.

"I'm self-taught!" she shouts back.

Not comforting.

Without any regard for other cars, she merges onto the street. I slam my foot into the floor, wishing I had a brake pedal.

"Relax!" she tells me. "This is fun!"

"We should talk about your definition of 'fun,'" I say.

"What?" she calls.

Before I can repeat myself, she steps harder on the gas, and we sail through the car in front of us. I throw my arms in front of my face as the other car passes through us. I slice through the front passenger seat, which is thankfully empty. Sylvie laughs beside me as we emerge into the headlights of the other car. They beam through the seats and across the dashboard. "The look on your face!"

She slows to a more reasonable speed, and I'm able to breathe again.

"What were you saying before?" she asks. "I couldn't hear you."

"Not important." I'm not used to someone actually hearing my commentary. I need to be aware now that my words can have impact.

Wait. So why *shouldn't* I say whatever I think? "What I should have said was, You're kind of an asshole."

Sylvie laughs as if this delights her. "It's official. I like you. I'm going to show you the best night of your life. It will be epic."

"Great?" I don't know that I want epic. I think of Jersey taking Leah to Sweet Venom—I hope Sylvie didn't have that kind of night in mind. That's not me.

"I'd rather be an asshole than a dream girl," she says, as if that's an explanation. Maybe it is.

"Whose dream girl are you?" I don't mean that to sound insulting. "Also, I thought you didn't believe we're dreams. Not enough ballerinas and astronauts."

"Near as I can figure, I am the invention of at least a dozen pathetic men. At first, I was their Manic Pixie Dream Girl. Later, I was their Cool Girl. I was their Unattainable Girl, their Girl Who Got Away. I'm the girlfriend they lied about having, the ideal woman who spoiled them for all others, the reason why they don't have a date. Because of me."

There's so much bitterness in her voice that I can taste it, like smoke that coats the back of my throat, but I latch on to the key word. "So you admit we *could* be dreams?" I don't know why that's so important to me—it is, in a way, a minor distinction from a lie.

Sylvie takes a turn without slowing down. I blink into the headlights of the oncoming cars. "A dream is something you want badly; a lie is—and I've looked this up in a dictionary, courtesy of a kid who never studied but claimed he did—'an untrue statement told with the intent to deceive.' A lie is told 'to create a false or misleading impression.' Go on, tell me that's not how you were made."

I can't say that.

I want to, of course, but the words clog my throat.

She waits.

And I say, "Mother didn't want me to leave her."

"'Mother'? Shit, that already sounds messed up. Do go on."

She's driving with the traffic now, instead of through it, which is an improvement. A few of the cars that pass are no more substantial than a cloud, and I wonder if we could drive them. Most likely they'd melt around us, I think, and leave us abandoned on the road. I don't want to talk about Mother. "Where are we going?"

"To the party of the summer, my darling." Sylvie flashes another of her smiles. "I am going to show you the life you should be living. And who knows? Maybe you'll find the answers to all those pesky questions you've been yearning to ask. Like, what is the meaning of life? Or what does it feel like to die? Or which is better, red wine or white?"

The "life I should be living," according to Sylvie, features two ice-sculpture swans sweating under the party lights, a pyramid of champagne glasses that looks poised to topple into a pool, women in flimsy overly expensive shoes, and men who seem averse to the top three buttons on their pastel-colored shirts. The party is half-outside, half-inside a summer home constructed of chrome and glass, with the Atlantic Ocean only a few steps away.

Careful to touch no one, I weave between the partygoers as Sylvie strides straight through them. She rolls her eyes as I suck in my stomach to squeeze between a tray of delicate lamb chops and a tanned woman with a sequined clutch. I gawk at her thin-as-a-pin stiletto heels.

"What? You've never seen Manolo Blahniks before? You really haven't lived." With an overly dramatic sigh, Sylvie grabs my arm and pulls me through the crowd along the pool.

"You can't feel like you fit in if you walk through them like a ghost," I complain.

She blinks at me. "Why on earth would we want to fit in?"

Of course, we want to blend, don't we? How else can you be a part of the world? "There's no point in a party if it only makes you feel more alone."

Sylvie stares at me for a moment. "Okay, there's a lot to unpack there. Just come on." She tugs me with her, toward the ice swans, and her grip is stronger than it should be, clamped onto my forearm so that I have no choice but to barrel through several tipsy college-age party-goers and a man with a distinguished mustache.

"Excuse me," I mumble to them, even though I know they can't hear me and that Sylvie must think I'm ridiculous, but I've spent so long pretending to be like them that it's hard to act as if ordinary people aren't there.

She halts in front of a vast buffet of hors d'oeuvres: shrimp cocktail, tiny quiches, prosciutto wrapped around melon balls, crab legs, bruschetta, and an array of sushi and dumplings. "Spot what we can eat."

Why can't she—Then I realize: "Are you testing me?"

Sylvie is smiling again, and I think she has a thousand smiles. This one says that I'm correct, though it doesn't tell me why. "I just want a baseline for where you're at."

"Fine." I begin to pass my hand through the table.

She catches my wrist. "Without touching."

"*You* just walked through—"

"Which can we eat?" There's an intensity in her eyes that's jarring. It's the first time she's seemed to care what I say. I wonder if she's hungry—and if so, for what? We don't need food, or at least I never have. She releases my wrist.

Placing my hands behind my back to show I'm cooperating, I scan the table.

Without warning, a man reaches through my stomach and picks up a bruschetta. I suck in air but otherwise don't react. Sylvie is watching me, and I can't help but want to please her, the way I always wanted to please Mother—except with Sylvie, she can see me and hear me and judge me and, if she chooses, reject me.

Focus.

There's a wisp of haze that clings to a plate of pastries shaped like stars. Certain I'm right, I point at them. "Those."

Sylvie picks one up and bites into it. Gravy oozes over her lips, and she catches it with her index finger. She licks her finger, her tongue darting out. "Wagyu beef. Excellent."

Now that I'm looking for them, I see others, shimmering into view amid the other real appetizers. I pick up a lobster-and-cheese pastry puff and pop it into my mouth. It tastes of cream and the sea and what I imagine the color golden green would taste like.

"'Alone' isn't such a bad word," Sylvie says. "You're lying to yourself if you think you can pretend to be one of them." She gestures toward all the partygoers with the half-eaten appetizer. It pales as if it's been bleached by the sun, and she shoves the rest in her mouth before it can vanish. "You need to find the joy, the beauty, and the fun in being as you are. Like I have."

She smiles at me as if she's hand delivered the secrets of the universe.

I don't think she has. There's a whisper in me, growing louder, wondering if I've made a mistake in coming here, in abandoning Leah, in leaving Mother's casket.

"Are there more like us?" Selecting another pastry puff, I try for a casual tone but fail dismally.

She shrugs. "Sure."

She doesn't elaborate, just glides toward the dance floor.

Following her, I try not to flinch as I walk directly through people. I can't help but shiver, though, as I hear their voices echo in my ears. A five-piece band is playing beach-themed music beneath an archway, and couples are showing off. You can tell who has taken ballroom dancing lessons and who hasn't. One man is counting his steps. Another is swinging a woman around like she's a scarf fluttering in the breeze. An older woman is shimmying by herself with a shadowy partner. I stare at the shadow man, wondering if he sees me the way I see him or if I look as substantial as I feel. There is so much I don't know. But maybe,

maybe, I'm on the cusp of answers, if I can just coax them out of my indifferent new friend.

"You want to know what it means to be a lie?" Sylvie says, with a smile dancing on her lips. "Rule number one: People don't matter, not to us—all they're good for is the lies they tell." She points to a haze that's building in one corner of the room by an abstract sculpture of fluid metal curves. "The rest of their lives we can't touch, so who cares? You can't let yourself care."

I let her draw me toward the growing haze.

"Rule number two: Use the lies you can. Avoid the ones you can't." She waves at a pool of toxic muck in the far corner. Undulating, it lurks in the shadows like a hungry predator, and I think of the ooze that seeps through the street gutters in Queens. "Make that rule number three: Avoid the ones you can't. Three rules. Only three that matter."

"A little cynical, don't you think?" Mother matters. So does Leah. Am I supposed to just not care about my sister? Not worry that she's ruining her future with Jamie, the kindest and most patient man possible? Not worry about the dream art that fills her apartment? Or the way her best friend, while trying to help her, is only making things worse?

Side by side, we watch the haze solidify into the shadow of a—

Wolf.

My heart seizes, and I poise to run.

"Hey, chill." She catches my arm again. She does that a lot. I'm beginning to dislike it as much as I love it. "Listen to the liar."

The liar in front of us is a bald man in his late sixties. His pants are spotlessly white, and he has a martini in one hand. "He loves it at the vineyard. Tolerates it in the city, but we have a walker that takes him to Central Park each day, so I'd say he has a pretty good life."

Looking again, I realize the haze is shaped like a Labrador retriever. His thick golden fur fades to wisps, but his silhouette is unmistakable now that I've calmed enough to see clearly. His tongue lolls out of his mouth as he pants.

Kneeling, Sylvie pets the shadow dog's neck enthusiastically. "Who's a good boy? You are. You're a good boy." He licks her cheek, and she laughs before she wipes the slobber off with the back of her hand. "I like the literal manifestations of lies the best. Unlike *that*." She nods at the woman that the man without a real dog is lying to, and I notice that her hand is wreathed in a smoky haze.

She has a miniature dog stuffed in her designer purse, and she's feeding it bacon-wrapped scallops with her haze-shrouded hand. The dog and the scallops are, as near as I can tell, 100 percent real, but the smoke curls around them.

"My guess?" Sylvie says. "She claims she never feeds her dog human food, negating an obvious truth. You want to steer clear of that. No telling what kind of toxic crap a blatant lie like that will produce if it goes on long enough to solidify. Should that be rule number four? Nah, let's make it a corollary of rule number three: Avoid toxic crap. Like the muck that politicians and talk-show hosts spew when they twist the truth and spread dangerous lies. Literally dangerous for us." Giving the dog one more pat, Sylvie stands up and links arms with me. We stroll away from the scallop-and-dog lady. "Since you're new—" she begins.

This time I interrupt her. "I'm not."

She snorts, clearly not believing me.

"I'm twenty-three."

"So? I'm twentysomething." She waves her hand. "Always been vague about that. Days. Decades. Whatever."

"My birthday is August twenty-third," I say. "I was an easy birth. Latched right away. Slept through the night . . ." I know all the stories. And from age two onward, I have my own memories. I remember learning to read and devouring all the Little Golden Books before graduating to an abridged graphic novel version of *Around the World in Eighty Days*. My favorite stuffed animal was a one-eared rabbit that I dragged everywhere, until Mother told a deliveryman it had been damaged in the dryer and told me it had gone to Bunny Heaven. My one-eared rabbit disappeared after that. I tell Sylvie a few of these memories.

She gawks at me as dancers, shadowy and otherwise, spin around us. "Wait. Are these your *actual* memories? You were born and you *grew up?*"

Of course, I did. Mother wanted me to grow up, so I did. She'd wanted a chubby-legged toddler, then a pigtailed five-year-old. I was a skinny teen who never had to fight acne and never had a sunburn, and then I became me as I am now. An inch taller than Leah. Same face, but I smile more, and I wear my hair the length that Mother preferred, just to my shoulders. And my eyes match hers—though in photos, baby Hannah had eyes like Dad's.

"But . . . if you aren't new . . . then why . . . ? No offense, but—"

I finish for her. "—why don't I know anything? Because I never left her side." It aches to use the past tense. I blink as my eyes fill. I thought I was done with crying, but saying this out loud feels like a fresh wound. In my mind's eye, I see Mother on the couch, so still, with the muck from the TV pooling on the carpet. The house wasn't silent, with the hum of the refrigerator, the whir of the fan overhead, the buzz of the voices on TV, and I can still hear it all roaring inside me. The casket was a relief after that.

"Okay, so then why are you here?"

"She died."

"Oh." Her eyes widen. "Oh!"

I take a breath and say what I've barely let myself think, the only question that matters now. "I'm here because I need to know: Can a dream outlast the dreamer?"

What happens to a lie after the liar is gone?

CHAPTER THIRTEEN

The morning after their "girls' night out," Leah woke with her head pounding and her mouth tasting like stale peanut butter. Running her tongue over her sticky teeth, she stared up at the ceiling of her apartment and attempted to reconstruct the night: She and Jersey had worked all day cleaning out her mom's house, mostly the kitchen and the bathroom, and then gone out to a bar called Sweet Venom, which specialized in a sickly sweet drink that she'd had decidedly too many of.

It had, for a while, made her feel better. Or at least it had distracted her.

Then Jamie called.

Outside a car alarm beeped, and she wished someone would turn it off. Or drop a dumpster on top of it or something. A second later, it stopped, and then a siren wailed. Sighing, Leah sat up.

And noticed the very naked man beside her, fast asleep.

"Shit," she breathed.

She hadn't . . .

She had.

She'd walked away from the first guy. Gotten another sweet venom. Downed it. Gone outside for fresh air. And then she'd told a nice guy that she wanted to forget. She didn't want to forget memories she had; she wanted to forget memories she *didn't* have—the ones she should have made if her life had been different.

Ironic that she had achieved selective memory after all. She couldn't remember chunks from the prior night. Like whether she'd even told him her name. She wasn't sure about his. Sam? He kind of looked like a Sam, with his tousled hair and a bit of drool in the corner of his mouth. He hadn't stolen the covers, which explained why she hadn't noticed him instantly. She'd woken bundled in her sheet, like normal, but naked, which was only normal when she and Jamie . . .

Shit.

Jamie.

She squeezed her eyes shut. What was she going to tell Jamie? Did she *have* to tell Jamie? Could she pretend it never happened? Jersey wouldn't tell, and they'd known no one else at the bar. Did Jersey even know?

That's low, Leah.

She couldn't keep this from him. That was nearly as bad as the cheating itself, which, if she remembered the bits and pieces correctly, had actually been pretty good. Except bad. Because she shouldn't have done it. Even if it was what she'd needed at the time. *Thought I needed.*

Leah buried her face in her hands. Maybe if she went back to sleep, she'd wake up and this would all have been a dream. Last night. Also, cleaning out Mom's house. And the funeral. And the call from the hospital—the kindly nurse was so very sorry to deliver the news. Everyone was so very sorry. Like the lawyer, when she told him about her sister. So very sorry. Leah didn't want their sympathy. Sorry didn't begin to fill the holes in her life.

Why, though, had she thought bringing home a stranger would?

Exhaling heavily, the man rolled closer to her. His arm flopped across her pillow. She had to get him out of here. She'd told Jamie she'd call . . . If she didn't, or if she'd missed his call and then he decided to come over . . .

She checked her phone. No messages from him yet, but it was only a matter of time. *What am I going to do?*

Yanking on clothes, she dressed. She wanted to shower. Her skin felt gummy; her hair was matted. But a shower wouldn't go far enough—she wanted to slough off her skin, not be the kind of person who'd cheat on Jamie.

A voice inside her whispered.

He'd been smothering me.

Not an excuse.

He hadn't understood.

Still not.

I felt so alone. I am *alone.* No mother. No father. No sister. *I didn't want to be alone last night.* Now she was anxious to be alone again.

Reaching across the bed, Leah shook the shoulder of . . . whoever this was. Sam. She didn't want to know if that was really his name. He lifted his head and blinked at her. She attempted a smile—this wasn't his fault. "Hey," she said.

"Hey, goldfish. Good morning."

He had blue eyes, which she hadn't noticed last night.

He stretched and didn't seem in a rush to dress and flee.

"So . . . that was nice?" Leah said. "Thanks?" She felt herself blush. This had to be the most awkward she had ever felt in her life. *Please leave.* "I'd offer you breakfast, but . . ."

"You want me out of here," he said.

"I . . ." She winced. "Sorry. I shouldn't have . . ." She had a sudden thought. "We used protection, didn't we? I don't . . ."

"Yeah." He sat up and gestured toward the used condom on the floor.

A tiny knot loosened in her shoulders. At least there wouldn't be any ramifications. She was on the pill as well. "I don't usually do this." Except when she met Jamie. But that hadn't been like *this.* It had felt right. Real, even. There hadn't been any betrayal. And there had been a lot less whiskey. Her eyes flickered around the apartment—at the laundry spilling from the hamper, at the dishes in the sink, at the unopened bills on the table, everywhere but at the man tossing the condom in the trash and then pulling on his clothes.

He offered a smile. "You don't have to be embarrassed. It was great."

"Yeah. It was." She had no idea if that came out sounding sincere. She reminded herself that none of this was his fault. He had been prepared to leave her after the gyro. She was the one who cajoled him to come home with her, to help her forget, to make her feel less terribly alone. "You were great." She tried to muster enthusiasm in her voice. It wasn't his fault that she was sabotaging her life.

"I'm Sam," he said.

She'd been right about that. "I remember."

"No goldfish memory for you today. As for me . . . well, there are moments I'd like to have again. Holes in my memory to fill . . ."

He doesn't know my name. God, this was humiliating. Who was she to sleep with a guy without telling him her name? Consensual sex, all great, whatever, but it was still supposed to *matter*.

"What I'm trying to say is, I'd like to see you again."

Shit.

It did matter. To him.

"Look, you seem like a nice guy, but I'm in a relationship . . ."

Gently, he said, "A relationship that doesn't seem to be going well." Then he held up his hands in surrender. "Absolutely no pressure. You need time. You need space. You told me that."

She had? She must have.

"Call me when you're ready?"

She wasn't going to be ready. This wasn't going to happen again. She wanted to pretend that it never happened, like Mom always did. It must have been nice to rearrange her memories so that they suited her. Unfortunately, Leah hadn't inherited that ability.

Why couldn't he leave already? Vanish like a dream she never wanted.

He crossed to the table that was squeezed between her sofa and kitchen counter. Scrounging around, he located a pen and a scrap of paper. "There. My name. My number. In case you want to—" Leah's eyes flicked to the bed, but Sam finished with—"get coffee. No strings. No expectations. No pressure."

He was a nice guy.

She already had a nice guy.

What I want is to be left alone. And then she felt awful for think-ing that. Sam had only done what she'd wanted him to. She'd invited him home; she remembered that much all too clearly now, how she'd practically pleaded, like a pathetic mess. And he was being gracious and gentlemanly and was actually interested in her. "I'm in witness protec-tion, and I'm not allowed to form attachments to anyone. You should forget you ever met me, for your own safety."

Oh, fuck, why did she just say that?

His eyes widened.

"Better if you don't know my name, remember where I live, or tell anyone about this, okay?" Leah said. She herded him toward the door. "You were fantastic, and I loved every second of last night, but we can't ever see each other again."

"Uh, okay . . . um."

Leah kissed him on the lips, very quickly. "I'm sorry. It wasn't meant to be."

He retreated into the stairwell, and Leah shut the door. Leaned against it. Winced at herself. That was not smooth. There was zero chance he'd believed her. She hoped he'd at least think she'd been kind. She hadn't begun the night intending to hurt anyone. She just wanted to escape her reality for a bit.

She wondered if that was how Mom had justified her lies—she'd meant no harm. It was only a cookie, only a birthday, only a daughter . . .

Her phone buzzed.

That would be Jamie, checking up on her, as he always did, because he cared. It shouldn't make her want to throw the phone out her third-floor window. She stared at his text. **Hope you're okay this morning. Love you,** it said, plus a kiss emoji.

She took a breath.

Exhaled.

And typed: All fine. Just about to jump in shower. Talk later.

She then deleted: Talk later.

Added a kiss emoji.

Deleted it.

Added: Love you.

Did not add: I'm sorry.

She wasn't going to tell him, she decided. He'd be hurt if he knew. If he didn't know . . . he wouldn't be hurt. It was that simple. Leah wouldn't breathe a word about this to anyone, and she had no intention of ever seeing Sam again. She would erase this night from her memory as if it had never happened.

Hit send.

She glanced at the scrap of paper with Sam's phone number but didn't touch it. Instead, she called Jersey. When her friend answered, Leah said, "Don't tell Jamie."

"Never," Jersey promised. "But Leah . . ."

"Don't say it. Don't say anything."

"Lips sealed."

Leah exhaled and sank onto her couch. Jersey was the best friend she could ever ask for. Every time she'd needed an escape from her mom, Jersey was there to offer a distraction, an ear, or a couch to sleep on. She was the one dependable constant in Leah's life. As for Jamie . . . what he didn't know wouldn't hurt him.

All I have to do is pretend that I'm not the worst person in the entire world, and everything will be fine.

She thought of her mother.

Maybe the apple didn't fall far from the tree.

No. I'm not like her.

A voice inside her whispered: *Liar.*

CHAPTER FOURTEEN

Sashaying through the crowd of partygoers, Sylvie plucks a wineglass off a table and then flashes me one of her sparkling smiles. "You want an answer? Here it is: Yes, you could wink out at any moment. Poof, candle extinguished." She waves her hand in the air dramatically. "It's beyond either your or my control, so it's absolutely pointless to worry about it. I'm certainly not going to."

Every word hits like a fist.

Sylvie swirls her glass and inhales, blissfully. She sips. "The host insisted he was serving a '57. He isn't, except to us." She holds the glass out to me. "You try."

I don't take it. "You don't care at all if I just . . . *poof?*"

Shrugging, she finishes the wine herself. Burgundy darkens her lips, and she licks them. "Either of us could wink out at any time. Can't predict it and can't stop it, so might as well enjoy ourselves. And this—a party of rich wannabes—is exactly the place for that. The rich and especially the wannabe rich are magnificently great at lying about who they are and what they have."

No. I refuse to believe that the only option is to just give up. I deliberately don't think about how I crawled into Mother's casket.

"Come on, look around you, Hannah. Look at all the beautiful lies!" Sylvie spreads her arms expansively, encompassing the fog that rolls knee high throughout the house. It's thickened since we've arrived, with swirls of smoky darkness in corners and a shimmer that mimics the glint of sunlight in others. Visions form and dissipate within the mist, like the shadow dog, who appears and disappears as he weaves between the legs of the partygoers, endlessly begging for attention that they don't—can't—give him. Nearby, one woman is cocooned in haze so thick that she looks blurred. Another has the faint shape of wings protruding from her back. When she turns, I see they are twisted and torn. It *is* beautiful but also sad. Sylvie doesn't seem to see that. "Shame to waste even a single second," Sylvie says, and she tosses the empty wineglass over her shoulder. It shatters on the pavement, but no one around us flinches. Only me.

She drags me through the party. "Not him. Not her. Definitely not him. Ah, *him*."

We halt beside a man named Gary. We know he's named Gary because he talks about himself in the third person. "—but that's not the way Gary rolls. And I said to him, 'Steven,' I said, 'you gotta man up. Back when I got my private pilot's license—'"

Sylvie looks as delighted as a kid elbow deep in candy. "Oh, please say you have a plane." *Please don't.* I have zero desire to ride inside an ephemeral airplane. If that's what Sylvie has in mind for our "epic night," then I am out of here.

He doesn't say it, but he also doesn't stop talking.

He has a woman and her date pinned between a marble column and a wide-leafed tropical plant in a large porcelain pot. It looks as if the woman is considering whether it would be rude to jump into the plant.

Gary is white, middle aged, and entirely certain he is fascinating. He sports a spray-on tan, a receding hairline, and overly bright teeth. His shirt is unbuttoned to midsternum to reveal a patchy lawn of graying chest hair, and his khaki shorts are tight. But what *is* fascinating is the mist waterfalling off him. It's spread around him to swamp the entire nearby area.

"Wait for it," Sylvie whispers.

In his booming voice, he says, "You've probably heard rumors, but once, there was this party where servers parachuted in with the appetizers. It was off-the-charts insane—"

"You were one of the parachuters?" the woman's date asks.

"Not exactly," Gary says, "but it inspired me—"

"I heard there were zoo animals there," the woman says.

"Oh, yeah!" Gary says. "Tigers in cages as decoration. Trained penguins as servers—"

The date scoffs. "Yeah, I don't think—"

"Scout's honor," Gary swears. "I was there. Hey, hey, Topher, come tell Skip and—sorry, what was your name again? Daphne?"

A muscle twitches in the woman's cheek. "Diane. We've met several times."

"Of course, of course, Diane. Topher, Diane here wants to know about the Split Rock Road party. You know, *the* one." He waves his friend over.

"I really don't—" Diane begins.

But Topher bounds over. "Preface this by saying, I wasn't actually there, but I heard from a guy who swears—"

Sylvie draws me back as the haze builds. It's hip deep around us and rising as Gary and Topher attract more people to their conversation. Usually, this was the point when I'd retreat to my bedroom and bury myself in a book that was never written while Mother spun her tales to the point of suffocation, but with Sylvie gripping my arm and practically vibrating with excitement, there's no retreating.

Eyeing the fog as it unspools, I say, "Maybe we're myths. Tall tales. Urban legends." It's a kinder interpretation, especially since stories can outlive the storyteller. I am a fan of any explanation that doesn't mean I cease to exist without warning and without chance of appeal.

"Watch," Sylvie breathes, delighted.

And the infamous off-the-charts party that never existed rises around us.

◆ ◆ ◆

There are, in fact, penguins, which I find more than a bit absurd. Also, contortionists suspended in hoops from wires that fade as you look toward the stars. Spangled in sequins, they twist their bodies as if they were made of rubber.

Around me, it feels as though the number of partygoers has doubled, with every available space filled with shadow-draped figures in tuxedoes and evening gowns. One woman has golden face paint that makes her gleam like a goddess beneath the lights. Another carries cement blocks on her shoulders in towers six feet above her head. I feel as though I've dipped into the center of a circus. The promised parachuters descend from above and vanish as their shadowy feet touch the lawn, only to descend again.

Sylvie clasps my shoulder. "Welcome to Wonderland." She looks immensely pleased with herself, as if she's created all this just for me. "Once one person starts . . . it spreads." She gestures to the knot of men and women in the heart of the haze. Gary's group has grown to eight people, and I'm certain that they're all talking about his mythical party.

It's spread to other pockets of partygoers too.

"I heard there were fire dancers in the pool . . . ," one nearby says, and their listener agrees, embellishing on how many and how elaborate their tricks were.

Sylvie smacks her lips and pulls me to the edge of the pool where there are, as promised, shirtless men dancing with torches as they balance on surfboards. Sweat drips from their muscles, and smoke spirals up toward the sky.

It's like nothing I've ever seen.

Or heard.

There's a cacophony of music overwhelming the live band. An Elvis impersonator strolls by, then vanishes, but I hear the croon of "Heartbreak Hotel" dovetailing a Rihanna song. The tiles beneath my feet vibrate with the bass beat, which dissolves into a rumble as six motorcyclists drive directly through the partygoers and then vertically up the columns onto the roof.

A few shadows scatter around the motorcycles, then re-form. As the motorcyclists disappear, the thrum of the bass returns. I've never seen a nonexistent world spring up so quickly. Mother's lies were built in a slow, measured way, formed from retelling after retelling, beginning as wisps of haze until, at last, they took solid form. Here, it feels as if the partygoers are breathing their imagination to life in the moment.

"How is this possible?" I ask Sylvie.

"Repetition." She grins. "The lie of the most outrageous party ever thrown has been told and retold and grown until enough people believed it. It pops up nearly every weekend out here if you can find a real party elaborate enough to remind people about it."

"You've seen this before?" I have to shout over the music and the laughter.

"Many times! This is just the latest incarnation. Ooh, that's new!" She drags me across the patio, directly through both people and shadows, to the lawn. "Ever ride an elephant?"

Sure enough, there's a goddamn elephant striding through the smoke across the manicured grass. Like us, it doesn't bend the blades. Whoever first invented this lie must have loved animals. I wonder if the party-that-never-was began with something plausible and tame before it took on this life of its own—literally.

I feel a smile pull at my lips.

I don't need Sylvie to tug me forward; I'm moving on my own. I'm not going to miss this. Riding an elephant wasn't on Mother's lengthy list of accomplishments and adventures from her pre-child life. I think she fed a giraffe once. According to her, there had almost been a camel ride on a trip to Egypt; if only she hadn't met a man with charming eyes in Greece that one summer . . .

But I have a chance to do what she did not.

I think she would approve.

Running across the grass, I laugh out loud as a pair of shadow hands hoists me into the air. I swing my leg wide to straddle the elephant. He's made of shadows, mist, and flesh, and he feels solid beneath me. His skin is coarse and dusty, like pavement covered in chalk. He smells of straw and honey.

As he lumbers forward, I shift from side to side. He flicks his ears, and they ripple, stirring the mist. I pat his neck. "You're an excellent elephant. Thank you for this."

Maybe Sylvie's right. Maybe this is the way to live. Enjoy whatever precious time I have. Go to impossible parties. Ride impossible elephants.

Not worry about whether or when I'll fade.

Just pretend that this is enough.

If I pretend hard enough, maybe it can be.

After lumbering across the lawn, the elephant arrives at the beach. The sand doesn't shift beneath his feet as he marches toward the water and wades into the shallows. He walks in the breaking waves, and they flow through him as if he weren't there.

I hear hoofbeats behind me and turn to see Sylvie on a black horse with a mane of wisps. She gallops past with a wave. I watch her shrink in the distance before she turns and gallops back. Her cheeks are flushed, and she's out of breath. "Come for a gallop!"

"I don't think elephants can—" But before I can finish, my mount lurches into a run. He thunders down the beach. Laughing, Sylvie matches our pace on her shadow horse.

An array of stars glitters above us, the lights from the party shine behind, and the moonlight splinters across the surface of the sea. I hear the howl of the wolves. Beneath me, my elephant falters, beginning to fade, and Sylvie pulls me onto the back of her black horse. Riding together, we turn and race back toward the impossible party.

CHAPTER FIFTEEN

Seventeen-year-old Leah clutched her RISD acceptance letter in one hand and didn't know whether to scream or cry. "Why did you let me apply if you were only going to say no?"

Mom was already crying. Great crocodile tears that she'd always been able to summon at will. Leah didn't believe her tears any more than she believed the words that had been coming out of Mom's mouth. "You had your heart so set on it . . ."

"You're right," Leah said, waving the letter. "It's only *the* best art school in the entire country. And it's only been my dream since I was, like, five years old."

In a small voice, Mom said, "I didn't think you'd get in."

Leah sat down on the kitchen chair with a loud thump. "You didn't?" All that talk about how much she believed in Leah, how of course she'd get into her dream school, about how she was destined for greatness. *Just more lies.*

"Of course not," Mom said. "Tons of kids draw and paint, like tons of kids play football or baseball. How many of them become professional athletes, really? You'll outgrow it, like you'll outgrow that ridiculous cat-eye makeup that I know you wear only to annoy me." She waved her hand at Leah's face. "Art is a fun extracurricular, sure, but it's not a career."

"It can be," Leah said. "If you're good enough."

"If you're rich enough," Mom corrected. "You have to be practical, Leah. Dreams aren't going to pay your rent or buy your groceries—do you know how many dreams I set aside to feed and clothe and house you and Hannah?"

Leah stared at her. "For fuck's sake, Mom."

"Language," Mom scolded.

"I can guarantee that it wasn't expensive to feed, clothe, and house my dead sister."

Mom let out a gasp.

Leah squeezed her eyes shut so she wouldn't have to see her mother's wounded expression. She couldn't believe this was happening. All this time . . . all these months . . . while she was working on her application, worrying over it, devoting hours to building a portfolio, agonizing over every brushstroke and every word in her essays, Mom had been cheering her on, making her believe it was possible, and now, this? They couldn't afford it? Shouldn't that have been a conversation months ago, back before the financial aid application deadline had passed? Before it was too late? "You told me that there was a college account. You've been saving ever since I was born. You said it would be no problem."

"I didn't want you to worry," Mom said. "It was meant as a kindness."

"Because you didn't believe I was good enough to get in," Leah said. She didn't know what hurt worse—the death of the dream, or the fact that Mom had lied about something so very important to her.

"There *is* a college account, and with financial aid—"

"Wait, you said I shouldn't apply for it," Leah said, "because we didn't need to. We wouldn't qualify. Because you had saved enough."

"I applied for aid from SUNY Stony Brook on your behalf, which, as a state school with a wide range of majors, is the more practical option—"

"I don't care about practical!" Leah knew she was shouting and that that wouldn't help, but she didn't know how to stop. The acceptance letter crinkled in her hand, and she forced herself to quit squeezing it. She spread it flat on the table. "This was important to me."

"I know you don't care about the practical." Mom was no longer crying, which made it clear that the tears had just been another tactic. Mom's voice was clipped, businesslike. "Which is why I needed to step in and think about your future. You can't spend money we don't have on an artsy-craftsy degree you won't use. You need to prepare for a real job in the real world—"

"When have *you* ever cared about the real world?" Leah shot back.

Mom pointed her finger at Leah. "I have worked. I have scrimped. I have saved. For you. I have given up dreams. Given up travel. Do you know I used to—"

"What happened to my college fund? All that money you were saving?" Leah crossed her arms. She couldn't help the tears from pouring down her cheeks, but at least she wouldn't stop trying. But what was she trying to do? The money was gone; the dream was dead. Maybe she just wanted Mom to admit for once that she hadn't done "what was best." She'd thought only of herself, yet again. "Where did it go? Clothes? Jewels? Drugs? Gambling? Where?"

"Nowhere," Mom said.

It had to be somewhere. She'd scrimped and saved. "Why are you lying—"

"There was never enough!"

Leah fell silent.

"How much do you think an admin assistant makes?" Mom asked. "There's never enough. Never was. Between the mortgage and the bills . . . you don't have a college fund. You'll go wherever we can afford, and you'll be grateful for it! Stony Brook is an excellent school. Your friend Jersey is going there. I'd think you'd be grateful for *that* at least."

"It's not . . ." Mom was twisting it again. Leah wasn't ungrateful. She'd just thought . . . Mom had said . . . She'd *promised* that Leah could attend the college of her dreams, that all she had to do was work hard and Mom would take care of the rest. If Leah had known, she could have applied for financial aid. She would have applied for scholarships. She would've gotten a part-time job. Done whatever was necessary. And maybe it still wouldn't have been enough, but she could have tried. Or worst case, she could have not applied and not gotten her hopes up. She could have avoided *this* moment, which felt like a knife thrust into her heart. "You lied to me."

Quietly, Mom said, "It was easier."

"Than what? This? Because this doesn't feel easy to me!"

"Everything's been easy for you!" Mom shouted back. "You've had everything that I could give you! Did I say you couldn't go to college? No, I didn't say that. Just that you need to be realistic about where you go and what you do. You need to have reasonable goals and reachable dreams. You can't bankrupt our family for nonsense!"

Standing, Leah hugged the acceptance letter to her chest. She felt herself beginning to cry again, and she didn't want this conversation to drag on. It was pointless. No words could change what her mother had done, and there were no words that would ever change her mother.

As she walked into her room, she heard her mother say, "Hannah understands."

Leah slammed her door as hard as she could.

The next day, while Leah was at school, her mother replaced her door with a shower curtain so that she couldn't slam it again.

◆ ◆ ◆

It was a long shot, Leah knew.

Dad might not be home. Even if he was, he might not open the door. *I should have called first,* but if she'd done that, he might have said no right then. It was easier to say no over the phone, when you didn't have to look your only daughter in the face. If she appeared in person and begged him . . . then maybe?

Exactly what was she going to say? She hadn't visited in years. After the court case, he hadn't wanted to see her. And then when Katelyn didn't have a baby, Leah hadn't known what to say. She couldn't ask if there had been a miscarriage, much less if Katelyn had ever truly been pregnant. They'd spoken on holidays, and he called every year on her birthday. But it was always stilted, always surface. She didn't even know what he thought of her art. Did he even know she still painted? She wished she'd brought samples. Even her college-application portfolio. Maybe she should go home. Come back another time with her art. Show him what she was capable of, and then see what he said.

As she turned to leave, the door swung open.

Dad stared at her.

She stared at Dad.

"It's a video doorbell," Dad said.

"Oh," Leah said.

She meant to say a lot more. Wanted to. Didn't know where to start.

"Hi, Dad."

He invited her in, and she gawked at the house. Katelyn, or whoever they'd hired, kept it spotless. It wasn't Dad unless he really had changed. There was a side table in the foyer with a painted wooden box neatly labeled "Mail." They even had an umbrella stand with umbrellas in it. There was no surface of her and Mom's house in Garden City that wasn't piled with stacks of mail, books, or whatever. Leah peeked into the dining room, which had candlesticks on the table, as he led her into the kitchen.

The kitchen looked as if it were out of a magazine: white marble everywhere, an island with an extra sink, lush plants in the window. Mom was fully capable of killing off cacti. Leah tried to imagine living in a house like this, photo ready all the time. She'd be afraid to breathe wrong. *This was almost my life.*

She didn't know how she felt about that.

"Water?" Dad offered. "Soda? We have ginger ale and Diet Pepsi."

That said a lot about their life right there. She shook her head. Tentatively, she perched on a stool adjacent to the kitchen island and folded her hands on her lap. She wished she'd said yes so she had something to hold, but he'd already seated himself on a stool at the end of the island.

"Are you all right?" Dad asked. "Is your mother okay?"

"She's the same," Leah said. *Worse.* She didn't tell him that, after their latest fight and coming home to find a shower curtain for a door instead of an apology or an explanation, she'd moved out and was living with her best friend Jersey's family—at least temporarily. She hadn't been able to bring herself to tell anyone but Jersey why she'd left. "I . . . well, I . . ."

His face was unreadable. She may as well have been talking to a marble statue. She tried to mesh this man in front of her with the father who'd read to her when she couldn't sleep, fought with her mom when he thought she wasn't watching, laughed so hard at TV shows that tears sprang into his eyes. "What do you need?" he asked.

She felt her cheeks blush. She *had* come because she needed something. Haltingly, she explained—about her application to the Rhode Island School of Design, about her dreams of being an artist, about her nonexistent college fund. She told him how Mom hadn't encouraged her to apply for financial aid because she hadn't thought Leah would get in and about how Mom wouldn't consider helping her take out a student loan.

"Art school," Dad said flatly. "You came to ask me for money for art school."

"I . . . Yes."

"You chose her," Dad said.

Leah flinched. All the words she wanted to say evaporated in her throat.

"You stood in court, and you chose her," Dad said. "You said it wasn't true, that she didn't lie, that she didn't claim over and over to everyone who'd listen that our daughter, that our Hannah . . ." His voice broke. "I offered you a home, a family, a chance to escape and start over, with me."

Leah couldn't meet his eyes. "You were too late," she mumbled. He'd waited two years to rescue her. By then, she hadn't wanted to be rescued, not by him.

Why hadn't she?

Fear?

Inertia?

Hurt.

After two years, how could she believe he really wanted to save her?

"And now you're the one who's too late," he said. Then he sighed. "Leah, you can't cut me out of your life and then show up to ask for . . . What's tuition? Sixty thousand a year? Eighty? For four years? You don't see me. You barely talk to me. Until you need three hundred thousand dollars, and now you come here?"

Leah felt tears on her cheeks. "You're my father." He was supposed to help her when she needed help and save her when she needed saving and *be there* for her, even though she'd made mistakes. "Please, I need your help."

"You chose her," he repeated. "And you lied to do it. For all I know, you're lying now. For all I know, she sent you to lie for her because she needs the money or wants it for some harebrained dream that she'll never even try to achieve. You're exactly like her." He stood up. "I think you should leave. Come back when you want to be my daughter, not when you want my money."

"Dad . . ."

"I'm sorry, Leah," he said. "The answer is no."

CHAPTER SIXTEEN

The shadow wolves call to one another.

Years ago, when they first hunted me, they ran in silence, spilling out of buildings and coalescing on the street around me, and I remember how chilling that silence was, as if it wanted to swallow all sound that I ever made and snuff out all thought and feeling. It was a smothering silence, like the quiet of the casket. For a long time after they attacked me, I hated silence and would try to fill it with my voice, even if no one but me could hear it.

This is worse.

Their cries echo in my bones, as if they're dredging a channel through my body. They pour through me until they're all I can hear. One howl lifted by another and another.

"Run," I say.

For once, Sylvie doesn't argue. She kicks her heels into the sides of the horse, and it springs across the sand toward the lawn, a streak of muscle and haze.

I can't see the wolves yet. Everywhere, shadows are thick and writhe with their ominous spirit. Clinging to Sylvie's waist, I'm knocked against her as the horse canters toward the house.

"Not there!" I cry. "We have to get away!" We need to flee along the beach into the open night. Leave the wolves far behind.

"They'll catch us! Trust me! I've done this before!" Sylvie yells.

The horse thunders onto the patio by the pool, and Sylvie flings herself off its back. She grabs my arm and tries to pull me down after her. "They'll tear us apart!" I cry. "Sylvie!"

Beneath me, the horse bucks, its eyes wild, as the first wolf leaps onto the arch above the partygoers. As I fall, I see the beast silhouetted against the night sky just for an instant, and then I crash against Sylvie.

We fall into the haze. It wraps its arms around us, and all I can see is movement: the shifting of the shadows. I hear Sylvie's exhale, hard and sharp in my ear, as she hits the ground. My elbow jams into stone, and pain lances through my arm.

"Don't scream," she hisses, her breath hot. "Stay silent. Stay low."

"We need to run," I whisper back.

"They'll chase us. We need to lose them."

She said she's done this before. When? How? The pain recedes to a throbbing. *Not broken. Phew.* I wonder if Sylvie's hurt beneath me. I think of the pain from the wolves' teeth; whoever said that time dulls pain has never contended with this memory.

"Crawl," Sylvie advises.

Side by side, we crawl on hands and knees through the haze. I flinch as legs and feet of party guests slice through me, but they feel no more substantial than the mist itself.

There are no more howls. Have they left? Seeing a crowd this size, did they retreat? I'd been a lone girl, solitary prey. Perhaps the wolves wouldn't attack a crowd?

I am wrong to hope.

The screams begin, discordant with the beach music that continues playing without a falter. Above the haze, the chatter and the laughter continue to flow, but it's punctuated by a scream that cuts off suddenly, horribly.

"Toward the house," Sylvie whispers. "Get inside."

Yes, inside. That saved me before, when I flung myself into my mother's garden. Except this isn't my home or Sylvie's, and I don't know if it will keep us safe. All I know for certain is that the wolves are out here and we need to be elsewhere.

"When I say so, get up and run as fast as you can," she whispers.

Fur brushes against my arm, and panic surges through me like fire through an oil slick. I spring forward without waiting for her. Swearing, Sylvie bursts forward next to me. The wolves are everywhere. They slip in and out of the shadows, hurling themselves at the silhouettes dancing by the pool. They've torn the contortionists from their wires. The tiger's cage is open and empty. I see no sign of the magnificent elephant or Sylvie's beautiful horse.

All around the patio, the shadows are shredded. Silently stalking their prey, the wolves weave between the laughing partygoers. Mixed with the real, not all the shadows have the sense to run, and I see two wolves knock into a dancing silhouette. The dancer vanishes beneath their paws.

I belt toward the house. Its lights blare, warm and welcoming. My heart is beating so fast that it hurts, and my breath tears at my throat. Beside me, Sylvie barrels directly through a man with a martini in hand.

I see a wolf turn toward us.

And then we are through the archway into the house. A trio of partygoers is playing a game of pool, and a shadow wolf is tearing a body apart at their feet. Only I can hear her screams.

There is no blood as she is torn, but that only makes it more horrifying. The dying shadow woman fixes her eyes on me. *She can see me.* I'm rooted to the ground as the wolf tears into her torso.

There's no safety inside.

Guard-like, a wolf blocks the doorway to the rest of the house. Wolves hunt in and beyond the archways that lead to the patio, lawn, and beach. There's no way out.

"Don't touch the people," I say. "We have to blend in."

Every part of me wants to run, but that would draw the wolves' attention. Spinning slowly, I run my hand across a tray held by an oblivious server and lift up an unreal glass. Its weight is solid in my hand, and the deep-red liquid sloshes against the sides, leaving a slow drip like a wave pulling back from the shore in slow motion. *Stay calm. Blend in.* I take a sip, and the wine feels as if it's scalding my tongue.

A wolf halts in front of the chattering woman with the miniature dog in her purse. Its jaw widens—and keeps widening, impossibly large, until its jaw is a swirl of shadows. It encases the woman's arm up to her elbow. She doesn't even flinch.

I feel a scream building in my throat, but I force myself to look away. Pretending not to see the horrors unfolding around me, I drift closer to the billiard table as if joining my very real and very inedible friends will somehow protect me.

"Corner pocket with the seven," the man with the pool cue says.

"He's never going to make it," I say to the woman next to me. My voice only shakes a little.

She tells him, "You can do it, Steve."

Steve bends over and eyes his shot.

She waves her hand. "Little to the left."

"A little more to the left," I say. "You're going to miss."

He shoots and misses as the white ball rolls past the seven.

"Told you," I say, and then my throat closes up as I feel a brush of softness against my left calf. I don't turn. Don't look to see if it's a wolf. Don't tense in any visible way, though my fingers close even tighter around the stem of the wineglass.

I don't know if it's possible to fool the wolves, but it's all I can think to do. Sylvie drifts closer. From the corner of my eye, I see she's holding one of the beef pastries, but her hand is shaking, and she isn't eating it.

"Tell me about your favorite sunset," I say to her.

"Sorry? Now?"

"Yes, now."

A wolf skirts the edge of the billiard table. My insides scream to run. But where? They stalk on the fringes of every exit. One halts in front of a man who drips with the same toxic ooze that filled the streets near Sweet Venom. *Dangerous lies.*

The wolf opens its jaws and inhales the muck at the man's feet, swallowing the acidic sludge in a single gulp. I shudder.

"Favorite sunset," I repeat.

"Um, okay." Sylvie swallows, her eyes also on the wolf that destroyed the muck. She forces herself to look at me instead. "It caught me by surprise. I was at a party. Much like this one, before the . . . you know. An ordinary party, in Great Neck, but there were actors there, a few almost-famous ones, and clumps of people surrounded them, trying to capture their attention. As if their fame would rub off, but the people were just as invisible as—" She freezes as a wolf sniffs her feet.

"And the sunset?"

"I saw a glimpse out the window: all reds and oranges. It looked as if someone had set the clouds on fire. I rushed outside and stared for an hour as the clouds shifted color. I swore at that moment that I'd never miss a single sunset."

"Have you ever missed one?"

Another wolf pads closer to me. I do not look. I feel its breath hot on my leg, beneath the hem of my sundress. I raise the wineglass to my lips and sip. It burns, and I nearly forget to swallow as the wolf's breath hits my skin.

"Once," Sylvie says. "I was in a wine cellar. Lost track of time. Came outside and saw that it was already that flat gray. I made myself stay outside until the next sunset. It's my one constant. The sun never disappoints me."

"Even when it rains?"

"I'm neither sugar nor a witch," Sylvie says, with a false laugh. "I won't melt. Even in the rain, even behind the clouds, the sun still sets, and the sky still changes. Always reliable."

I never paid too much attention to sunsets. Mother was my sunrise and sunset. But Sylvie never had anyone like that. *She also never had to lose anyone.*

"Hannah." Sylvie's voice pierces.

I try to focus on her, but she looks blurry. Everything looks fuzzy, as if the edges have been blurred by an eraser. The voices of the pool players are muffled. What's happening? Is it the wolves doing this? Is it me?

"You're fading," Sylvie informs me.

I hold my hand up, and it's translucent. *No! Not now! Not yet! I'm not ready to go!* The wineglass slips from my grip. It vanishes before it hits the floor.

"Now we leave," Sylvie says. "Walk with me. Very, very quickly."

She grips my hand hard, so hard that the pain shocks everything into crystal clear lines and the lights flare so bright that they pierce my eyes. Suddenly, I am here again. As solid and real as ever. We move quickly between the people, still weaving, still averting our eyes from the wolves.

One wolf watches as we pass by, and its gaze feels overly hot, like a fire in the summertime. *Can it tell?* I wonder. Are we tinged with smoke like the false wine? Can it see through me? But then a spiral of black smoke drifts up like a signal from a group of partygoers, and the wolf shoots after it.

We break into a run.

The door is open to the driveway—to the world. Outside, light spills onto blue flagstone but doesn't pierce beyond it. I don't know how many wolves wait outside, or if they're all inside, destroying the remnants of the party that never should have been.

"Don't show fear," Sylvie says.

I am all fear. My heart is fueled by fear. It pumps through my veins, but I skirt around a valet who does not see me and say, "Excuse me," then laugh lightly, pretending Sylvie has said something that amuses me. We cling to each other's arms, as if holding one another up after too much alcohol, and spill onto the flagstone.

There are cars parked two or three deep on the circular driveway. A few are tucked on the lawn, perilously close to the flower beds. I don't see any wolves, but that means nothing. I know they're nearby. My skin prickles, and my stomach feels like a clenched fist. We walk between the cars, looking for one with the telltale haze, praying for it.

All the cars are solid, steady. Real. Untouchable. I let my fingers fall against them, hoping against hope that one will feel solid to me, but my fingertips glide through their haze-free surfaces.

"There," Sylvie whispers.

She's looking directly at a bloodred car that's tucked into the shadows beside the hydrangea bushes. It's mostly haze and wheels. "It'll dissolve around us," I object. What we need is a car that's been fully imagined.

"It'll hold long enough to get us away." She strides toward it.

"And if it doesn't—"

"Do you see a better option?"

I don't.

She places her hand on the car door. Wisps of haze curl around her wrist, and I see a wolf burst from the bushes several yards from us.

I meet its eyes.

Yellow eyes. Jaw open.

Instantly, I know I've made a terrible mistake.

"Sylvie!" I cry.

She yanks open the car door and jumps in, scrambling to the driver's seat. Caught in the wolf's gaze, I freeze. Follow Sylvie or run? The wolf flickers out of view, and a stream of smoke flows across the driveway and then solidifies. I jump into the car.

Sylvie is patting above the sun visor, searching for the keys. "Shit, shit, shit."

Quickly, I pop open the glove compartment.

Keys fall into my hands, and I shove them at Sylvie.

Her hands are shaking as she jams them into the ignition and twists. *She's terrified.* And that scares me more than anything else. I thought nothing would faze her.

The car jolts as a wolf lands on the hood, and we both scream. Its jaw drips with saliva, and its eyes burn as yellow as the sun, the only constant in its shifting bulk of fur and shadow.

"Drive!" I shout.

Sylvie throws the car into reverse.

We sail backward, directly through another car—it liquifies around us like wet tissues. She spins the steering wheel, and the wolf dissolves into smoke as it's thrown from the hood of our car. She slams on the gas, and we shoot forward, directly through the parked cars.

The wolf runs through the hydrangea bushes that line the gravel driveway. It's lifted its muzzle into a howl, but I hear only the silence. Our ghost car makes no noise. The window mists and then clears, and I see the wolf alongside us.

It lunges toward me, and I scramble away from the door, crashing into Sylvie.

"Watch it!" she cries.

The car jerks sideways.

The wolf snaps its jaws, and the shadow of its teeth stretches toward me like fingers and grazes my skin. My arm burns, and I hear myself scream.

"Hang on!" Sylvie cries.

She whips to the left, and the car blurs around us. I cling to the solidity of the seat. My arm throbs, and I don't look at my skin. I don't want to know what those teeth have done. Sylvie bears down on the gas pedal so hard that it feels as though we're flying.

I am no longer screaming. My breath has left my body. The wind assails my face, and tears stream from my eyes.

Sylvie shouts over the wind, "Have we lost it yet?"

I twist my head and see a stream of shadows following us. "Drive faster!"

Hunched over the wheel, she bears down on the pedal and races through the other cars, and then suddenly pulls the wheel right, and we are driving through a house. Clouds burst around us as we shoot out the other side.

I see the ocean ahead, dark and flat and lit by the moon and stars. She pulls the wheel left and we sail over a sand dune and bounce onto the beach. The car rattles as if it will shake into pieces.

I look behind us again.

It is dark and still. If there are wolves in the shadows, I cannot see them.

CHAPTER
SEVENTEEN

The beach is black, and the ocean blacker. I can't see any shadow wolves in the darkness. The car jolts and jerks as it propels down the beach. I hear the tires spin in the sand before we lurch forward, free again.

"Did we lose them?" Sylvie asks.

I look behind us for the hundredth time.

Still can't tell.

"Maybe?"

"Not the answer I'm looking for," Sylvie says. "How about 'Yay, Sylvie, you saved us! You're my hero! I will eternally worship you, at least until I involuntarily abandon you for the cold of oblivion.'"

I shudder. "Not funny."

A few of the houses behind us spill pools of light onto the beach and illuminate the edge of the waves, but it's not enough to determine if we're safe.

"Brace yourself!" Sylvie says.

I turn forward and see she's speeding toward a jetty of rocks. "Sylvie, turn!"

The rocks stretch from the dunes out into the water. She can't turn anywhere fast enough to avoid them. Instead, she speeds up.

"Stop!" I cry.

We hit the rocks, and the car flies in the air. Beside me, Sylvie shrieks as if on a roller coaster and loving every second, but I sound as if I'm being murdered. We crash onto the beach—and then keep falling as the car dissolves in wisps around us. My knees scrape against the sand as I tumble into the shallows.

I feel the kiss of a wave on my arm, thigh, back. It tangles my hair before it recedes. I'm flat on my back, looking at the stars. Everything aches. I don't think anything is broken, but I haven't tried to move yet.

Nearby, I hear Sylvie laughing.

Gingerly, I peel myself up out of the surf. Another wave crashes, and the water stains the sand around me, but there's no trace of me ever having lain on the beach.

"Now *that's* the kind of thing that makes this all worthwhile!" Sylvie jumps to her feet. "Hands down, closest escape I've ever had. God, makes me feel almost alive!"

As another wave crashes, I retreat from the water's edge. "That was horrific and terrifying and six kinds of wrong. Why didn't you slow down?"

"Because then we wouldn't have flown," she says, with the air of someone stating the obvious to the oblivious. "Crashing without flying is no good. All pain, no joy."

"Rather avoid the crashing at all. And the fleeing. And the terror." I stare down the darkened beach. There could be dozens of wolves back there, waiting to catch our scent.

"We escaped—that's what matters."

"I managed to go years without seeing those monsters." I achieved that by staying in Mother's house. It hits me how exposed I am now without her. I think of Leah. *It was a mistake to leave her.* If I'd tried harder, I could have found a space for myself in her life. Maybe her apartment could have been my refuge and sanctuary.

Or maybe not. Leah knew I was a lie from the start. She was so angry with Mother for clinging to me, for choosing me. Maybe . . . she had a right to be? Given what I am?

"You couldn't stay that lucky," Sylvie says. "Or that sheltered. The wolves always show up eventually. You just got to be ready and quick and not let it freak you out so much. We escaped! Focus on that. Yay, us!"

"How often have you seen them?" I ask. "Do you know what they are? Are they . . . lies?" I still don't like saying the word. It tastes sour on my tongue.

"Often, and no."

I think for a moment that she isn't going to say any more and that I'll have to pepper her with questions she won't answer yet again, but she continues. "You can't trace them to a particular kind of lie the way you can with other hazards, like sinkholes that appear in a road but aren't really there or shards of glass that cover the floor. People with their hearts torn out. Or missing heads. All of them, you can trace back to a person and their words if you try. Not the wolves, though."

She falls silent again.

"So what are they?" I ask.

Sylvie shrugs. "They hunt lies."

She turns her back on the darkness and begins walking east. I match her pace but don't ask where we're going. "Away" is enough of a destination.

"As far as I know, no one created the shadow wolves. They just exist. Like rocks and clouds and like actual wolves. Anyway, they're drawn to lies, and the lies they destroy . . . well, they don't come back."

I think of how the wolf swallowed the untouchable toxic muck. *What they catch, they destroy.* My arm—the wolf's teeth had grazed my skin. And the ache in my leg mimics the pain from when the wolf bit me years ago.

I always hoped the wolves had forgotten me, even though I was incapable of forgetting them. It looks as if their memories are as long as mine. "They were after me."

"They were after all of it," Sylvie corrects. "A lie as big as the party-that-never-was—it's as irresistible as catnip. Or wolf-nip. Of course, they'd attack."

Slowing, I gawk at her, then hurry to catch up. "Wait—you knew they'd come? We went to that party, and you knew it would be attacked?" Why did we go in the first place? You don't walk into a lion's den. What had she been thinking?

"Well, yeah, I knew they'd come *eventually*. Teens know the cops are going to bust up their parties. Same deal. You gotta make your exit at the right time. I admit, I didn't think they'd come that quick or in those numbers. That was a narrow escape, but wasn't it awesome? So exhilarating!"

"It was *not* 'awesome.' It was terrifying and pointless. We could have died—been destroyed, painfully—and for what? A party?"

"*The* party."

"No party is worth that risk."

"It had an elephant."

I am so angry, I'm shaking. "You could have warned me."

"You might not have wanted to go. Plus, I thought you knew. Who doesn't know about the wolves? You've been alive for years, you said."

"I knew about them. I avoid them."

"So do I! Hence the running!"

"That's not what 'avoiding' means." I am aware that I am arguing with one of the only two people I've ever met who has been able to hear me, but I'm livid. "'Avoiding' means you don't go places where you know they'll be. It means not tempting fate."

She scoffs. "It means hiding from everything you want to do? That's not the way I roll." Spreading her arms out, Sylvie twirls on the sand. She tilts back her head and shouts toward the stars, "Risk it all, baby, or what's the point?" She grins at me as if she expects me to be charmed or delighted or won over—I am not.

"The point is not dying!" That's so basic and obvious that I don't understand why she doesn't understand. My hands are clenched into fists, and I want to scream. Oblivion has never felt so close, whether it will come by darkness or teeth, both nearly ended me tonight.

Her expression is full of pity. "That's not the point at all. The point is to live. Have you ever truly lived, Hannah? Or have you been so consumed by not dying that you missed out?"

I have lived. I lived with Mother. Happily. For years. Growing up, growing into the person I was meant to be. It's just *this* existence that I don't understand. "You take too many risks. And fine, that's your choice. But you had no right to decide for me."

I think she's going to wave my words off, but instead, she seems to deflate. She looks forward again, and it's harder to see her expression when she isn't facing the moonlight. "You're right. I didn't. It's just . . . this has been my life for so long that I assumed it was yours too. Obviously, not the cars and the parties. But the wolves. I've always run from them. You haven't?"

"Once. Yes. And then I hid from them. It worked for years." Until Mother died. Until I left Leah. "We need to find a place to hide. Are the houses safe, the ones without parties?"

"Not in the slightest," she says with all her old cheerfulness. She flashes me a smile as bright as the stars above us. "Nowhere is. You'll get used to it."

I don't want to get used to it. I just want to be safe.

◆ ◆ ◆

We walk for what feels like hours.

Sylvie dismisses one house after another. "After the party, the wolves might be satiated, or they might be jazzed up to hunt some more. We don't want a house that looks like a sumptuous birthday cake."

There are a lot of birthday cake–like houses in the Hamptons. We walk past sprawling estates and faux castles and houses with more turrets, balconies, and chimneys than seemingly plausible. Most shimmer like they're lit with a thousand candles, but a few look 100 percent real.

At last, Sylvie selects one: it looks as if it's been overlaid with gauze. "I present to you: a house filled with lies but not actually constructed from them, a rare find in this area. We should be safe here."

"Should be?" I repeat.

"I wish you'd quit acting like all of this is my fault. We are what we are, and they are what they are. Just deal with it, okay?"

I have a half dozen retorts on the tip of my lips, which all boil down to: *I don't want to deal with it.*

We glide through the glass doors into a living room filled with plush white couches. One wall is covered in masquerade masks, each more elaborate than the last. Another has a pencil sketch of an extended arm, housed in an ornate gold-painted frame. I think of Leah, but this sketch doesn't shift or change. It simply exists within the weight of its frame, lit by a single light as if this were a museum.

Sylvie flops onto one of the white couches. "Love white sofas. Absolutely everyone lies about how they keep them unstained. Makes them feel gloriously new and clean. Yum." She stretches as she kicks off her shoes and sprawls across the cushions.

Skirting the glass coffee table, I choose the other sofa. The cushions sink beneath me, which means Sylvie is right—this sofa is wreathed in lies—but I'm more concerned with whether the wolves will follow us here than with the furniture.

"What else do you know about the wolves?" I ask.

"God, Hannah! I swear if you ask me one more question, I'm going to scream. I know nothing! I am nothing! Go to sleep." Closing her eyes, she laces her fingers together on her chest. "If you aren't here when I awake, I won't miss you. So you know."

I'm not sure if that's a hint for me to leave. Obviously, I'm not going to ask.

I may owe her an apology.

My excuse: I have twenty-three years of unasked questions built up. I'm not used to having someone who can hear me. I've spent plenty of time criticizing Leah, Dad, the neighbors, and everyone else in my little corner of the world with zero ramifications, but I never had to worry about someone else's reactions before. I wonder if Sylvie has. She never really said how long she's been here, living like this, alone in false, glittering houses with pristine couches, swimming pools, gourmet appetizers, and the constant risk of violent death.

I always wanted to see the world, but I never wanted to run through it, terrified for my life. If the wolves descend on every party . . . the simple solution is to not set foot in one.

I don't understand why Sylvie hasn't reached that very obvious conclusion.

Not going to ask her.

Instead, I choose, "I'm sorry."

"For what?"

Many things, but primarily squandering my first experience with someone who can see and hear me on worry, on frustration that she's not seeing me clearly enough or hearing me loudly enough, that she's not giving me the answers that I want and crave fast enough—as if she exists in reaction to me. She doesn't. She's her own person, or whatever she is, someone's dream girl or not.

"Wait—I'll answer for you," Sylvie says. "You're sorry for badgering me with questions I can't answer. You're sorry for being high strung. You're sorry for not saying thank you when I showed you the best night of your life. You're sorry for not saying thank you when I saved your life by getting us away from the shadow wolves. You're sorry for not appreciating that I don't have to spend time with you—my precious time that could end, *poof*, at any moment. I don't know how many minutes I have to waste, and I've wasted too many on you."

"All of that." I want to explain that I have zero experience with other people. This is new, and I'm terrible at it. But she knows that, so I simply say again, "I'm sorry."

She's silent for a moment.

Her breathing is even. I wonder if she's fallen asleep.

But then she says, "Okay."

"Okay?" I repeat.

"Okay, I don't hate you." She adds, "I don't *like* you either. But I don't hate you."

That's a start.

I try to make myself comfortable on the white couch. Outside, the waves and the wind merge into an undercurrent of constant noise. I listen for aberrations: any hint that the wolves are coming.

Sylvie's voice rises out of the darkness. "What was it like being a kid?"

I startle. I didn't expect her to speak again, much less to ask *me* a question. It's such a broad question too. "It's . . . not so different from being an adult? Except when you're a kid, you flip-flop between feeling as if everything is out of your control and having no power to feeling like everything will work out fine."

Sylvie lets out a laugh. "And that's different, how?"

"Now I feel like everything is out of my control and it's *not* going to work out fine."

She quiets. It's not as if I have a lot to compare my childhood to. It was what it was. A lot of it was wonderful. A lot was lonely. I never considered that it was unusual that I had a childhood, that I grew and changed—but I suppose that was exactly the point of me. I am the Hannah who is able to grow and change, who wasn't forever frozen in time, relegated to memories. Sylvie interrupts my thoughts. "Did you play with Barbies and all that shit?"

154

I grin. "Yes."

There was never a shortage of toys or books. "I had a dollhouse," I say, "that would rival one of these mansions. It had a tiny breakfast nook, with tiny food on the table. Little bowls with grapefruit molded out of clay, and tiny spoons. Lemonade glasses with plastic lemon wedges. Each room had a chandelier, and the foyer had a grandfather clock that chimed every hour."

No one could play with it but me, of course, but it was okay. I remember I spent hours crafting stories around the dolls that lived in each room. I'd come up with different voices for each of them. Make believe they were talking to each other. And to me. I remember they'd argue a lot, but they never left. None of them ever walked out the door. I don't even know if the front door opened. I suspect it did. Everything else in the dollhouse functioned perfectly, right down to the tiny light switches, the water in the faucets, and the blender in the kitchen. It wasn't real, but it was accurate. I played with that dollhouse nearly every day until it disappeared—*Like I almost did.*

It was replaced by a vanity with a mirror decorated with red roses. A jewelry box sat on the table, the kind with a ballerina inside that spins when you open it. It overflowed with necklaces, bracelets, and rings. Sometimes, I'd put them all on at once and pretend to be a princess.

Mother liked to give me the things she couldn't give Leah, as well as the things she thought that Leah should want. Briefly, we had a dog, as ephemeral as the one at the party. And once, there was even a pony in the backyard, but it didn't stay long. Those weren't lies that Mother was interested in maintaining. She didn't want to be tied down with a pet. Can't travel with a pet, she'd say, even though she didn't travel anywhere.

"I was happy, mostly," I say.

Sylvie snorts. "You just didn't know any better."

"Maybe. But I knew I was loved."

Did Leah know that she was? Or did she only see the love Mother spent on me?

The couch creaks as she sits up. I can feel her staring at me in the darkness. "The dead toddler with your name was loved. *You* didn't fucking exist. How could you have been loved?"

"Mother loved imagining me." I wonder what would have happened if she'd stopped, if she'd moved on like so many told her to do. I shy away from that thought.

"And now she's dead."

"Thanks for the reminder." As if I could forget. I suspect I'll be aware of it every second of every day until I fade—or get torn to pieces by the shadow wolves.

"Sorry," Sylvie says. I can't tell if she means it.

I try to see her face across the room. Moonlight falls on the carpet but doesn't touch her. She's a silhouette on the couch. She might as well be a shadow herself. "Did you ever have anyone like that?"

"I've had at least a dozen adore me."

"Anyone you loved back?"

"Obviously not. Do you know how horrific that feels, to be the image of so many people's adoration? Like being pulled apart in a dozen directions. Guess you wouldn't know." Then she sighs. "There was one. He's the one who made me who I am now, so to speak. I could have cared about him. His name's Jason, and he's sweet—the kind of person who notices when someone is sad. He invented me so that he'd avoid breaking his best friend's heart. She was desperately in love with him, and he wasn't ready to tell her he's gay, so he told her stories about a girlfriend who lives out on Shelter Island. I love riding bicycles, and I can skip rocks. My record is thirty-five skips. I don't even know if that's possible, but that's what he said . . ."

"He's your liar?" I ask.

"One of them. The only one left actually. He was the only one who invented me for the sake of someone else."

"Is he still lying about you?"

She may have shrugged—the shadow on the other couch shifted—but I couldn't see her well enough to tell. "Haven't checked, but I'd say yes."

"You cared about him, though, so how could you leave?"

"Easily. I stole a car that his neighbor never owned and drove east as far as I could. Been out on the South Fork ever since. Years now. He's probably graduated college by now. Gotten a job somewhere that's working him too hard and underpaying him while claiming to give him 'valuable experience,' and he's telling himself it's what he always wanted while living in a shitty apartment that's always too hot or cold, and his parents nag him to come and visit, but he's too embarrassed to tell them that he's alone and lonely and nearly broke."

"You've got his whole life figured out."

"Seen it before."

"You could visit him and find out if it's true."

"And then what? It's not like I could talk to him, and even if I could, what would I say? Everything's going to be fine? I don't want to be the kind of person who lies to anyone."

The words linger in the air. It's a beautiful thing to say. Made easier by the fact that no one can hear us.

Far easier to tell the truth when there are no ramifications or consequences.

At dawn, I wake, which is miraculous in and of itself. Sunlight streams through the skylights in the vaulted roof, and I hear people puttering in the kitchen—the telltale rattle of dishes and the vacuum-sucking sound of a refrigerator door being opened. A slosh of liquid. Milk? Orange juice? Or maybe this is the kind of family that jumps straight to a mimosa or Bloody Mary. All I know about them so far is that they have a Michelangelo sketch in their living room, and they lie about keeping their white sofas pristine.

Sitting up, I pat at my hair, trying to flatten a clump of frizz that's plastered into an angle. There's a cat on the hearth, and I freeze as I realize it's staring straight at me. "Can you see me?"

It flicks its tail and stalks off.

"Never can tell with cats," Sylvie says.

I feel a rush of relief. I purposely didn't look over at her sofa before. I didn't want to see it empty because she'd faded or because she'd left. Either was possible.

"Want to see if they have anything for breakfast?" Sylvie asks. "Occasionally you can score homemade pancakes in a place like this." She levers herself off the sofa. Her hair looks perfect, and her eyes are bright and alert. I'm fairly certain I have crusted drool on my cheek.

I'm also fairly certain of something else:

"Sylvie, I can't live like you do."

Bouncing into the kitchen, she doesn't look back at me. "You've barely given it a try. It's not always as exciting as last night. Sometimes it's downright boring—you'd love that."

The family is in the kitchen. A teenage girl with ripped jeans and a crop top is perched on a stool. She's typing on her phone as she shovels cereal into her mouth. The father is scowling at the dishwasher as if it's offended him, and the mother sits in the bay window with her laptop. Outside, the beach and ocean sparkle in the sunlight. A few beachgoers stroll along the shore. Gulls circle, and a tern plummets from above. It splashes into the waves and then emerges, empty beaked.

Sylvie sticks her hand into the fridge and flails around. She ignores the father who paces back and forth in front of the dishwasher. "I think it's the latch," the man says, gesturing at the dishwasher. "I'll order a replacement part—"

"You'll call a repairman," the woman says without looking up.

"Nah, I know what I'm doing," the man lies. "I can fix it myself." For a brief instant, I see the shadow of tools in his hands and a toolbox beside him, but then they vanish in smoke.

Sylvie scowls at the fridge, hands on her hips. "Seriously? Not even a yogurt?" The father walks through her, and she doesn't flinch. *She's done this a thousand times.*

"My kitchen counter used to be filled with pastries," I offer. Croissants. Muffins. Cupcakes. So many cupcakes. I don't think I'll ever be able to eat a cupcake without thinking of Mother. "Do you need to eat?" Just because I don't doesn't mean she's the same.

"Need. Want." She waves her hand in the air. "Does it matter which?" She runs her hands through the cabinets.

"Do you *like* that this is your life?" I ask. "Always on the run?"

"Sure. It's great." She seizes a jar and pulls it through the cabinet door, then wrinkles her nose. "Either homemade peanut butter or vomit, unclear which." She tosses it onto the floor, and it crashes. The family doesn't react. They're immersed in an argument about who can repair their dishwasher. "So many mundane lies. Couldn't they have lied about caviar? Let's try the next house."

"This is what you do? Go from home to home, scavenging? Stealing?"

"Hey, it's not stealing if they don't know it's here. Bonus: there's some messed up, hilarious shit you can find when you're scavenging. Once, I found an entire barrel of eels. Why? Who knows? Why do people lie about anything?"

Leaving through the sliding glass door, Sylvie trots down the beach toward the next summer home. I catch up to her. "Don't you ever want a different life?"

She halts. Sunlight glints in her hair, and I have to squint to see her. Hands on her hips, she demands, "You think there's a choice?"

Yes.

I think this is not the only way to live.

And I tell her about the man in the bar who wore all white. He's like us, I tell her, and he may have found a different way to live. If I can find him, I'm going to ask.

CHAPTER EIGHTEEN

"So he's your White Rabbit," Sylvie says, "and you chased him into my fucked-up Wonderland. And now, you want to leave me to find him."

"Or you could come with me."

Without thinking about it, I take her hands in mine. Her hands feel warm and soft, and my fingers instinctively close around them. It feels like I'm holding a bird, fragile and soft and about to take flight. My breath hitches in my throat, and the waves sound extra loud on the shore. I am overly aware of the rough sand, the salty wind, and the cry of the gulls.

"Or *you* could stay," she counters. She doesn't remove her hands from mine.

"He might know how to live without fear of the wolves or of fading away." I want her to understand. He could hold the answers we both need.

"You don't even know where he is," Sylvie says.

He boarded a train—or at least I think he did. He could be any-where by now. Or nowhere. *He could be gone.* Vanished. Rotted. But I don't believe that. He said the words "over the years." He must still exist if he's already lasted for years.

"I know where to start looking," I say. The key is the bar. He visited Sweet Venom frequently, he said, as well as other nearby bars, so it's likely he'll return again, especially if that woman is there, the one he was trying to save. It's possible he has some connection to her, similar to how I'm connected to Leah. *If I can't find him, then perhaps I can find her.* She was at Sweet Venom by herself; she could live in the area—and she could lead me to him, even if it's unintentional on her part. At least it's possible. "We can't just keep going to parties and pretending there isn't a problem."

"Come on. You have to admit that some of last night was fun. The elephant? You liked the elephant. You don't have to like *me* to like this life." She looks, for the first time, younger. Vulnerable. As if she's asking a larger question, beyond not wanting me to go search for my White Rabbit.

"I have to try," I say. "I'll come back."

She lets go of me. "Yeah, sure."

My hands feel suddenly cold, as if doused with water. "I will," I promise. I don't know why she doesn't believe me. I haven't lied to her. Not about anything, and I've answered every question she's asked me, though there haven't been many. It occurs to me that all the questions I've asked her relate to me; I don't know that much about her life. "Why do you think I won't?" But I have a guess. "Have you had someone not come back before?" It's a clumsy way to ask, I know. I am now sympathetic to every person I've ever heard stumble through a conversation. It's easy to be eloquent when no one can hear you. Less easy when you know your words matter.

She looks out at the ocean and doesn't answer.

I look too. The waves are higher today, crashing like punches onto the sand. The water then pulls back as if the shore had offended it. The sky is blotchy with clouds, and the seagulls call to one another incessantly, their calls raw.

"Everyone leaves," Sylvie says at last. "It's just how it works."

"You've lost someone too."

"No one I didn't expect to lose." She's still not looking at me. Her eyes are on the horizon. On the south shore, there's no land to break the line of ocean. It's simply layers of blue, smooth and unending, blending into the matte gray sky.

"Who?" Perhaps someone with more experience talking with people would have asked with more finesse. She might not want to talk about it. I don't know what she's feeling as she gazes at the horizon, and I wish I could inhale the question and swallow it.

"Others. Like us." She sits and pulls her knees up to her chest and hugs them. "You asked once if there were others like us, and there are. Or were. Probably are, but the ones I knew . . ."

"What happened?"

"Some faded. Some left."

I wonder why she outlasted them. I wonder what they were like. I wonder how they came to be, how they felt about their lives, if they ever tried to change what they were. "Is that why you—"

She interrupts. "Why I have trust issues? Why I don't open up to you? Why I live in the moment? Why I think your little quest is pointless and a waste of time?"

Yes, to all that.

"Look, you seem like a very nice person—slightly desperate, definitely needy, but nice. You don't know me, though, and I don't care. See, that's the piece you're missing: *I don't care.*" She stands up and walks straight toward the water, then spins to look at me, and her skirt flows around her. "People come, and people go. I don't get attached. So, go find your Rabbit or don't. But don't feel like you need to come back here. I'm *happy* alone. I don't need anyone."

I'm not needy.

Desperate, yes.

But not needy. How could I be when I spent my entire life invisible? I've learned to be alone too. I've simply not learned yet to be untethered, the way Sylvie is, and I don't *want* to learn that. I want to belong somewhere, with someone who wants to be with me. Is that so wrong? I want a life. Just because I'm not technically alive doesn't mean I don't deserve that just as much as anyone else. I think; I feel; I exist. I have every right to keep doing those things if I can. I don't want to worry about shadow wolves devouring me or about fading away or winking out of existence. If I have to fight to find out how to stay in the world, then I will. I'm not going to spend my life in constant fear, scavenging nonexistent treats from people who don't appreciate what they have.

"You don't have to *need me* to come with me," I say. "You could just come. For fun."

"And get stranded in Islip, or whatever, when you fade away? No, thanks. I'm good right where I am, doing what I'm doing." She strolls away and wades ankle deep into the water. The waves crash into her shins and then through them without breaking.

"We'd be a team." I've never been part of a team before. A family, yes, at least according to Mother, but never a chosen team. Leah never had that either, now that I think about it. She never played on a sports team or auditioned for a school play. She did her art mostly by herself. She took classes. Stayed after school sometimes for extra time in the studio, until Mother insisted that she get an after-school job. She scooped ice cream and hated every second of it, according to the many arguments that I tried to block out.

"Adorable, but no, thanks. I'm a lone wolf." Sylvie howls at the sky. A seagull veers away, and I can't tell if it's in reaction or a coincidence.

"Hey, I'd rather you didn't make that noise, especially after last night."

"Oh? This noise?" She howls again.

"Shush, you're going to attract them."

"Go then. Before they can come." She howls a third time, louder, lifting her head up. It sounds more like a scream this time. "Run away, Hannah. Go!"

She's pissed at me. It doesn't take a genius to figure that out, but it's beyond me to know how to fix it, except by agreeing to not go, which I'm not willing to do. Not after the wolves. Not after nearly fading away. Not after losing so much time. I feel the seconds ticking away as steadily as my heartbeat. "I'm sorry I've disappointed you."

"I'd have to care to be disappointed. Leave already."

She howls again.

This time, I leave.

◆ ◆ ◆

It isn't a long walk from the beach to the Amagansett train station. I have no idea what the schedule is, but there's an electronic sign near the tracks.

Luckily, there's a train scheduled in five minutes.

Unluckily, it's delayed by an hour.

Enough time for second thoughts, and third. Enough time to return to the beach and try again to convince Sylvie to come with me? *She doesn't want to see me.*

Sitting cross-legged on the ground, I wonder why I am leaving a woman who can see me and hear me to find someone who may not even exist anymore. I should be content with what I have. But I'm not, because it feels like all I have is smoke in my hands. If I don't *do* something, it will slip through my fingers. I spread my fingers out and study them. Do they look dimmer? Less distinct? Maybe.

A train whistle shrieks in the distance.

Startled, I glance at the clock. It's early. What kind of delayed train comes early? The silver box curves as it chugs toward me, wreathed in a haze so thick it blots out the view of all the nearby houses and trees.

I know what Sylvie would say if she were here: Someone lied about the train being on time. Perhaps multiple someones lied often enough that it made it true. The false train chuffs its way into the station, and with a metallic shriek, the doors slide open. Smoke pours onto the platform, but no one disembarks.

If I was afraid that driving a car would draw the wolves, then boarding a nonexistent train is equally stupid. On the other hand, it's here, and it could get me to Queens faster, if this train is, as I suspect, created to be perfectly on time.

It chimes two notes, the signal that the doors are going to shut soon. *Decision time.* I hold up my hand, and I can see the train *through* my palm.

I don't have time to deliberate.

I dart through the doors just before they close. They shut with a sucking noise, and I'm standing hip deep in haze. The train jerks forward, and I catch myself on a pole before I have the chance to wonder if it's solid. It is. The fact shouldn't surprise me—the whole train is like me. I shiver, not sure if that's reassuring or terrifying.

A lot of people believe the train will be on time. Or they wished it were?

Dreams or lies?

Does it matter? *How can it not matter?*

I notice that I'm not the only passenger. A man in a suit reads a newspaper. The images on the page blur as I look at them, and the words squirm, unreadable. Shifting, I peek around the paper. He's faceless, a blank swirling void where his features should be.

Click, click, click.

A few seats away, two hands are visible, twisting a pair of knitting needles back and forth. The knitter has no real body. Just a woman's silhouette, hunched over her work. No features. No discernible clothes. She's a nondescript gray from head to toe, but she's knitting a scarf with every color of the sky from sunrise to sunset. It unfurls from the needles and pools on the floor and then snakes throughout the train car, weaving between all the seat legs. My eyes trace it through the train. On one seat, the scarf shifts to blue then black, like a storm overtaking the sky. It lightens. Gray clouds give way to yellow, and I wonder how many days or years are knit into this scarf. I'm careful not to touch it as I make my way down the train car. I wonder if I can find answers here. Perhaps I don't need the man in white.

"Can any of you hear me?" I ask.

No one answers me.

I don't know if they can't or they choose not to. In my experience, most shadow people aren't aware of their surroundings; they're caught up in their unique prisons. But if Sylvie and I can exist, there could be others that I've overlooked. It's a nice thought, but as I walk through the train car, I see no one who looks, for lack of a better term, fully formed. They're all fragments. Bits of memories, wishes, dreams. *Lies.*

As I reach the end of the train car, it occurs to me that we haven't stopped in a while. I try to look out a window, but the glass is fogged. I rub my sleeve on it and peer outside.

I expect to see ordinary Long Island: houses, roads, towns, maybe a stretch of trees, but I see none of that. Only open plains with vast stretches of what looks like wheat.

My heart thumps faster. I don't know what this means, except that I never should have boarded this train. Hurrying to the opposite side, I climb onto one of the seats and peer out. Only ocean outside. There shouldn't be. The Long Island Rail Road should be inland by now.

Heart thumping harder, I look around, trying not to panic. There has to be a way off. An emergency button? A cord to pull? I remember being on a bus with Mother once, and there was a blue cord you could pull when you wanted the driver to stop. A little girl yanked on it continuously until the bus driver implored her to please stop.

Drawing a deep breath, I try to regain composure. Maybe there's a way to signal whatever phantom conductor is driving this monstrosity.

Methodically, I search the train. Shouldn't there be some kind of emergency intercom? What if there's a fire? Or a medical emergency? A speaker from which the next station stop can be announced? The train has none of that.

All it has is a scarf.

I finger the yarn. It's soft, solid. Feels like a sweater should. Real, with a hint of the greasiness of lanolin. It's also the closest thing to a cord that I've seen on the train.

It isn't logical, I know, but neither is this train's existence. I begin to coil up the scarf. I chase it around seat legs, winding it as I go. It fills my arms. The scent is both sweet and mildewed, like a heavily perfumed towel left balled up and sopping wet. Collecting the scarf, I travel up and down the train car. At last, I stand in front of the knitting hands. They haven't slowed.

"I'd like to get off this train," I say.

No response.

"Sorry if this is a terrible idea," I say, and then I yank hard on the scarf. The loops jerk from the needles, and the hands freeze. A keening noise emanates from where a body should be, and the train squeals in response.

Dropping my armful of yarn, I rush to the door. The window is coated with grime, but I think I catch a glimpse of trees and brick. Are those buildings? Is it slowing?

Yes, it's slowing!

It squeals as it lurches to a stop, and the train exhales as if it's alive. I wait for the doors to open, but they don't. I tug on them, trying to worm my fingers between the rubber to pry them open. They resist.

Glancing up, I see there's an emergency pull that I swear wasn't there before. Jumping, I reach for it. My fingers graze it—I miss.

The train chimes two notes, the "all aboard" signal.

I leap again, and this time, my fingers connect. I yank as hard as I can, and the doors lurch open with a squeal. I throw myself outside and stumble onto a street. A car drives straight through me. I scream, but I slide through it untouched. It continues on through the train.

The nonexistent train pulls away with haze billowing around it. Only when it clears do I see where I am.

No place I recognize.

◆ ◆ ◆

Starbucks on one corner.

Cloud 9 Hair Salon on another.

Across the tracks, Garden City Automotive.

Garden City! Home. I don't recognize this street or the stores, but Mother's house must be within a few miles. I'm not sure which direction to walk, but if I follow the train tracks, they'll lead to a station. From there, I can catch an ordinary, non-horror-show train to Queens.

Stick to the plan, or run home?

It's not home. It's the shell of home. Leah has almost certainly continued to gut it in the two days I've been away—or has it been longer? How much time have I lost? Regardless, I don't know that I'm ready to see the house, or her. Especially, if Sylvie's right about who we are, then that means that Leah was right about Mother: she was a liar.

I'm not ready to unpack that. "It's complicated" doesn't begin to cover it.

Train tracks it is.

Skirting the edge of them—I'm not stupid enough to walk on them, especially not after just having been on a train that could touch, trap, and potentially kill me—I stick close by them. It's inching toward dusk, which means I lost more hours than I thought on the ghost train.

I check my hand again. Still solid. For now.

Guess I got scared back into existence, if that's a thing that can happen. Or perhaps it's merely luck that I continue to be here. I wish, for the billionth time, that my existence came with a rule book. Regular people complain that their lives don't come with a manual, but that's not true. They have other people to teach them the rules. Books, hundreds of thousands of books, devoted to exploring every facet of their lives and deaths. Physics textbooks. YouTube videos. A million explanations at their fingertips. Some of them contradictory, yes. Some, flat-out wrong.

Some, lies.

But so many answers around them for the plucking!

Sylvie might be right about what we are, but she can't be right about what we become. I won't let myself believe that I'm destined to dissolve into nothingness. Mother didn't give me this life for me to just fade away. If she did, then why do I continue to exist after her last breath? There must be more for me, a reason why I persist.

There must be more.

My White Rabbit may know.

If I can find him.

I have lost all sense of time. It was morning when I left Sylvie; then I was trapped on the ghost train for the bulk of the day. By the time I catch the real train, I should, I hope, reach Sweet Venom by nightfall and still have several hours before the bars close to track down Rabbit or the woman he seemed to know.

I keep an eye on the nearby houses and apartments. Shadows are growing between them—a change in the light, or is it wolves? I walk faster. *This was a mistake.* If the wolves come for me, what do I do? Sylvie isn't here to pull off some miraculous trick with a nonexistent car. Can't run home either. It's not the sanctuary it was. That's been stripped away, memory by memory.

Out of the corner of my eye, I see the silhouette of a wolf. It materializes, then dissipates.

It could be my imagination. Or my fear. My heart beats so hard that I feel it down to my fingertips.

Don't panic. If you run, they'll chase.

It occurs to me that I'm doing exactly what I wanted to avoid: running from wolves. Maybe Sylvie's right, and it's inescapable. Maybe this was what I was always destined to be. Prey. Because I'm not supposed to exist.

Who says, though? I think! I feel! So why do I have any less right to live than the people who tell the lies that make us? I've persisted beyond my mother's death. Doesn't that mean that I'm meant for more?

Find the White Rabbit; find answers.

I repeat it like a mantra and walk on. The wolves watch from the shadows.

CHAPTER NINETEEN

Leah chose Whisper White as the new paint color for the living room walls. She thought Margaret Addleman of Premiere Homes would approve, if that woman ever approved of anything. Her other choices were Swiss Coffee, which had light-brown undertones, or Cameo White, which was . . . well, frankly, also white. All the ultrabland options were a variation of white, off-white, beige, or gray.

"Huh, white," Jamie said as he pried the lid off the first can.

I cheated on you. "Whisper White."

"Oh, of course, obviously. You can tell because of the . . ."

"Blue undertones?"

He had blue eyes, his name was Sam, and he tasted like whiskey and sweat. I washed the sheets twice afterward.

Jamie smiled at her. "Exactly what I was going to say. Blue undertones and a fruity aroma, with a hint of oak."

She knew he wanted her to laugh, so she did, then offered to stir. Mixing the paint, she wished she could have bought any other color. Magenta. Aqua. Beach Foam. Jamie spread drop cloths over the carpet. They'd already moved the bulk of the furniture into the bedroom and draped the piano in a sheet.

He'd volunteered to help her paint in preparation for the open house. The real estate agent had scheduled it for two weeks from today, pending the finalization of all the paperwork with the lawyer. Leah had wanted to say no. She didn't want to see him, to look him in the eyes. He would be able to read her guilt—it permeated her the way the scent of cigarettes clung to a smoker for days.

But so far, nothing.

As the minutes ticked by, it became easier to keep her tone light, to act normal. "Second choice was Swiss Coffee, which had a touch of brown, but I worried it would look too—"

"Brown?"

"Exactly."

"And you wanted white."

"She said to make it as boring as possible," Leah said. "Apparently buyers want a blank slate so they can imagine themselves in a home, but not so blank that it doesn't look like a house." Leah had avoided him for as long as she could after her . . . mistake. Any longer, and he would've shown up at her door and worried until she broke down and told him the truth.

She was determined not to do that. He didn't deserve to be hurt. So she said yes to his help with the house and told herself that she would forget that night ever happened, as if she could erase it from existence by sheer force of will.

I slept with a stranger, and I'm so, so sorry.

Leah poured paint into a tray and dipped a roller.

"Guess this is different from your normal painting?" Jamie asked.

That wasn't a topic she wanted to discuss either. "Yep. You know, I found a painting I did in high school hanging in her bedroom. I didn't think she kept any of my art." What did it mean that Mom had kept it? She couldn't have been proud of her art, could she? Wait, she didn't want to talk about her mom either. What the hell was a safe topic? "My dad never did."

"You've never talked much about your dad."

Usually, she steered clear of that topic, too, but today it felt like everything was quicksand. *I walked away after you called, but then I went back. My fault. My choice. If you knew, you wouldn't look at me the same. You wouldn't forgive me.* Her father hadn't been able to forgive her mother for her breaking her promises. Oh, she never cheated—*That low is reserved for me*—but Mom betrayed him in plenty of other ways, and he hadn't been able to forgive a single one of them. He hadn't understood her. Had he even tried? She remembered the ultimatums: *Get help, or I leave. Change, or I leave. Heal, or I leave.* If he had tried harder, if she had wanted help, if she'd been able to admit she was broken, would things have been different? *Would it have been different if I had tried harder to understand her?* "He left when I was twelve. Died when I was twenty-three. Last saw him right before he died, when he was in the hospital. His second ex-wife called to tell me he was dying."

She remembered that phone call. She was working at a coffee shop that thought it was trendier than it was, and she'd let the call go to voice mail because she didn't recognize the number. She'd listened to it on her break, after confusing an order for a mocha latte with extra milk with one for a mocha espresso with extra who gives a shit.

"What did he die of?" Jamie asked.

Leah let out a bark of a laugh, even though there was nothing funny about the question. "I don't know. Cancer? He did the whole I-didn't-want-you-to-see-me-like-this speech, and he didn't want to talk about medical stuff." Those weren't the details Dad had wanted to discuss. He'd wanted to talk about how he hadn't been as shitty a dad as she'd thought. He'd wanted to tell her that he'd tried to be there for the big moments of her life. He'd sneaked into the neighbor's backyard to see her posing for prom pictures—her mom had told him that Leah hadn't wanted him to see her. Leah hadn't even known he'd wanted to come. She hadn't known that he'd watched her college graduation either. All those moments, lost . . . She hadn't known.

Jamie spread more paint on the wall as she talked. She was aware he was listening and grateful that he was looking at the wall, not at her.

"I didn't find out until my dad was dying in the hospital, a decade later, that his wife had never even been pregnant." She remembered the hospital had smelled like overripe lemons, and he'd smelled of soap and plastic. She'd wanted to throw up when he told her the truth. Katelyn hadn't been able to conceive. There was no baby and was never going to be.

"Your mom told you she was?" he guessed.

"Bingo."

But she didn't want to talk about her mom. How had they gotten back to that? Everything circled back to Mom. "Fact was he was a crap father, and I was a crap daughter." *And now I'm a crap person. And you deserve better. Can't you see that?*

"You got dealt a crappy hand," Jamie said.

"You did too," Leah said. *You met me.* "Your father isn't peaches and sunshine."

He dipped the roller and attacked another section of the wall, covering up the dingy, stained whatever the prior color had been. "Yeah," he agreed. "Toxic masculinity ruined him. Or his parents did. He thinks the world is out to get him. Listens to way too much talk radio. You don't ever want to talk politics with him. You'll come out of it feeling like you need to shower in scalding water. He believes every conspiracy theory . . . Hey, what are we supposed to do about electrical outlets?"

"Eek." She'd forgotten about those. "I'll get a screwdriver. Hold on." She retrieved a screwdriver from her box of supplies and removed the cover from the electrical outlet.

"The worst part about my dad, though, is how he treats my mom," Jamie said. "He gaslights her constantly. Convinces her that everything wrong in their relationship is her fault. He's never to blame. She apologizes about a dozen times an hour for things that aren't her fault."

Leah had met both his parents and hadn't seen any of that. They must have a lot of practice hiding that side of their relationship. "I just thought she must be Canadian."

He laughed.

I can do this—be normal with Jamie. So long as she kept her secret buried, it didn't need to destroy them. It could be a blip that was never repeated. A tree that fell in the forest and wasn't heard.

"Told my dad once that the absolute worst insult was to tell me I'm like him," Jamie said. He paused and examined the wall. "That didn't go over well."

"Yeah, I imagine not."

"Felt damn good to say, though. The truth shall set you free and all."

Fuck.

I can't do this.

Leah put down her roller. "Need to go to the bathroom." Scooting across the living room, she shut the door and took deep breaths. It still smelled of cleaner. She'd scrubbed at the tiles, but it hadn't made much difference with the grout. It remained stubbornly stained gray and black.

She splashed water on her face. All she had to do was keep her mouth shut about the other night, and everything would be fine. She could do this. *It doesn't make me a terrible person. It only makes me a person who made a terrible mistake. And then decided to be an utter coward about it.*

She thought of Jamie telling his father exactly how he felt and didn't know how anyone could be that brave. She knew she wasn't.

For the first time in her entire life, Leah wished she were more like her mother. Mom wouldn't have had any problem lying her face off to Jamie for decades if it made life easier. Leah looked in the mirror and saw her mother's eyes, her father's nose, her lips, and she hated all of it.

CHAPTER TWENTY

By the time I make it to the Garden City LIRR station, I am drenched in sweat and my heart feels as though it's ricocheting inside my throat. Is this how it's going to be from now on? Forever in fear, until I fade or am destroyed?

I don't want this.

Any of it.

I want Mother back. I want my safe cocoon. Even if it was a lie, it was mine. Standing on the train platform, I close my eyes and picture my bedroom—the bed swathed in petal-pink sheets, the vanity with the *Snow White* queen's mirror, the closet full of clothes just for me, the stacks of books, the teddy bear large enough to serve as an armchair. I felt so safe there. I wonder if I would have felt content forever if Mother had lived, or would I have someday ventured out into the world, longed for the unknown? Would I have minded that I never saw the ocean, despite its closeness?

Swaddled within the press of real passengers, I board the train. Spreading my feet for balance as the train lurches through thickening neighborhoods, I'm careful to touch no one, especially if they're coated in the toxic sludge. Unlike when I rode the ghost train, I can see out the windows into the backyards—some tiny but with aboveground pools or a square of vegetable garden; some piled high with rusted bikes, empty cans, concrete blocks. We pass by a lot filled with school buses, then a warehouse with broken windows wreathed in translucent vines. One street is jagged with shards of glass that have burst through the asphalt, but the cars drive through them unimpeded. A woman pushes a stroller through a cloud of smoke and bees. The swarm follows her down the street. She is either unconcerned or unaware.

The train squeals at my stop in Queens, and I'm grateful there's no knitter in control this time. Making my way off the train, I insert myself between commuters as we tromp down the platform and spill onto the street.

The walk back to Sweet Venom is punctuated by landmarks only I know: the street that was filled with umbrellas and the one half-swallowed by muck, then the gyro cart that served a beating heart. It doesn't take long to find the bar again, which feels like the first thing to go right in a while.

Maybe this will work. Maybe I'll find him.

Sweet Venom looks as I remember it with its faux-blood sign, grimy window blurred with neon, and bored bouncer at the door. I slide past him and wait for my eyes to adjust to the dim light. It's a different crowd than when I was here with Leah and Jersey, and it feels slathered in shadows. The ocean in the corner of the bar has thickened. It's not water anymore; it's black and viscous, like tar—the muck has invaded the water. When it laps the wood, it leaves a greasy film behind. Several of the patrons are wrapped in so much dense smoke that I don't know how they can see their way across the bar.

It's more crowded. More people, more lies. More lies, more smoke and more muck. A busy night, after hours.

I scoot closer to the bar. The bartender is swathed in a haze, nearly invisible. Only the bottles and glasses are crisp, as is her reflection in the mirror. She doesn't speak as she mixes drinks and runs credit cards.

A TV hangs over one corner of the bar, muted, but tuned to the news, a close-up of a red-faced man yelling soundlessly. Black gunk drips from the screen and bleeds onto the floor, seeping toward the tar-like ocean. I skirt the filth and slide onto a stool.

Beside me, a man is hunched over a half-finished beer. The level of liquid in his glass rises and falls without him bringing it to his lips. I can't tell what the actual level of beer is or how many he's had. When he turns his head to signal the bartender, I see that his eyes are swollen shut with cobwebs. Shuddering, I look away.

On my opposite side, a woman is being chatted up by a man in khakis, and she looks as if she'd rather be miles away. I slide closer. The man is chattering about politics, and the black ooze that drips from the TV also leaks from the corner of his lips. It has seeped into his eyes as well, clouding them with a gray film. "You'd have to be a naive idiot to think there won't be election fraud next time too. It's rotten to the core, the whole system, from school board to presidential."

The woman is looking right and left, desperate to escape the conversation, but he has her pinned against the bar, blocked by a press of people trying to get the bartender's attention. There's no way for her to slip away.

He's spraying droplets of the black gunk onto her shirt as he talks more and more animatedly about a lost election as proof of the corruption that has to be stopped, even if it disenfranchises a few people—it's because of the deep state, he says before launching into a tirade about how the moon landing was a hoax. The tar-like ooze is pooling beneath the man's feet, but he doesn't notice.

Scanning the bar and the benches beyond him, I look for my White Rabbit. He should be easy to spot if he's wearing the same white-knight outfit. Even if he isn't, I remember his face. Anyone that handsome can't be forgotten. But I don't see him, or the woman he tried to help.

I shouldn't be disappointed—the odds were low that he'd be in the same bar at the exact moment on the exact night that I decide to look for him. I can't give up too quickly.

I venture outside again and take a deep breath. *I can do this.*

The next bar is across the street.

◆ ◆ ◆

Six bars.

Six failed attempts to find the White Rabbit.

I do find a man with skin consumed by mold, a woman with knives for fingers, and a shadow that shatters into a hundred butterflies. Also, dozens of tipsy ordinary people whose lies form just a tissue of haze around them. And more who seem swaddled in the same oozing tar—it makes my skin crawl to look at them.

I hate bars, every last one of them. The reasons: the buzz of voices making me feel as if hornets had taken up residence in my skull, the dim lights causing faces to blur when I try to see through the crowd, the way everyone wants to be seen and not be seen at exactly the same time. Makes my head ache. And then there's that toxic crap everywhere. Every time I look at it, it seems hungry. It doesn't flow naturally; it oozes, amoeba-like, as if it's hunting for prey.

I wonder how Leah feels when she goes to a bar. Does she feel anonymous and invisible or anonymous and free? I wonder how she is, whether she's reconciled with Jamie or mourned our mother yet.

Outside, I breathe in the night air. I could keep searching. There are many more bars in Queens. I could look farther afield, or I could revisit these same bars, see if he's arrived at one of them while I was elsewhere.

Or I could give up this foolish search.

"Come on, Hannah," I say out loud. "Keep it together." All I need is patience. And time. Checking my hand against the streetlight, I wonder how much of that I have. A few more nights, or only a few more hours? I'm partially translucent again.

Returning to Sweet Venom, I tuck myself into a corner, well away from the boiling muck. It's after midnight, and the after-work crowd has cleared out. A handful of college students and a few careworn regulars remain. The bartender still appears predominantly invisible. I wonder if that's how she sees herself or how others see her.

The tar-like ooze is nearly everywhere now, and a knot of six early-twenties men in too-tight T-shirts are coated in a thick smoke with the same greasy quality as the boiling ocean. Where should I spend the night? Before now, I assumed I'd curl up on a bench here and just wait, but I'm not wild about spending the night with the muck. It could consume me while I sleep.

I don't pay much attention to the knot of belligerent guys until I hear a female voice from within. "Sorry. Can't. I've got a very large and very jealous boyfriend."

"Yeah, baby? I don't see him here."

"He's—"

A familiar voice says, "He's right here."

I leap off the stool.

My shoes dip into the ooze and sizzle. Swearing, I jump back.

I skirt the edge of the muck, careful to step on tiles that are free of it. It reminds me of the game Leah used to play when she'd pretend the floor was made of lava. Sometimes if she played it for long enough, I could play, too—the carpet would bubble and turn bright red, reeking of sulfur and bubble gum. It was the closest we ever got to playing together.

This is not nearly as much fun.

Where is he? I know I heard him.

The men are talking over one another. Laughing too loudly. They're pressed too tightly for me to see anyone, and the black smoke swirls thick around them. "Bet you just haven't had a real man. What's your boyfriend like? One of those snowflakes?"

I don't hear the woman's answer. Nor do I hear Rabbit's. I wonder if he walked through the door or if he just appeared like some kind of fairy godmother. No idea if that's possible, but then it would explain why I wasn't able to find him on the train before.

With an awkward lunge, I leap onto a table, then perch like a crow before jumping onto a bench. I feel ridiculous, but I don't want any more contact with the toxic muck than absolutely necessary. I also don't want Rabbit to leave. Gritting my teeth, I crawl along the bench while the ooze licks the floor beneath me. A surge threatens to flow over the top, and I slide along the wall.

At last, I reach the knot of men. The woman has squirmed her way out of the center. She's smiling as if her life depends on it and laughing lightly as if they've said something extremely amusing. There's nothing I can do to help her; I know that. But where's—

A man in white jeans and a white T-shirt stands behind her.

But he's not my White Rabbit.

He's not the same man at all.

CHAPTER TWENTY-ONE

He's at least six inches taller than my Rabbit, and he's Black, not Asian. Just as heart-stoppingly handsome but definitely a different man, even though he's wearing similar clothes. In fact, the exact same clothes.

Odd.

Now that the woman is clear of the knot of men, he begins to stride away, and I know in an instant that he is not like me. He doesn't flinch as he walks through the thick layer of muck on the floor.

I look down at his shoes. *Holy shit.* Bubbling around his soles, the muck eats at them like acid. Holes are spreading, but he doesn't appear to notice. I planned to approach my White Rabbit casually, so as not to scare him away. Offer him a drink, the way he did to me. Start a conversation like a normal person. But instead, I scream, "The floor is eating you!"

Sometimes I think it's a good thing that I haven't been able to communicate with people before now. I'm obviously not good at it.

Everyone ignores me except the man in white. He looks down and swears. He lifts one boot out and then hops to the other, which only splashes the muck onto his laces.

"Get on a bench!" I call.

He strides to the nearest bench and jumps on. Deprived of its prey, the ooze belches as it sloshes against the legs of the bench. The man in white flattens against the wall, staring at the bubbling gunk, as I make my way over. It requires stepping directly through a couple making out sloppily on the bench.

"Hi," I say.

"Hi. Thanks for the warning. I like these shoes."

For an instant, all I can think is, *I'm talking to another person.* So what if he's not the same White Rabbit from my first time at Sweet Venom? He's like me and like Sylvie. I feel giddy. I wish Sylvie were here so I could say, *I found him!* Or someone like him. It wasn't as if I knew the other man anyway. "They're nice shoes," I say.

I really am terrible at talking to people. Is it possible to get better at this? I resolve not to bombard him with questions as I did with Sylvie, but of course, the first thing out of my mouth is "Who are you?"

"Jared. You?"

"Hannah Allen." My name tastes delicious as I roll it across my mouth. I love saying it out loud to someone who can hear me. I will never tire of the sensation. "Nice to meet you."

"I'm Jared . . ." He stops. "Jared . . ." Again, he stops, and his face twists into a frown.

Sylvie was surprised I had a last name. Maybe many of us don't? "It's okay, Jared," I say quickly. "Nice to meet you." I don't ask: *Can you tell me how to stay alive?*

He still seems unsettled, but only for a moment. Soon his eyes widen, and he grips my hands, engulfing mine. My breath stops in my throat. The music, the laughter, the shouts—all of it fades, and it feels like the world only consists of this man and me. "I know you," he says, his voice low and intense. "I remember you."

Wait—he does? But how . . .

"You were here. In this bar. Sweet Venom. I *remember.*"

"I . . ." I shake my head. Yes, I was here, but he wasn't. I know what the man I chased looked like. I can conjure his exact features. You don't forget the face of the first person who ever saw you.

"I handed you my drink." He stares down at our clasped hands and then opens his. My hands rest in his palms, and he looks at them as if they're a revelation.

"You, uh, look different." I cringe. There had to be a less awkward way to phrase that. He has to know it was an entirely different person who—

He frowns. "I wore white. I always do."

"You must have changed your hair." And eyes, nose, lips, chin, skin, body. I have no explanation for how this other man remembers me.

He drops my hands. Beside him, the woman he wanted to rescue has curled herself onto a stool and is signaling the bartender. "I was at the bar, and I handed you my drink, and then . . . What did I do next? Why did I leave you?" He turned to face the door, as if it had the answers.

"You tried to help a woman who was being harassed by an asshole." Like he tried to do just now.

But he dismisses my words. "Jessica wasn't here that night." He gestures at the woman—she must be Jessica—as she pays for her drink and then gulps it down. "I handed you the drink . . . and then I left? Because Jessica wasn't here and didn't need me." He sounds more certain, as if telling his story makes it the truth.

"You did help a woman. Not her, Jessica. It was a different woman. Really pretty. Korean American, I think? I never caught her name." If it was him. "You said you do this all the time, help women who need an excuse to ditch assholes who won't leave them alone. That's how I found you again." If I did. How can this be the same man?

He looks lost. He runs his hand through his hair. "You found me," he repeats. "You were looking for me?"

"Because you can see me and hear me and touch me." I lay my fingers on his arm and then remove them. "And I can see, hear, and touch you. You know they can't, right?"

"She's heard me and seen me," he insists, gesturing toward Jessica. "She likes when I cook her dinner. I completed a year of culinary school, and she loves my gnocchi. I make it with butter and sage. Pair it with chardonnay."

Not possible. "You're a cook?"

"Now I'm in management. Stable job. Good hours."

None of this makes sense. If he's not like me, why did the ooze eat his shoes? Why didn't anyone react when he leaped onto the bench? Why don't they notice him now, talking to a nonexistent girl? Jessica can't see him now; how could he have cooked for her? "Okay, Jared, you're in management. What do you manage?"

"Work. It's my job."

I touch his arm again. Still solid. "What's your job?"

Could he have found a way to interact with them? *That would be a trick worth learning,* I think. Imagine if I could talk to Leah, to anyone, meet anyone, have dinner, have sex, travel, see the world and interact with it. God, the possibilities! How could it be possible?

But at my question, Jared seems to crumple in on himself. He stares again at the woman. "I . . . don't know. I'm in management, and I work decent hours. She's happy because I'm home in time to cook dinner. I make her butter and sage."

"Forget I asked," I say, soothingly. "Doesn't matter. What matters is that you remember me. You handed me your drink."

He smiles at me, and I feel as though I have been wrapped in the softest, warmest blanket. Whatever made him anxious when I asked about his work has dissipated. "I did," he agrees. "I'm glad I did, and I'm doubly glad you found me again. I've thought about you since then."

I don't know what to make of that sentence. "Great," I say brightly.

"I should have stayed and talked to you. I don't know why I didn't . . ."

"You left, after you helped that woman, and you got on a train." My cheeks feel hot. Am I blushing? His eyes are fixed on me, and it feels as though he can see every thought, feeling, and memory I've ever had. I notice that the muck on the floor is moving in shallow waves. Congealing, it's deepest around the knot of guys in the corner, the ones who were bothering Jessica. They've switched from harassing women to expounding on politics—spouting conspiracy theories—and the greasy ooze rolls off them like sweat.

Following my gaze, Jared shakes his head and clucks his tongue. "It's those kinds of lies that create the worst mess, the ones full of hate and fear, the ones that spread wide." The ooze bleeds into the pool of muck and bubbles more vigorously.

He knows about lies. What else does he know?

"Let's get out of here," he suggests, "before it floods the place."

"Does that happen often?"

"Often enough these days," he says grimly.

Fine. We'll talk when we're away from the muck. "Follow me," I say. We walk on top of the benches that line Sweet Venom. I step straight through the same couple making out, and Jared does too. At the end of the benches, I pause—there's an ankle-deep pool of toxic muck between us and the door. I think I can make it in a few strides, maybe? Or we could go from stool to door and shorten the distance *if* the stool is solid enough to support us. Most things in the bar are solid, hardened with lies.

But if I'm wrong, I'll crash into the ooze.

"I'm going to try it," I warn him.

"Try what?"

I crouch down, gauging the distance. It won't be a graceful leap.

But I don't have much choice.

I jump.

And am caught in a firm grip as Jared darts in front of me.

Carrying me, Jared barrels through the door onto the sidewalk. "Sorry, sorry, I should have asked. I know you didn't consent."

I have never, ever been carried, and I can't begin to sort out what it felt like to be lifted and cradled and taken out of harm's way. Gently, he sets me down. My knees feel wobbly for no rational reason. Taking a breath, I begin to say he didn't need to apologize—

But he doubles over, a jagged cry tears from his lips, and he drops to his knees.

"Jared, what's wrong?" I wrap my arms around his shoulders. The muck. It must have burned him. "Are you okay?" His entire body is vibrating. I feel his shoulder blades shift beneath my fingers. "What's wrong?"

Pedestrians walk right through us.

"Jared?"

He raises his head. "Who's Jared?"

Pale skin, strawberry hair, with a cleft chin and blue eyes that rival the sky just after dawn. White jeans. White T-shirt. Different man. "I . . ."

"Sorry, Hannah. Must have tripped. I'm a klutz."

He knows who I am even though I have never seen *this* man in my life. My brain feels as if it's stuttering, trying to make sense of what just happened. "You remember me?"

"Of course. I handed you my drink." He gives me a quirky smile. "I'm not offended that you don't remember my name. I don't expect to have made the kind of impression on you that you made on me."

"You said your name is Jared."

"I couldn't have. My name is Michael."

"Sure. Michael." I'm aware that my voice sounds shrill, and I feel as though a thousand questions are battering inside me like birds against the bars of a cage.

"Great to see you again, but I have to go."

"Can I come with you?" It feels strange to ask rather than to simply accompany him—like with Mother. Jared—Michael—whoever he is.

Rabbit. He's smiling at me, and I can't look away. It's the same warm smile.

"I'd be delighted," he says with a charming bow. His voice is a low, soothing baritone, nearly the same as before, but now with a trace of a British accent. I wonder if he sings. He must have the most soothing singing voice.

He takes my hand. Are his fingers longer than before? They close around mine gently, as if he's afraid of breaking me, and he sets off, his strides longer than before. I half jog to keep up. He's taller than he was. Thinner. As if he's been stretched out, taffy-like.

He walks around a couple stumbling along, laughing together. "Excuse me."

They don't acknowledge him.

"Doesn't it bother you that they can't see us?" I ask. As soon as the words are out of my mouth, I wish I'd asked a different question. I have a thousand, and I don't know how many I'll have the chance to ask before he tires of me. I think of Sylvie and how my questions irked her.

He looks surprised at the question. "Why should it? It's not their fault."

"Well, no, but . . . Why walk around them and not through them?" Granted, I always walk around people, but that's because I don't like to feel different from them. I have a suspicion that his answer will be different.

"Because. Well, it just doesn't seem right." He sounds as if he hasn't thought about it before. "Ah, here we are." He stops in front of a bar called the Plaid Pig. It has neon signs in the window for various types of beer and whiskey, and there are Christmas lights strung around the sign. The bouncer is a woman with antlers, and I wonder what kind of lie she told that resulted in sprouting them.

Rabbit gives her a nod as we enter the bar. She doesn't even blink, of course. He strides across the floor as if he knows exactly where he's going. Ahead, there's a woman: late twenties, smoky eye makeup, pixie-cut hair, black jeans with artful rips. Her arms are crossed, and she leans backward as a drunk man leers at her. "Hey, she has a boyfriend," Rabbit says. "Leave her alone."

This bar is similar in setup to Sweet Venom, but thankfully, no ocean of ooze. There's a half-moon stage on one side, with a microphone stand and a stool. A guitar leans against the wall. It has a familiar haziness.

I pick up the guitar. It feels solid in my hands. I strum discordantly. I have zero idea how to play; I didn't inherit Mother's musical knowledge or talent. I wonder if she could have given me that skill if she'd chosen to. How much did her lies shape me, and how much did I shape myself?

I look over at Rabbit. Am I witnessing how lies shape him?

He's with a different liar, and she envisions him differently. Could that explain it? It's an interesting theory. I press down on some of the strings and strum again, just as discordant as before, and then notice that my hand looks faded. Not translucent yet, but the edges of my fingers are blurred. I put down the guitar and watch as knives sprout from the wall above a couple talking in low voices. One of the knives connects with the man's head. He doesn't flinch.

Across the room, Rabbit screams.

Spinning around, I spot his white jeans and T-shirt. He's fallen against the wall, curled into himself with pain. Then he straightens. He's a different man again. Black hair sweeps across a dark forehead, and he's broadened, with wide, muscular shoulders.

Leaving the guitar, I approach him. "Michael?"

"Ravin," he corrects.

"Of course. Ravin. Sorry. I forgot."

"That's all right." Charmingly, he adds, "If you'd like, I can pretend I forgot your name, Hannah. So we'll be even."

I glance at the woman he left. "Is she going to be okay?"

"Is who going to be okay?"

"No one. Never mind." He's forgotten her. *But he remembers me.*

"I'm thinking of heading to another bar. Want to come with me?" His smile is the same—warm as the sun, radiating joy.

"Why another bar?" I ask.

As if the answer is obvious, he says, "Because Helene needs me."

"Helene." This must be the name of the woman at the next bar, another who's conjured up an imaginary boyfriend. "How long have you known Helene?"

His smile slips. "I . . . I'm sorry, but I can't remember."

"What do you remember? Where are you from? Where do you live? What do you do during the day when there's no one who needs you in a bar?" I glance at the clock. It's inching toward two o'clock. The bars should all be closing soon. "Where do you go after the bars close?" And why can't I stop asking questions? I promised myself I wouldn't, but they just spill out.

He frowns. "I'm Ravin. I live in Brooklyn. Born and raised in Connecticut. Parents from India. Second generation. I went to college in New Jersey. Graduated cum laude. I work for a hedge fund in downtown Manhattan. I don't mind the commute; I use it to catch up on my reading."

"What are you reading?" I ask him.

"I . . ." He stops. Frowns. "That's odd. I read every day. Why don't I remember?" Fear creeps into his eyes.

I'm beginning to understand. I think. "It's all right," I say quietly.

"Favorite food is sushi. Favorite color is green. I can't remember where I live."

"You said Brooklyn." Gentle. Calm. As if I don't think at all that there's something terribly, terribly wrong with him. I haven't had much practice controlling my expression.

He nods but doesn't look convinced. "I have to go. Rose needs me."

"You said Helene."

"Helene. Yes. Or Astrid. Joanna? Ji-Yoon." He's trying out names as if they're shirts and he wants to see if they fit, but he's growing more panicked.

I stop him with a hand to his chest. "Do you remember your name?"

"Michael," he says. "No, I'm Evan. I'm from Queens. I work in finance. No, management. I'm a car mechanic . . ." And then he contorts in pain as his features shift in front of me, his face melting and re-forming, until at last, he resembles the man I first met at Sweet Venom, the one who handed me his drink. I want to flinch, scream, or run away. But the look in his eyes makes me freeze:

Pure terror.

"Please help me," he whispers.

CHAPTER TWENTY-TWO

Eighteen-year-old Leah trudged from the LIRR station across the Stony Brook University campus. She wore a backpack, carried a duffel bag, and dragged a suitcase bursting with everything she could cram inside. She hadn't wanted to leave a speck of herself in that house.

Fresh start.

It wasn't art school, but at least it wasn't home.

She hauled her belongings up to her new dorm room. Squaring her shoulders, she stuck the key in the lock and opened the door. A girl bounced to her feet from where she'd been sprawled on one of the two twin beds. "Hi," Leah said. "I'm your roommate. Leah."

The girl beamed. "Hey, roomie. I'm Mindi."

"Oh. Um, I thought my roommate was Bethany." The housing office had sent a letter, complete with contact information for a Bethany Sullivan, but Leah hadn't reached out. She hadn't known what to say besides *Don't care who you are so long as you aren't my mother.* Leah waddled her suitcase inside and tossed her duffel bag on an empty spot by the unclaimed bed. She hoped she was in the right room.

"Well, yes, that's me, but . . . new school, new leaf, new life, new name! I've decided that from now on, I want to be called Mindi." She added, "It's my middle name."

Looking around, Leah saw that Mindi had already decorated her side of the room: a pink plaid comforter, a poster of the pi symbol carved into an apple pie, and several photos taped to the wall of what looked like her family—she looked like she had at least three older brothers and two sisters. All of them were smiling.

"If you want to switch sides, that's fine with me," Mindi said, sitting cross-legged on her comforter. "I probably should have waited until you got here—but I wanted it to feel like home."

Definitely don't want it to feel like that. "It's fine." Leah dug into her duffel bag for her sheets. There was a limp pillow on the bed, and she wished she'd brought her own. It hadn't fit, though. *I'll make do.* Mom had told her to come back on the weekend if she forgot anything, but Leah had zero intention of returning until the obligatory Thanksgiving vacation. She felt a sharp pang of jealousy, thinking of Mindi's smiling family, and immediately buried it.

"Are you sure?"

"One hundred percent."

Mindi watched as Leah unpacked. "So what's your story? Who are you? Nerd? Cheerleader? Band geek? Let me guess—theater kid?" She held up a finger. "Before you answer, you don't have to be whatever you were in high school. That's the beauty of college. No one knows who you were before. You get to invent yourself anew. For instance, I was a math nerd."

Leah thought of her mom, trying on new personalities and stories as if they were clothes. Somehow it seemed different with Mindi. Maybe it was because she was being so up front about it. She wasn't lying about her past; she was choosing a new future. It felt like an important difference. "And now?" Leah asked.

"Still a math nerd," Mindi said. "But I'm planning to also try on 'party girl' and see how it fits."

A knock sounded on the open door, and Jersey stuck her head into the room. "Did I hear someone mention a party? Hey, Leah, glad you made it."

Grinning at her friend, Leah abandoned her bedsheets and hugged Jersey.

"You two know each other already?" Mindi asked. "I mean, obviously, yes."

Jersey said, "We're practically sisters."

For an instant, Leah felt like she couldn't breathe. She should have had a real sister. If Hannah had lived. Would they have been best friends? Whispering together late at night as kids? United against their parents? And would she have left her behind to begin a new life at college? She let herself imagine all that, just for an instant, how different everything would have been if she hadn't been alone. *At least I had Jersey. Practically a sister. And she's here with me now.*

"You haven't answered me, though: who are you?"

Not a sister.

She knew the answer she wanted to give. She wanted to say, *I'm an artist.* The words formed on her tongue, but they didn't make it past her lips. She wasn't one yet. How could she claim that label before she'd proven it? She wanted to be, but it wasn't who she was.

And she wasn't going to lie. Not about that.

"I don't know yet," Leah said.

◆ ◆ ◆

The party was fine.

Leah had no clue who the host was, but it didn't seem to matter to anyone. There were beers in the bathtub, chilling in a mix of water and a few stray ice cubes. The music was loud enough to shake the floor, and at least a few people had yet to be introduced to the concept of soap and showers. But it was better than being alone.

She was snug in the middle of a group chattering about last summer. Both Jersey and Mindi were there, as well as a couple of new friends and a few could-possibly-become friends.

"Hey, Leah, you've been to the Hamptons, right?" one kid—Joel— said. He was in her art-history class. Usually propped his feet up on the seat in front of him.

"Sure," she said. And then she wondered why she'd said that. She hadn't ever been to the Hamptons, even though she'd grown up on Long Island. Mom hadn't wanted to face the traffic and didn't like the beach, and Dad . . . "I mean, no," she corrected.

But he didn't hear her over the thrum of the music.

"You know that seafood place with the shark-head entrance? Can't miss it. It's on Sunrise Highway. No idea what town, but you know the shark-head place?"

"I don't, but go ahead."

"How do you not know the shark-head place? Seriously. The door—" He mimed the shape of a giant shark head around him. "It's, like, iconic."

"She doesn't know it," Jersey said, jumping to her rescue. "Get to the point."

He wouldn't. "One-lane highway at that spot. Gotta go past it." He was glaring as if her lack of knowledge of this restaurant had offended him to the core of his being. Worse, everyone else was staring, too, waiting for her to fix this logjam in the middle of their conversation.

"Sure, yeah, sorry. Forgot."

The words felt bitter on her tongue, and she thought of her mother. Mom would have claimed that not only did she remember the restaurant, but they'd dined there multiple times and had them cater an event at their summer home in Southampton.

One white lie does not mean I'm becoming my mother.

But she felt as if she'd dipped herself in pond slime. While Joel babbled about the restaurant, Leah turned to Jersey and said loudly, "Do you know if Mulligan grades the final on effort as well as execution?"

"No, but I know the secret to acing it," Jersey said.

Cutting himself off, Joel asked, "What?"

Jersey smiled at him sweetly. "Don't be Joel."

Mindi whooped. "She got you!"

All their friends laughed, and Leah relaxed, the subject successfully changed—thank God for Jersey. She was always there to shield Leah from whatever—or, more accurately, whoever—was hurting her. Leah listened as her friends vented about homework and finals and grades, and she wondered if she was ever going to reach a point where she could get through a conversation without thinking about what her mother would have said. *She's not here. She doesn't get to live in my head rent-free.*

Leah downed another beer and tried to focus only on the here and now.

This was her life, and it was going to be what she made it.

◆　◆　◆

By the end of junior year, Leah had taken enough prerequisites that she was certain she'd be one of the select students allowed to do independent work in studio art senior year.

Yet when she checked the student portal, it wasn't listed as one of her classes.

She waited outside the Art Department chair's office, clutching her folder of recent samples. Leah stared at the bulletin board opposite his office. It was coated in flyers for study-abroad art programs, gallery showings, internship opportunities. She fixed her eyes on a blob of red paint, a print of an abstract that was appearing in one of this year's senior's final projects.

It's just a mistake.

A clerical error.

A simple fix in the computer system.

She needed this course. It was the culmination of everything she wanted, everything she'd worked for. Plus, studio art was a requirement for the major. *Obviously, an oversight.*

Leah checked her phone. Five minutes late. She knocked. No answer. She heard the professor's voice, muffled through the door. And then he went silent. She knocked again. Shifting from foot to foot, she tried to be patient.

At last, he opened the door. "Oh, sorry. I didn't know you were out here."

Given that she'd knocked twice, she thought that was unlikely, but she didn't say that out loud. She scooted inside. "Hi, Professor Corden."

His office smelled like oil paint, the pungent odor permeating the air so that it tasted greasy. Above his desk was a print of a Picasso, *The Old Guitarist*. She stared at the figure's neck, bowed over the guitar, weighed down by the blue around him but still playing. The shelves on either side of the print overflowed with art books and stacks of sketch-books. Her fingers itched to open one and see what the Art Department chair drew in his spare time.

"I think there's been a mistake in my schedule," Leah said. "Um, I . . ."

He waved his hand. "The Registrar's Office can fix that."

"They sent me here." Leah had tried to talk to the registrar first, then the department secretary, and finally she'd ended up here, in the chair's office. "I was, um, hoping to take Independent Studio Art. I'll be a senior next year."

He picked up his glasses and placed them on his nose. "Ah, Leah Allen, yes?" He tapped on his keyboard. "Let me just bring up your file . . . You took . . . hmm . . . okay, yes, I see. You didn't qualify. I'm sorry, my dear."

"But I've taken all the prerequisites." She juggled the papers in her hand to pull out the nice copy she'd printed of her transcript. She knew he'd have access to her files, of course, but she wanted to be prepared.

He didn't even glance at it. "Yes, but you need the courses *and* a teacher recommendation."

She had wondered if that was the problem but had convinced herself that it would all be fine. Her last professor hadn't seemed impressed with anything she'd done—she'd squeaked through with a B minus— but that was the opinion of one person. She still didn't understand what she'd done wrong. She'd completed every assignment, and all he ever said was that her work "lacked spark." Surely one subjective opinion wasn't enough to keep her from her dream. "I brought samples of my work. If you could maybe, please . . . I really think I can do this."

He accepted the portfolio.

She stood, barely breathing, while he flipped through her work. She stared at his eyebrows, wondering if how they raised and lowered meant anything. He had white hairs mixed in his bushy eyebrows, and they curled at willy-nilly angles.

Finally, he heaved a sigh. "Independent work is for our top students. Please understand that it's a highly competitive course of study and requires a high degree of self-motivation—"

"I'm motivated," she burst in. Her eyes felt hot. She knew exactly how to keep tears from falling. Curling her hands, she dug her nails into her palms. "I promise I won't let you down."

"You completed all the assignments, but I am seeing the same comments over and over from your teachers. From Professor Cunningham: You lack originality. You lack trust in your own creativity. Professor Malley deemed your work 'prosaic.' Professor Lasner . . . The consensus is that you are trying to please them rather than finding your own voice, and the independent study program is for those who have already discovered their voice. If I could direct you to one of the more academic classes, you might find it beneficial." His voice was kind, and that made the words a thousand times worse. He knew they had to feel like a trowel digging holes into her heart, but he still said them.

Prosaic.

Lacking originality.

She'd read all the negative comments too: She was going through the motions, one had said. Too intent on pleasing others, said another. And the worst, lacking a spark.

How the hell did one find a spark? What did that even mean? Wasn't it all subjective? She knew she could draw. And paint. Maybe not sculpt. But she had the technique. Wasn't that enough? Couldn't she find her "voice" if they just let her try? She'd had positive comments too! Why hadn't he looked at those? Professor Lasner had complimented her use of color. Professor Cunningham had given her an A for technique. Only Professor Malley had panned her work entirely.

God, what if he's right?

"Have you considered art history as a major?" Professor Corden said helpfully. "You've completed enough courses that it would be easy to switch your major. And your GPA in those courses is excellent. If you switch now and complete a research project for your senior thesis, you have a high chance of graduating cum laude."

She took back her portfolio. Her fingers felt numb.

"It's not that I'm trying to discourage you, but a career as an artist is a difficult undertaking in the best of circumstances. We try not to set our students on impossible paths. I know this level of honest feedback is difficult to receive. Please understand that, as difficult as it may be to hear, this is meant as a kindness—I'm trying to help you."

Of course, he was, or he thought he was. She nodded. He could be right. What if she wasn't good enough? She'd never wowed any of her professors, and here the chair of the Art Department, a professional artist who'd seen countless student portfolios, had flipped through all of what she thought was her best work.

What if I've been lying to myself? All her dreams were just castles in the clouds. She'd been fooling herself for years, thinking that she had a chance. She felt her cheeks heat up.

At least Professor Corden hadn't lied when he broke her heart. *Unlike my mother.* She fled his office, clutching her artwork, with tears stinging her eyes and cheeks on fire. She wasn't sure which "kindness" was worse.

CHAPTER
TWENTY-THREE

"Please help me."

I laugh, even though it isn't funny. "You were supposed to help *me*."

"Anything you need. What can I do?" He sounds so genuine and intense that tears prick the corners of my eyes. Here I thought the problem would be convincing him to cooperate. I was prepared to drag answers out of him—though, maybe not bombard him the way I did with Sylvie—but that's not the case at all. I'm certain that he is 100 percent willing to help me.

I am equally certain that he can't.

He can't even hold on to his own name.

"Who are you now?" I ask.

"David. Same as I've always been." He sounds amused, as if I'm flirting with him by playing some kind of get-to-know-you game.

"I'm just going to call you Rabbit. Do you mind that? Ever had a nickname?"

He hesitates. "Most call me David. Just David."

"Let's stick with Rabbit," I say firmly.

He smiles as bright as the sunrise.

For an instant, I forget everything else I wanted to say—his smile is so . . . the only word I can think of is innocent. *He'll help me, if he can.* "Rabbit, I need to figure out how I can keep from fading away *and* how I can avoid spending my life running from the shadow wolves. How do you keep yourself, you know, *alive?*"

He looks confused by the question.

I look at his beautiful, perplexed face. *He's broken.*

"Running from the shadow wolves?" he asks.

Scanning the street, I look for one to show him. With so many lies around, there must be at least one wolf. And I'm correct. Half a block away, a shadow wolf slinks along the sidewalk beside a stream of ooze. Thankfully, it hasn't noticed us. "Like that," I say.

"Oh, yes, them." He shrugs. "They don't bother me."

I stare at him. "Why not? You're like me."

"I don't know. They've never shown any interest in me."

What makes him so special? Other than the fact that he changes who he is multiple times a night—could that be it? He transforms so thoroughly that the wolves don't recognize him? No, there has to be another explanation.

As we watch, the wolf lunges at the muck.

As if alive, the ooze retreats. It swirls and swishes, crashing against the curb. Like the ocean hitting a rock, it curves up into a wave—and the wolf slams teeth first into it. The muck crashes over the wolf's body, and the wolf dissipates into smoke and then solidifies on the other side of the wave. Spinning to face the sludge again, the shadow wolf crouches, teeth bare.

The muck retreats—there's a tear in its gelatinous wave from where the wolf ripped it apart, and then it knits itself back together before collapsing into a puddle and slinking away in the gutter. The wolf attacks again as the first bit of ooze reaches a drain.

"That crap isn't easy to destroy," Rabbit says, "but the wolves can do it. They perform a service, keeping the city from becoming overrun with muck and other malignant lies."

I'm not malignant.

We watch as the wolf attacks again and again. It tears hunks of muck away like taffy and swallows them. Sludge smears the wolf's muzzle, and the muck stretches thinner as it tries to escape, slipping down the drain.

The wolf blocks the drain, gobbling the muck as it tries to escape.

"Do they not hunt you because there's tastier prey?" I ask.

Behind me, Rabbit hisses, and I spin to see him double over in pain again. His fists clench, and his muscles shift in his arms as they thicken. His hair bleaches, fading to blond, and when he lifts his face, sweat drenched and panting, his features have changed again.

"Who are you now?" I ask gently.

Straightening, he smiles at me as if he hadn't just contorted in pain. "You said you were going to call me Rabbit." He starts walking down the street at a brisk pace.

Lightly, I ask, "Where are we going, Rabbit?"

"I just need to check on Justina," he says cheerily, as if nothing were wrong with him or me or the world, "and then I promise I'll help you find a solution to your problem."

I have no choice but to follow.

Inside the Shaggy Hound bar, I am not at all surprised to see yet another woman, now a short white woman in a skintight purple dress with a tattoo of a willow tree on her shoulder, fending off yet another unwanted advance. Glancing at her phone, Justina says in a bored tone, "My boyfriend is on his way to pick me up."

The man is thirtysomething, with slicked hair and a face that would have been handsome if it weren't curled into a sneer. "Yeah? Why wasn't he here with you?"

"He wanted to watch the game," she replies promptly.

"I did," Rabbit agrees.

"What game?" I ask him.

"*The* game," he answers.

"You don't even know what sport," I marvel. "Do you have any of your own thoughts and feelings, or are they all put there by these women who invent and reinvent you?"

His face crumples.

Instantly wishing I'd kept my mouth shut, I put my hand on his arm. "Sorry. I shouldn't have said that." At least I shouldn't have phrased it so bluntly. I'm not used to thinking before I speak. I've never been able to hurt anyone with my words before. It makes me feel as if I'd dipped myself in that boiling ooze.

He summons a smile and covers my hand with his. "My thoughts about you are clear."

I feel myself blush. It's hard to think straight when he smiles at me like that. He *has* remembered me through each of his changes, which means that even while his brain is being stirred like soup with false memories, he is able to retain what actually happens to him.

The slicked-hair man leans closer to the woman. "I don't think you have a boyfriend. I think you're faking it so you won't have to go home with me."

She sighs heavily, leans to the side of her stool, and shouts, "Roger?"

The bouncer waddles from the door. "Yeah, Justina? This guy giving you problems?"

"He says I'm lying to him," she says in a bored tone, as if she's been through this conversation a hundred times. Perhaps she has. I wonder how long Rabbit's been her imaginary boyfriend. Weeks, months, or years?

Roger cracks his knuckles. "Justina only lies to dickheads, and I don't like dickheads in my bar."

"Your bar?" The guy snorts.

"Yeah, my bar," Roger says. "And Justina's our patron saint. So you'd best find yourself another place to drink."

Oozing hostility, the bartender says, "Last call."

The guy glares at all three of them and then backs toward the door. He trips over a stool, half falls, and catches himself on the table. "You." He aims a finger at the patron saint. "Aren't that hot anyway."

"Thanks, Roger," Justina says after the asshole leaves. "You're my hero." She slings her purse over her shoulder and blows him a kiss as she heads for the door.

He trails after her to resume his post. "You know, if you weren't here by yourself so late at night, then guys like that wouldn't assume—"

She levels a finger at him. "Going to stop you right there. I should be able to go where I please, by myself or not by myself, and not have some rando think that my choices have anything to do with him."

He holds up his hands in surrender. "You're right. Get home safe." With a wave, Justina exits the bar, and the door swings shut behind her. The music continues to play, vibrating the floor, and the other customers vie for the bartender's attention.

Beside me, Rabbit says, "She shouldn't have needed his help."

I agree. "The guy should've gotten the hint on his own." It was lucky she comes here often enough to know the owner. Lucky too that he was serving as bouncer tonight.

"*I* should have been enough," Rabbit says.

He's staring at the closed door as if she's walked out on him, as if she even knew he was there. I take his hand. "Hey, you know they couldn't see you, right? You remember that?"

He blinks. Holds my hand tight. "You know what I remember? You. Clearer than any of my memories of her. Or my memories of anything else. You, shining through. Why is that?"

"I'm . . ." I almost say *real*. ". . . like you."

Fervently, he says, "I'm glad you found me." His eyes are so intense that I feel as if I'm swimming in them, and I realize we are standing mere inches from each other.

Taking a step back, I try to remember how to breathe. *Focus on the problem at hand,* I tell myself. "Where . . . um, where do you go after the bars close?" His life is a jumble. How does he make the pieces of himself fit together?

"I go home and sleep." He then squeezes his eyes shut. "No. I don't. I . . . I wander. Until I'm needed again. I take the train sometimes. Until it stops running. Out east."

It's not such a terrible idea. I could bring him back with me to Sylvie. She might know what to do with him, how to help him. She doesn't shift her appearance, even though she was invented by multiple liars. If Rabbit could learn how to remain as one person for more than a few minutes, he might have a shot at sorting through his memories. And maybe then he could explain why he's so uninteresting to the wolves. "Then let's go together," I say. "We can help each other. How does that sound?"

He's still looking at me as if I'm his water in the desert, and I don't know how to feel about being the subject of such intense regard. "Together sounds perfect," he says.

We walk side by side through the streets of Queens. The ever-present muck flows in roiling clumps through the gutter beside us. In places, it has spilled from the gutters to swamp the asphalt. Watching it, I shiver. It smells of rot, and I think of Mother's kitchen as Leah and Jersey emptied it. This stench, more than the scent of Mother's body or her casket, smells like death.

"Don't touch it," I warn Rabbit.

He catches my hand in his. Like he's known me for years. Like it isn't extraordinary that he can hold my hand. I wonder if he's as amazed by it as I am. "I know," he says. "That stuff is toxic. It burned holes in my shoes."

He remembers that. "Where's it going?"

"Everywhere. Near as I can tell, its sole purpose is to spread. Anything it can corrode in its path, it will. As I said, toxic."

He's still holding my hand. I can't tell how much he knows about what we are or what he believes. Sometimes, he seems fully aware, and I don't know if now is one of those times. "How long have you been alive?" I'm certain there's a better way to phrase that, but those are the words that come out of my mouth.

"Since I was born." He grins at me.

It's an infectious grin, and it makes me want to smile back, but I can't. The muck is writhing, forming tiny whirlpools, and splashing over the curb. I glance around; for the first time ever, I actually *want* to see shadow wolves, but none come to devour the growing muck. Was he born? Sylvie wasn't, and she didn't grow up. "Do you have any memories of your childhood?"

"Of course," he says; then his grin fades. "I think."

There's a *lot* of sludge.

We should walk faster.

I pick up my pace to a trot, which forces him to lengthen his strides to match. "I remember learning how to fix a car engine," he says. "Wrench in my hand. Smell of grease, oil, gas, and sweat. But . . ."

"But what?" I prod.

"It's not a clear memory, you know? I couldn't tell you the type of car or who was with me or how I learned to hold a wrench. It's like I can only see through a pinhole. A few details. Like I can remember ice-skating, the sound of a blade on the ice, the spray of ice, but that's it. I don't remember who taught me. I don't even remember lacing up the skates. I think I was skating with someone. I was holding a hand." He lifts up our clasped hands. "I don't know whose. Guess all memories are like that. They fade."

I have plenty of clear memories, and I know which ones are mine and which are manufactured by Mother's stories. Mostly. "Are they wreathed in fog?"

"Yes," he says, a note of surprise in his voice. "How did you know?"

False memories.

"Do you have any memories that aren't cloudy?" I ask. "You remember handing me your drink. Do you remember that clearly?"

He brightens. "Absolutely. Every second with you is clear."

I was right. He retains true memories, even when he shifts.

We walk on, still holding hands. I wonder what time it is and what Sylvie's doing right now. All the bars are closed, so I know it's late. Did she find another impossible party? Has she holed up in another fancy, nonexistent house? Is she safe? I hope she is. "Do you remember what you did after you handed me the drink? Where you went?"

"I . . . I'm not sure."

I'm upsetting him. I try a different tack. "What draws you to the bars?"

He shrugs, clearly more comfortable with this question. "It just feels like the right thing to do. Besides, I like the music. The drinks. The hum of people. I'm a people watcher. I like to guess their stories. Like that guy—" With his free hand, he waves at a man in shorts and a hoodie. He's walking fast, his eyes glued on his phone and one hand shoved in his pocket. "Going home? Meeting friends? Late-night job? Late-night drink? Where did he intend to be tonight? He's obviously not happy where he is, so where is he going?"

I watch the stranger walk by and think that Sylvie would be amazed that I found someone who asks just as many questions as I do.

"You want to know a secret?" Rabbit says. "Sometimes I follow them." He releases my hand and holds up both of his in surrender. "I know, I know. Sounds creepy."

He drops his arms. My hand misses his warmth. "You aren't doing it to hurt them, so I vote not creepy." I don't know that regular people would agree, but regular people don't have our . . . limitations.

Really, what was I doing with my life except following Mother around without her knowledge? It's what I tried to do with Leah. I don't think she would have been happy if she'd known I was there while she and Jamie . . . I shy away from the details of that memory, especially the sounds. I wouldn't mind having that memory wrapped in a fuzzy cloud.

"Thanks," he says. I hear the relief in his voice. He cares what I think of him, and that thought warms me. He continues. "They just . . . all have stories, you know? Their own set of memories and their own dreams."

"And their own set of lies," I say.

"That too."

"Do you think we're made of lies?"

I am not sure I want to know his answer. I'm also not sure I should have asked the question. But it's out there, the words floating like invisible bubbles that I wish I could pop.

"Of course," Rabbit says, "but that doesn't mean we're bad." Ahead, the sidewalk dips into the street; the muck has pooled in the depression. "Now *that* is evil." We stop at the end of the sidewalk and stare across the river of muck.

A pretzel cart rolls by, pulled by shadows. Taxis splash through puddles but do not disturb the ooze. It flows in all directions in the gutter and rivulets across the street. There are dry patches between. If we leap . . . Okay, some will require a large leap. I'm not certain I can make it. Not certain even a prima ballerina could make it. "Is there another way to the train station? Maybe we can go around?"

We take a right. A left. Another right.

And I slow. "Rabbit."

He slows with me. "What's wrong?"

"Look."

Muck cascades sluggishly down the stairs that lead to the train platform, a toxic waterfall that we cannot pass. Passengers walk right through without seeing it, and the tar-like muck clings to their skin and clothes after they pass.

"Guess the train is out," Rabbit says, sounding far calmer than I feel.

It's everywhere. It'll swallow us. We have to get out of here. Back to Sylvie and the Hamptons, where it's safe. I think of the shadow wolves at the glittering false party. *Safer.*

"We need to steal a car," I say.

"We—sorry?"

I scan the street for one that's wreathed in fog. There must be at least one—I spot a blue car that looks held together with mist and duct tape. Can't even tell what kind it is, but I pull Rabbit toward it.

But Rabbit screams.

I spin around abruptly. The muck must have burned him—but no, he's changing again, shifting back into David, the man who handed me the drink.

The ooze, though, is creeping closer down the sidewalk, as if drawn by his scream. It comes in waves, mimicking the ocean, and I wonder how fast it can flow and how high the waves can rise.

"Come on, Rabbit," I order him.

Yanking him with me, I race across the street and pull the car door open. *Not locked. Yes!* No need to lock an imaginary car—Sylvie was right. Again. I dive into the driver's seat. The keys fall into my lap as I tilt the visor. "Get in!"

"Do you know how to drive?" Rabbit asks.

"No. You?" How hard can it be? You press on the gas and turn the steering wheel.

"Plenty of times."

"Clear memories or foggy ones?" What does it matter? He has more experience, even if it's entirely false. Mother never claimed I'd gotten my driver's license, and I've never tried to drive any kind of car, real or fake. I climb into the passenger seat as he comes to the driver's side.

A wave of muck crashes into the side of the car. It sizzles as it hits. A scream builds in my throat as I watch the side mirror sag. The glass and plastic drip as if melted.

"Drive!" I order.

He shoves the keys into the ignition, puts the car into drive, and stomps on the gas. The muck slips from the window as he shoots down the street. Glancing over my shoulder, I see the sludge pool on the pavement. It slinks backward, and I see a shadow wolf form in an alleyway and run toward the waves of muck.

I breathe again.

◆ ◆ ◆

Sunrise Highway.

It's well named.

We watch the sun rise over the road ahead as we continue east. Rabbit drives as if he's been doing it all his life, though I don't know how long that life has been. A week? A month? Years, like me?

I don't want to ask him. It could cause another memory crisis, not ideal while he holds the wheel. Better if he doesn't probe too deeply into *how* he knows what he knows.

"Want to listen to the radio?" Rabbit asks, breaking the silence.

"Sure." I study the console for a minute and locate the on button. Static blares from the speakers, and we both jerk back. I twist the volume. It feels strange to manipulate the dials. Wisps of smoke dance around my fingers as I push buttons, trying to find a station. It settles on a song I've never heard before, pulsing with static but still a good beat. *Good enough.*

I wonder if it's a real song or if it's like Leah's sketches. Nonexistent music.

It exists for me. I wonder if the singer who never sang this song would appreciate that. Somewhere out in the world, there must be countless albums that were never made, books that were never written, symphonies never played. Is there a library somewhere filled with stories never imagined? What about a school of facts never learned? A museum of treasures never saved? A theater of plays never performed?

Looking at the lemonade sky, I wonder what else is out there. Maybe there's nothing left to see. Maybe everything good and glorious has been destroyed by the ooze and the shadow wolves.

"What's your favorite thing about the world?" I ask Rabbit.

"Meeting you," he says without hesitation.

I laugh. "You can't mean that. You just met me."

"You are my clarity," he says simply.

He sounds as if he means it. I try to imagine what it must be like, to have all my memories wrapped in a fog, never certain which are real and which are mine. It's entirely possible that I am the first person who has ever persisted in his memory through his varied identity shifts.

"Also, you asked for my help," he says. "I've never met anyone who directly asked me for help, and I like to help people."

"Uh-huh. Anyone ever tried to help you?"

"You," he says. He smiles at me so brilliantly that I'm transfixed. I want to tell him to keep watching the road, but all I can do is stare at his eyes. They slide between colors: brown irises flecked with gold become greener and greener; then the green shifts to blue. More gold flecks as brown leaks into his irises, and they darken to near black. Extraordinary.

It's like watching the sun set. I wonder what Sylvie will think of him. I think about watching the sunset with her and Rabbit tonight, if we can all survive that long. "I have a friend who loves sunsets," I say. "I never paid much attention to them before I met her."

"I'm usually inside around sunset," he admits. "I can't remember just watching one, especially with a friend." He faces the road again, and a frown creases his forehead. "I should remember."

"Don't worry about it," I say quickly. "Just focus on the road. It'll turn into Montauk Highway at some point. We'll keep following it." And then? How do we find Sylvie? Will she even want to be found?

"Tell me about yourself," Rabbit says. "You said you needed my help. How can I help?"

I don't know if he can help me. Don't know if anyone can. Holding my hand up against the rising sun, I think I look solid. Light glows around my fingers but not through them. I can feel the seat of the car, smell the scent of old french fries and plastic. "I was my mother's lie, and now . . . I don't know what I am."

I want to keep seeing sunrises and sunsets. I want to hear songs that were never played. I want to see places beyond that cramped, rarely vacuumed house in Garden City with the baked goods that no one ever baked in the kitchen that only gleamed for me. I want to see more oceans. A part of me also wants to find a nice, safe hole to crawl into and never feel fear again. I don't want to be afraid anymore. No more muck. No wolves. No shadow trains that hold me captive or cars that dissolve around me. I want an ordinary life, the kind I can never have.

"I don't understand the problem," he says.

"Me neither. And that itself is the problem. There's no rule book for the way we are. I don't know if I'll fade, when I'll fade, *why*. I don't know where the wolves came from, or why they hunt me but not you. I don't know how to live without . . ." My throat clogs, and my eyes feel hot. I never even imagined having to live without her. Ordinary people might plan how to move on. They know things change. They expect to grow up and begin their own lives. But my life was never mine before now. "When did you know what we are?"

"We're just people, albeit different in some ways, but we think and feel and are," Rabbit says. "I'm sorry, Hannah, but I don't know what you mean. I've always known what I am."

That seems blatantly untrue since his name has changed several times on just this night, but I don't want to argue with the man driving the impossible car. I stop asking questions, for now. Instead, I focus on the road, with the sun rising above.

◆　◆　◆

Once we reach the Hamptons, I drag Rabbit from fake mansion to fake mansion. Check every imaginary swimming pool that I can find. Pop into gleaming kitchens overflowing with banquets' worth of food.

But no Sylvie.

"Maybe she's gone somewhere else?" Rabbit ventures.

Maybe the wolves caught her. Maybe she's jumped in a car and driven somewhere else entirely. Maybe I was an idiot to think she'd wait for me. Maybe there are just too many lies to search through.

Maybe I should never have left.

I think of the first day we met, how she barely waited for me to watch the sunset. I remember how surprised she was when I reappeared. *She didn't believe I'd come back.*

I suddenly realize that I know, if not *where*, then at least *when* I can find her. "All we have to do is find the best place to view the sunset."

We climb back into our stolen car, and I can feel Rabbit's doubt, without him having to voice it. "There's less than an hour to sunset."

"It won't be as much of a needle in a haystack as it sounds," I say. "Most of the views here are north, south, and east. West is land. All we have to do is find where the beach curves so that it faces west."

"Or someplace high," he says. "A roof?"

Possibly, but there aren't any skyscrapers out east. And it's not like there are random towers around for viewing. She could find a balcony on one of the mansions or a widow's walk. Rabbit points to a sign along the road, a brown sign for historical landmarks. "How about a lighthouse?"

Montauk Lighthouse.

She's most likely already done that, probably her first evening in Montauk. Then again, it has to be one of the most dramatic places to view the sunset from around here, and Sylvie is nothing if not dramatic.

"She'll be there," I say.

I don't know how I can be so certain, but I am. She feels she's been abandoned. Again. She'll go to the lighthouse, the most dramatic view around, to match her mood.

He drives farther east. There aren't as many mansions, real or otherwise, beyond the Hamptons. We see a seafood restaurant with a plaster shark at the front entrance, its open maw framing the door. We pass fruit stands with glowing, unreal peaches mixed with real fruits and vegetables. A pickup truck zooms past. It's wreathed in wisps of haze.

My eyes are drawn to the water. It teases, peeking between trees with its sparkling blue, and then suddenly it's splayed out on both sides as the island narrows down to a strip. Then the island widens again, and the two-lane road veers inland.

The farther out we go, the more color fills our view. Light-blue sky, deep-blue water, dark-green trees, beige sand, but most striking are all the colors in between.

"I never knew it was so beautiful," Rabbit says.

He parks the car in an open lot surrounded by grass and crowned by the red-and-white-striped lighthouse. It rises above a building clad in weathered shingles that's now a museum. The CLOSED sign is clearly visible from the car. That won't stop us.

"Have you ever seen the ocean?" I ask him.

"Never. I never knew I wanted to."

"What do you want?" I ask him.

"To be useful," he says immediately.

"Useful" was never an adjective that I considered much when I thought about my future, if I ever thought about my future. I suppose I was useful to Mother in a way. She needed me, or the idea of me. I filled some hole in her that was empty. A Hannah-shaped hole.

I wonder if I ever could have been enough to fill that hole. Leah didn't think so. She thinks I tore a bigger hole in their family, though it wasn't my choice or my doing.

Maybe it's best for her that I left. Or maybe she feels my absence. I've always been there, a part of her family, and now . . . I'm here. And it's near sunset.

"Let's get to the top," I say.

We cross the parking lot with the sun behind us. I don't bother to try the door at the base of the lighthouse—the sign says CLOSED—instead, I slide right through the wood. That's one thing that Sylvie has taught me: to be less self-conscious about how I move within the world.

Rabbit follows me.

Inside, light still spills through a round window high above us. We're in a silo-like cylinder with red brick walls coated in chipped white paint, and a spiral staircase fills the entire area. I climb and try not to worry that the steps will fade beneath me.

It's the kind of stairway where you can see between the steps, and I become dizzy as we climb up and up. There are window nooks every so often that provide light. The rest of the tower is in shadow, but even in the darkest stretches, I can still climb higher.

The stairwell narrows slightly around us, and I wonder how many steps we'll have to climb. I'm huffing, and my side aches. I've done entirely too much running and fleeing and being afraid in the last few days.

At last, we reach a landing. It's utilitarian, with electrical boxes on the wall, a fire extinguisher, a metal chair flecked with rust. Another staircase, a short straight one this time, leads up one more flight.

I climb to the top.

There are windows facing every direction, separated only by strips of metal. Ocean in three directions, a strip of land against the sinking sun in the other.

And against that backdrop is Sylvie.

"You found the best view," I say.

She doesn't turn around. "I always do."

"I told you I'd come back. You could have waited someplace more apparent. Feels like I searched all of Long Island."

She shrugs. "You seem to have found me just fine. Did you—" She twists her head and sees Rabbit standing behind me. "That would be a yes. You found him. And he's wearing all white, exactly as you said he would be."

"Hi, ma'am," Rabbit says. "I'm Jared." Then he stops. "Evan."

"He's Rabbit," I say. "And he—"

I don't have to explain his issue because he seizes in pain again, his face changing as he silently screams. He waves me back when I rush to his side.

"What the hell?" Sylvie says.

He drops to his knees, his fists tight as his body ripples. When he stands up, he's muscled and tanned, like a surfer in Malibu. His straw-blond hair droops into his eyes, now blue. How many versions of him are there?

Sylvie purses her lips in a whistle. She says nothing. No questions. No answers. Behind her, the sun kisses the blur of distant trees.

"You're missing the sunset," I say.

Rabbit straightens. Exhales. "Excuse me for that," he says politely.

Sylvie flashes him a smile. "You're weird. I like that. But I don't miss the sunset for anyone." She turns her back on him—and me.

I stand beside her. "I found him in a bar. He had a different face and name—"

"Hush," Sylvie said. "Watch."

I quiet. Rabbit joins on my other side. He doesn't speak either. I resist the urge to study what he looks like now, whether it's one of his prior faces or a brand-new one, and instead watch the clouds as they shift above the dying sun.

I notice how free of haze it is up here. I take a deep breath and then another.

I am here.

I made it back to Sylvie and the sunset. I found my White Rabbit. We escaped the muck, and now there's just the beautiful world framed by the ocean.

Maybe this is enough. For now.

Then the world goes dark around me.

CHAPTER
TWENTY-FOUR

Get it done. Everything will be better when it's over and done.

Leah came alone this time. It had seemed like a good idea when she left her apartment but felt decidedly less of one now. She breathed in the sharp tang of lemon, bleach, and new paint. The scent pierced like a needle through the skull, but it was vastly better than the sickly sweet stench of rotten food and the taste of stale air. She told herself this was progress.

God, it was so damned quiet.

It was never quiet at home. Mom always talked, talked, talked, as if she could fill the holes in her life with a garbage truck full of words.

"You know Mr. Eiderman down the street? I think he deals drugs."

"Last week, Beverly—remember Beverly? You clipped her mailbox when you were learning to drive. Last week, I saw her put out a baby swing with the trash, and I think—"

"We almost adopted, after Hannah. Always said we would. There are so many kids out there who need a loving home."

"If your father hadn't left, we would have had a whole houseful of kids."

Leah shook her head. She was here to work. She picked Mother's bedroom as the next one to gut. Ruthlessly, she hauled clothes out of the closet and stuffed them into garbage bags to donate or toss, whichever was quickest. She could put them on the curb with a "free clothes" label. If no one wanted them, then she'd leave them for the garbage the next time she came.

Ugh, how many "next times" were there going to have to be? It wasn't that big a house, and in the end, only one person had lived here. Why had Mom kept all this crap? Leah wedged old purses into another garbage bag and then yanked open the dresser drawers.

So much crap.

Everything Mom said, crap.

Everything she did. Everything she touched.

Leah swept all the items into the trash bag: photos, brushes, knickknacks. She opened Mom's jewelry box. Fake pearls. Fake gold. Plastic and glue under all the glitter. "How fucking poetic," she said and then dumped all of it in the trash.

She spun around, looking for something else to toss. Her eyes landed on her mother's bedspread, and her fingers itched to tear it into shreds. Instead, she stalked out of the room to calm herself.

She was supposed to leave the house so that it looked as if it *could* be lived in, not like it was lived in. Leah's gaze swept around the living room with its fresh coat of paint, the sofa where Mom had died, and the piano she never played.

She took a deep breath.

Fucking lemon scent.

Another deep breath.

You can do this. It's just a house. Just a wall. Just a sofa. Just a piano. Mom had tried to teach Leah to play. She remembered sitting side by side. Mom would frown at the music book, plunk out the notes, and then Leah would imitate her. Dad was the one who insisted they pay for lessons with Mrs. Murphy.

Mrs. Murphy. Leah hadn't thought of her in a long time. She'd kept going to lessons up until Dad left. After that, Mom said Leah was never going to be a concert pianist, so why waste the money when they could save for college?

Yeah, that had worked out well.

Leah's phone buzzed in her pocket and she jumped. *McCormick and Taylor.* She winced. Considered letting it go to voice mail but knew that would be a mistake.

"Hello," she answered.

"Leah, this is Chantelle from Steven McCormick's office."

"Sorry I didn't call—" She'd hoped they'd still give her leeway. She hadn't shown up to work since her mother died. Hadn't called either. She hadn't wanted the sympathy, to say all the things they expected her to say.

"We know it's a rough time for you, but we had you scheduled for today. We don't want to be insensitive, but we need to be able to rely on you. Our clients were expecting your return—"

"I've been sick," Leah said. "Since the funeral. I think it's the stress. I've been throwing up all day. Just really nauseous. I know I should have called, but I wasn't thinking straight." She cringed as she lied. She shouldn't have answered the phone.

Chantelle said a stream of sympathetic things but stressed that Leah should return to work as soon as she felt well enough. Tomorrow? Could she count on her tomorrow? Leah agreed to tomorrow.

"Because we want to be understanding, but—" Chantelle said.

"I'll be better tomorrow," Leah said. "You can count on me."

She slid the phone back into her pocket.

Tomorrow she'd return to work. Make herself sound cheerful. Shuffle columns around in a spreadsheet. Prepare a PowerPoint. Pour herself some coffee. Smile through the client meetings. Pretend that this was in any way what she'd meant to do with her life.

"You made me this," Leah said to the piano. "I could have been more."

The piano sat there. Sad, dusty, out of tune.

"I could have been better."

Leah reached into her box of supplies—Lysol spray, Clorox bleach, paint rollers, trash bags, a screwdriver, a wrench. She pulled out the wrench. It felt solid in her hand. Real. She'd come here to fix up the house.

She'd fix it.

She'd fix it all.

Make it all disappear. And then she'd continue with her life as if none of this had ever existed and her mother hadn't turned her into a lying, cheating failure whose dreams had been smashed, whose father had left her, whose baby sister had died when the doctors had said—had *promised*—they'd save her.

Leah slammed the wrench down on the piano keys. Again. And again.

Fix it, and then she'd be fine. Everything would be fine. She hit the piano over and over, shattering the keys and chipping the wood, and then she took a step back and stared at the damage she'd caused.

CHAPTER TWENTY-FIVE

It's night.

I was watching the sunset at the top of the lighthouse with Sylvie and Rabbit. And now I'm alone. Still in the lighthouse.

"Sylvie?" I call. "Rabbit?"

I'm afraid of what might answer.

Unlike when I faded before—in Mom's living room and at the Babylon train station—I cannot deny what happened. There's no ambiguity this time. Both the sun and my friends are gone, and I don't know if I've lost hours or days or weeks.

I have to find them.

I have to leave, to live.

I have to . . .

I don't know what, but I know I can't stay here. My heart is beating so hard that I can hear it, pounding like waves on the sand. Spinning, I spot the stairwell. It's a gaping maw of darkness, but it is, of course, the only way down.

The lighthouse strobe flashes in my eyes, and I flinch, both at the light and the dark. It prods me forward. Taking a deep breath, I touch the wall lightly and am relieved that it's solid beneath my fingertips. However real this place is, it also looms just as large in people's imaginations.

The first few steps are visible, lit by the moon, the stars, and the lighthouse beacon. But after that, the stairwell is drowned in shadows. I feel my way down. At the landing—the control room, I remember—I inch along the wall to the spiral staircase and continue my descent. I didn't count my steps on the way up, but I know there are a lot. Just need to be patient. And careful. And calm. How, though, can I be calm when any second everything could disappear again? I'm the opposite of calm. I'm so tense that my skin feels electrified.

Every so often, a sliver of moonlight spills in through one of the recessed windows. It casts the steps in various shades of gray, and I'm reassured that all the shadows seem to be motionless. I have no plan for what to do if a wolf or other hostile shadow appears in the stairwell. There's nowhere to run. I'm trying hard not to think about why I'm alone, presumably hours later, with no memory of any time passing.

I faded. Again. I can't stop it, control it, or predict it. *And next time, I might not come back.*

I push that thought away.

Keep walking down.

Keep watching the shadows. Glancing behind myself, I note that it's just as dark where I came from as where I'm going.

I begin to wonder if I'm anywhere.

Have I faded already?

Is this the darkness that follows life?

I think of Mother and the darkness of her casket. This doesn't smell the same. It smells of mildew and stone and rust. It smells of salt and sea. It smells of bodies that passed this way so long ago that their breath has become a part of the lighthouse.

When at last my foot touches the floor, I feel as though I've passed through a kind of liminal space that doesn't exist in any world, real or imagined. I feel for the door in front of me but can't find it.

Instead, I walk straight through it into the night.

I hear the kiss of the waves on the shore far below and know there are cliffs nearby, dropping into the ocean. There's a highway somewhere behind me, and I see the stars in the dusty sky above. They are beautiful—and I've never felt more ephemeral.

◆ ◆ ◆

Hurrying through the lighthouse parking lot, I spot them: Sylvie and Rabbit. She's in a shimmering car—another convertible, top down—with her skirt hiked up to her thigh and the wires of the steering column spilling onto her lap. Rabbit faces the highway, his back to me. Neither senses my approach.

I consider waiting there, ghostlike, but as always, the questions are pressing so hard against my lips that I cannot stay silent. "Can you see me?"

Sylvie swears as she jumps, jostles the wires, and drops her wire cutter.

Rabbit embraces me. "You came back!"

He wraps his arms around me, and it feels like being enfolded in a cocoon. He smells like cinnamon—warm cinnamon sprinkled on top of hot chocolate. He releases me, and I feel more chilled than the air warrants. His skin is dark again, and his hair is buzzed short. He has the cheekbones of a model, as well as the lips, which are currently in a frown. I don't remember which name went with this face, but it doesn't matter. He's Rabbit. He's here, he's real, and with his eyes on me, I feel real. "You scared us," he says.

"Not me," Sylvie says.

"You scared *me*," Rabbit amends. "I thought I lost you."

"I was right there." I don't remember anything after the beginning of the sunset. Same as before—the hours are simply lost. I shiver, and he plucks a leather jacket from the back seat of the car and drapes it over my shoulders. The weight of it surprises me, as does the warmth. "Why are we stealing another car?"

"Yours had zero style," Sylvie says with a sniff.

Both of them seem okay. Sylvie is the same as ever. I may as well have strolled down to the post office for all she seems to care. "What happened to me?" I ask. "From your point of view, what was it like? What did you see?"

"You were there, and then you weren't," Rabbit says. He's still staring at me as if he's afraid I'll disappear again should he blink. Honestly, I'm afraid of that too. I wish he'd wrap his arms around me again. I feel as if I can't disappear when he's touching me.

He was right next to me when I disappeared in the lighthouse, though. So was Sylvie. She glances up at me. "Sorry you missed the sunset."

"I won't miss another," I promise.

"Don't lie," she says.

The two words hit like two punches.

Sylvie returns to her wires, stripping the brown ones and then tucking her wire cutter back into its holster. "Here we go," she says and then touches the live wires together. The car rumbles to life. "Hop in."

I want to rage, scream at the universe that this isn't fair and I don't deserve to fade away—but instead, I just climb into the passenger seat as if I'm fine.

Rabbit slides into the back seat. "Where are we going?" he asks politely.

There's no place we can go where I'll be safe, no place with the answers I need. All I can do is keep existing until I don't anymore. Like Sylvie. Like Rabbit.

"Nowhere," Sylvie says. "Everywhere."

She steps on the gas.

Sylvie doesn't take us to a pool party this time. No mansion. No summer house. Just a bonfire and a lot of tipsy people with a whole mess of haze around them. Most of the women are in bikinis, and most of the men are shirtless. No one looks as if they're over thirty, and a few look far too young to be here. Sylvie doesn't pay attention to any of them. She minces across the sand and straight through the bonfire.

Rabbit flinches. On the other side of the flames, Sylvie scoops up three bottles in one hand and then saunters back directly through the bonfire again. "I wish she wouldn't do that," he complains.

Sylvie grins. "You should always do whatever gives you the most joy. Only way to live." She hands each of us a bottle.

He scowls at her, then at the bottle. "Your life isn't just about yourself; it's about what you can do for others."

Sylvie clinks the top of her bottle to the neck of mine. "Those 'others' can't even see us, so why do they matter?"

I think of Mother. I think of Leah. They matter to me. But it isn't enough to keep me from fading away. Three strikes already. Soon, I'll be out.

"They need us," Rabbit says.

What do we need?

That's the question I can't answer.

He crosses the sand to a girl seated on a driftwood log beside a shirtless, very drunk guy. She can't be one of his liars this far from Queens, but he clearly considers her a damsel in distress. "He can't help being the way he is," I tell Sylvie. "He's the boyfriend—the one that will always protect them, listen to them. The one who always says yes, who cares more about them than himself."

"Ugh," Sylvie says. "Boring."

"It's noble," I correct.

"Looks painful." She shudders.

I take a sip from the bottle as I watch Rabbit. It tastes like liquid bubble gum, carbonated. I wrinkle my nose and wonder if this is the last thing I'll ever taste. "Was it like that for you? With all your liars? You said you were created by multiple liars, like Rabbit. Did you change like he does?" I wonder if I've changed. *Yes. Mother wanted me to change.* But with me, it was more gradual. She wanted me to grow and live, the way baby Hannah never could.

Sylvie doesn't answer. Instead, she says, "I didn't think you'd come back."

I don't know what to say.

I watch as the other guy stalks away, leaving Rabbit with the girl. Sylvie grabs another wine cooler. The girl on the log stands and sways, and Rabbit jumps to his feet to steady her. He doesn't quite touch her. His eyes meet mine through the bonfire, and he smiles at me. To Sylvie, I say, "I don't think he has the answers we were hoping for."

"*You* were hoping for," she corrects. "I'm fine as I am."

She's not. And neither am I.

I am a light bulb, sputtering before it goes dark forever.

"Who did you lose?" I ask. "Before me."

She hesitates, and I think for a moment that she's going to dodge the question like she did before, but then she answers, "Her name was Lily, and she and I were inseparable. Went to every party together, every night. Like Bonnie and Clyde, if they crashed parties instead of robbed banks. Anyway, inseparable. Until we weren't. End of story. That's that."

I'm quiet for a moment, watching the flames spark and writhe. The partygoers are dancing in the sand to tinny music from one of their phones, shaking their bodies, and holding their beers and wine coolers in the air. "What happened to her?"

"One night, she said her liar had quit lying, and she announced that she was done: no more vapid and pointless parties. Then she . . ." She trails off and chugs another gulp of the wine cooler.

"She left you," I finish. *Like I did.*

Sylvie stares out at the black water, formed of moving shadows. "She vanished, like you, but she didn't reappear. One week after she began to change her life, we were having breakfast together and—" Her voice has begun to shake. She tries to flash me a smile. "Maybe it was just a bad scrambled egg."

"She stopped partying, and she vanished?"

"I haven't missed a night since then," Sylvie says. "Always a party somewhere. Always a summer home to crash. A pool to swim in. A spread to filch food from." She wiggles the half-drunk bottle in the air. "Free drinks."

She's trying to save me, in her own way.

Rabbit begins to saunter back to us, and then pain wipes the beautiful smile from his face. He's beginning to shift again, in the grip of yet another liar.

And suddenly, I understand.

We're shaped by our liars. Rabbit is proof of that. Sylvie's friend didn't vanish because she stopped partying; she vanished because her liar quit lying. Specifically, one week after.

A lie can't outlast her liar.

This is the answer I've been looking for—the answer to what will happen to me and also when. It hits me all at once:

I know what I need to do.

My voice shakes. "I need to leave."

My disappearance in the lighthouse was a warning, possibly my final one, my third strike, but at least I've been given a warning. Or a gift. I can't waste it. I have to do what Sylvie's friend could not.

I have to save myself.

How many days do I have? Or is it hours now? I examine my hand. It looks blurred. Can I see the fire through my flesh? The need to act *now* feels urgent and terrifying, like fingers wrapped around my throat. "I need to go home."

"I thought you don't have a home anymore," Sylvie says.

But I could. If I tried.

I have to try.

"Yeah, but I have a sister. She might *be* my answer."

With tears blurring my eyes, I face her. "I'm sorry. I . . ." I don't know what to say. How do I leave the only two people in the world who have ever been able to see and hear me? But if I don't, then what happened in the lighthouse, what happened to Sylvie's friend Lily . . . I want to thank them, to hug them, to explain, to stay, but I have to leave them. "I need a new liar. Now. Before it's too late. And I think I know who it has to be."

Sylvie's eyes widen. She understands. "Take the car."

◆ ◆ ◆

As it turns out, I am a terrible driver, but it doesn't matter much since I sail through everything I hit. Other cars, fine. Streetlamps, fine. A few mailboxes.

A lot of mailboxes.

It's the headlights. They pierce my eyes, and I start to empathize with moths. So bright, I can't look away. If it were daylight, it wouldn't be so bad, but faced with all the headlights blazing out of the darkness, I keep drifting more and more to the right, toward the multitude of mailboxes. Luckily, there's no reason for anyone to lie about them, and my car zips through them unscathed.

After about a half hour, I start to get the hang of it. A good thing because the speed of traffic is starting to increase, and it's harder to judge which cars are real and which can crunch mine like a trash compactor. Clutching the steering wheel, I stay in the right lane, trying not to flinch every time another car or truck passes me.

I can do this. Mother drove all her life without a second thought. Even Leah learned to drive, despite Mother's stories—accidents that had happened to her or to people she knew. Twenty-car pileups. Run-ins with electrical poles. A landscape truck that landed on top of her car or her parent's car or the neighbor's car or her fifth-grade teacher's car.

Occasionally she lifted her stories directly from movies, and Leah would call her out. Mother would laugh and say she was merely making the story more personal. It had more impact that way. Leah worked extra hard on her parallel parking to avoid having to take the driver's test twice and listen to any more of Mother's stories. I may never have gotten practice behind the wheel, but I listened to them all. Unfortunately, remembering them was not helping me relax.

It's a two-and-a-half-hour drive to Leah's apartment, which means I have plenty of time to think. I wish I didn't. It would be easier if I could just party like Sylvie and not think about the future or the past, but I can't. I'm not like her.

She still has her liar, spreading the story of the Girl He Once Dated, and Rabbit has his multiple liars, keeping him alive as the Protective Boyfriend. Me, I have no one. The only solution is to cultivate a new liar, one who already knows about me. Leah.

There is a clear problem: how to convince her to lie about me. I can't communicate with her. Can't leave her a note. Can't affect her world. I tried to catch Leah's attention when we were children and failed spectacularly. I don't know what makes me think I'll fare better now.

I need her more.

I didn't *need* her then. I *wanted* her to acknowledge me. I wanted a real sister, a connection, a family relationship. I wanted to be heard and seen. I wanted to tell her that I hear her and see her. She didn't have to have a lonely childhood. She could have had me.

I like to think that, on some level, Mother knew I was there. Yes, she told Dad that I was a lie. She knew she was manufacturing my life when she talked to neighbors and friends. But sometimes, when we were alone, it was different. I remember sitting beside her with my hand over hers, pretending to hold it. She'd talk about everything we would have done together and all the memories we would have made. Once in a while, she'd even act as if she heard my side of the conversation, and I'd have to rush through words to make them fit in the time she allotted:

"We went to Niagara Falls once. He refused a raincoat. Said a little water wouldn't hurt him. You wouldn't believe how drenched he was." She laughs out loud. "It was as if he'd stood under a showerhead for an hour. He was soaked to the bone."

I wonder what that felt like. "Sounds unpleasant."

"We meant to see other waterfalls. Like in Peru or Costa Rica. Travel the world to see every magnificent waterfall. And garden. He promised me flowers from all over the world. I always wanted to see the tulips in Holland."

"You could still travel," I say.

"I know I could still travel," she'd say, and I felt that glorious little shiver that she anticipated my words, or I anticipated hers. "But not on my own."

"I'd be with you."

"You'd be there, Hannah."

I would, I thought.

I would have, I think now.

Leah needs me, and I need her.

If this works, I'm not leaving Leah. Not ever again.

CHAPTER
TWENTY-SIX

A fresh start. That's what Leah thought as she dropped the final box on the floor.

Finally, at twenty-six, she had her own apartment, even if it was up a dingy stairwell and had patchy heating and a steady drip from the kitchen faucet (which doubled as a bathroom sink). At last, she'd jettisoned all her various roommates. Not that she didn't like them. She'd had some great ones that she knew she'd stay friends with, like Mindi and Jersey, plus the usual few she hoped never to see again. But this. *This* was her own space.

Hands on her hips, Leah surveyed her new domain. She'd have to put up a screen if she didn't want it to feel like she was sleeping in the kitchen. She'd need a couch. A secondhand one would be fine. If it was short enough, she could squeeze a little table between it and the kitchen counter, and it could serve as both a dining table and a desk.

She could hang her art on the walls, once she started painting again. *I will start again.* Now that she had her own place, she'd be able to breathe and think and not feel as though her every brushstroke was being observed and critiqued. With roommates, everyone was in each other's business all the time, and with even the least judgmental person, it felt like they were breathing down her neck. *It'll be different now.*

Tomorrow, she'd hunt down an art store. Buy some supplies . . .

Her phone rang.

She pulled it from her pocket and stared at the screen. Mom. Her finger hovered. If she didn't answer, Mom would keep calling, leaving more and more frantic voice mails about how she was certain she was dead and why did she insist on worrying her poor mother so terribly?

Bracing herself, Leah answered, "Hi, Mom."

"Leah! You're there! Thank God. I was watching the news, and I thought I saw your face flash up on the screen."

"Yes, that was me. I've been kidnapped and murdered. I'm famous now, and they'll be featuring me on all the true-crime podcasts." She tried for a breezy tone and failed.

"Don't even joke about that."

"What do you want, Mom?"

In a cheerful voice, as if they had normal conversations all the time instead of the painfully stilted, once-a-month obligatory calls, Mom said, "I wanted to see how you're settling into your new place!"

For a second, Leah forgot how to breathe. She hadn't told her mom she was moving. In fact, she'd instructed her roommates, her friends, and her coworkers *not* to tell her mom. If they didn't feel they could lie, then they were not to answer her calls, respond to her emails, or reply to her texts. Under no circumstances were they ever to give her mother this address.

This was supposed to be her place—a safe space, a calm place, without all her mother's complications.

"Leah?"

"Yeah. Um. Everything's fine. Gotta go. Got a million things to do." She knew she shouldn't ask. Her mother *wanted* her to ask, and Leah didn't want to give her the satisfaction, but she had to know. "How did you find out?"

Mom laughed. "Oh, that! I called your work."

"You . . . what?" Leah felt light headed. She sank to the bare floor of her new apartment. That was so beyond the bounds of okay. "What did you say?" Also, who did she talk to? The front desk? HR? God forbid anyone in management . . .

"Don't worry," Mom said. "I didn't tell them who I was."

Louder, Leah asked, *"What did you say?"*

"Calm down," Mom said. "I just had to make sure my girl was all right. I'd stopped by your apartment to bring you some cookies I'd baked—"

"You don't bake." What was she doing stopping by the apartment? Leah had told her again and again that she couldn't just drop by. She had to call first. Her roommates didn't deserve to be trapped by her mother and her endless stories. Mom wouldn't pick up on any of their hints that it was time to leave. She had never respected anyone else's life as having value. It was only about her own needs and whims.

"Imagine my surprise when I saw your room was empty! No sheets on your bed! No clothes in your closet! All your hair gels gone from the bathroom cabinet."

Leah closed her eyes. She could picture her mom barging in, flinging open the door to her former bedroom, and one of her poor roommates trying to stop her. It must have been Mindi; Jersey knew Mom well enough not to answer the door. Ugh, she even searched the medicine cabinet! "You shouldn't have done that, Mom."

"I was concerned! And when that girl wouldn't tell me where you'd gone, I told her how important it was with your health history."

Crap. "I don't have any health history."

"You could! For all she knew."

Leah gritted her teeth and then took a deep breath. "What did you tell my work?"

"Well, the conversation with what's-her-name, the girl who always looks like she's seeing cartoon stars circling over her head—"

"Mindi," Leah said.

"Her," Mom said. "The conversation with her gave me an idea, so I told your work that I was calling from your doctor's office and that I needed your current address."

Leah exhaled. That didn't sound so bad. "You didn't claim I had some terrible illness?" She wondered what sort of story she'd have to unravel. At the very least, she owed Mindi an apology. Maybe even a drink. Or several.

"Annoyingly, the man wouldn't give it to me," Mom said. "I asked to speak with his manager, but he said it was company policy to not give personal information about any employee out without the employee's explicit permission."

Maybe Leah should also buy a drink for whichever HR person wrote that policy. "Mom, I don't want you calling my work ever again." It wasn't her dream job, but it was fine. Her company did PR for events, and while her job was mostly tweaking PowerPoints and shuffling columns in Excel, at least some of their clients were art galleries. Plus, her coworkers were all fine. Not a single one of them ever microwaved fish for lunch or hit "Reply All" unnecessarily. She was lucky to work there, as she told herself repeatedly. "Especially don't call them and pretend to be someone you're not. You could get me in trouble, and I could lose my job, which means I'd lose my salary; then I really would be out on the street, probably murdered, or I'd develop a terrible illness that I can't treat because I no longer have health insurance."

"A mother should know where her daughter lives."

"I'm house-sitting for a friend in the Hamptons," Leah lied.

"Oh, how lovely! But the commute—"

Leah hated herself for every word, but it was the lesser evil. Besides, lying to Mom didn't feel the same as lying to other people. It felt like survival. At the very least, it bought her some time before her mother remembered how much she enjoyed injecting herself into Leah's life uninvited. "Worth it for the view."

"Must be," Mom said. "But you know you could take some time off. Turn this into a mini vacation. Or use the time to work on your art. Have you been painting?"

She was already lying. One more was easy. "Yes."

"You know, I've always believed you had talent," Mom said.

Leah gripped the phone so hard she thought it would shatter in her hand.

"Such a shame you didn't pursue it."

◆ ◆ ◆

Leah abandoned the idea of unpacking after the phone call. Instead, she texted Jersey and Mindi and met them at their favorite bar, a place called Rissi's, which served excellent apple martinis. She was on her second when she hit upon an idea. Why did she have to talk about her mother? She'd wasted so much of her life worrying about what Mom would say or do. *When does it get to be my turn?*

She swiveled on the barstool. "I'm going to do it."

"Do what?" Jersey asked.

"Good for you." Mindi toasted her and downed a gulp of her martini. "You know, that guy has been watching you all night."

Leah rolled her eyes. "Not a guy. I'm talking about living my own life without worrying about what anyone else says, does, or thinks of me, especially my mom." She was not going to let the past define her anymore. Beginning today, she was going to be a new Leah. She thought Jersey, whose hair was blue this week, would understand that.

"I'm talking about the one with the tattoos and the piercings," Mindi said. "Tasteful tattoos. Can't see any misspellings." She was craning her neck to look behind Leah.

Leah refused to turn. She wasn't here to pick up guys. She was here to put her mother behind her. "I'm going to talk to one of the gallery owners. See if they'll hang one of my pieces. When I finish one that I like enough."

"You've been painting again?" Jersey said. "That's great!"

"I'm going to start," Leah said. "It's a studio apartment, right? So I'll use it as a studio."

"You know that's actually just code for 'smaller than a closet,'" Mindi said. "And whoa, he's coming over here. Stop rolling your eyes at me, Leah."

Leah took a fortifying sip of her martini and turned to face the tattooed guy. She wasn't in the mood—but okay, he was cute. The guy smiled. He had nice eyes. Kind eyes. With a sheepish smile, he said, "I've been trying to think of a line, but everything sounded cheesy." He had a nice voice, smooth and deep; it sounded the way whiskey tasted. "I figured I'd better just say hi before the night ended, and I missed my chance. So . . . hi."

"Hi." *As lines went, that wasn't terrible.* Leah took another sip of her martini. "So, did you have a plan for what we'd talk about after 'hi'?"

"I hadn't gotten that far." He considered it for a moment. "Movies? Books? Sports? Art? Food? How about, Do you butter your toast before you put it in the toaster or after?"

"After, clearly. I'm not a monster." Leah felt a smile tugging at her lips. "When you eat an Oreo, do you bite into it or eat the top cookie first, then the filling?"

"Depends. Is there milk?"

"Not enough for the whole sleeve of Oreos."

"Then I dip as many as I can and bite them," he said immediately, "and I twist apart the rest and eat them cookie first and filling last."

Mindi leaned over. "Correct answer. You may sit." She vacated her barstool and gestured for the guy to take it. "Got to powder my nose. Come on, Jersey." She tugged their friend's arm.

"But what if she—" Jersey began.

Mindi hauled her toward the ladies' room while the tattooed guy sat. Leah swiveled to face him, took another sip, and discovered she'd reached the bottom of her glass. He offered, "Can I buy you another one?"

"Sure," she said.

He signaled the bartender.

"You said we could talk about art," Leah said. "Did you mean that?"

He smiled at her, and she liked how genuine he looked. He had one crooked tooth, one of his canines, and even that was cute. "Absolutely."

"Seriously?"

"Seriously. I'm just glad you didn't pick sports. Who do you like better: Manet or Monet? While you ponder, I'm going to Google them so I know the difference."

She laughed.

"My name's Leah."

"I'm Jamie."

◆ ◆ ◆

This is a colossal mistake. Leah and Jamie were parked outside the restaurant. She never should have agreed to introduce Jamie to her mother. But after eight months of dating, things were getting serious. Plus, she'd already met his family. Lovely people who didn't talk much. His mother was a doctor who didn't seem to mind that Jamie wasn't, and his father taught economics at a local community college. Lovely, nice, emotionally stable, normal people, as far as she could tell.

She'd given her mother strict instructions to be on her best behavior. Mom seemed shocked, but then she always seemed shocked when someone implied her behavior was anything less than exemplary. Leah had picked a restaurant with zero memories attached—a new Italian restaurant in Hempstead, the town next to Garden City—on the theory that Mom wouldn't have a single story to tell about it. Also, lower odds that her mother would spot anyone she knew. Aside from warning Jamie, which she'd done, many times, there was little else she could do. Except flee.

"We can still ditch," Leah said. "I can call and tell her one of us is sick. Mild cold but we don't want to pass it on to her. Or we were in a fender bender. No one hurt, but we won't be able to do dinner tonight."

Jamie reached over and squeezed her hand. "I swear I won't embarrass you."

"Definitely not you I'm worried about."

"But I might lick all the butter."

"Yeah, that wouldn't be the worst-case scenario," Leah said. "She's . . . a lot."

"You've warned me," Jamie said. "It's going to be fine."

It's not going to be fine.

As soon as she stepped through the door, the scent of garlic smacked her in the face. The lights were dim, and fake candles were on each table beside fake pink roses. Jazz music pumped through the restaurant, beneath the overlapping conversations. It was, she was happy to see, not crowded. Only half the tables were full. Fewer people to overhear if this all went downhill.

Mom was already seated. She waved enthusiastically, and every muscle in Leah's body tensed. She wanted to run like a zebra spotted by a lioness. Bob and weave through the traffic so that Mom couldn't catch her.

The hostess said, "Welcome to Ruvo. Do you have a reservation?"

Still frozen, Leah didn't answer.

Jamie stepped in and, pointing to the waving woman, said to the hostess, "I think that's us."

Leah took a deep breath. *You can do this.* It had been, after all, her idea. Her very terrible idea that she regretted down to the soles of her shoes.

"If you really want to leave," Jamie whispered in her ear, "I can fake a heart attack."

She let out a hiccup-like laugh. She hadn't expected to laugh at all tonight. She would feel lucky if she survived the evening with her relationship intact. He had no concept of Mom's capacity for ruining her life. "I love you," she whispered back.

"I love you too," he said. "Relax. It'll be fine."

Leah snorted but led the way, threading between tables until they reached her mother. Mom popped out of her chair.

"My sweet Leah." She wrapped her arms around Leah and squeezed.

Surprised by the hug, Leah froze again. She managed to force her lips into a smile as she lightly patted her mom's back. "Hi, Mom." They hadn't hugged in years. Usually, Leah sidestepped the rare attempt of an embrace with ease. It worried her that she hadn't predicted this one.

Mom released her. "You must be Jamie." She ambushed him with a hug, too, but Leah noted that he didn't freeze.

"I've already ordered us appetizers."

"Mom . . ." She hadn't budgeted for appetizers. Also, she didn't want this dinner to be a second longer than it had to be, but she bit back the words. All she wanted was to survive the meal, and then she could tell everyone who asked that, yes, of course, her mother had met her boyfriend. It was profoundly irritating how many people cared. Virtually every one of their friends, as well as Jamie's parents, had asked about it. Apparently, most people considered this a relationship rite of passage.

Simpler to get this over with than try to explain her mother.

Plus, there was always the chance that her mother had changed.

Ha.

Both of them were seated opposite Mom in the center of the restaurant. Leah was grateful they weren't stuck in a corner without an easy escape. She spent an enjoyable few seconds imagining herself clambering over the other tables and bursting through the window like an action-movie hero.

"So, Jamie, tell me about yourself?" Mom asked.

As Jamie talked, Leah tried to relax. It was only one dinner. Not even Mom had the ability to torpedo her and Jamie's relationship over a single meal. Worst she could do was embarrass herself and confirm what Leah had already told Jamie—about her stories, about her need to craft the perfect life, about her narcissism.

She tuned back in when the waiter stopped at their table for their drink order. Jamie ordered a Coke, while Mom ordered a merlot. Leah got a ginger ale. "Aw, upset tummy?" Mom asked her. When Leah was a kid, Mom would feed her ginger ale and crackers any time she had an upset stomach. Tonight, it seemed the safest option.

"I'm fine," Leah said.

After clearing the unused wineglasses, the waiter began to take away the empty fourth table setting. As he scooped the utensils onto the plate, Mom instructed, "Leave that."

"You're expecting a fourth?" the waiter asked.

Leah felt her face flush bright red. She refused to look at Jamie. Instead, she kept her gaze fixed firmly on the waiter. "We're not," she said.

Mom smiled pleasantly. "We might be."

"Mom . . ."

"Leah?"

She felt Jamie's eyes flicker back and forth between them. The last thing she wanted was to explain why Mom always insisted on an extra place setting. "We probably won't use it," Leah said to the waiter, "but if you could leave it . . ."

"Of course," he said and departed with the excess wineglasses.

Leah began to wish she'd ordered wine. At least a bottle.

Jamie was smiling an I-don't-know-what's-going-on-so-I'll-just-be-polite kind of smile, and Leah felt sweat beading on her skin. She squeezed her hands in her lap so hard that her nails made crescent indents in her palms.

Mom lifted her menu. "You know, they have cannoli for dessert here."

"I've never had a cannoli," Jamie said gamely.

"Well, then we have to try one," Mom said.

"With an appetizer and an entrée, we'll be too full," Leah tried.

"Nonsense," Mom said. "Everyone knows that dessert goes into a different compartment." She smiled at Jamie over the rim of her menu and looked so pleasantly normal that Leah wanted to scream. She didn't know which was worse: Mom acting like herself and driving Jamie away, or Mom acting like a normal person and making Leah seem overly dramatic. "I once had the best cannoli in Florence, Italy . . ." And Mom was off and running with amusing anecdotes about a trip that may or may not have taken place before Leah was born. According to her, she'd danced in a fountain and posed with every naked statue she could find until a street artist agreed to paint her surrounded by Renaissance sculptures.

"Is that where Leah gets her love of art?" Jamie asked.

"She certainly didn't get it from her father," Mom said. "All artistic talent comes from my side of the family. And musical as well. Did Leah tell you that I was almost a concert pianist? Leah showed promise, too, if she'd stuck with it. She has a habit of not sticking with things."

Leah gritted her teeth. Her hands were clenched beneath the tablecloth. She would *not* let this dissolve into another screaming match with Mom. Not in front of Jamie.

"Like her painting," Mom continued. "She showed so much promise."

"Leah still paints," Jamie said. "All the time."

"Oh, that's wonderful to hear!" Mom beamed at her, and so did Jamie. Mom continued, "Did you know that Leah almost went to art school? If only her father had contributed to her college fund as he'd promised—"

Leah shot to her feet.

Both of them looked at her expectantly.

"I . . . have to go to the ladies' room," Leah said.

And bolted.

In the bathroom, she splashed water on her face, glad she hadn't gone for the cat-eye makeup that Mom hated—the way she would have when she was sixteen. She held on to the sides of the sink and tried to steady her breathing.

So far, she was the only one acting erratically. Mom hadn't done anything wrong, at least on the surface. Yes, leaving the fourth place setting was a strange quirk, but nothing that couldn't be laughed off or explained away. Leah could claim that Mom liked to have access to an extra fork in case she dropped one, if Jamie asked later. He probably wouldn't even ask. It was only a blip. It just loomed large in Leah's mind because she knew what was behind it. Certainly, he'd missed all the passive-aggressive jabs. He didn't have the context to know what Mom was truly saying.

She could do this. She could get through this. One dinner, and then it was done.

Mother can't ruin this. Not unless I let her. Whether her relationship thrived or failed was in her own hands.

"Stop expecting the worst," she ordered her reflection.

Thankfully, her reflection didn't answer.

After drying her face, she made her way back to the table. She could see Jamie laughing at something her mother said, and it occurred to her that she shouldn't have left them alone. It had only been a few minutes. What harm could her mother have done?

As she sat down, Jamie said, "I didn't know you have a sister."

Leah still hadn't finished a single painting. It had been a full year since she and Jamie had started dating, and she'd barely even sketched anything. Problem was she'd told Jamie that she had. Scads of pictures. Just none ready to show him yet. And he'd believed in her—said she could show him whenever she was ready; he respected her creativity, loved that she was an artist, blah, blah, blah. She didn't know why the lie had come out of her mouth—she'd been scrupulous about never lying to him—but when it came to her art . . . And once the lie was out there, she didn't know how to walk it back. She felt as if she'd coated herself in filth and couldn't shower it away.

She'd start sometimes. Mix paint and dip her brush in. But then, she couldn't think of what to paint. Everything she pictured seemed so prosaic.

On Sunday, the day after Jamie had asked if they could move in together, Leah sat at her table desk, squeezed between the kitchen counter and the secondhand couch, and waited for a bolt of inspiration.

All I need is one painting.

Just one.

She could hang it over the couch, say it was her favorite, and that would be that. It wouldn't even be a lie—it would have to be her favorite since it was the only one—and then they could start the next phase of their relationship, whatever that was going to be. But none of it could happen until she painted at least one damn painting that she didn't hate. She wouldn't say yes to moving in together while she was lying to him.

She stared at the canvas with her brush poised. She'd have settled for a spark of inspiration. Just a trickle.

Maybe a landscape. Or a portrait. Or a play of light on leaves. Every image she conjured was of another work she'd seen. She wanted just one speck of originality. Something that was only hers.

Her phone rang.

She dunked her paintbrush into the bowl of water and answered. "Hey, Jersey."

"Hey," Jersey said. "Any news for me?"

Leah stared at the canvas, willing it to fill with color and shapes. "What news would I have?"

"Ugh, please," Jersey said. "Did he propose?"

Oh. That news. "He did not."

"But he had that rom-com look in his eyes!" Jersey said.

"He didn't propose." She'd actually breathed a sigh of relief when he only brought up moving in together. Every time she thought about marriage, she thought of coming home to see her father loading up his car, promising he'd have a place for her. At one point, her parents had thought they'd be forever, too, a perfect family with two kids and a garage. "He did ask if we could move in together."

"Woo-hoo! That's awesome! And you said yes? Or wait, you didn't because he has horrible hygiene habits that you haven't told me about?"

"His hygiene is fine," Leah said. "I said I'd think about it."

"Ahh, okay, cool, I get it." She paused. "No, I don't get it. You love this guy. I thought you were ready for the next step?"

"I am," Leah said. "Almost. There's this thing . . . It's silly. There's this small, unimportant thing that I've been lying to him about, and I just don't want to start our lives together with a lie between us." It didn't feel small. It felt like an elephant she'd allowed into the room with no plan for how to get it out.

Jersey sighed heavily. "Listen, Leah, I know how lying makes you feel, given everything with your mom, but just come clean! You can do it. You aren't her! It'll be okay. He'll understand. Come on, Leah, he loves you, and you love him."

"Yeah, but . . ." She could do that. Just confess that she'd been lying this whole time, that her closets weren't filled with finished canvases, and that, on days she hadn't cleaned, the apartment wasn't ankle deep in sketches. She always neatened up the apartment before he came, she'd said once, otherwise he would have seen them, and she wasn't ready for him to see her drafts. He'd said he understood. Jamie always understood. Sometimes that was infuriating. She occasionally wished he'd call her on the lie, tell her to produce all this artwork, and then everything would be out in the open, and he could either hate her for the perpetual lie or not. "I don't want us to be like my parents."

"You and Jamie are *nothing* like your parents," Jersey said.

Nice of her to say, but . . .

"You have them as a cautionary tale in front of you. You won't be like them. Leah . . . the only one who can screw this up is *you*," she said gently.

"Exactly why I have to do this," Leah said. "I have to make the lie into a truth."

"Leah!" Jersey said. "You can't have a relationship without a few lies. And it doesn't mean you're like your mother. What if someday you put on a dress that makes you look like shit, and you ask him what he thinks? You really want him to tell the truth?"

Leah laughed, even though she didn't feel like laughing. She couldn't explain why this was so important to her. It was just . . . She burst out, "What if my mother screwed me up for all relationships forever?"

That was it. That was the fear.

What if she was, by either nurture or nature, destined for unhappiness?

Her primary example of married life had been a complete and utter disaster. What if she turned out just like her mom? What if Jamie left her because of that? Or worse, what if he wasn't strong enough to leave her? She could destroy both their lives.

"You can't let your past sabotage your future," Jersey said. "Pretty sure I read that in a fortune cookie. If not, it should be in one. Hey, that's my new career: fortune cookie writer. But seriously, Leah, you deserve to be happy."

"Okay, okay." She sighed. "Thanks, Jersey."

"Call me if you need me."

She returned to staring at the canvas. Where was her spark? What did she want to paint? And why did it matter so much if she painted or not? Jamie loved her. They were good together. Why wouldn't she want to continue that? Except that she didn't believe it would last, especially if they began with a lie.

It's her fault.

Maybe what she needed wasn't to paint some perfect picture. What she needed was reassurance that she and Jamie wouldn't be the same as Mom and Dad. There was one person who could provide that reassurance, if she chose to.

Studying her phone, Leah imagined saying everything she'd wanted to say to her mother: about how screwed up her childhood had been, about how Mom's lies had cost her any kind of relationship with Dad, about how Leah feared she was doomed to make the same mistakes. Leah was finally in a healthy relationship, and she was terrified she'd blow it up. She was afraid she'd turn out like Mom, who was unable to let go of lies to save her relationship or protect her living daughter. But if she could get some kind of closure from Mom . . . even half an apology. An acknowledgment that mistakes were made. Anything. She needed that. Just to hear Mom's voice tell a smidgen of truth. And then she'd be free.

Leah dialed.

This was, she realized, the first time in years that she'd *wanted* to call her mother. Perhaps this was a sign that she was ready for things between her and Mom to finally change.

As it rang, she formed the words in her mind. She'd tell her about Jamie and her nonexistent art and the legacy of lies that Leah didn't want and wasn't going to accept. If she said it out loud to the woman who taught her to lie, then maybe it would become true. And then she could move forward and *be* the person she always said she'd become.

The phone rang again and again.

No one answered.

It wasn't until the next day that the call came. Her mother had died, alone in her home, undiscovered for twenty-six hours.

CHAPTER TWENTY-SEVEN

As I climb the steps, I see that Leah's apartment is overflowing in a miasma of soupy haze. It waterfalls down the narrow stairway that leads to her apartment. Once I slide through the door, I'm enveloped in it. I wait for the haze to dissipate enough for me to see the outline of furniture.

I listen.

I'm not alone. Leah? "Are you here?"

I know she won't hear me, but it feels strange not to try. It's late. Very late. I lost hours during sunset, another to the party, and several more to the drive. She could be asleep. But then I hear her. She's muttering to herself, and I hear her bare feet shuffling on the fake-wood floor as she pads back and forth. A creak—the kitchen cabinet? A clink of glasses. I hear water gush from the faucet. She swallows.

"Just call," she is saying. "You have to do it."

A phone beep, then a succession of beeps—it begins to ring. She pads back and forth again, and then a single beep as she disconnects the call.

"You know you have to do it. For him. For you."

She mutters that a few more times.

What the hell happened? I wasn't gone for that long. The haze was nothing like this. Yes, there were the sketches and canvases, but this is beyond anything I ever saw in Mother's house, even when she was spinning her tallest tales. "Leah, are you okay?"

She dials again, and this time she lets it ring. "Jamie?"

There's a pause.

"Sorry. Yeah, I know it's late . . . yeah . . . yeah . . . Can you come over? I need . . . I need to talk to you. I don't want to wait until morning, if that's . . . Okay. See you soon."

She says bye and hangs up, and I wonder if all the haze and mess have anything to do with Jamie or if there is something more. I think of how I left her in the bar, on the lap of a stranger. She paces again, and I move around the apartment to see if there's an area that's clear of fog.

By the window, I'm able to see more. Leah is by the foot of her bed, shrouded in so much haze that it looks as if she's wrapped in clouds. Her face is blurred like a painting that someone smeared with their thumb.

"What have you been doing?" I breathe.

How many lies do you have to tell to look like this? And what is she lying about?

I remind myself that this is not why I'm here. Most likely I only have a handful of minutes before Jamie arrives. If I want to try to reach her, this is my opportunity—if I can make her tell Jamie about me, if she can become my liar, then I can live. This is it.

I position myself directly in front of her. I take a deep breath and put my hands on her shoulders. I can feel her, but she can't feel me. "I am Hannah Allen, your younger sister. Your mother wanted her second child to live so badly that she willed me in to being. That lie broke her marriage. It made her a terrible mother. I was created out of her pain and need. I am not the child that died; I am the one born of grief."

She wanders to the sink again and pours herself another glass of water.

Her hair is unbrushed, and her eyes are rimmed in red. I wonder if she's been drinking. I wonder if she's been sleeping. Her sheets smell like stale sweat and old cologne. What bad decisions has she made since I left her?

I continue. "I may not exist, but I am real. The specter of me tormented your childhood. You worried that Mother would mention me to one of your teachers or your friends' parents. And sometimes she did. Mother's lies twisted reality around you. Do you remember when you were sent to the school counselor with a note from the teacher, saying they believed you had deep psychological issues because you kept talking about your dead sister? They called Mother, and do you remember what she said? That your sister was alive and well, and she didn't know why you were behaving the way you were. She promised to take you to a psychologist. And what did she do? Nothing. Our mother did nothing because she knew it wasn't you. It was her. And it was me."

Leah swallows the water. She's staring at the wall. I don't know what she sees, but I see it covered in canvases. This time, the art is clear. Ugly red slashes. Swirls of black and gray. The images shift and morph, but in them, I can see her pain. She painted her pain with lies instead of brushes.

I wonder if she ever told anyone the full extent of it:

How Mother would tell people Leah was damaged, that she was the problem child who shoplifted and stole drugs from her medicine cabinet. Leah never did any of that. Instead, it was Mother who made mistake after mistake. "She made you lie," I say. "For her. And she lied to you, to keep you, because she was afraid of losing you too. You thought that it would make a difference if she knew you chose her over Dad. But it didn't, did it? You were still her second favorite."

I hear footsteps on the stairs.

"I ruined your life. I am as real to you as if I were flesh and blood. All you have to do is admit it. Tell Jamie. Tell him I ruined your life. It's not even a lie."

I feel, bone deep, that if she talks about me, if she admits the impact my nonexistence has had on her life, then I can continue. I have no proof, but it *feels* right. "Tell him," I plead with her. "Tell him everything about me, and let me live!"

She opens the door, and Jamie comes in. With him, there's a rush of air, and for a moment, the haze clears, then reappears heavily, beneath the couch and the sofa.

"Thank you for coming," she says.

He crosses his arms.

He does have a lot of tattoos, I notice. He also seems more worried than angry, despite his pose. It's difficult to see Leah's face through the haze wrapped tightly around her skull.

"You haven't answered any of my calls since we painted your mom's house," he says. "I even tried calling you at work, but they said you haven't been in."

"I can explain," Leah says, and she launches into a tale that begins with losing her wallet in an Uber and ends with her wandering by the Empire State Building in bare feet.

She learned from Mother after all.

He shakes his head. "You could have called me. I was worried about you. If Jersey hadn't said to give you space . . . Are you okay?"

"I wanted to call," Leah says. "Phone was broken."

The haze thickens around her ankles. It's tinged with the greasy kind of smoke that comes from an ugly lie, the kind that can hurt. I keep an eye on it, thinking of the toxic muck—this is a cousin to the kind of lie that births that filth, a lie that harms. Is that why she called him here? To lie to him?

Out loud, I say, "You can do it. Tell him."

"Really, I just needed some time to think," she says. "It's been a lot, with my mother and—"

"Me. Mention me."

"—the house. The lawyers. All of it. It's just been a lot of memories, and I haven't had room in my head for us." She's telling the truth now. I can taste it in the air. It's less sour. Maybe she's going to do it.

I drift closer to her, keeping an eye on the greasy smoke. I'd rather it not touch me. *Tell him the truth. All of it.* It wasn't just Mother's death, the house, and the lawyers; it was Mother's life, Leah's childhood, and me.

"I know," he says. "But I worry about you. You don't need to go through any of this alone. You should know by now that I'm here for you. Even if you want to rage. Or just sit on the couch and say nothing—you don't have to be alone."

She takes a breath, and I hold mine. "That's the thing, though," she says. "I *am* alone, and I think that's the way it has to be. I don't know how to say this without hurting you, but I . . . don't need you. Frankly, I'm not sure if I ever did."

The haze is spilling out of her lips. It drips down her neck.

She's trying to drive him away.

I press closer to her, my lips near her ears. "You don't want to do this. Don't break up with him. You need him."

"Jamie, I know you want to be my knight in shining armor—"

He doesn't. I've met a knight in shining armor, and it isn't Jamie. Jamie is just a person, a real person, who cares about Leah. She doesn't understand what she's giving up. He wants to connect with her, to see, hear, and understand her, and he could, if she'd just let him.

"—but I don't need to be saved."

Jamie cups her cheek in his hand, and she pulls back. "Leah, what are you saying? Are you breaking up with me?"

"Tell him it's my fault," I say. "Tell him, tell him how messed up Mother was again." It hurts to say that out loud. Especially to say it in the past tense. But the evidence is everywhere in the apartment, from the canvases on the wall, to the redness around her eyes. The evidence is in all that Leah has become and all that she hasn't become. "Tell him the truth! Now!"

And she blurts out, "I cheated on you. I . . . wanted to forget . . . everything, everyone, *me*." She grabs a slip of paper and shows it to him. "His name is Sam. He wrote this." She crumples it up and tosses it into the sink. Water erodes the words. "He left me his number after I slept with him, after I went to the bar with Jersey. Now do you understand?"

I take a step back.

Did I do this?

Leah hadn't planned on telling him that truth, I'm certain. Did I somehow reach her? Did she hear me? I begin to shout in her ear. "Talk about me! Tell him your sister exists! Please, Leah, hear me! You know I'm here! All you need to do is tell him I'm real! I'm real to you! Say it! Say I'm your sister!"

CHAPTER
TWENTY-EIGHT

She does not mention me.

Sitting on the edge of Leah's bed, I stare at my hand. I can't tell if it looks less solid or the same. It just looks like my hand. Leah is confessing to Jamie: truth chased with promises. Close to lies but not quite.

"Just the one time," she says.

"It won't happen again," she says.

"I'm fine now," she says.

"You're not fine," I say to her. The haze in the apartment hasn't dissipated, and I don't know what will help. It's not as simple as opening a window. Leah still has clouds wrapped around her like a scarf.

Jamie echoes me: "You don't seem fine. Have you slept? Eaten?"

She laughs, brittle. "You're mothering me again. After what I told you? Why? Do you want someone you can coddle? Protect? Save? Well, you can spare yourself the bother. I don't need to be saved. I need . . ."

Help.

". . . space. Okay? I've said it a thousand times, but you keep not hearing me. Just space. Can't you fucking give me that? Or are you trying to smother me? Control me? Is this a power trip for you? Today's to-do list: save the messed-up failure in apartment 3C."

I was foolish to think I could reach Leah, that she could change my fate. She has never known me, never cared about me, never heard me. Only Sylvie and Rabbit ever have. *I shouldn't have left them.* At least I could have spent my last moments with those who can hear me. But what's done is done. You try to make the best decisions you can with the information you have—and sometimes, you choose wrong. That's just how it is.

"You're grieving," Jamie says gently.

"I'm celebrating! Ding-dong, the witch is dead! I'm finally free! No more childhood trauma, because I can't be hurt anymore. All my problems stopped with her breath, and now I'm free and it's over."

I close my eyes, take a breath, and open them again. "It doesn't work that way, Leah." I can see plain as day, clear as sunrise, that she has not dealt with one iota of her pain, not from her childhood or from Mother's death. Or Mother's life. Or mine. Just like Mother never did.

She can't help me. She can't even help herself.

Mother is gone, and that's it.

Shaking his head, Jamie steps back. "I love you, Leah, but I don't love how you're treating me. I came over when I got your call, despite how late it is, because—"

"You came running because you thought I needed you," she interrupts. "I don't. I don't need anyone. I've been taking care of myself for a long time, and I don't—"

I yell, "Stop lying!"

She breaks off midword.

I stare at her.

That's twice now. Twice she was mid-lie, and I stopped her. At least, I think I did. It could have been a massive coincidence. "Tell the truth," I say, standing up.

"I just . . . I need to be alone," Leah finishes. "I don't want to break up with you, but I don't . . . I cheated on you! I don't know how to be who you need me to be. Or how to be who I want to be."

A truth.

"Okay," Jamie says, quietly.

I can reach her. "Leah, listen to me! Tell him everything! Tell him —" Darkness eats at the corners of my vision. Lifting my hand, I stare at the smoke *through* my fingers.

Not now. Please, not—

I fade anyway.

CHAPTER
TWENTY-NINE

Leah dressed for her mother's funeral. All black, which was easy. Respectable black, which was not. Shredded black jeans wouldn't work, and neither would any of her T-shirts. She didn't want to wear any of her work clothes. Whatever she put on would forever be the clothes she wore to her mother's funeral. *I'll burn them after this.* Or, more likely, shove them in the back of her closet and never look at them again. She selected gray pants and a black short-sleeve sweater that never fit right in the shoulders.

Staring at the mirror, she debated makeup. Half of her wanted to do the cat-eye makeup that her mom hated, but it felt petty. She applied eye shadow and a touch of mascara, only enough to make it look as if she'd slept last night.

"Fuck this," she said to her reflection.

She felt as though she was giving a performance that she'd never agreed to give. The funeral—it was supposed to give comfort and closure, but she knew full well that she wasn't ever going to get that. Not after the lawyer's call.

It almost felt as if Mom had died on purpose, to deny Leah the chance to resolve things with either of her parents and move on.

Mom hadn't had much: the house, mainly, and she'd left it to her two daughters, fifty-fifty. How nice. How fair. The lawyer had only been briefly flabbergasted when Leah informed him that Hannah was her baby sister who died twenty-one years ago. After all, Mom's will had been updated and notarized ten years ago.

"She never—" the lawyer had started to say.

Leah hadn't let him finish that sentence, hadn't let him feel pity for Mom, for the woman so unable to cope with the past that she ruined the present.

She'd need to produce a death certificate, of course. *I'll have to call the hospital.* They kept records, didn't they? She knew Mom wouldn't have a copy at the house. Not when she had a chair at her kitchen table for Hannah and insisted on place settings at restaurants. She would've tossed any proof that negated her favorite lie.

The worst was when the lawyer asked, "Are you certain?" As if Leah could be the one who was mistaken.

Tell a big enough lie, and everyone will believe you.

The buzzer broke through her thoughts.

Jamie was here.

Jamie, who deserved better than her, who had no idea how messed up she truly was, who thought she was here painting every day and pursuing her dreams, who didn't know her dreams had died years ago, who didn't know all the terrible choices she'd made or hadn't made, who saw her as someone other than she was who saw her today as a woman mourning her mother, when all she really felt was empty and pissed.

She waited for him to come upstairs. His eyes were full of concern. "How are you doing?" he asked; sympathy infused every syllable as if he could possibly understand what she felt. He, with his lovely parents and normal family. He, who was kind to a fault, who apologized to curbs when he tripped over them and gave up seats on the subway without a second thought. He, who believed every word she'd ever said, because they were in love and why should she lie to him?

"I'm fine," she said.

All she'd say when anyone asked today was, *I'm fine.*

My biggest lie:

I'm fine.

If she said it often enough, she'd make it true.

CHAPTER THIRTY

The sun is pouring through the window. Jamie is gone, and Leah has sunk to the floor, face in her hands. The fog whirls around her. An easel leans against a garbage bag. That wasn't there before.

What did I miss?

My heart is beating so hard it hurts. I kneel next to her. "Leah! You have to hear me! Please, I need you!" I shout at her. "Call Jamie back! It's not too late! You can still save me! Save *us*!" I plead with her. I try to shake her. But I can't touch her, can't reach her.

She's not thinking of me. She's not thinking about anything but how much she hurts right now, and there's nothing I can do about that.

I keep yelling until my throat feels shredded. "Call him back. Tell the truth. Please!"

But she is silent. The haze of her lies wraps tight around her like a shroud, and eventually I have to admit the truth:

Nothing I can do to save me.

Nothing I can do to save her.

I'd almost reached her before I faded. She stopped lying for a moment, but the moment has passed; Jamie is gone. It's over.

I look at the street below and watch the haze of lies drift between pedestrians and cars. "I'm sorry, Leah," I say, "for everything."

◆ ◆ ◆

Outside, I take a breath.

It tastes like a city: a mix of old pretzels, rotten fruit, and exhaust from taxis, buses, and too many cars. It sounds like one too: a cacophony of TVs and radios playing through open windows, the chattering of voices, the rumble of the subway.

It's midday now, and Queens is bustling with people and their lies.

I know I only have a little time left.

I think of Sylvie and Rabbit and wish I could tell them how close I came—Leah heard me, at least enough to stop lying.

I halt in my tracks.

Sylvie said she used to have many liars but now only has one—that's the primary difference between her and Rabbit. What if that's why he transforms but she doesn't? He is continually reshaped, tormented by how his many liars twist his reality to suit whatever they please.

If Rabbit only had a single liar, would he stop shifting?

If liars can be stopped, can he be helped?

Can they be stopped?

I have to test this. If I can't save myself and I can't help Leah, maybe I can save Rabbit. Stop his liars and stop his pain. At least then I'll have done something.

It only takes me a few minutes to find my first liar.

Ahead of me, a man with hunched shoulders is walking his well-groomed dog. He carries a crunched-up plastic bag in the same hand as the leash. "You better not leave your dog shit on my flowers," a woman shouts from her window.

"Absolutely not!" The dog walker holds up his unused bag. "Never would."

Lies fill his bag until it looks puffed up with haze.

Coming close, I say in his ear, "Don't lie to her. She clearly loves those flowers." Each flower has its own label, and the bed is guarded by a garishly painted statue of a gnome.

"Only time it happened was when I didn't have a bag," he says. "But never again."

The bag deflates as the haze dissipates. The man grunts as he bends down to scoop up his dog's business. He makes a show of tying off the bag so she can see.

She glares at him, grunts, then closes her window.

Was that me? Did I cause that extra bit of honesty, or was it the woman's glare? I follow the dog walker until I spot a couple, deep in an argument.

One of them gestures enthusiastically as he talks, and the second man looks shrunken in on himself. He nods every once in a while, and with each nod, a layer of gauze seems to wrap around his eyes.

"Why are you lying to him? You don't need to lie. You know you shouldn't," I whisper to the man talking.

He falters.

And then he continues, wrapping his lies like a scarf around the other man's head.

But for an instant, he faltered. I saw it.

I press closer, keeping pace directly behind him. "You don't want to do this. He doesn't deserve to be lied to. Look at him. You're hurting him with your lies. You're better than this."

This time, the guy stops. His shoulders slump. "You know I get carried away. Just . . . yeah, we used to date. And he—"

"Tell him," I whisper.

"He broke up with me, not the other way around. But just because he beat me to it doesn't mean I wasn't going to end it. I would've waited until after the holidays, because I'm not an asshole," he says.

I can't control what they say—couldn't make Leah talk to me or even about me—but I *can* influence them, at least a little. Like a conscience. Liars can hear me mid-lie, to a degree. It's a revelation in both its simplicity and its implications.

Is it enough, though, to help Rabbit—if I silence his liars?

There's a man ahead in a red baseball cap and camo shirt, and the boiling black muck spills from his mouth, staining his lower lip and neck. It gathers around him, and I know it's not safe for me to stay.

But even the muck can't change what I'm feeling:

It isn't fear.

It's hope.

CHAPTER THIRTY-ONE

I've traversed the length of Long Island more times in a few days than is reasonable. It adds up to more miles than I've ever traveled, but it doesn't feel like nearly enough. Stepping hard on the gas, I power through the other vehicles in my way. I want to see more, feel more. I formed to satisfy someone else's needs and wants, and now that she's done with me . . .

Maybe this is how Sylvie feels, why she is the way she is.

What would I have been like if I'd felt this way sooner?

As the speedometer rises, I wonder what real Hannah would have been like if she'd grown up, lived, breathed, lied, like everyone else. That Hannah wouldn't have feared fading away.

Gripping the steering wheel, I pray to whoever is listening—God, Mother, even the shadow wolves—to let me last until I can reach my friends. If only I can tell Sylvie and Rabbit what I've figured out. *Please, let me stay just a little longer.*

Perhaps someone hears me, because I stay alert and alive as I drive the hours east.

I find them at sunset on the stretch of beach where Sylvie and I first watched the sun dissolve into the earth. For all her proclaimed wildness, she is rather predictable.

Maybe I am too, I think as Sylvie pats the sand beside her as if she's been saving me a spot. "How was the family reunion?" she asks. "Are you all fixed now?"

"Still dying. Leah is a mess," I say, mimicking her extra-cheerful tone.

Rabbit sits a few feet from us on the sand. He's changed again, but I don't remember the name that matches this face. "Rabbit . . ."

His eyes flick open, and he jumps to his feet.

"You have to take me back. She needs me! You have to take me to her!"

Sighing, Sylvie flops back onto the sand. "He's been like this, off and on, since you left. Can't tell me who 'she' is or where 'home' is, but . . ." She waves her hand at him. "See?"

He paces to the edge of the water, and then contorts in pain again. We watch as he writhes and then stands, dusts himself off, and walks back to us—but with a different face. I haven't seen this one before. His eyes have shifted to a deep brown flecked with gold. In a polished voice, he says, "Sorry for the theatrics, Sylvie, but I have to go back. If you would be so kind . . ."

"I'm not missing sunset," Sylvie says.

Rabbit focuses on my face. "Hannah, you're here! It didn't work?" He takes my hands, and I squeeze his, grateful for their warmth and solidity. "No. It didn't work, Rabbit."

"You should have stayed until you were fixed. Why did you come back?"

"She just can't stay away from us," Sylvie says. "We're that irresistible."

"Your sister—"

I blurt out, "We can stop them mid-lie."

Both of them stare at me.

"The liars. While they're lying, they can hear us. Sort of. It's not like we can have a conversation. It's more like, we're their conscience. At least, I think." I describe to them what happened and how I tested it.

As I talk, the sun dips lower in the sky and tints the clouds the color of blush wine. *This could be the start of my last sunset.* I wonder if Sylvie thinks that with every sunset.

"If you're right . . . ," Sylvie says when I finish. "I mean, it seems super unlikely and definitely like grasping at straws because you're desperate, but if you're right . . ." She grins impishly. "It means we can mess with liars. Ooh, the possibilities! I want a Ferrari or a helicopter with its own landing pad. Also a pilot."

I laugh as she kicks her feet into the air. "Not sure it works that way."

She waves at me like this is a minor detail. "You don't know how it works."

"I wasn't able to convince Leah to lie. Only *not* to lie. Believe me, I tried."

"Okay, that's less fun," Sylvie says. "All this time, it never crossed my mind to try to *stop* them from lying."

I smile at Rabbit. "You know what this means, right?"

He looks at me blankly.

"It means we can help you! Think about it: You're shaped and reshaped by a multitude of liars. Silence as many of them as we can, and maybe you won't keep shifting. Maybe you can keep one face, one name, one set of memories."

"At least until you can't," Sylvie says cheerfully.

"But I have to—" His breath hisses through his teeth again as his face contorts. He drops to his knees. Still gripping my hands, he looks as if he's proposing. Or praying.

"I can't swear it will work," I say louder, as if I could shout over his pain. "But we can try. We go back to your bars, find some of your liars, and then—"

Strawberry blond and freckled, he straightens. "And then I'll save her."

"And then we'll save *you*," I say.

Sylvie jumps to her feet. "Cool. What are we waiting for? Let's go mess with some humans." She turns her back on the horizon and walks toward the car.

The sun hasn't finished setting.

◆ ◆ ◆

Car window down, I listen for parties as I drive—it's likely there will be someone spewing out lies that we can test my theory on. As soon as we're sure . . .

Agitated, Rabbit fidgets in the back seat.

In the rearview mirror, I see his face undulating, his hair lengthening, his shoulders broadening. His teeth are clenched hard against a scream. "She needs me," he grates out. "I have to help her." He tries the car door.

Both Sylvie and I shout, "No!"

"Don't do that!" Sylvie yells. "Car, moving!"

Slamming on the brakes, I steer toward the side of the road, and we run through a fruit stand. Twisting in the seat, I grab for Rabbit as he throws open the car door.

"Not good," Sylvie says, bolting after him.

I unbuckle and run after him. He's jogging toward a lit-up house. His body is continuing to change as he runs, his legs shifting their length. He stumbles. Crashing down on his knees, he catches himself on his palms and then rises. There's blood on his chin, his cheek, his hands, but he doesn't stop.

"What the hell is wrong with him?" Sylvie asks.

"You used to have multiple liars. Did this ever happen to you?" I wonder if it's the time of day or the distance from his liars—he's far from all of them, so maybe they are all pulling on his body and mind with equal strength.

"No. Don't know. Yes, probably? I never had to watch it from the outside, so who knows? It's seriously disturbing."

He plunges through the wall of the house, and we follow him. He doesn't see the shadow wolves, but I do. "Sylvie!" I grab her arm.

"Shit."

"We have to get him out of there."

"Car," she says.

We spin, but the car, half stuck into the fruit stand, has already drawn their attention. One of the shadow wolves stands on its hood. The wolf lifts its head in a silent howl. A shiver dances across my skin.

"Another car?" I suggest.

"I'll find one," Sylvie promises. "You get him."

We split up, and I aim for the door. Surest way to avoid drawing the wolves' attention is to behave normally. Rabbit, however, races right through the side of the house, through an ivy trellis. I skirt around a hydrangea and slip in between a pack of partygoers.

One of the wolves is already inside, stalking between them. I don't know if he can sense me or not, but I know he's following Rabbit.

I can't lose him just as I've found a way to save him!

He's integrated himself into a conversation with a group of men and women. All the women have carefully applied makeup. Half are holding drinks. There's a man talking loudly and standing close to another woman, who is shying away—perhaps Rabbit's latest damsel in distress. I drift closer, listening to their conversation, then realize Rabbit has shifted farther away. I overhear a man say, "You hear about that party where they had elephants?"

The wolf snarls and pads closer.

Hurriedly, I say to the man, "Don't lie. You don't need to lie."

"I don't think it actually happened," the man amends, "but if it did . . ."

"The owners hired a private circus," the other man said. "Contortionists. Trapeze artists. Even a trick motorcycle rider. Yeah, I heard about that. There were elephants."

The wolf bares its teeth.

Quickly, I switch my attention to the other man. I press close and say, "You don't know that. You shouldn't spread lies."

He gives a nervous laugh. "But I wasn't there either. Can't swear to it."

"Yeah, hey, did you hear what Angela told Tony last Tuesday?"

"Zero work talk," the first man says. "Promised my wife."

The wolf withdraws.

I exhale and check on Rabbit. He's the same as when I first met him: movie-star handsome, Asian American with cheekbones that could shame a classical Greek statue.

"I have to find her," Rabbit says.

"I know. It's okay," I say soothingly. "We'll take you to her, but you have to come with me now. Sylvie's getting a car, and we have to leave." I glance again at the wolf, careful not to make eye contact. I hook my arm through Rabbit's and escort—or more accurately, drag—him toward the door.

The wolf trails behind. It definitely noticed us.

"Get ready to run," I tell him. And I hope that Sylvie hasn't already run. She survives by letting the wolves chase other prey. *She wouldn't do that to us.*

I listen for the sound of a car. That will be our cue. Any second now, Sylvie is going to hot-wire another unreal vehicle. She'll swing by the front of the house—

The wolf streaks past us, and I tamp down a scream. I feel its fur brush past me, soft as a breath of wind, and it plunges through the wall outside.

A car engine revs.

"Run," I tell Rabbit.

We race side by side, straight through a table with an antique lamp and then a wall covered in silvery wallpaper, and we burst out into the middle of a bed of ornamental grasses. Ahead, the wolves are circling a car that is wreathed in haze. Through the windshield, I catch a glimpse of Sylvie. She's hunched over the steering wheel. I can't see her expression: fierce, terrified, neither?

"Split up," I order.

Releasing his arm, I run in one direction while he runs in the other. Waving my arms in the air, I call to the wolves, "Hey! You! Over here! Look at me, a tasty lie!"

All I have to do is clear the way for them to escape, and I will have succeeded in doing more than I dared hope when I left Leah and drove back east. Rabbit saw me stop that liar; he knows it can be done. Sylvie will help him get back to the bar.

"What are you doing?" Rabbit calls to me.

"Just go! Get out of here! Tell Sylvie to take you to Sweet Venom!" If they find his liars, he can change his situation. I never had that chance with Mother. He can take control of his life. Stop any more lies from forming. At least then he'll have peace. He can be one person, like Sylvie, like me. He can be whole and make his own memories.

The wolves twist their heads as I deliberately run through cars, demonstrating exactly what I am. One of them pivots and runs toward me, fading into the darkness and then rematerializing beside me. I catch a glimpse of Rabbit jumping into Sylvie's car as the wolves blend together, thickening into a wall of smoke.

I run, knowing that this time I won't escape, and I tell myself that this is right, this is my choice—my only and best choice. A chance to make my life matter for someone.

Or a chance to be eaten by wolves.

Spotting a car laced with haze, I clamber onto the hood. Slowing, the wolves pace around me. There are three—no, four. It's hard to count because they blend into one another. They have me surrounded. No need for them to rush; they can dismember me whenever they choose.

I very much want to live.

I didn't have that feeling when I lay in Mother's casket. But now I have things to do. People to take care of. Sunsets to watch. Rabbit to save. Sylvie to care for.

Waving my hands in the air, I shout, "Sylvie! Over here!"

The unreal car barrels through parked cars. It's another convertible, of course—Sylvie can't resist them, and liars can't either. "Jump!" she calls to me.

She sheers close to me as the wolves hurl themselves, jaws open, at the car. I throw myself off the car hood and into her back seat. I crash into Rabbit, and he folds his arms around me.

The wolves chase after us as we speed away.

◆ ◆ ◆

"Confession: I almost left you," Sylvie says as she speeds down Sunrise Highway.

It shouldn't hurt, but it does. Still, I don't let her see that. "I almost wanted you to." I am temporary, after all. She shouldn't risk her future for me. She could have decades ahead of her.

"Well, I needed you," Sylvie says. Then before I can react to that extraordinary statement: "You're the only one with a clear idea of where we're going. He's useless."

In the back seat, Rabbit writhes again. His breathing is shallow; the pain is written clearly across his face as his features change. I don't know how many liars we'll need to find to help him or how we're going to find them all, but at least we can try.

"You don't hate me for almost letting you become dog food?" Sylvie asks.

She's glancing at me anxiously in the rearview mirror. I've never heard her sound insecure before. "You didn't," I reassure her. "You saved me."

"Because of Rabbit. He kept screaming until I turned around." For an instant, I think she actually feels guilty; then she adds, "I don't want you to start thinking that we're friends or anything. I just wanted him to shut up."

I grin at her reflection in the mirror. Now she sounds more like herself. "I can't tell if you want me to forgive you or not. You definitely seem like you don't want to be the hero here."

"Not a hero," Sylvie says quickly. "Never wanted to be. But I also enjoy being adored, and it makes me equally uncomfortable to think you might have the wrong impression of me. I *am* a selfish coward, but I don't want you to think that's a bad thing."

I laugh. It's the only reasonable response. *We're all a mess. Rabbit just wears his damage on the outside.* "I do adore you."

I see her visibly relax. There was truth sprinkled in with all her denials and deflections.

"Hang in there," I tell him.

"What's the plan?" Sylvie asks.

"Bring him back to the source, to his liars," I say. I've been giving this some thought. "We should be able to find one in a bar called Sweet Venom, the one I met him in. There's a woman who visits the bar nearly every night, and her go-to lie is about Rabbit. That's the face he reverts to the most often."

"You want to stop her lie?"

"I want to set him free," I say.

"Huh. Do you think that will work?"

"I think he can't live like this," I say. "Look at him."

"Rather not. Looking at the road."

She drives, and I focus on trying to make Rabbit more comfortable. This is one of the worst episodes I've seen. He writhes. He screams. His whole bone structure changes beneath my hands, and I don't know how to make it better. Maybe I shouldn't have taken him so far from his liars.

"If we get her to stop," I say, "then he'll stabilize."

"Or he'll vanish," Sylvie says.

Rabbit, covered in sweat, manages to say, "It's not her fault." He then arches his back as another shift takes him. It's like a tug-of-war, with his body as the prize. "She doesn't know, they don't know, what they do to me. I just need . . . to help them . . . to be with them . . ."

At last, the shifting stops. He's settled into another face, and his breathing becomes easier. I wrap my arm around his shoulders, and he leans against me and just breathes.

"You okay back there?" Sylvie asks.

"Better," he says.

"Less suicidal, now that you're not in pain?"

He doesn't answer, but he does wrap his hands around mine. I'm becoming used to the way his hands feel different every time he touches me. Longer or shorter fingers. Wider or narrower palm. Softer or rougher skin. But his hands are always warm and gentle.

We drive in silence for a while.

I check my hand. Still solid.

I wonder how long my luck will hold.

"You know, all real people are mortal," Rabbit says to me softly. "They don't know how many days they will have. It could be decades, or it could be hours. That makes them not so different from you."

He didn't say "us."

Because he *can't* fade, even if he wants to. He's bound to the liars who keep him perpetually shifting. Funny that I'm trying to bring him closer to the one thing that I have and don't want: an end.

I try to instead enjoy holding his hand. It will always feel miraculous to me to hold someone's hand. As miraculous as a sunrise. I think of Leah and how hard she's pushing Jamie away. She's a fool for not appreciating what she's got. You need to hold close the people who can truly see and hear you.

◆ ◆ ◆

Reaching Queens, we navigate the streets by avoiding the boiling ooze. Left, right, another right, straight. Rabbit points past Sylvie's ear. "Watch that puddle."

"I see it." She's gripping the steering wheel, and her jaw is clenched.

I'm surprised she hasn't demanded we leave the car and walk, leaving her free to return to Montauk. Continuing onward, deliberately endangering herself, doesn't fit her style. Then again, being reckless does. She steers like she's driving in a video game, crashing into lampposts and trees ringed by concrete.

"It's Saturday night," Rabbit says. "More people near the restaurants and bars. It concentrates the muck."

"Why haven't the shadow wolves stopped this?" Sylvie wonders. "They're supposed to keep lies in check. That's their entire purpose."

We all stare at the mess that clings to the pavement. "It's too much," Rabbit says. "Believed by too many, and it spreads too fast. The wolves can't keep pace. There are pockets like this all over New York City, probably all over the world. Every year, every week, it seems to get worse." He seems much more coherent now that we're back near the bars. I might have been right about distance being the problem—he's tied to his liars. *All the more reason to sever him.*

Looking at the ooze, I shiver. "What happens if the wolves can't beat it back?"

"I assume it will keep spreading," Rabbit says.

"Well, that will be unpleasant," Sylvie says.

I eye the ooze with revulsion. It sloshes through the gutters and spills across the street. On the sidewalk, it's swallowed a food cart. If it spreads too far, there'll be no place safe for us to go. For the first time in my life, I find myself rooting for the wolves.

"Can we get around it?" I ask.

"With some creative driving," Sylvie says.

That sounds alarming.

Before I can protest, Sylvie swings the wheel hard to the right and aims directly for an apartment building. I know from Leah that apartments can be stuffed with lies, so I don't think—

There isn't time to think.

She barrels through the lobby. We hit a cluster of chairs, and they careen off the windshield, oddly silent. I twist to see behind me. The actual chairs are still in position, but they're much shabbier than the ones we hit. Someone must have lied about a renovation. I hope no one ever lied about the walls because if—

We slide through the walls between the elevators and mailboxes and burst onto a sidewalk. The street here is only marginally less filled with ooze. I can see it dripping from some of the windows. Thankfully, not all the windows—not everyone has been sucked into the same lie—but enough to make an impact. About half the windows have a waterfall of gooey, bubbling ooze spilling into the sidewalks and running through the gutters.

Sylvie keeps to the center of the street, trying to avoid the rivers on either side.

"How close?" she asks.

"Close," Rabbit says.

Sweet Venom is on Baylor Street. "Fifteen more blocks."

"That's not close," Sylvie says.

We have to make it. Rabbit needs the pain to stop, and I need to do one thing, just one thing that I choose, before I fade. Otherwise, what was it all for? What was the point of lingering beyond Mother's death? I have to make this life that she gave me matter. If all I do is help

Rabbit, well, at least it's something. More than I've ever done. "I need to see this through."

"Yeah, I get that, but . . ." She gestures, one hand still on the wheel.

There's a sea of muck in front of us, and the wolves are in full attack mode, tearing at the sludge. I spot three wolves battling the ooze. They leap onto cars, fade in and out, and reappear to attack the waves. Working together, they take one wave, but the muck simply spreads.

Sylvie throws the car into reverse.

We try another street. Deliberately, carefully, painfully, we pick our way through Queens. The seconds feel as if they're slipping by too fast, and I don't know how many I have left to spare.

Rabbit lasts another ten minutes before the next change hits. I pin myself against him, trying to hold him steady so he doesn't flail and hit Sylvie. She needs to drive. "Hurry," I beg her.

"What do you think I'm trying to do?"

"You're doing great," Rabbit encourages her, between gasps.

"Shut up," she tells him.

"Turn right!" I shout.

She turns right, avoiding a deluge of ooze that rushes like a flash flood down a narrow side street. Twisting in my seat, I watch it out the back window. I can't imagine how the wolves are going to fight against this much toxicity.

"It'll play out eventually," Sylvie says. "Not our problem. Our problem is *that*."

Ahead of us, between our car and Sweet Venom, is a whirlpool of muck. It swirls ominously in the center of the pavement, hungry, and the real cars and taxis drive through it as if it weren't there. It feels like it's waiting especially for us, though I know it would cheerfully devour whatever presented itself.

"Hang on!" Sylvie barrels through another building, this time a café. I see the coffee mugs in a flash. We drive directly through a storeroom and then out the other side.

We're heading in the correct direction again, but a seven-foot wave of muck looms directly over us. Our car slams into it, and we jerk forward as all motion stops. The toxic sludge melts around the hood of the car.

"Everyone out!" I yell as the ooze devours the windshield.

CHAPTER
THIRTY-TWO

The piano was smashed.

There was no hiding it.

Leah led Jersey to the damaged piano—her friend had come fast when she called.

"You just have to help me move it to the curb," Leah said, trying to sound upbeat rather than like she wanted to hide in a corner and cringe for all eternity. "It'll create more open space in the living room. The real estate agent will like that."

"Gah," Jersey said.

"It'll be heavy, but if we take it slow . . ."

"You did this?"

Feeling herself blush, Leah crossed her arms. She'd hoped that Jersey wouldn't ask questions, except how she planned to lower it down the porch stairs without destroying the steps, a detail that she hadn't worked out yet. "Yes."

"With . . ."

"A wrench."

"Okay. Um . . ." Gently, Jersey asked, "Do you want to talk about it?"

"I was having a moment," Leah said. "I'm fine now. Just a lot to clean up. A lot of mess. You know how you can just get frustrated sometimes? With all that needs to get done, and you're tired, and there's just a lot."

Jersey pressed her lips together. She opened her mouth and then shut it again, seeming to think better of prying. She crossed to the side of the piano and examined it. "You want to just put it on the curb? As if it's not, you know, a piano."

"It's not a grand piano," Leah pointed out.

"Still as heavy as fuck."

Leah laughed, a brittle laugh that didn't sound or feel right. Her throat felt thick. *People lose their temper all the time. It's not a big deal.* It didn't make her a terrible person. Unlike cheating and then lying about it . . .

Jersey knelt next to the piano. "Well, it does have wheels. If they move over carpet. Not sure what we do when we reach the door. It would be a lot better if we had additional muscle. Did you call Jamie?" She looked back at Leah.

Leah looked away, and her eyes landed on the freshly painted walls. "I . . . didn't. If I do . . ." She took a breath and plunged on: "I need to break up with him. For his sake. He deserves better than someone who inexplicably smashes pianos and sleeps with guys named Sam." There, she'd said it out loud. That made it true.

Jersey nodded gently and circled to the other side of the piano. She attempted to yank it away from the wall, but the piano didn't budge. "Does Jamie know? About Sam. Not about the piano. Or also about the piano. Did you tell him about either?"

"He doesn't know."

"Why break up? You're not planning on seeing Sam again, are you?"

"No, but . . ." That wasn't the point! The point was . . . She looked at the shattered piano keys and pictured her mom's fingers, haltingly showing her how to play a beginner piece. *What kind of concert pianist only knows how to play do re mi?* "I'm a liar. Can't stop. It's in my blood, I guess. Jamie deserves better." So did Sam, for that matter.

"Fuck your 'blood.' What do *you* deserve?"

I deserve to be alone. "If we can find a piece of plywood, we could make a ramp down the stairs. Get it down that way."

"Do you want to break up with him?"

She didn't know. "I don't want to see him again." She'd made it through painting the wall, but she didn't know if she could do it again. Just thinking about it was painful. Like swallowing glass. "He'll ask me how I am."

Jersey gave her a look. "Yeah, I see how that's so terrible. Leah . . . I'm not sure distancing yourself from people who care about you while you're going through shit is the most sensible move. Look, I can tell him you need space if you want— buy you some time to process all of this—but I think you're wrong. You can't isolate yourself and hope that'll make you feel better. Leah, you have people who care about you, who love you. You can lean on us."

Leah didn't know how to explain. "He just worries about me all the time." It was too much. It made her feel as if she'd been wrapped in layer after layer of blankets until she couldn't breathe and wanted to burst out—

Jersey laid a hand on Leah's arm. "Hey, *I'm* worried about you. Have you even been back to work since your mom's funeral? Or have you just been here, smashing innocent musical instruments and plotting how to implode your life?"

Leah shifted her weight so that Jersey's hand fell away. She didn't meet her eyes. "I was just taking out my frustration. I'm okay now. Really, I'm fine."

"Innocent musical instrument," Jersey repeated.

Leah laid her fingers on the keys, a C chord. "It was out of tune anyway." She managed a smile so fake that it felt as if her face was plastic. "You don't need to worry about me."

"Really? Look, I'm all for distracting yourself and escaping the world—Sweet Venom is my favorite coping mechanism—but . . . are you sure you're thinking clearly? Not about Jamie, but about what *you* want, what *you* need? Maybe it's time to let yourself feel without beating yourself up for having emotions?" Peering closely at her face, Jersey asked, "Leah, you know I'm always here for you, right? For the tough stuff as well as the fun stuff. And so is Jamie."

"I know you are," Leah said. "But I told you, I'm *fine*. I don't need to be saved. Not by you, not by Jamie, not by anyone."

CHAPTER THIRTY-THREE

"Go, go, go!"

I shove Rabbit toward the car door. Sylvie springs onto the sidewalk. The ooze has seeped across the street, and it's impossible to avoid. I feel it sting my feet through my shoes. I yank Rabbit, pulling him with me.

He doubles over in pain as another transformation takes hold.

We've got to stop this—it's torture, no other word for it. I run in the direction of Sweet Venom, but I don't know if we'll be safe there. Last time, the ooze nearly consumed the floor. Still, I see it as a beacon—a lighthouse, guiding me, except you aren't supposed to steer a ship toward a lighthouse. You're supposed to go around it because it's surrounded by rocks. Still, I hope we find answers for Rabbit—and me—inside that bar. I have to accomplish something before I fade. If I can accomplish just this one thing, save this one man, then my existence won't have been pointless. I will have been more than the embodiment of one woman's grief.

Ahead, I see it, the neon sign blazing in the murky window. "There!"

We jump from dry patch to dry patch, and when we need to, the toes of our shoes dip into the muck. Sylvie hisses as it sloshes over her bare toes, and without a word, Rabbit scoops her up.

"Hey, I'm not in need of rescue!" Sylvie says. But when he wades through a puddle of muck, she quits struggling and lets him carry her. "I'm only doing this because I made a poor choice in footwear," she says. "Also, I like my toes and don't want them corroded."

"They're very nice toes," Rabbit says.

She wiggles them in a little dance.

We're going to make it. Just a little—

A wave of muck rises so suddenly that I stumble backward. Rabbit begins to run with Sylvie in his arms. She swats at him like he's a horse. "Faster!" he cries. "Hannah, dammit, keep up!"

We belt down the sidewalk and hurl ourselves inside Sweet Venom. Finally, we breathe.

"We did it," Rabbit says.

"This place is a shithole," Sylvie says.

Thanks to Sylvie's speed on the highway, it's only eleven o'clock, and the bar is still clogged with people. Several are drenched in the muck—it pours from their mouths and eyes—but it hasn't flooded the bar yet. It only stains half the floor. We skirt around the ooze, and Sylvie squirms out of Rabbit's arms to stand on her own.

The music is cranked up so loud that it crackles, and I think I hear other melodies trapped within it, other beats that clamor to be heard. Unsung songs. I scan the area, and it's only after I look at everyone in sight that I realize that I'm looking for Leah.

"How long will this take?" Sylvie asks. She's eyeing the ooze, clearly calculating how long we have until it builds toward a tidal wave. We have at least a few minutes.

"Depends," I say. If there's one of Rabbit's liars here. If there's an asshole who needs to be repelled. If she chooses to lie tonight. "Might not happen at all."

Sylvie snorts. "That was far too much to go through for nothing."

"Let me get you a drink," I suggest.

She brightens. "Why did I think we wouldn't be good friends? Oh, wait, I remember, because you just wanted to ask me questions—you didn't really care about me. You know, I can't believe I let you drag me here. I live out in Montauk for a reason, you know. All the parties on the South Fork are pretty. *This* is not."

She's right about that. There's an ugliness to the bar that tastes like gasoline, a greasy kind of desperate flavor. Rabbit warned us that there's a different clientele on Saturdays. I slide my hands through the glasses until my fingers close on a drink. I hand it to Sylvie, and she downs it in a single gulp. I reach through the bar to find a second for myself, but my eyes are fixed on a man spewing black muck. The woman he's talking to can't see it stick to her eyes and drip down her cheeks. I look toward Rabbit.

He's weaving his way to the benches. Has he found her already?

Abandoning my search for another glass, I cross directly to Rabbit—I don't weave through the crowd. Just walk straight through.

Opposite a clump of people, I see the Asian American woman from the first night. She said that she was a frequent visitor. "This is perfect!" I crow. "It's her!"

As I scoot next to her, Rabbit catches my arm. "Wait."

"Why?"

She's feigning politeness as a semidrunken man lurches toward her. I wonder why she frequents this bar if this keeps happening, but then I think of that other woman and the bouncer—it's not on her to stop going places just because someone else is behaving badly. She has every right to be here. Maybe I shouldn't stop her. But no, she's hurting Rabbit. She'll just have to find another way to protect herself. "Rabbit, I have to do it now if—"

"I have a boyfriend," she tells the man, with an apologetic smile.

Rabbit hisses as he begins to shift.

Leaning closer to her, I open my mouth to say, *Don't lie*—

But Rabbit stops me. Fighting through the pain, he says, "Hannah. Don't."

"But she's hurting you." She has no idea of the cost of her lie. She thinks it's harmless, kind even, but the effect on Rabbit—

"Don't," he spits out. He's on his knees, gasping for air. The muck is creeping toward him—it's sent out tendrils like ice spreading across a window.

Sylvie bounds over. "Hannah, what the hell are you doing? You're supposed to stop this. Remember why we risked our necks to come here?"

His transformation complete, he straightens and watches as the man scoots away, having lost interest in the woman. The woman resumes sipping her drink and looking at her phone. She looks content. And safe. Because of Rabbit. "He told me not to."

"Jesus Christ," Sylvie says.

My cheeks flush. I shouldn't have lost my nerve. Rabbit doesn't know what he wants or needs—he barely knows who or what he is from one moment to the next. Still . . . "If she stops lying about him, what happens?"

"Maybe the guy learns not to be an asshole?" Sylvie suggests.

"Or maybe he doesn't."

A few feet away, the drunk man downs another beer. He's scanning the bar, looking for another prospect. If she hadn't lied . . .

"She'll find another way," Sylvie says.

Rabbit shakes his head.

He wants *to protect her,* I realize. It shouldn't surprise me. Knight in shining armor—I said it myself, yet I'm surprised all the same. He must remember the pain he's been in, how we came all this way for the express purpose of ending that pain.

The woman looks up from her phone and glances at the drunk man, calculating whether she's safe now. He swings toward her, and she quickly looks back down. She's holding her breath, I can tell. *I can't take away her protection.*

"Leave this liar," I say. "We'll find another."

"Fine," Sylvie says. "How many faces did you think he wears?"

"I've counted at least six so far." Five more women to find, at a minimum.

"Gotta be more than that," Sylvie says.

He frowns at us. "I don't know what you mean. This is my girl. I need to protect her. She's . . ." He shakes his head. "Sorry. Yes. But . . . no."

"Clear as mud." Sylvie snorts.

I take his hands. I am *not* giving up on him. Just . . . I can't take him away from this woman. *We'll stop the others instead.* "Let's go to the next bar."

"Come on," Sylvie says. "This is for your own good."

◆ ◆ ◆

In the third bar, we find the next liar.

Rabbit doubles over in pain the instant we enter.

"I see her," I say. Leading the way, I wade through grasses that tickle my ankles until I reach a woman surrounded by three men who are bristling with glass shards. One shard protrudes from the closest man's throat.

The woman (midtwenties, blonde hair, ripped jeans) has a smile plastered on her face. "Love to, boys, but I have a boyfriend, and he's a bouncer—as soon as his shift is over, he's picking me up here."

This time, I'm not letting her hurt Rabbit. I need to stop her lie. Set him free.

Catching up to me, Rabbit grabs my arm. "Please."

"You're a lie," Sylvie says harshly. "Rule number one: People don't matter to those like us, because we don't matter to them. That woman can't see you, hear you, or feel you."

"You're wrong," he says. "She needs me."

I shake my head. His brain is like stirred soup; he can't know what he's saying. "Remember the pain? Remember how you change? You don't remember, but it happens."

"I remember *you*. I remember every second with you. Hannah." He takes my hands, the same way I took his, and gazes directly into my eyes. It feels as though he's melting into me. "You are wonderful and amazing, and you have opened my eyes to a whole world beyond. I remember *that*."

Sylvie snorts. "Hey, all she showed you was a beach. I was the one who found the bonfire."

Ignoring her, he raises my hands to his lips and kisses my knuckles. "But I also know this. I can give her a way out."

"You don't need to save all of them," I say. It feels as though he is slipping away from me. This was our whole purpose in coming here. I pull my hands away and place my palms on his cheeks. "Look at me. You deserve a life."

"I have one."

"You're in pain! Every time you change!"

"Would you have traded a day with your mother for all the freedom in the world?" he asks me. "Knowing how much she needed and wanted you?"

Releasing his face, I back away. It's an easy answer. I've already answered it. I went back to Mother the one time I tried to leave, and I never tried again. I didn't want to leave, until I had to, because I had a place there. I had a purpose.

Oh.

That's it.

"You have a purpose," I say.

He smiles a little sadly. "I knew you'd understand."

Hands on her hips, Sylvie says, "Well, I don't."

"I know," he says. He sounds placid. Calm. *Resolved.* "And that's part of your charm."

She isn't mollified, though she does mutter, "I *am* charming." Then louder: "But what are you saying? Did we come all this way for *nothing*? Did you see how I drove? It was amazing. Miraculous. You're going to waste that?" She turns to me. "Hannah, you have to insist. This is idiotic."

"You're choosing this?" I ask him. *Over me, over whatever future we could have had, for however long we could have it.* I keep that to myself.

"I want this," he affirms.

His hand is warm on my arm, holding me in place, preventing me from interfering with his liar. I don't know if he remembers the pain, but I believe he remembers being with me. And still, he chooses this.

"If there were just fewer liars . . . ," I say. "All we have to do is stop some of them. You can keep the rest. Three. How about three? That would be more manageable, wouldn't it?" It isn't fair for him to have to suffer like this. The liars don't understand the cost of their lies.

"I can't choose who is worth helping," he says. "It's okay. Hannah, you've given me memories to hold on to. There's a *me* here that wasn't here before. Because of you." He kisses me, and his breath tastes as sweet as a ripe apple. I feel his arms around me, warm. And then he releases me, and it's as if a wind brushed between us.

He doesn't need me to save him. Yes, who he is tears him apart daily, but it's not as simple as stopping the liars. They need him—he keeps them safe, their knight in shining armor. Real or not, dream or lie. It's his existence.

I take a breath. "Okay then."

He smiles.

Sylvie shrieks, "Okay? It's not okay! Hannah! You realize he's always going to be like this if we don't help him. I thought you wanted to help him. You wanted to be his savior."

"He doesn't want saving," I say.

She steps back from both of us. "You both. I can't. Just can't. Next time you're in Montauk, do me a favor and don't come find me." She pivots and stalks toward the door.

"Sylvie, wait!"

She holds up a hand. "Don't follow me. I'm done with both of you."

I begin to chase after her, but then Rabbit doubles over in pain again. He holds up a hand, takes a breath, and straightens. "I'm fine."

Glancing at the door, I'm torn, but Sylvie is already gone. "I can help. Whatever you need to make this easier." Maybe watch for the muck and the wolves. Keep him safe while he does what he needs to. Until I fade.

But he shakes his head. "How much of a life can I offer you, watching me fracture myself again and again?"

I'd do it. For him to see me and hear me and remember me. "Rabbit . . ." All those years I spent looking out the window, watching other people find one another. And now I'm supposed to walk away? "You can't tell me you'd rather be alone."

"I'm not alone." He turns to his liar and smiles at her. And I know I have no choice. This is what he wants and what he needs, and he's not willing to pay the cost for freedom.

I have no place in his life.

He doesn't even notice as I walk out, alone.

CHAPTER THIRTY-FOUR

"You're grieving," Jamie said quietly.

No, no, no, he didn't get to forgive her while she was breaking up with him. She'd called him for the first time since they'd painted her mother's house together, begged him to come over even though it was late, but instead of any of the things she'd planned to say, out poured a lie about losing her wallet in an Uber and walking barefoot by the Empire State Building. And then, when she did tell him the truth about cheating on him . . . *He can't forgive me. How can he? He can't understand when he doesn't understand.* There was no excuse that made what she'd done okay, especially an excuse that wasn't even true. Leah *wasn't* grieving her mother, the woman who'd messed up so much of her life. "I'm celebrating! Ding-dong, the witch is dead! I'm finally free! No more childhood trauma, because I can't be hurt anymore. All my problems stopped with her breath, and now I'm free and it's over."

Shaking his head, Jamie stepped back.

The look in his eye—as if Leah were a monster—almost derailed her. But he didn't understand what it was like to live with that kind of toxic person. She felt *relief*, not grief. Her mother had no power over her anymore. Leah couldn't be hurt or humiliated or disappointed ever again.

"I love you, Leah," Jamie said, "but I don't love how you're treating me. I came over when I got your call, despite how late it is, because—"

Because he thought she'd be in pain? Because he thought she was broken and needed him to fix her? "You came running because you thought I needed you," she interrupted. "I don't. I don't need anyone. I've been taking care of myself for a long time, and I don't—"

She broke off midword.

What was she saying?

Why was she trying to drive him away? Because she didn't want it to be true? She felt as if her entire brain were screaming at her to stop lying to him. *I am* broken.

But I'm not grieving. And I don't need him to fix me.

"I just . . . I need to be alone," Leah finished. *That's* what she'd called to tell him—yes, that was it. She had to explain that this wasn't about him; it was about her. She knew that sounded like a line, but it was the truth. "I don't want to break up with you, but I don't . . . I cheated on you! I don't know how to be who you need me to be. Or how to be who I want to be."

"Okay," he said.

Just okay? That was it?

"I'm toxic right now," she pressed. "You deserve better." She was messing up everything, right and left, and she didn't know how to stop. It wasn't fair to him.

"Okay."

He wasn't going to fight or yell? He wasn't angry? She felt like yelling. Her skin itched. She wanted to scratch it all off and let her insides spill out so they wouldn't hurt anymore. "Okay," she said. "I guess that's it?"

"If it's what you want," he said.

"It is," she lied. And then: "I'm sorry."

"I know."

He glanced around the apartment as if he were committing it to memory—or saying goodbye. And she wanted to say a million other things: *Don't go. I need you. I love you. Please help me.* But she didn't say any of that. Whatever urge she'd had to spill her guts had faded. The last thing she needed was to make herself vulnerable to someone who, with his own lovely and perfectly normal family, was incapable of understanding. No, he'd be better without her in his life. And she . . . *I'll be fine.* She watched him walk out. Flinched when the door closed.

She exhaled.

The silence pressed in on her ears.

It's over. Staring at the door, she knew she could still run after him. She pictured him walking down the dingy staircase. But she wasn't going to do that.

She'd done what she set out to do: cut him free. He'd be better without her, and she didn't need him. He was continually trying to fix her. He saw her as someone she'd never been and could never be. It was better that they were apart.

Cut out all the parts of her life she didn't need. Leah marched to her closet. She threw it open and began yanking out all her unused art supplies: canvases, sketchbooks, pencils, paints, brushes, pastels, chalk. All the mediums she thought she'd try and never did. Her easel, folded up for months, maybe years.

She spilled it all on the floor, faster and faster. A jar of paint shattered. She sopped it up with paper towels, though she knew it would stain. It was appropriately red. Like blood.

She dumped paint thinner onto a cloth and scrubbed at the linoleum floor. Harder and harder. The acrid smell pierced like needles. She kept scrubbing.

She looked at her unfinished artwork.

Grimly, Leah began wiping the canvases with paint thinner. It wasn't the recommended method, but it accomplished her goal: obliterating her failed, prosaic, unfinished attempts to do what she never should have tried to do.

Then she spread the canvases out to dry and opened a window to air out the apartment. Leah breathed the air in. She looked out at the Queens night, at the life still bustling on the street, at the cars still going by, the people weaving to and fro. Only a few of them were alone.

She should have felt cleansed. Ready to begin the next stage of her life. She told herself that's what she was doing. Starting over fresh, without anyone or anything from her past. She could reinvent herself however she chose.

Maybe once it was all gone, she'd feel joy again. She'd be herself. Find herself. Or whatever. But first:

Get rid of it all.

Bury it.

She piled all her art supplies into a black garbage bag and set it next to the splotchy, drying canvases with the stained remnants of her failed life.

Sinking to the ground, Leah told herself this was for the best. Jamie. Her art. Her life. Why didn't she feel better? She'd done the right thing. *I'm fine. I'm free.*

But she didn't feel free.

She felt empty.

CHAPTER
THIRTY-FIVE

I am alone.

It's an odd realization to have in the middle of a crowded sidewalk, people streaming in and out of bars and restaurants. Hugging my arms, I look for any sign of Sylvie—the flash of her smile or the roar of her stolen car. But I only see taxis and shadows filling the street.

The ooze rises and falls as if it's a tide pulled by the moon. Looking back at the bar, I see the white of Rabbit's outfit through the grimy window. He's back where he belongs. *He didn't need me after all.*

It feels unbearably sad to just stand there on the sidewalk, waiting to be consumed by lies—or the lack of them. So I walk. I'm careful to step only where it's safe, but that's where my care ends. I don't look up from the sidewalk to see who or what I'm walking through.

People slide through me, and I wonder about who they are. What they dream. What they lie about. Whether they need lies to keep themselves safe, like Rabbit's liars, or whether lies have eaten them alive, like Leah. I wonder what they'd think if they knew I was here, walking through them. To them, I'd be a ghost.

I suppose that's what I am now: a ghost of my mother's dreams. Her lies. Her hopes. I was part of a life she never led. And now, I'm a ghost of that unlived life. Strange.

I wish I had a purpose, like Rabbit, or a conviction that the world is mine for the tasting, like Sylvie. But I have only me. And that isn't enough.

The wolves will tear me apart if I let them.

The toxic muck will consume me.

I keep walking.

◆ ◆ ◆

I could have stayed in the casket.

I could have stayed with Leah.

I wanted . . . I don't think I ever let myself articulate what I wanted, or even the idea that I could want. But I did. Like my mother or because of my mother, I wanted *more*. I wanted sunsets and sunrises. I wanted oceans and mountains. I wanted friends and lovers and enemies. I wanted to shout, to sing, to be heard. I wanted to be more than a shadow. I wanted to be someone who cast a shadow. I wanted to leave footprints in the sand. And now?

I failed.

With Rabbit. With Sylvie. With Leah.

With Mother?

She died thinking she was alone in the end. She didn't know I loved her as fiercely as she loved me. She was my world because she never let me go. I never left, but she never knew.

And now this is where I end.

I'm standing on a corner in Queens. Not sure in which direction I walked. My feet just led the way, and here I am. There's an overflowing trash can next to me. A snake mostly made of shadow slithers along the gutter. There's far less muck here, just a trickle running down the side of the street. Even fewer people. I've found a residential area. It's almost quiet, except for the continuous whoosh of cars on adjoining streets.

A woman slams a door open and stalks out. She's followed closely by a second woman with the same nose, eyes, and chin—her sister? "You always do this. Just admit you need help."

"I'm fine," the first woman says. "You're delusional. I miss one month—one!—and you have to make a federal case out of it. I said I'll get you the rent, and I will!" Fog pours out of her mouth as she speaks. I see it curl around her like a boa constrictor, tightening around her neck.

"It's not about the money—"

The other woman snorts.

"—it's that I'm worried about you!"

Someone opens a window and shouts, "Hey, keep it down! Trying to sleep here!"

Both sisters shout, "Sorry!"

They glare at each other.

If I'd been able to talk to Leah . . . God, the things we could have said to one another. If I had someone to go through childhood *with* rather than just adjacent to . . . if we could have been there for each other at Mother's funeral . . . "Talk to her," I say to the first sister. "Not everyone gets this chance. Don't waste it. Don't waste a single moment. Tell her the truth."

She flinches. "I don't want to talk about it." Her lie manifests as a scarf of mist that wraps around her mouth.

I move closer. "Yes, you do."

"You wouldn't understand," she says.

"Not if you don't tell me what's going on," her sister says. Both of them have lowered their voices. They're not shouting at each other anymore. "Come back inside. I'll make hot chocolate. With milk."

"I'm not six."

"So? It's hot chocolate."

She should say yes. Not every sister gets this chance.

Leah is going to need to find her own way, without a sister to make hot chocolate.

I've tasted hot chocolate before, when Mother claimed she made it for her daughters on the first snowfall every year. She'd done that once when Leah was maybe five years old. She hadn't done it since, but one winter she told that story, and a steaming mug of hot chocolate appeared by my bedside table. It had a homemade marshmallow, floating like an iceberg, and tasted like a melted chocolate bar with a hint of peppermint. The next winter, I waited for the tradition to be repeated, but Mother must have forgotten that lie. I never had hot chocolate again.

I step even closer, touching the scarf of haze around her mouth. It's as soft and sticky as a cobweb. Experimenting, I tug at it, and it responds to my touch, same as other lies. I begin to unwind it. Then faster, I unspool it, wrapping the strands between my fingers.

As soon as I've finished, I step back, the lie strands twirled around my hand and her mouth free. Freed from the haze, the woman says, "We could talk, I guess, if there's hot chocolate."

Her sister smiles.

They go inside as I watch them.

Huh. I shake off the cobweb of lies, and the strands fall apart as they drift down. They're gone before they touch the sidewalk. I think about following the sisters inside to watch them drink their hot chocolate. To hear their conversation and pretend it's me and Leah.

Instead, I walk on and wonder when the fading will overcome me. Will I simply vanish as if I'd walked off into the sunset? *That would have been a good way to go. Into the sunset.* If I'd stayed at the beach with Sylvie, then I could have walked toward the sunset, and she could have watched me disappear. As it is, no one will know I was here, and no one will know I'm gone.

That's rather depressing.

I look at my hands and think of how the lie cobwebs felt. I'd been able to make a difference, even if the sisters would never know what I'd done.

I think of Rabbit. I want to tell him I understand. He's able to make a difference in the world. He's a necessary lie.

◆ ◆ ◆

My feet take me back to Sweet Venom. I'm not going to interrupt Rabbit; I only want to reassure myself that he's okay. I won't even talk to him.

The bar buzzes with people, the late-night, drink-until-last-call crowd, but it's obvious that Rabbit isn't here. Maybe that's just as well. We've said our goodbyes. He's moved on. Just because I'm still here doesn't mean I have the right to intrude on his decisions.

Finding a stool that I can touch, I slide on and grab a leftover drink. It tastes fruity and has a wedge of pineapple. I eat the pineapple first, enjoying the sting on my tongue.

Men with glass shards, like the ones in the other bar, are here in a cluster. I wonder . . .

Abandoning my drink, I slide off the stool and cross to them.

I pluck one of the glass shards from the closest man's cheek. It slides out, and after a moment's thought, I toss it into the ooze that lurks beneath the benches. It's swallowed by the muck, melted as if it's fallen into lava.

Pressing my lips together, I focus on each shard, plucking them out. Is it my imagination, or is he breathing easier? I can't tell if it's making any difference, but I'm able to see his skin beneath the glass, smooth and unbroken.

There's a cluster of glass on his chest, poetically impaling his heart. I grip the largest piece with both hands and tug. It's in deep and won't budge. He turns away when his buddy points to the bar. They laugh.

I'm panting. This is more exhausting than I anticipated, but I don't want to leave the job unfinished. I circle around the man, brace myself against the floor, and tug on the shard in his heart. It begins to shift.

I pull harder, putting my full weight into it.

At last, it slides out.

I feel a bite on my palm. Dropping the shard, I look at my hand. A thin line of red runs across my left hand. I squeeze my hand into a fist. Open it again. No fresh blood wells up. It wasn't a deep cut, but my hand is now smeared with red.

I wipe my hand on my skirt and turn to the second man. Diligently, I remove every shard of glass that I can find. And then the third man. I don't know if it helps. I doubt that it will magically make them better, happier people. But by the time I've removed half the shards from the third man, the first says, "Think I'm going to call it a night."

"Yeah, not feeling it tonight," the second man agrees.

The one I haven't yet finished says, "What the hell? Night's not over yet."

"It is for me, man." The first finishes his beer and abandons the glass on the table. He heads for the door, and the second follows him with a wave to the third.

Without his friends, the third man seems to deflate. I reach to remove another shard, but he stalks out the door. I think of following him, but another liar has caught my eye. He has ooze spilling over his lips and out of his eyes, and I wonder if there is something I can do about *that*.

I position myself in front of him and say, "You know you're lying."

He keeps talking, and the ooze keeps spewing from his lips. It spatters on the table in front of him. He leans on it, oblivious to the fact that his sleeve is dripping in gunk. The droplets swim around as if looking for something to cling to.

I reach for the glasses and connect with one. Dumping its contents over the ooze, I wash it away. I say in a louder, stronger voice, "You know you're lying, and you should stop."

He falters, ever so slightly, midsentence.

I position myself next to his ear. I can smell the ooze. It reeks like gasoline. It's as if he's poisoning himself and those around him. Exactly like that. "Stop," I tell him. "Think about what you're saying. Do you know if any of it is true?"

He hesitates again, and this time it can't be a coincidence. But then he dives in again: "I heard it can cause infertility. And birth defects. Plus, it causes blood clots and heart problems. It's all about the pharmaceutical companies making money—"

Grabbing another glass, I throw the alcohol in his face. He doesn't react, but the ooze washes from his eyes and lips.

He adds, "At least that's what I heard. I'm not a doctor."

It's a start.

Interesting that the ooze can be washed away. It's not invincible or inevitable.

Contemplating the puddles of muck in the corners of the bar, I wonder if there's something I can do about that—there are at least some glasses I should be able to touch. But why am I bothering. I can't make a dent in the ooze flowing through the streets, so what's the point? Besides, I'm going to fade anyway.

But maybe, maybe I can make a tiny impact before I go. Maybe my existence will have mattered, even if no one ever knows or remembers.

Maybe that's enough.

CHAPTER
THIRTY-SIX

I am alone.

It's better this way.

Leah forced herself to get up and haul the trash bag with her art supplies as far as the apartment door. She should drag it downstairs to the dumpster—*I'll do it later.* Having accomplished this much, she felt sapped, as if she'd expended a week's worth of effort all at once, which didn't make sense since all she'd done was empty one lousy closet.

Outside, the sun was just beginning to rise.

Maybe she just needed some caffeine. Yes, that would fix everything. She'd make coffee. Or maybe a glass of wine. She still had the dregs from the merlot Jamie had brought the other night with dinner—she pictured Jamie, his little frown of concentration as he tried to uncork the bottle. Laughing at himself, he'd handed it to her to uncork properly.

He was so damned *healthy*, so well adjusted. *Well, some of us aren't so miraculous.*

Not that she could blame her mother for Sam. Oh, no, that was all her. And Jamie had been so understanding about *that* too. If he'd raged at her . . . So goddamn understanding. *Maybe some people don't deserve understanding. Or forgiveness.*

Maybe I don't want it.

Maybe I'm fine exactly as I am.

Really, this was best for everyone. She couldn't hurt him if he was gone. All her lies and secrets. It was better for Dad when he left. Once he'd escaped Mom's toxicity, he'd started a new life and been happy, at least for a while. The same would happen for Jamie.

And for me.

She'd be able to move on.

Yes, that was all she needed: a fresh start. Leah crossed to the kitchen sink. She didn't need someone micromanaging her feelings and telling her to feel what she didn't. She didn't need someone who smothered her with kindness.

She heard Jersey's voice: *Yeah, I see how that's so terrible.*

The apartment felt hushed, even though outside the world was waking up with the sounds of car engines, a distant siren, voices, and footsteps from the apartment above. Leah had the nearly overwhelming urge to call him, tell him she didn't mean it, tell him she was sorry, tell him everything—but she squashed that instinct down.

Grabbing a wineglass, she began to scrub it. She thought of the dirty dishes always in Mom's sink and still piled high after her death.

"I'm fine without her." She squeezed the glass as she rubbed the sponge on the stubborn red stain at the base. "Without *him*. I'm fine without him. And he's better off without me. I've done both of us a favor." The burgundy stain just would not fade. She leaned against the counter and scrubbed harder. "I'm *free*."

This was the life she wanted. She chose this. Being in a relationship with a nice guy, being loved, being happy—that wasn't possible for someone like her. Just like she'd failed at art, she'd also failed at having a nice, normal, healthy relationship. She didn't deserve either art or love. *This* was what she deserved, the legacy her mom had left her, along with that cursed house made of memories she didn't want—

The wineglass shattered in her hand.

CHAPTER THIRTY-SEVEN

I am a lie.

I cannot touch the real world or real people.

But I can touch other lies. All my life, I've seen that as a lesser skill, a consolation prize. I can't touch what's real, can't leave a footprint either literally or metaphorically, so what does it matter?

It *does* matter, though. I've read books that were never written, eaten food that was never made, heard songs that were never sung, seen art that was never painted. I can touch and feel, and I can destroy other lies.

So, I do.

I begin with Sweet Venom. After the glass shards, I work my way through the other customers, unraveling the fog that attaches to them and releasing it into the air. I don't touch the shadow dancers, but any of the lies that look painful or wrong—those I dismantle.

After the final customers leave, I turn my attention back to the puddles of tar. I wonder . . . if I wash it away, will it simply filter into the street and join the rest, becoming fuel for the oceans and rivers of muck? Is there a way I can get rid of it more permanently? Can it burn?

I can touch ample cigarettes and lighters strewn across the bar—so many people have lied about smoking that it's easy to find a supply. I flick a lighter, watching the flame glow. Yes, this is worth doing before I fade.

One of the puddles belches a bubble. "Let's see if you burn," I whisper. I lower the flame. If it is as full of gas as it smells . . .

The flame hops to the ooze. It spreads quickly, the fire snaking beneath the benches. I don't worry about the bar itself; it's real and can't be touched by false flames. But as the fire spreads, I begin to worry about the other shadows in the bar, lingering after the real customers have left for the night.

I shoo the dancers toward the door. Many don't understand, but I am insistent. They're doing no harm; they don't deserve to burn.

Once all the shadow dancers are outside, I watch as the flames lick the windows. Every bit of muck is burning, and it is beautiful.

Even more beautiful than a sunset.

I know exactly what I want to do with the last moments of my life. I'm going to watch it all burn.

As the fire wipes the inside of Sweet Venom clean, I rip the bottom half of my skirt from my sundress and wrap it around a branch from a tree that was never planted along the sidewalk. When the flames begin to die down, I venture back inside. I hold my arm over my mouth as if that were enough to shield me from the smoke. Already, it's dissipating, the fire only burning in one corner.

I dip my makeshift torch into the flames. The fire leaps onto the strips of skirt, and I carry it outside, grateful that the wind cannot touch me or my fire.

Outside, the muck runs through the gutter. I kneel down and submerge my torch. Immediately, the flames chase along the ooze. I grin wolfishly.

Behind me, the shadow dancers are returning to Sweet Venom. I don't speak to them, and they don't thank me. I follow the flame as it spreads.

I walk the streets of Queens, lighting them on fire as I go. Soon, the sky is stained orange and black. I feel as glorious and awful as an avenging angel. I have soot marks on my legs and burns where sparks have landed on my arms. I don't care.

I laugh as I burn a street full of ooze.

I wonder what Rabbit would think of my newfound purpose. And Sylvie. Mother? She didn't make me for this. This was all me, and it feels good. I wonder what else I could do if I weren't about to fade. I suppose I'll never know. But at least I can do this.

Turning a corner, I find a sea of muck so deep it swallows the entire street. Its waves lap across the sidewalk, reaching for the apartment steps. Grinning, I advance. I'm holding my flame aloft. I wonder if it knows what I've done, if it can feel the heat from the fire the way I can from the streets behind me.

Out of the corner of my eye, I see a shadow wolf slip along the wall ahead of me.

A coldness settles into the pit of my stomach, and I wonder if I should run.

I don't want my quest to be interrupted by wolves before I've done all I can. Maybe I've accepted that my days, perhaps hours, are numbered, but I still don't want to be torn apart by those teeth. The memory of their pain haunts me more than any other memory.

I begin to back away, but then I notice that the muck is flowing toward the wolf. It thickens as it coalesces and spills onto the sidewalk where the wolf is making its stand. The wolf is trying to attack it, but there's only one wolf, and the muck has already risen to its knees.

The wolf is exactly like the others—made of haze and smoke— exactly like the ones that hunted me when I was younger, exactly like the ones that crashed the party with Sylvie. I owe it nothing, and if I were to help it, then it would undoubtedly turn on me. It is, as I've been told, a defender of truth. That's its purpose.

It's lucky to have a purpose.

I look at my torch. All I'd have to do is lower it to this batch of ooze. The fire would spread, and the wolf would have the chance to escape.

And come after me.

There are plenty more streets with ooze that I can attack. According to Rabbit, the muck exists all over NYC, not just in a few streets in Queens. It's not a localized problem; it's a societal-level toxicity, caused by nation-size lies. In other words, I could simply skip this street and leave the wolf to its fate and still have plenty more to burn.

The wolf is tearing at the muck around its legs, trying to rip it to shreds and devour it, but there's too much. It's obvious that the sludge is going to overwhelm the wolf before it can destroy enough to escape.

"Dammit," I say.

I lower the torch to the ooze. Jogging, I circle around the muck, lighting it on fire as I go. The flames spread, and the ooze switches direction, reaching toward me—it's too abrupt a change to be anything but deliberate. Whether by instinct or intelligence, it knows I'm a threat, which pleases me.

"Run and leap!" I call to the wolf. "You can escape! Go!"

Lighting the ooze in as many places as I can, I don't realize that the muck has spiraled around me. Its intent is clear: to swallow me.

By the time I realize I've been surrounded, it's too late—the ooze is circling me, closing in tighter and tighter, too wide for me to jump over and too deep for me to wade through.

This is it.

I've done as much as I can.

The fire is spreading through the ooze but not fast enough. The muck will reach me before the fire can consume it. I'll die in ooze and flames. *Overkill.* I feel a hysterical laugh bubble in my throat.

This was not what I expected when I climbed out of Mother's casket. Was it worth it?

Yes.

I don't have to hesitate.

I would do it all again if I had the choice. Well, maybe I wouldn't have let myself get trapped while trying to save a goddamn wolf. But the rest . . . Sylvie. Rabbit. Even Leah.

I wave the torch in front of me, and the whirlpool hesitates.

Then a shadow flies through the flames and lands beside me. As if defending me, the wolf plunges his muzzle into the ooze. Encouraged, I swing my torch at the sludge, but it doesn't retreat. It continues to creep closer, so I thrust the burning torch directly into the muck, plunging the fire into its heart.

It tries to retreat, like the tide pulling back from the shore.

I yank the torch sideways, dragging the flames through the ooze, spreading the fire. The wolf is decimating another wave as it rises to consume us.

At last, a break in the muck! I seize the moment and run through the low-burning flames. I scream as the fire and toxic sludge burn my ankles, but I don't stop. And then, I'm beyond it.

Standing, I hobble away. The skin on my ankles is a painful red, and it feels as if a hundred needles have stabbed my flesh, but I'm not on fire anymore. Could be worse. I'll scar, if I live long enough to scar, but I don't think I've done any permanent damage. Behind me, the wolf is doing real damage to the shrinking pool of toxic muck.

Steadying myself, I walk faster.

I don't notice at first that the wolf is following me. I'm on the hunt for another branch and more fabric that I can use for a new torch.

Catching a glimpse of the wolf, I wish I had my torch. Wolves don't like fire, right? I don't know about these wolves. As I understand it, they aren't lies; they are made of shadow. They hunt lies. Like me.

"Leave me alone," I say loudly.

As if that will frighten him off.

As if he's an ordinary animal.

He continues to pad behind me, silent as a shadow. Oddly, he doesn't attack. I try to ignore him. I don't want to run—that will make me prey.

I find a cashmere sweater balled up on a step. It's shimmering, so I know I can touch it. Lifting it up, I wonder how flammable it is. Worth a try.

Holding up my lighter, I wait until the sweater catches fire.

The wolf snarls.

I freeze.

There is a river of muck creeping toward me. The ooze immediately catches fire. Brushing past me like the wind, the shadow wolf launches at the muck, and together we destroy the lie.

The shadow wolf walks alongside me now. I carry the fire. He's the teeth. Together, we burn the ooze and hunt the muck. I'm careful not to let him out of my sight. I don't know when he will decide to turn on me, and I don't understand why he hasn't, but I'm grateful for it.

Dawn comes to Queens.

It spreads like my flames, changing the sky first to a dull blue and then to a pale matte gray. I hear birds. More voices. More cars. There will be more lies today. More ooze from people's lips. More glass shards. More gauze that obscures eyes and silences mouths.

There's a lot to do.

CHAPTER THIRTY-EIGHT

Leah wrapped gauze around the cuts on her hand. She'd left the shards of blood-speckled glass in the sink but couldn't muster the energy to clean up the mess. Her hand throbbed, but she couldn't bring herself to care. It felt distant, as if it were someone else's flesh that had been cut. *It's fine. I'm fine.*

She felt numb, as if her innards had been hollowed out with a spoon. She wondered if this made her a deficient person—she couldn't feel her own pain.

She was fine.

So what, if her mother had died? So what, if she'd ruined the best relationship she'd ever had? So what, if she was on the verge of losing her job because she just didn't care enough to show up?

Maybe she was monstrous, but she felt nothing.

I don't need anyone.

Better off alone.

I deserve to be alone.

I will never be happy.

I don't deserve happiness. It's not in my blood. Better to be alone, where no one can touch me, and no one can hurt me, and I can't hurt anyone. I am my mother's daughter.

Lies are in my blood.

I am made of lies.

CHAPTER THIRTY-NINE

I am searching for more sludge to burn when a car—a convertible—pulls alongside me. Sylvie leans out the open window. "I leave you alone for one night. What the hell happened to you?"

Glancing down at myself, I smile wryly. My dress is in tatters. My arms and legs boast glaring red burns that still sting, especially when I touch them. My shoes are also ruined. And there's a shadow wolf walking placidly beside me. It bares its teeth at Sylvie.

"Jesus, Hannah! What the fu—"

"Don't hurt her," I tell the wolf.

He relents, still eyeing her balefully.

She stops the car. "Did you . . . I have so many questions I don't know where to begin. Really thought I was coming to save you, but . . . Okay, it's unclear. Do you need saving? Because I have a new getaway car. It took me a while to find just the right one." She pats the outside of the door. "Had to find one that didn't clash with my dress."

She's wearing her black-as-a-shadow dress, and the wolf sputters at her lie. "Maybe don't tempt him?" I suggest.

She shrugs. "I'm in a car; he's not."

"Except you aren't going to drive away and leave me here, right?" I don't say the word "again." How did she even find me? I've wandered far from Sweet Venom. Glancing at street signs, I realize I don't know exactly where I am. Still somewhere in Queens, I assume, but I have no gauge on where.

"Might leave you here. We'll see." She drives slowly, matching our pace. I'm not entirely sure where we are walking. Just that I didn't want to stop. "I only came back because I was curious. Not because I care."

The wolf bristles again.

Interesting that he can detect a lie even when it's told by a lie.

"You do care," I say, "but don't worry—I won't tell anyone."

Sylvie points a finger at me. "Hey, don't tell me what I do or do not feel. Only I'm in charge of me. No psychoanalysis shit on me, you hear? It won't work. It'll roll off like water off a duck's back, which is not an expression I ever intended to use."

"Really? Just curiosity?" I ask, eyebrows raised. "Curiosity led you to search all over Queens, for hours, despite the muck and the wolves?"

She glares at me.

"You could've been back in Montauk by now."

"I'll be there by sunset," she says. "Got plenty of time. Or maybe I'll go into the city and watch the sunset from the top of the Empire State Building. That has to be a spectacular view. Classic even."

"There will be more toxic muck there," I warn.

"Lots of it," Sylvie agrees. "More people, more lies; more lies, more muck, and God knows what else."

We pause and stare at each other.

"You haven't faded," Sylvie says.

I lift my hand and stare at it. It looks solid to me, and I'm oddly certain that it will stay that way. "I think I was wrong about what I needed."

"Oh?"

"I didn't need a liar," I say. And then I feel myself smile. "I needed a purpose." That's what Rabbit had that I didn't, when the wolves were hunting me and not him. Now . . . everything has changed.

She studies me, and I think she's about to say something profound. But instead, she retrieves a pair of sunglasses from within the car and puts them on. "Cool. So, are you bringing your new pet? If so, we need a few ground rules. Namely, he doesn't eat me."

"Wait—you really want to go to Manhattan?"

"You know me. I like the best view." She glances at the sun, just rising at the periphery of the sky. "Got a bunch of hours to kill before then. Maybe we should find you a new outfit?"

"Actually, there *is* one thing I'd like to do first, if you wouldn't mind giving me a ride."

"Side quest? Sure, I'm in."

Before getting in the car, I turn to the shadow wolf. It doesn't speak, so I have no real idea how much it understands. "Do you want to come with us? You can't hurt Sylvie. She's my friend. Or the car. I know it's not real, but it will help us stop more lies."

Sylvie whistles. "Huh. So you're, like, an honorary shadow wolf?"

I suppose I am. Whatever that means.

Guess I'll just have to figure it out as I go. Like I have with everything else in my life.

I kneel in front of the wolf. It's weird, I know, but I want him to come. We've made a good team against the ooze, and I don't know . . . It's nice not to be afraid of him.

He saunters toward me, his jaws close to me. I tense. The shadow wolf licks my cheek. It feels like a breeze. His breath smells like the ocean and forest, which surprises me. I was expecting more like sulfur and brimstone, but instead, it smells like nature, like seaweed and salt water, like the breeze after the rain.

"When you think you've seen everything . . . ," Sylvie mutters.

"I've barely seen anything," I say.

But that's going to change.

◆　◆　◆

We drive to Leah's apartment, and Sylvie parks in front of the building's door, beside a fire hydrant. Above, the sun is peeking through clouds, as if trying to see the world clearly. "Wait for me?" I ask her.

The wolf growls.

"Not going to hang out with a lie killer," she says. "You take your new pet with you."

"Come on," I say to the wolf. He jumps from the back seat onto the sidewalk. His body shimmers between solid and shadow as he lands. I shiver. His silhouette still sends a stab of fear through me. "You'll wait?" I ask again.

"Not sure," Sylvie says. "We'll see."

She'll wait.

I know it's the truth.

Squaring my shoulders, I gather my courage and walk through the door into the apartment building, then climb the stairs. The wolf pads up silently behind me. I am thinking so hard about Leah and Sylvie and everything that I don't check to see if he's following me.

I glide through the door to Leah's apartment. She's home. I can tell from the way the wolf is snarling. I am hip deep in artwork, and I wade through it as I cross to Leah.

This time, I know what to say. More importantly, I know what she'll feel.

"You've been lying to yourself," I say to her. "Probably for years, but certainly since Mother has died." As I talk, I begin unraveling the cocoon of gauzy lies bundled around her. "You haven't let yourself grieve." Pulling the lies away, I feed them to the shadow wolf. He swallows them gulp by gulp. "I know you don't miss her, but you *do* miss who she should have been to you. You miss the family you were supposed to have and the childhood you deserved. You miss me, or at least the me who could have been. You need to admit that before you can move on. Your life isn't what you think it is. You need to see Jamie clearly and decide if you want to be with him and how you want to treat him, but more importantly, you need to see yourself clearly so you can figure out how to treat yourself."

Leah doesn't hear my words, of course, but she also doesn't walk away. She is sitting on the edge of her bed. Her shoulders are hunched, and her hands are clasped in front of her.

"Once you see yourself clearly, maybe then you can move on. Try art again. Draw. Paint. Whatever it is you want to do. Whatever you want to be. But first you need to stop lying to yourself. See yourself the way I do, as someone to forgive and as someone to love."

She stands up and crosses to the mirror.

She looks at herself.

I am behind her, though the mirror does not show it. I am still unwinding the gauze. There's so much of it. I am now at a lower level, where it's tattered and torn. Some of it looks like lace. All of it goes down the wolf's gullet. She won't be able to wrap herself in these lies again. It won't stop her from creating new ones, but this is what I can give her:

A fresh start.

She can begin again and build whatever life of truth and lies she wants. But she won't be weighed down by all the lies she's told herself about her past, or her present and future. She will face her thoughts and emotions, and then she will choose what she wants to do with them.

"This is my gift to you," I tell her. "Because I love you. Because I am your sister."

I think maybe she hears me. Not as me. But perhaps, as a voice in her head. A conscience. A memory. A dream.

Or maybe I am only fooling myself, and she has no sense of me at all. That's okay. Because I am nearly through unraveling the lies wrapped around her. She will begin this next stage without lies—and without me as well. I hope it's enough, because it's all I have to give.

As I unwrap the very last strand of cloudlike cotton from over her eyes, I stare at her face, unblurred for the first time in as long as I can remember. I hold the lies in my hands for a moment before surrendering them to the wolf.

Leah, at last, begins to cry.

CHAPTER FORTY

Leah touched her cheek with her fingertips. Felt the tears. "Mom," she whispered.

For the first time, she felt her rage slip away, replaced with a sense of grief that washed over her. Or maybe it had been there all along, and she was finally acknowledging it for what it was. She'd lost her mother, both the one she'd had and the one she'd wished she'd had. And it hurt like hell, like a hurricane bashing her insides.

She'd lashed out because it hurt so badly. It was so obvious now how badly she'd treated Jamie and why. She'd hurt him because she'd been so intent on denying her own pain.

How could she not have seen it before?

Jamie had seen it.

Jersey had seen it.

You're grieving.

She'd rejected that. Because it wasn't what she'd thought grief was supposed to be, or maybe because she didn't want to grieve for someone who'd done so much damage and caused so much pain.

She'd rejected both Jamie and Jersey—they'd both tried to help her in their own ways. Yet they still stuck with her. They still cared about her and supported her. She'd made herself a new family and hadn't even noticed.

I'm noticing now.

Mom had been a shitty mother, Dad had been a crappy father, and her little sister Hannah had died far too young, and nothing was ever going to change any of that. And it was *sad*. It sucked. It made her angry, and she felt that she was understanding all this clearly for the first time.

She was *not* fine.

And finally, that was okay. She didn't have to be fine.

If only Mom had realized that. Like fireworks inside her chest, Leah felt a burst of pity for her mother. Mom had been hurting so badly but had never let herself recognize her pain. *Not that it excused anything, but it explained so much.*

Mom had never stopped lying to herself, and that was the saddest of all.

Leah stood up shakily and moved across her room. She unfolded her easel and set it by the window. She then picked up one of the still-damp canvases.

Unloading her supplies from the black garbage bag, she selected paints, as well as a few brushes. She positioned them by her easel. Then took a breath.

In sure and steady strokes, she began to paint her truth.

Reds and yellows dripped down the canvas. Patches of paint failed to soak in, the paint thinner still damp in some places. She kept going. A face appeared, warped, her mother's. At the base, tendrils reached toward the sky . . .

She channeled it all—her pain, her grief, her hope—into the canvas. It was the first time in her life that she was completely raw with her art. Tears trailed her cheeks as she painted. And when she at last finished, she dipped the brush into water and stepped back.

Then she dialed the phone. "Hi, Jamie? I know I have no right to ask this, and I will understand if you say no. But could you come over? There's a painting I'd like to show you."

❖ ❖ ❖

As Leah continues to paint, I walk out of her apartment and down the stairs. The wolf follows me silently, and when I step outside into the daylight, Sylvie is waiting. She smiles bright as the dawn when she sees me.

"Plenty of time before sunset," Sylvie says. She pats the passenger seat beside her as the wolf jumps into the back seat. "Ready to see the world?"

I look back at Leah's apartment. "Ready to save it."

ACKNOWLEDGMENTS

I'd tell you where I got the idea for this book, but it would be a lie.

It grew inside me like a mushroom, feeding on the debris of other stories and the remnants of other ideas—a woman who doesn't exist, an artist who doesn't create, a sunset, a train, muck that spills from the lips of a lying politician—until suddenly, it was its own story, drastically different from anything I'd ever attempted to write before. Until suddenly, I had to write it. And I couldn't stop.

Sometimes that's how stories work.

But they don't grow in isolation. This book wouldn't exist without the encouragement, support, and love of my family and my friends. I am profoundly grateful for all of you, and I love you with all my heart.

This book also would not exist without my extraordinary agent, Andrea Somberg. Thank you for always believing in me! And thank you to my magnificent editor, Erin Adair-Hodges, and my wonderful developmental editor, Laura Chasen, as well as all the fantastic people at Lake Union. Thank you all for bringing this book to life!

And a special thank-you to my readers. May you always find the truth in the lies.

ABOUT THE AUTHOR

Sarah Beth Durst is the author of over twenty-five books for adults, teens, and kids, including *The Bone Maker, The Lake House,* and *Spark.* She won an American Library Association Alex Award and a Mythopoeic Fantasy Award and has been a finalist for the Andre Norton Nebula Award three times. Several of her books have been optioned for film/television, including *Drink Slay Love,* which was made into a TV movie and was a question on *Jeopardy!* Sarah is a graduate of Princeton University and lives in Stony Brook, New York, with her husband, her two children, and her ill-mannered cat. Visit her at www.sarahbethdurst.com.